D1606192

Praise for *The Coalition Rebellion* Series

"[*Lord of the Storm* has] so many sparks that it's a wonder the book doesn't set itself on fire while you're reading it."
—*LikesBooks.com*

Rebel Prince is the long-awaited conclusion to The Coalition Rebellion Series

First two books in trilogy recognized as *Romantic Times* 200 BEST OF ALL TIME!

Lord of the Storm's Accolades and Honors:
Romance Writers of America's RITA Award
Romantic Times Reviewer's Choice Award
Romantic Times Career Achievement Award
Reader's Choice Award
RRA Book Award
BTC Bookstore Network Award

Skypirate Accolades and Honors:
Romantic Times Reviewer's Choice Award
Romantic Times 5-Star review !

Praise and Awards for Justine Dare Davis

Romance Writers of America's RITA
4-time winner, 7-time finalist

RT's Reviewer's Choice Awards
5-time winner, 19-time nominee

RT's Career Achievement Awards
3-time winner, 6-time nominee

Authored 4 books selected for
"Romantic Times 200 BEST OF ALL TIME."

Other Justine Davis Books from Bell Bridge Books:

The Coalition Rebellion Novels

Book 1: Lord of the Storm

Book 2: Skypirate

Book 3: Rebel Prince

The Kingbird
(A Coalition Rebellion Short Story)

Also:

Wild Hawk

Heart of the Hawk

Fire Hawk

Rebel Prince

Book 3: A Coalition Rebellion Novel

by

Justine Davis

Bell Bridge Books

This is a work of fiction. Names, characters, places and incidents are either the products of the author's imagination or are used fictitiously. Any resemblance to actual persons (living or dead), events or locations is entirely coincidental.

Bell Bridge Books
PO BOX 300921
Memphis, TN 38130
Print ISBN: 978-1-61194-556-0

Bell Bridge Books is an Imprint of BelleBooks, Inc.

We at BelleBooks enjoy hearing from readers.
Visit our websites
BelleBooks.com
BellBridgeBooks.com
ImaJinnBooks.com

10 9 8 7 6 5 4 3 2 1

Cover design: Debra Dixon
Interior design: Hank Smith
Photo/Art credits:
Man (manipulated) © Aleksminyaylo1 | Dreamstime.com
Woman (manipulated) © Branislav Ostojic | Dreamstime.com
Background (manipulated) © Leeloomultipass | Dreamstime.com
Ship (manipulated) © Philcold | Dreamstime.com

:Lprt:01:

Dedication

For twenty years, I have waited to write this story.

For twenty years, readers have asked for it.

For twenty years, rarely a month went by without someone asking if I was please ever going to write it.

Twenty years is a very long time.

Thank you all for waiting with me, for asking, for remembering.

(And for a particular group of you—you'll know who you are—yes, the epilogue is just for you.)

Prologue

"I'M GOING AFTER her. I'll take the next transport." Dax Silverbrake was pacing the floor of the Triotian royal palace's private quarters, covering the same twenty feet of floor time and again. Barely suppressed energy nearly crackled around him.

King Darian of Trios watched his best friend in obvious amusement. "Are you sure confrontation is wise just now?"

The pacing continued. "What I'm sure of is she has no business scarpering off like that. Off world, without even a word of explanation."

Dax half expected a reminder he himself had done much, much worse. But Dare looked as if he were considering his next words so carefully that Dax knew what was coming, and hastened to forestall it.

"I know, this is my doing. Perhaps it wasn't the best decision, but I only wished her safe, and free of pressure, for as long as possible."

"Lying to your child is rarely the best decision," Dare said.

"I didn't lie," Dax said. "I just . . . omitted something."

"Spoken like the skypirate you once were."

Dax winced. And there it was, he thought, stopping in his tracks.

Dare pressed the point. "You omitted something indeed. The biggest thing of her life. Her destiny. And she is, in fact, an adult now," Dare added.

Dax spun around then, glaring at his oldest, closest friend. "You are not being any help, Dare."

"I am a father too," he said.

"But not of a daughter. They're . . . different."

"That I cannot argue with," Dare agreed with a grin. "Women are thankfully different."

"Califa's too damned calm about it," Dax muttered.

For the first time Shaylah, Dare's mate, spoke. "That's because she's not worried about Shaina's welfare."

"How can she not be?" Dax spun around to look at the queen he so admired, the woman he loved like a sister as he loved Dare like a brother. She was smiling so serenely that Dax felt a spark of irritation.

"Because she knows Shaina is safe."

Dax blinked. "What? How can she know that?"

"Shaina was upset, furious really, and feeling betrayed."

Again Dax winced, but this time the feeling went clear to the bone. He was beginning to realize the scope of the mistake he'd made.

"Califa knows because she knows her daughter. She knows where she would go. Where she always goes when something goes wrong in her life. Which is why she will be safe."

Dax frowned. "Are you saying . . . ?"

"Of course. She went to Lyon."

Chapter 1

AS LONG AS THEY didn't know who he was, he had a chance of staying alive.

Lyon held to that hope as he sat in the darkness of the tiny room they'd thrown him in. His head ached where the cudgel had caught him, and his shoulder ached where he'd gone down on the taproom floor, but nothing ached quite as much as his pride. He'd been taken like a green cadet, by one of the oldest ruses of all time.

But the worst part was that when Shaina heard about it, she'd be able to say, "I told you so."

And say it she would. She'd hold this over him until they were both old and gray, and for Triotians that was a very long time.

All this assuming, of course, that he was alive for her to say anything.

Instinctively he checked the chain around his neck. The heavy ring bearing the royal crest lay safe against his chest. He'd taken it off before he'd arrived. The ring was too recognizable, and he'd wanted this bit of anonymity before the rest of his life began.

How long had he been out? Minutes? Hours? It had been daylight when he'd risen to wander Galatin, the capital city of Arellia, his mother's home world. And now it was—

His thoughts broke off at the sound of approaching footsteps. The door rattled. He leapt to his feet, ignoring the pain that shot through his head at the swift movement. He'd already felt around in the darkness, knew they hadn't left him anything to fight with. This was going to be hand to hand.

So be it, he thought.

He backed up against the wall. He raised one knee, bracing his foot against the wall. Light poured in as the door swung open, and he blinked reflexively as it stabbed at his eyes.

"Awake, are you? Good. I was afraid you were out permanently."

The cheerful voice didn't fool Lyon this time, as it had when the jolly-looking round-faced man had approached him asking directions. That had been just before the man's unseen companion had bludgeoned him senseless. He'd awakened to find his money pouch gone and a lump on his head the size of a whisperbird egg. So much for being the pride of the Triotian War College.

"Not feeling talkative?"

He could make him out now, an unprepossessing man with a tendency to wear an absurd grin. Lyon contemplated making a run, and tensed the leg braced against the dank wall, ready to push off, thinking he could bowl over the rotund man and be gone before he could recover. Except for one little problem. He didn't know where the second man was, the tall one who was altogether too handy with his cudgel.

"Well, that's fine, you just stay quiet, and when the man with the coins arrives, we'll just be on our—"

A hollow thump in the corridor was followed by the thud of something heavy falling. The man in the open doorway looked toward the sound.

"Rickel," he called. Silence. "Eos, that man," he muttered. His voice rose a notch. "Rickel, don't play any of your silly games now."

The man took a step in the direction the sounds had come from. Lyon knew he had to take this chance—he might not get another. He shoved away from the wall, lowered one shoulder, and ran for the light.

The man wasn't nearly as soft as he looked. Lyon heard a grunt as his shoulder took the man at kidney level, but he didn't go down. His hands wildly clawed back at Lyon. Grasping fingers tangled in his long mane of hair, and yanked fiercely. Lyon winced. Twisted away. Struck out at the round man's face.

Lyon heard another thud, just like the first. The round man jumped, yelped explosively. He glanced down the dark hallway, as if facing a secondary attack from the rear. The glance was only a split second, but Lyon didn't waste the opportunity. He drove a precisely aimed foot sharply into the man's ample gut. Air whooshed out of him. Lyon swept the man's legs out from under him with a swiping kick. Swiftly, he grabbed his own blade from the man's belt and used the hilt to send him to sleep.

One down. Now for the other. I'll relish paying him back for this headache.

"Cub! Over here!"

He froze.

No. It was impossible. She had sworn she wasn't coming. She was home, on Trios. There was no way in Hades that Shaina Silverbrake could be here.

But he knew that voice too well. And no one else dared use that childhood nickname any longer.

"Come on! These skalworms will be coming around any minute—you'd better get moving!"

He spotted her the instant she spoke the second time, from the shadow of the large archway. She was grinning at him, that insufferably taunting grin he'd seen directed at him all too many times in his life. She'd always seemed more vividly alive than anyone he knew, and now she was fairly crackling with life. She was fire and spirit and beauty afoot. She took his breath away.

She doesn't want you except as her loyal companion, so stop even thinking about it.

"Will you move, Cub? I'm out of rocks to throw. Don't mess up my chance to rescue *you* for a change."

He'd deal with her unexpected appearance here later, he thought. In the meantime, she was right—as she so often was—and he'd better get moving.

She led the way unhesitatingly, and just as unhesitatingly he followed. She wasn't the exact navigator their beloved Rina was, but she knew the way and he didn't, given he'd been unconscious when they dragged him in here.

They ran until they reached the alley behind the taproom. And that, too, brought back memories. Shaina had always been quicker, and able to outrun him, until a growth spurt had given him the height and stride to beat her. And their instructors in the warrior arts hadn't been above using their competitive natures to get the most out of each of them.

And of course his father had advice.

Don't get cocky. A smart woman doesn't need muscle or strength to get the better of you. And Shaina is very, very smart.

The words had been delivered in a wry voice, interrupting Lyon's crowing over his first-ever victory over her in a footrace. The comment had been followed by a teasing comment from his mother, and then his parents had exchanged That Look that told him they'd be disappearing into their chamber for a while. He'd been just old enough by then to realize what that meant, and had quickly gone back to his crowing to hide his embarrassment at his parents' lovesickness.

And his father had been proven right in their next race, when Shaina had distracted him at the start and gained herself a ten-stride lead he hadn't quite been able to overcome. Their race now was to get clear of this dark, rather dank alley—he'd swear he'd seen a fanged flymouse hanging upside down in that high corner—and it ended at the street. A street that was full of rowdy Arellians, reveling in remembrance of their declaration of independence from the Coalition.

They merged into the crowd, thankful the celebration seemed to still be going full speed. As they worked their way down the street, Lyon watched celebrants who clearly gave little thought anymore to the years-long war that the declaration had caused, a war that left many dead and more wounded, some permanently. Judging by the people he'd talked to since his arrival, looking forward, not back, was the Arellian wont. He had the odd thought that he, only half-Arellian, probably knew more about their history than they did, thanks to his parents' insistence.

But this was not the time to be thinking about history. Or even the future, that distant time when he'd be dealing with the burden his father now carried. Life was interesting when your father was the man who saved worlds and you were set to follow in his footsteps.

But right now he should be focused on saving his own backside. And Shaina's. Not that her backside was something he wanted to even let into his mind. It was enough to deal with the fact that she, the very person he'd come here to get away from, was walking beside him, apparently completely unaware of his turmoil.

To her you're just the big brother she never had, he told himself.

And you'd better remember it.

"HERE, CUB," SHAINA said, pulling her long, dark hair free of the cap she wore, "stuff that mane of yours under this."

Lyon was sitting across the small fire from her, on the folded thermal cloth he'd pulled from the pack he'd retrieved from his hired room once they were sure they'd eluded his captors. They'd escaped to the high ground above the city, at the base of the ancient mountain, camping as they had often done at home while exploring the slowly healing face of their world.

He caught the cap she tossed. Frowned.

"I don't need it."

It came out more sharply than he'd intended, but he was on edge. Not so much from the narrow escape as because that nickname was beyond wearing on him. But he knew if he said anything, she'd just use it more often. She liked being the only one who could really disconcert him.

"Wrong. I'm the one who doesn't need it. I blend in here."

She had a point, he thought. With her dark hair and pale skin, she looked as much Arellian as both their mothers. It was he who stood out. His father's genes threw true.

"Unless, of course," she added, "you'd rather keep walking around as a target."

"It's not as if anyone knows who I am," he said, grimacing as he put the cap on, shoving long strands of Triotian gold hair out of sight under the heavy blue cloth, taking care not to touch the still very tender lump behind his ear.

She scowled at him across the fire. "Have you been drinking too much lingberry, Cub?"

"Have you been bitten by a bark-hound?" he retorted. Damnation, he didn't know if he could take much more of this. She treated him as if he were indeed that cub—perfectly safe, utterly tamed—while he felt anything but tame right now, fighting urges she clearly didn't feel in turn.

No wonder the nickname was starting to slice at him.

"I could be any Triotian," he said with an effort at calm. "You know there are lots of people traveling between here and Trios since the MIP was signed." The Mutual Interest Pact had been a triumph of his father's negotiating skills, even if there were doubts on Trios that Arellia would hold up their end.

That all this would someday be his responsibility was a knowledge he'd grown up with. Yet somehow the coming changes in his own life and position, which had once loomed huge over him, seemed less important right now than the change in his feelings toward his best friend.

Shaina ignored his words. "Of course they know who you are. You look just like your father. You know, the guy whose face is right next to your mother's on all those placards all over the planet?"

He signed inwardly. She was right. Of course his father was everywhere. As was his mother. The Graymist family was as famous and revered on Arellia as his father's was on Trios. Many had died heroically during the first Coalition invasion, and had been secretly venerated even as the Coalition became the way of life. The rest of the Graymist family on Arellia had been wiped out in the rebellion. So when a surviving member of a most beloved family bonded with a king and became queen of the most revered planet in the system, he supposed the fame was inevitable. Especially when together they had waged the battle that had ended the Coalition's evil on Trios, which in turn had inspired the rebellion here on Arellia.

But two of the biggest heroes of that rebellion were Shaina's own parents.

"Look who's talking," he said. "Your parents are right next to them on practically every sign."

"Yeah," she said, rather glumly. "And before you ask, yes, I saw the statue."

Lyon managed not to laugh at her tone. His edgy mood faded. He'd seen it, too, that larger-than-life sculpture commemorating the flashbow warrior of Trios and his remarkable weapon, the gleaming silver crossbow that could only be used by him, firing bolts of incredible power. The new statue was the reason this year's celebration was even bigger than usual. It made sense, he supposed. This had always been a tribute to the warrior as much as to the decision to fight.

That warrior also happened to be Shaina's father, the near-mythical Dax Silverbrake, former skypirate, now Defense Minister of Trios, a title he ignored for the most part, saying being the flashbow warrior amounted to the same thing.

"Quite a party," Shaina said, looking toward the glow of lights and the faint sounds of celebration still coming from the city. "You'd think they'd just signed the declaration this morning."

"My father says it's important that they remember. If you forget, you get soft—and ripe for the picking all over again."

Shaina grimaced. "My mother says the same thing. She says the Coalition, or people like them, will never, ever give up, not really. Even if you wipe them out, more like them will reemerge, somewhere, and take the same path all over again."

Lyon didn't say, "She would know," although it went through his mind. Shaina's mother, also Arellian and the former Major Califa Claxton of the Coalition Tactical School, had been both famous and honored in the

Coalition before she committed the unpardonable sin of betraying the High Command for a friend—his mother.

Like everyone on Trios, Lyon knew the story inside out: A prince become king and his new queen working with the prodigal flashbow warrior and his tactically brilliant mate, standing together in a way that inspired them all. The Coalition, which had expected to crush the upstart rebellion easily, had instead been driven out of its most prized conquest.

He was incredibly proud of them. The responsibility of being their heir was heavy at times—hence his desire for anonymity on this trip—but he wouldn't trade being their son for anything.

"—stay here. I may never go back."

Lyon snapped out of his reverie at Shaina's words, and the edge that had come into her voice. "Never go back?" he said, afraid he'd missed something crucial.

"Well, maybe not *never*," she amended, "but come on, Cub, you have to admit living out from under our parents' legends has . . . a certain appeal."

Since he'd just been thinking something similar, he couldn't deny it. Nor could he deny the tense undertone he was still hearing as she spoke. As always, she used the bedamned nickname, which he'd only allowed because it had pleased him to have at least one person eschew the royal deference.

That at twelve she had refused to allow him the same privilege with her own name had amused him. Now he only used the shortened "Shay" in his mind, when his thoughts strayed into territory he tried to avoid. When someone thought of you as their brother, thinking of them as something much different than a sister only made things worse.

And taking off for another planet hadn't helped much, even before the source of his disquiet had turned up in person.

"Do you really think it would be different here?" he asked, feeling his way carefully, not knowing what was eating at her. "They're as celebrated here as they are at home. Especially your father."

She grimaced. "If they only knew."

There it was, Lyon thought. Whatever was eating at her was surfacing now. He'd grown up with her, and he knew her expressions almost as well as he knew his own.

"Knew what?"

"That my father, their vaunted, adored hero," she said, her voice now nearly dripping with a bitter note, "is a liar."

Chapter 2

SHAINA LOOKED as if she'd expected him to react exactly as he had, with shock. She turned her head and let out a compressed breath.

"What are you talking about?" he asked.

Shaina did what she often did when she wasn't ready to talk about something. She diverted.

"Never mind. Do you really believe those slugs who grabbed you didn't know who you were?"

"If they did, they never let it slip. Just cleaned me out. Except for the ring," he said, thankfully touching the bulk of it through his shirt. "They didn't see it."

"If your coin is all they wanted, why didn't they just leave you on the street once they had it? Or just kill you?"

She sounded so matter-of-fact about it, he couldn't help but wince inwardly. Sometimes she carried cool logic a bit far. He had no answer, but her words had something tickling at the edge of his memory, something he couldn't quite put his finger on. Thinking the best way to remember was to stop trying, he circled back to the beginning.

"What did your father lie about?"

He'd thought he'd kept his tone fairly even, but she flared up anyway. "Oh, I know. Why would the great, the heroic Dax Silverbrake lie? His whole story, every detail of his time as the most famous skypirate in the galaxy, is public knowledge, right? He came clean about everything, so what could he possibly have to lie about now, right?"

"Did I say any of that?" he asked mildly; not for nothing had he grown up with this girl, who had inherited her mother's fiery temperament as well as her courage.

"You didn't have to, I know you were thinking it. Like everyone else."

"And here I've always thought I was so exceptional."

He said it teasingly, trying to nudge her out of her mood. She didn't even smile, but lapsed into silence, her jaw set. He sighed. She could go from cool and calm to fierce and impetuous faster than anyone he'd ever met. The trip back to cool and calm wasn't always so quick.

He tried another path. "Why are you here anyway? I thought you weren't coming." Because this was the last place she'd wanted to be. He wondered if she realized he'd guessed that.

"You're bedamned lucky I did," she muttered.

He owed her this much, he thought. "Yes. I am."

Her gaze flicked to his face, searching, as if looking for any sign of falsity, or any hint he was patronizing her.

"All right, then," she finally said, apparently satisfied that his acknowledgment had been genuine.

"Thank you," he added because it seemed appropriate. That, at least, embarrassed her enough that she smiled awkwardly.

"Had to," she said. "Who would I torment if anything happened to you?"

"Whoever he is, I wouldn't wish it on him."

He said it wryly, although underneath he supposed he was glad to see his teasing, impish companion back. It made it easier for him to keep his thoughts under control. But at the same time, he didn't know how long he could keep going like this, as the safe, harmless playmate of her childhood.

"And I'm sure those thuggers will be loath to admit they were bested by a mere helpless girl." He made himself smile as he said it, and she made a childish face at him. It was an old, familiar exchange between them, and made them both laugh.

"You better be more careful then," she said, her tone changing.

There was something in the way she said it, some deep concern that might even be worry, that tugged at him. It warmed him. No matter how crazy his life was, Shaina was always there. Sometimes chiding him, sometimes teasing him, sometimes encouraging him. And now he had to add rescuing him to that list, he thought. It was usually the other way around.

But she understood, in the way only another child of legendary parents could.

Which brought him back once more to what she'd said in the first place. Her father, a liar? It didn't seem possible. Certainly not necessary. As she'd said, his godfather's entire history, some of it much less than pristine, was out there for people to see and learn. And while the general consensus was that by his actions as a skypirate he'd done more single-handedly to harass and frustrate the Coalition than the entire band of rebellious Triotian survivors, there were some who wished he'd found another way. Mostly these were parents of children who were fired with the stories of his adventures and were determined to run off and become skypirates themselves.

But Shaina felt much differently about the flashbow warrior, and she wasn't ready for him to poke what was clearly a raw wound.

"When did you get here?" he asked instead.

"This morning," she said. "It took me most of the day to track you."

He was well dressed, but didn't look outwardly wealthy. Once, just being Triotian would have been enough to draw a thief's interest, but that time had passed with the Coalition's near destruction of a world that had given so much to other worlds. But wealth, he supposed, was relative. It could well have been a simple robbery of someone they thought had more than they did. Leftovers from Coalition philosophy.

"How did you find me?" he asked.

She shrugged. "Lots of questions. Finally found someone who saw you with those skalworms. After you took that knock on the head. He thought they were just helping a friend who'd partaken a bit too much."

His brow furrowed. "You asked around for me by name?"

She gave him a disgusted look. "Of course not. I knew you didn't want to be held to ceremony yet. I just kept asking about a pretty Triotian walking around looking like he wanted a fight."

He blinked, drew back slightly. "I wanted no fight. They started it."

"I didn't say you wanted a fight, just that you looked like it."

"And I'm not pretty."

"As you wish. Ugly then."

She grinned suddenly. She was definitely back, his little pest of a companion. So he risked going back to his earlier question.

"Why did you come?"

She let out a long breath. For a moment she just stared into the fire. He thought of warning her she would temporarily destroy her night vision that way, but held his tongue. They'd both been taught by the greatest warriors of the rebellion. She knew.

Her lowered lashes were dark sweeping semicircles against her pale Arellian skin, skin so different from his own golden, Triotian tones. In an odd quirk of fate, he who looked so much like his father had inherited his mother's Arellian blue eyes, while she who looked so much like her mother had in turn inherited her father's jade green ones.

"I had to get away," she finally said, sounding tired—enough of an oddity for her that concern spiked through him.

"Why?" he asked, his voice soft.

"I was so angry I was . . . afraid. I've never been so enraged. I was in a fume like I've never felt before."

"So you left before you could say or do something you'd regret? How full-fledged of you."

"And I hope a zipbug finds your ear," she shot back.

"Easy. I meant it nicely. Learning to walk away is hard." *As I know all too well. I had to walk away from you.*

"Oh." She grimaced. "I didn't, though. Not before I . . . said some things. Did some things."

"To who?"

"My father. And my mother, too, but mainly him." Her jaw tightened, and her voice was fierce when she added, "She just went along because she had little choice. *He's* the one who lied."

And now they were at the point of truth.

"About what?"

"He—"

She broke off suddenly, her head whipping around to look behind them, her hand streaking to grab her dagger from her boot almost simultaneously with his own movement. He'd heard it too, the faintest of rustles.

Animal? Arellia had some dangerous creatures with more than two legs: slimehogs with tusks as long as his arm, the dangerously fanged flymouse, and jumpspiders the size of your fist. The fabled Arellian dragons were a myth, of course, but then many had thought the golden horses of Arellia a myth, too, until his several-generations-back uncle had found the last surviving herd. Arellia abounded with such mystical, magical tales, scoffed at and banned during the Coalition years, but clung to and repeated in the hidden corners.

Silence continued, and he wondered if it had merely been a bit of stray breeze they'd heard, rustling leaves. It was a still night, but perhaps up in the trees air was moving faintly.

He didn't believe it, not really, but whatever it was was holding fast now.

Shaina seemed to reach the same conclusion, and turned back. Or almost. Just as he had, she kept her head slightly turned, one ear aimed in that direction. And the dagger stayed unsheathed, within easy reach.

"Maybe it's that nasty slimehog we saw earlier," she said in a conversational tone that was a little bit too loud. He glanced at her, saw her expression, and realized what she was doing.

"Maybe," he agreed cheerfully. "He certainly was a bad-tempered thing. Looked like he'd go after anything that moved."

Shaina grinned at him. If the watcher was of the two-legged variety, thinking an ill-tempered—although that was a redundancy—belligerent slimehog was around would make him start thinking of his own welfare as much as whatever he was here for. And if it was indeed an animal, their voices would keep any but the most aggressive or crazy at bay.

"Maybe we should hunt him," Shaina said. "Since we're too insolvent to even buy food and lodging."

Lyon grinned at her; that easily she'd put out the possibility of a greater threat, and in the next breath announced they had nothing worth stealing. His father was right—she was a very smart girl.

"Ho, the fire!"

Lyon's dagger was back in his hand in an instant. *So. Two legs.*

He flicked a glance at Shaina. She was as ready as he, and when it came down to it, she was a bigger threat with the blade than he, not technically, but because no one expected a wispy little girl to be a threat at all. But she was frowning, and gave a slight shake of her head to indicate she hadn't sensed anything in that way she had.

"Approach," he called out, with every bit of command he could muster, "with your hands in full view."

"That's it, put your royal on," Shaina whispered.

"Quiet?" he suggested; no one ordered her and got very far.

The rustling came again, from the same place, more definite this time.

"And if you have friends, best they come with you now. We will not take it kindly if they eschew our hospitality by hiding and watching."

"I swear," Shaina muttered, "sometimes you sound more like your father than he does."

He hushed her again, although he appreciated the compliment, whether she'd meant it as one or not.

"Alone," came the answer out of the trees. "And I come with a gift to share, if you're truly without food."

So he had heard them. Clever, clever girl.

A man stepped out of the shadows of the trees and into the outer edge of the light cast by the small fire. He was small, wiry, and his face held the wrinkles of advanced years. One hand was held up, palm out to display its emptiness. The other hand held a fat, skinned, and ready-for-the-spit brollet. The thought of a juicy steak made Lyon suddenly realize he'd had nothing for two days now but one of the life bars he always carried in his pack.

The man spread his hands wider, revealing the large knife tucked into his belt. "I have but this blade, which I will put down if you wish, but I will not hand it over to you."

Fair enough, Lyon thought. He glanced at Shaina. She shrugged. Apparently nothing was triggering her warning instincts. He motioned the man to join them. "You are generous to offer," Shaina said, eying the large brollet. The things ran rampant on Arellia, and it was as well they were good eating or there would be even more of them, devouring all vegetation in sight and starving other creatures. "That would feed you for a few days."

"I welcome the company," the old man said.

For a man of such age, he moved easily enough, if slowly. He dropped down to sit before the fire, reaching out to it. His hands, Lyon saw, were gnarled, his fingers long and thin. They were almost delicate looking, with veins visible beneath skin that seemed oddly translucent.

It wasn't until the brollet was roasting nicely on the spit they'd improvised that Lyon finally asked, "Why are you not down with the revelers in the city?"

"I might ask the same of you, young prince."

Lyon froze. Shaina grabbed her dagger.

"I am no threat to you," the old man said. "Everyone knows the Prince of Trios is to make his first official appearance at the ceremony five dawnings hence. It is only natural that he would wish to see something of his mother's world. And you look a great deal like your father."

Lyon grimaced and barely resisted yanking off the apparently useless cap.

"Oh, you might fool those who look but do not see," the old man said, as if he meant to reassure.

"Which is most," Shaina said.

"Indeed, you are correct." The old man smiled at her approvingly. To Lyon's surprise, she looked pleased. Shaina didn't usually care what anyone else thought of her, save those she knew and respected.

The old man looked back at him. "You do have the look of your father," he said. "But your eyes, those are Graymist eyes."

Lyon drew back. "Do you have a name?"

"I am called the old man of the mountain," he answered.

"I did not ask what you are called," Lyon said.

A wider smile came over the man's face. He nodded. "My true name," the old man said, "is Theon Talberon." He looked at Lyon. "And," he added, "years ago, I knew your mother."

Now this, Lyon thought, was getting interesting.

Chapter 3

CUB DIDN'T QUITE believe it, Shaina realized, although she doubted anyone but her would have known that look. She didn't blame him. People from far-flung places across the system often tried to claim some kind of connection to the royals of Trios. It seemed to give them some sort of distinction they craved.

"I see your doubt," the old man said cheerfully. "But 'tis true. I knew the Graymist clan, even before your mother was born." He shifted his gaze to Shaina with eyes that were alert and bright, for all his age. "And I stayed with them through the rebellion, that was won thanks to your father, the greatest flashbow warrior yet seen."

Although she was surprised he knew who she was, she let it go for the moment. "He is," she said, her chin up proudly as she hid the grimace she might have let Cub see. To outsiders she showed only the greatest respect and admiration for her father.

"But do you know the story of the first conquest?" the old man asked.

Cub shrugged. "It was like any Coalition conquest. Bloody, deadly, and short."

"A succinct and sadly accurate assessment," he said.

"Creonic Age history," Shaina said.

"Not quite that old," Theon said mildly.

"Long before even my mother's grandparents were born," Cub said. "You say knew the Graymists."

"Yes. Of course, I have nothing to prove it but my word, a tale or two, and this," he said, holding something out to Cub. "A gift from . . . let's see, it would be your great-uncle? Or is that great-great? Time does slip away, children, I warn you."

Cub shifted his gaze to the object the old man held. Shaina quickly turned hers back to the old man; somebody needed to keep an eye on him at all times. He might be old, but her father—damn him—had always told her that sometimes threats came in the unlikeliest forms. The fact that she hated him just now didn't negate what he'd taught her. He was, after all, the greatest flashbow warrior, just as Theon had said.

She heard Cub suck in a breath sharply as he took the object from Theon's hand. A quick glance told her it was a small carving, some sort of feathered creature rising out of a curved base.

"The Sunbird," Cub whispered.

The old man gave him a pleased nod.

She saw it then. The Sunbird. The mythical fiery bird of Arellia. And the name of the ship his mother had flown in her glory days with the Coalition, before the truth of what they really were had become clear to her.

Unlike Trios, whose king had seen the truth from the beginning. The old king, Lyon's great-grandfather, and his son after him, had held out long after every other world in the sector, making Trios the last to finally fall. And his grandson had been the one to lead Trios back to the freedom they had lost. A fine, noble tradition, set by those kings. A tradition that would one day fall to Lyon.

Shaina sighed. It was hard to think of her lifetime companion as the king. To her he was still the boy who tolerated her knack for getting herself—and him—into trouble, and then managed to talk their way out of it. Tonight had been a dream, one last adventure, her rescuing *him* for once, before. . . . Maybe that's why she clung to the childhood nickname that so irritated him; calling him Cub enabled her to forget he was indeed Prince Lyon of Trios. Destined one day to be king.

He would be fine; he had learned what he needed, his parents and her own had seen to that. He was tough, strong, and smart, with his mother's quick mind and his father's cool temperament. And he possessed, she had to admit, although not to his face, some not inconsiderable fighting skills.

But she still couldn't picture the strong, powerful, regal King Darian not being around forever. Her head knew it would happen, that someday even Triotians passed from this realm.

Even her father would, someday.

Pain jabbed at her. *Not now*, she ordered herself. *Do not think of this now.*

"I believe our meal is ready," the old man said.

This last was directed at Cub, and after a moment's hesitation, he reached out and gave the old man back the carving, that remarkably detailed image of a creature that didn't really exist.

"This is not proof," he said. "Many lay claim to a connection to my family."

"As practical as your mother, I see. Except, it seems, when it comes to keeping our dinner from burning."

Shaina grabbed the roasted brollet and pulled it onto the flat rock on the edge of the fire. It smelled so good, her stomach reacted with an audible growl. But Cub didn't tease her as he usually would have. He was still staring at the old man.

"Did your mother ever tell you of their home here?"

"She has spoken of it, yes."

"Thanks to her service her family was able to keep it, until it was destroyed in the rebellion you are here to commemorate."

Shaina's gaze shot to Cub's face. His mother's service in the Coalition was not his—or his mother's—favorite subject. But his expression stayed even as he lifted a brow at the old man.

"Yes."

She thought she saw a smile flicker across the old man's face. This lovely brollet was going to wait, she thought with a sigh.

"Did she tell you of the mural?"

Cub drew back slightly.

"I see that she did. It was from that mural of a sunbird that she drew the name of her ship, was it not?"

"Yes."

The old man leaned back, smiling fully now.

"Why don't you portion that out, my dear?" he said to Shaina. "Less for me, my old bones don't have much meat left, so they require little."

She was hungry enough that she didn't quibble, but hesitated at putting her only weapon at hand to such use. With a wink, the old man took his own blade, carefully and pointedly still sheathed, and held it out to her. "You are your father's daughter, aren't you?"

"As fate would have it," she said neutrally as she took the knife and began to carve.

"How do you know of the mural?" Cub asked. "You were in that house?"

"I know of the mural," the old man said as he took the meat Shaina held out to him, "because I painted it."

Shaina stopped in the motion of handing Cub his portion.

"You?" she said, then grimaced as she heard how disbelieving she sounded. "No insult intended."

"None taken," the old man said easily. "It has been years since I have painted in such detail. And," he added with a sigh, "there is little market for such these days on Arellia."

Shaina took a bite of her own meat, and barely managed not to sigh aloud at the taste of it. The men began as well, although the old man was true to his word and did not eat much.

"Now Trios," the old man said as they ate, "is a place for such work. A place of freedom and good. And a beauty it will soon regain. But Arellia . . . Arellia is a place of wonder and mystery. Some would say magic."

Shaina nearly snorted aloud. Inelegant, she thought. But then, she was. She'd made her peace with that long ago, yet it still rose now and then to irk her. Her mother was tough, battle experienced, and a tactical genius, yet when moved to do so she could put on a show of feminine beauty unmatched by any save the queen. Shaina herself had the toughness, was working on the experience and tactics, but she was also inelegant, impatient, and a little wild. So be it.

"So, my young friends," the old man said, after handing back at least half of what Shaina had given him, leaving it to them, "what brings you to my mountain? Are you searching for the famous Graymist coffers?"

"The what?" Shaina asked.

Cub smiled. "It is an old legend among my mother's family. Of magic and lost treasure. I've not thought of it in a long time."

"The tales are commonly told here, and have been even more so of late. The visit of a prince of Graymist blood has renewed interest." He looked at Cub steadily. "But then, your people have been a trifle too busy to be telling stories, haven't they?"

"It happens when evil strikes so deeply," Cub said. "Rebuilding takes time."

He was quoting his father again, Shaina realized. Her Cub did pay attention.

"Did you ever wonder why," Theon said, "of all the worlds they conquered, the Coalition tried to erase only the people of Trios? Other worlds, the people were kept for conversion, or failing that, slaves. But Triotians were to be exterminated."

"My mother says they knew," Shaina said. "They knew that of all their conquests, it was the people of Trios who would be most likely to cause trouble. They would be the most stubborn, because they were the most dedicated to their freedom, their way of life. The High Command wanted no one left for the rest of the system to rally around."

"And they were right," Cub said softly.

"Indeed, they were," Theon agreed. "Your father rallied people the Coalition long assumed subjugated. He was exactly what they feared he was."

Lyon smiled. "Yes. He was. And is."

"What is this treasure?" Shaina asked. "I've not heard of it, and my mother is Arellian as well."

"It is particular to the Graymist family," Cub said. "Supposedly accessible only to them."

"Including you," the old man pointed out with a grin. "And who doesn't love a tale of hidden treasure?"

"My mother told me the story often when, as a child, I would not go to sleep," Cub said. "It is supposed to be in a secret cave on a mountain, undiscoverable by anyone who does not have the right."

"It has always belonged to the Graymists. And in fact," the old man put in, "it is said to be on this very mountain that looks over us now. That is why I asked if you were off to search. Seems an exciting adventure to have before you settle down to your duties, Prince Lyon."

Shaina saw from Cub's expression that the man could have said nothing more likely to stoke the desire to do exactly that.

"Are you searching yourself? Have you run out of strength or coin, and now must replenish either or both?" Cub asked.

Theon laughed. "You are as astute as your father, I see."

"If by this you mean suspicious, yes, it is a lesson I've learned at his knee."

"And no doubt learned well. As your father had to."

Shaina knew from her own mother's experiences as a collared Coalition slave more than she cared to about lessons learned hard. That history was in part why she held her king in such awe; she doubted very much she had the kind of forgiveness in her that had allowed him to forgive, accept, and even come to honor her mother—the woman who had once thought she owned him.

"I have no need of it," the old man said. "I live a simple life. 'Twould do me no good anyway, since if the legends are true, I could not take it. But were I younger, as bold as you are—and a Graymist—I believe I would find the hunt irresistible."

Shaina understood the man's words. And indeed, she found the idea almost irresistible herself. She turned to Cub, studying him intently for a moment—and thought she saw an answering urge.

"Shall we, Cub?" she asked. "One last adventure before you must start carrying all that responsibility on your shoulders?"

He turned to her. She saw the gleam in his eyes, and knew the answer before he spoke it.

Chapter 4

NO ONE SEEMED to notice him. Wrapped up in their revelry, smugly celebrating. They thought they were safe. They did not look beyond this day. Their minds were too small, too narrow to envision the scope he, so much wiser and experienced, saw so clearly.

The tall, thin man pulled his cloak closer around him. It was a warm day, yet no one seemed to think it odd that he was wearing the heavy garment.

These fools do not think at all, he told himself. *They are but insects, an annoyance, but not a hindrance.*

That they had, once, defeated the mighty Coalition was a part of history he chose to ignore. In fact, he had only a vague memory of the truth of that battle, so completely had it been supplanted by the official version—that the retreat had been a tactical decision only.

He pondered this new opportunity. He knew everything would change soon anyway. Not soon enough to suit him, of course. It chafed at him that things were moving so slowly. He had plans, important plans, and they could not begin until the move was begun. But they would move, his plans would work, and he would soon be back in the inner circle, where he rightfully belonged. He would regain his position and be honored as was his due, with the apology owed him. All the time he'd spent here in the last weeks, studying, learning, waiting for his opportunity, would culminate soon, and in personal triumph. And it would taste doubly sweet, after the years of disgrace and humiliation he had so unjustly suffered. It was not his fault that his commander had been a bumbling fool.

He had thought he would have to wait for the coming storm for his chance, that only then could he decide the best moment and action. And now it had been unexpectedly handed to him, as if on a golden platter. He had his key back into the empire within his grasp. And when he was back, those who had dismissed him, or declared him too crazed or disgraced by his late commander's idiocy to matter, would pay.

He dodged a knot of revelers, swirling his cloak around him to keep from touching them. The smell of wine and lingberry liquor met his nose, which wrinkled with distaste at the odor. They reminded him of nothing less than the unwashed Sowerths, whose reputation for filth was unmatched in the system.

Yet he nodded, smiling, at them. The fools would think him just another of them, mindlessly seizing the anniversary of their silly declaration as an excuse for drunken frivolity. But his smile was not with them, it was at them, even as he pitied them their blindness and relished the thought of their shock at what was to come.

He kept moving, taking a certain pleasure whenever he saw a trace of the scars left behind by the war. The repaired places in the roadway. The patched wall next to the Galatin city gate. Even the bright white finish of the Council Building brought him gratification, for he knew it had had to be repaired and repainted after the siege.

The thought of the man who had caused that siege to fail pricked the rising bubble of enjoyment, and he scowled. That man had gotten away with far too much. Who would have thought Arellia, this world of foolish tales and legends, would have spawned such an unpredictable and unorthodox fighter?

Yes, along with the others who had orchestrated this temporary setback—and it was temporary, he insisted silently, even if it had lasted years—in the glorious design, that particular Arellian captain would be dealt with once and for all. He should have died long ago, had in fact been reported dead. Only when he had come back to Arellia had he learned the skalworm had survived.

Perhaps as reward for the coup he was about to manage, he would be permitted to kill the man. That would be a nice start.

He hurried on. He went past the statue in the square, knowing better than to look at it now. The very image of that arrogant, brash, swaggering skypirate made him faintly ill. Silverbrake, more than anyone, even that upstart Arellian, was responsible for the ills he now suffered, for his status as outcast. And once he was delivered from this Hades, he would make it his mission to destroy him, too. Silverbrake had been within his grasp once, and escaped. He would not be so lucky this time. By Eos, if he had to go to that damnable Trios itself, he would see that Dax Silverbrake paid.

LYON WELCOMED the physical tiredness after the long day's hike, even though it brought on a faint echo of his headache from that blow. Much of their journey had been uphill as they worked their way up the mountain that overlooked—and some said watched over—Galatin. It was an old singular peak among the hills, not particularly tall or wide, but rugged and varied in terrain.

But they were in no hurry. The journey itself was the purpose, so they were taking their time. Still, this expedition would be much easier if the path were wide enough or cleared enough for an airspeeder, he thought.

But easy, he reminded himself, was for the soft. Mental preparedness for the job ahead of him was important, but so was the physical. He had the example of his father, an imposing figure in his Triotian prime, to follow—a difficult pinnacle to reach and an inspiration at the same time. But he would reach it. Trios deserved no less than the best he could give.

He finished the last bite of the rockfowl Shaina had snared. Coupled with the fish he'd caught from the mountain stream nearby, it had been a good meal. They would rest in the open tonight, on the lee side of the large rock their fire warmed. They shouldn't need more, since the weather seemed to be holding fair. He would prefer the softness of Triotian grass to lie upon, but that was merely indulgence.

Shaina was gathering bones to discard safely away; if there were animals to be drawn, better at a good distance. And since they were off looking for a mythical treasure, who was to say they wouldn't encounter one of those equally mythical Arellian dragons?

He smiled inwardly at the whimsy. Soon enough he would have no time for such things. He was certain his father did not. No doubt the propensity for anything whimsical had been destroyed the moment the Coalition had slaughtered his family and enslaved him.

His parents' story was indeed legend; it had all the elements of the stories handed down over generations. War, death, tribulation, love, and finally triumph. His own life, lived in relative peace, seemed dull by comparison.

A peace, he reminded himself, bought for Trios by eternal vigilance. And the constant guardianship of her king.

A yawn overtook him, and with an effort he rose and began to gather wood—enough to keep the now banked fire going—as much to keep those suspected animals clear as for warmth.

"Alternate?" Shaina asked when he returned.

"As usual," he agreed; they'd done this so many times, it was a routine. They would take turns checking the fire, so neither of them had to stay awake for too long.

She began to pull the thermal envelope out of her pack. "I suppose I should be thankful for your father's law about preparations," she said as she spread it out. "I was able to just grab this and run."

"There's reason for it," Lyon agreed as he pulled his own out of his similar pack, but left it folded and sat atop it as it warmed. He wondered if finally he was going to learn the truth behind Shaina's sudden, unexpected appearance here.

"Still, every year at the gathering, there are grumblings it's no longer needed."

"People feel safer now, at least enough to envision the future again. That Corling is long dead, and his lieutenant cast out of the High Command doesn't hurt."

The Butcher of Trios had been executed by his own, for failing to crush the Triotian rebellion. To this day his father regretted not having had the chance to handle that task personally. And Corling's lieutenant had failed to capture her father, the skypirate who had not only plagued the Coalition into a frenzy, but had come back to haunt them when he helped lead Arellia's own rebellion.

"Mordred should have fallen to the blade as well. I'm surprised he did not," he said.

"My mother says he knew someone, or was related to someone."

"That would be typical, for the Coalition."

"And now they've retreated to the very edge of the system."

"Are you saying you believe it is over?"

"Of course not. I'm my mother's daughter," Shaina said wryly.

And there it was again, the absence of her father in the equation.

"She knows Trios is the biggest prize in the galaxy," she said. "And the Coalition will never accept their defeat. She firmly believes they will one day return to regain all they have lost. From Daxelia to Trios."

"Trios would be the hardest to retake"

"It might not come to that. Arellia might fight, this time," she said.

"With your father to lead them once more?"

He said it without thinking. It was something he would have said before, when she'd been so proud of her father she would have near burst with it.

"Oh, he will lead them again, if necessary," she said, bitterness adding a slice to her voice. "They, at least, can trust him."

Lyon stifled a sigh. He was through letting her go at this sideways.

"Out with it."

It was not only worded like an order, but even to his ears his voice had a ring of command that eerily echoed his father's. For a moment Shaina looked startled, as if she'd heard it as well. Something flickered in her eyes, something he couldn't quite name, but he liked it.

"Do you remember your Selection Ceremony?" she asked.

"Of course I do."

It was one of the longest-held traditions of Trios, that every child that became of age would go through the rite. Every year those who qualified would gather in the square of Triotia, the capital, near the ceremonial stone. One by one they would approach, lay a hand on the cool, smooth rock. And wait. Most years, nothing happened. It had been so his entire lifetime. The last time the stone had awakened, the selected child had been slaughtered along with most of the population of the city in the invasion. And the time before that the stone had lit with a brightness no one had ever seen before, heralding the strongest in many generations. It had been for Dax Silverbrake, the greatest flashbow warrior ever seen.

"No one expected it to awaken to you," she said.

"Of course not. You know it never goes to a member of the royal family, any more than it goes to a member of the current warrior's family."

"Exactly. Yet you participated."

"Of course," he repeated. "It's tradition."

And the royal family of Trios was different than others he knew of; they ruled only by the consent of the people, and were granted no special treatment or benefits they had not earned. And so their children always took part, as did everyone's.

"Then why is it not tradition for the current warrior's children?"

His frown deepened as he wondered where she was going with this. "Because it would not work, everyone knows this. But for us it is . . . a gesture. Necessary to show that the royal family does not hold itself above the people who have chosen them to rule. Shaina, what is it?"

She drew in a long, audible breath. He found himself holding his, waiting.

"I was at the arena, watching the airspeeder races." She shot him a sideways glance. "Macario won, without you there to trounce him."

"Don't remind me," he said. "Go on."

"I cut through the square to go home. Kalila—you've met Fleuren's great-granddaughter?—her pet leecat got away from her and was hiding under the notch of the stone."

He knew where she meant, it was the spot on the stone where the first flashbow bolts had been carved out, before the main lode the stone had come from had been discovered to produce even more powerful bolts. But that stone in the square was still the center of the flashbow legend, the once-in-a-hundred-year-generation warrior who could use the crossbow that glowed with a strange energy, could fire those incredible, explosive bolts that were more powerful than even most modern weapons.

But what he didn't know, still, was what this had to do with her mood, her fight with her father, or anything else. He waited. She stared into the embers. He should stir up the fire, he thought, but he wasn't about to interrupt her now that she'd finally gotten to it.

"I went to retrieve it for her," she said. "She couldn't reach."

He barely managed to hide his exasperation when she stopped again.

"And?" he finally prompted.

"And I touched the stone. I never had before."

"I know. There was no need, the ability isn't hereditary."

"Wasn't hereditary."

He blinked. "What?"

"It wasn't hereditary." She lifted her head then, and met his gaze. "Until now."

It was so unexpected, it took him a moment to get there. When he did, the impossibility of it made his brow furrow with doubt.

"What are you saying?"

"It awoke, Cub. The stone came alive and glowed, the moment I brushed it."

"But—"

"Don't say it. It's impossible. It's never happened. I know all that."

"Maybe it's some sort of . . . bleed over, from your father. He is that powerful."

She laughed. It was a harsh sound. "That's what I thought. But the moment I confronted him with what had happened, it was obvious."

"What was?"

"That he already knew."

"You're guessing, Shaina. He couldn't have known, it's never—" He broke off before he repeated what she'd asked him not to say.

"No. He admitted it, finally. That he'd always known. Since I was a baby, and he'd found me playing with one of the bolts, and it was live. He tested it, different ways—removed himself to be sure it wasn't just him. But it always happened."

"My God," Lyon breathed. She took heart from the fact that he sounded almost as distressed as she felt.

"I'm the next flashbow warrior, Cub. And my father has been lying to me all my life."

Chapter 5

"WHAT ARE you doing?"

Rina Carbray paused, looking over her shoulder at Dax.

"Unless you've gone starblind, you can see what I'm doing."

She went back to stuffing clothing and gear into her pack. More gear than clothing; she had, after all, spent her formative years on the infamous Dax Silverbrake's *Evening Star*. Prepare for everything, and enjoy it if none of it happens.

"Why?"

"It's what you do, when you're going somewhere."

"Where are you going?"

She turned on him. She might be nearly a foot shorter, but she faced him fearlessly, shoving her bangs back so she could glare at him more thoroughly. "Your legal guardianship of me terminated long ago, brollet-brain. I go where I please."

For an instant pain flashed in his jade-colored eyes, and she regretted her sharp words. But he was acting as if he were no smarter than that ubiquitous creature, so he had it coming—even if she did owe him her very life and adore him as if there were blood between them, not merely the connection of choice.

And she had, she realized, jolted him out of his preoccupation. He was studying her now, as if that discordant note had snapped on his tactical brain.

"You're going to Arellia."

"Give the man a withal," she said, barely resisting the urge to flip one of the rare Romerian coins at him as she stuffed her small navigation projector in her pack's outside pocket, if for no other reason than she felt off balance without it. She added the small hairbrush that was all she required for the blonde locks she kept defiantly short, in tribute to the days she'd flown with the man she was facing down now.

"Rina—"

"It's the biggest celebration in the system, given Trios isn't in the habit of throwing huge, interplanetary parties. Why shouldn't I go?"

He ignored the obvious feint. "You're going after her."

She snapped the outside flap closed with a flick of her wrist, and with perhaps a bit more energy than was required.

"Someone has to, and it can't be you."

"I—"

"She wouldn't even talk to you right now." She glared at him. "And I don't blame her one curlbug's worth."

Dax sighed. "I was only trying to protect her."

"You protected me when you didn't always tell me what idiotic scheme you were hatching, when you denied what was obvious to everyone, that you were trying like Hades to get yourself killed. If you can't see that this is different, that you had no right to deny her this knowledge, then there's no hope for you."

He was pacing now. "She's my little girl."

"She's nearly the age you were when the Coalition finally took Trios."

"And we all know how well I handled that." His voice was sharp.

"You did the only thing you thought you could do," she said. "And no one knows that better than me, because I lived it with you."

"I thought you were angry with me."

"I am. That doesn't change the truth."

For a long moment he simply looked at her. Then, at last, he said softly, "You've become all I knew you could be, Rina. And more."

She flushed, unable to stop the rush of pride that filled her. This man had once been her world, the only stable thing in her life. He'd rescued her from death and worse; he'd kept her safe, and brought her home to Trios. And then, as her guardian, he'd given her a home, seen to her education, and taught her how to live a normal life even as he struggled to relearn it himself—as normal as life could be, after years flying the far reaches with the most infamous skypirate in the galaxy.

And when the time had come, she'd fought alongside him in the war for the liberation of Arellia.

She was grown now, long an adult, and strong enough to stand without him. The question was, was she strong enough to stand against him?

"Do you not see how she feels, Dax? I do. You're the closest thing to a father I have. And I think of how I would have felt had you kept something like that from me. If, perhaps, I had been too young when you found me to remember I was Triotian, and you had kept it hidden from me."

"I might have," he said, rather grimly. "It was a dangerous time to be Triotian, no matter how far from home."

"And if you had put it off until I discovered it on my own, how do you suppose I would have felt?"

His mouth twisted. "About how Shaina is feeling now?"

"Exactly."

It was a moment before he asked, "Have you talked of this trip with Califa?"

Rina held up a pocket-sized disrupter. "She loaned me this, just in case."

Dax smiled. And Rina smiled inwardly. The tough, ruthless skypirate, now once more the heroic warrior of Trios, was soft around the edges when it came to his mate. She sensed the moment when he gave in.

"She will listen to you."

"She always has." She tucked the disrupter into her belt. "And if she's with Lyon, you know he'll see to her."

"Yes. He will."

"At least he's always known who he was," she said, unable to resist a last jab.

Dax winced. "All right, stop, I accede." He sighed. "I didn't want to face reality. Heredity had never been a factor in the selection before, and I did not want it to be true now. Not my child."

"Why is it, this time?" she asked.

"I don't know. It shouldn't be. That's half the reason I never told her. I kept thinking it had to somehow be a mistake."

"That," Rina said, "was not the mistake."

She shouldered her pack; the transport she meant to catch left the skyport in less than an hour. But she had one more thing to say to him.

"Perhaps you were chosen because of what you would do, when the time came. Trios had become lax, complacent, content with our place in the system, never thinking anything could overtake us. There was no way we could have stood against the Coalition, weakened as we were. So who is the chosen warrior at that time? Probably the only man who would do what you did. So perhaps Shaina is the only one who can do what will be necessary in the next generation."

She could feel his surprise washing over her. "When did you become so wise? You truly have grown up, little Rina."

"And so," she said pointedly, "has Shaina."

He let out a heavy sigh. His mouth quirked upward at one corner. "Come, then. I'll take you to the skyport."

"In your airspeeder?" she asked hopefully.

He laughed. She had always been able to give him that, and it warmed her that she could still.

"I'm glad to see you haven't completely grown up."

"No more than you have," she said.

"Come, then." He gave her a sideways look, and the grin that he had passed on to his daughter. "I'll let you drive."

She let out a whoop of excitement. And ran.

SHAINA BREATHED easier, the knot she'd carried in her chest since the moment her father had admitted the truth loosening for the first time. As usual, unburdening to Cub relieved her tension. It didn't solve the problem, but it made her feel better. And it was clear by his expression that he was truly shaken. More than she'd even expected. He looked almost as shaken as she had felt when her father's admission had blasted her every perception of herself—and destroyed the future she'd hoped to build on her own choices. So many things she'd wanted to do, to try in her life, that now were lost to her. Because now she had no choices.

When Cub pulled her into a hug, she drew both warmth and strength from this, her dearest and oldest companion.

"Why?" he asked simply.

She sighed heavily. "He said that being the warrior came with a cost he didn't want me to start paying before I had to."

"It does come with great risk," he said, sounding as if he were keeping his tone neutral with an effort.

"He still had no right. If this is to be my life, my birthright, I had the right to know. How can I be prepared if I don't even know?"

"He would have told you, eventually."

"When? When an attack comes and it's too late?"

"I'm sure he wanted to protect you. You can't blame him for that."

"Can't I? My mother, at least, trusted me," she said. "She wanted him to tell me as soon as I was old enough to understand. He wouldn't."

"Your mother," Cub said, "would not be an easy person to stand fast against." His voice was tinged with admiration and respect, and while she agreed about her mother, right now she didn't want to hear it about her father.

"In this, she gave in. She had no choice. Because he is the flashbow warrior, it is his decision when the training begins for the next one."

"Your father is in his prime. He will remain the warrior for decades yet. Madoc stood with the flashbow into his hundredth year, and lived fifty more."

"And he had trained his successor for thirty of those years," she pointed out.

"Contention valid," he agreed. "What happened when he told you?"

She sighed. "We fought. Loudly. Long. And I . . . hit him. Pounded on him, really."

"And he did?"

"Nothing."

She grimaced. The idea of someone striking any flashbow warrior with impunity sounded ludicrous. And striking Dax Silverbrake even more so.

Her lying father, however . . . "He just stood there and took it. So he knows how wrong what he did was."

"Or it speaks of how much he loves his daughter."

She sat bolt upright in her anger, forgoing the comforting warmth of his arm around her. "Are you defending him?"

Cub threw up his hands. "No, just looking for an explanation."

"There is none," she said hotly. "Nothing he could say would make this right."

"Agreed," he said.

"So I caught the first transport. Rickety old cargo ship I wasn't sure was going to make it."

He was silent for so long, she thought he wasn't going to respond at all. Finally he said quietly, "Why here?"

"Why not? The big celebration is here. It will distract me."

He was silent again for a moment before saying, "Yes, a huge celebration. A great deal of it in honor of your father."

She stiffened, opened her mouth for a sharp retort, then stopped. For it was true, and she knew it.

"And my mother," she finally said. "Perhaps I came in tribute to her."

"Perhaps?"

For a moment, she wanted to pound on him as she had her father. She doubted Cub would be so obliging as to simply take it, however. And in the end he would make her think, make her work out in her mind exactly what she was so fumed about.

Cub always made her think.

Why had she come here? Was it truly just the lure of a big gathering, of revelry and merrymaking? The chance to get caught up in it all and forget the shattering of her entire life? But Cub was right—this celebration was as much tribute to her father as it was to the banishment of the Coalition. Back in the beginning, they had even considered calling it "Dax Days." A fact that had, according to the queen, sparked endless teasing.

While having a drunken bacchanal named after me might once have seemed the pinnacle of achievement, I find myself a little less appreciative these days.

Her father's voice, speaking words she had then been too young to understand, rang in her head. But later she had understood, had regretted she had been born too late to know the rakish, bold skypirate he'd been. But she had adored him nonetheless, even if she wished her mother hadn't tamed him quite so well.

She'd said as much to her one day. And her mother had laughed. "If you can't tell the difference between a man who's tamed and one who's curbing himself out of love, then you have much yet to learn, my sweet. Your father is far from tamed. And he will ever be so. And I would have him no other way."

Her mother's explanation had never left her, and had only fired her adoration even higher.

And, she thought bitterly, had set her up for the pain and fierce anger she was feeling now, that the man she had so worshipped had betrayed her. Had been betraying her since before she could even walk.

So why had she come? Here, where indeed the celebration was as much about that man as anything else?

Because Arellia was Trios's closest ally, surely. Trios was her home, and the hold it had on her was unbreakable, as it was with all who lived there. But being half-Arellian herself made her curious. She wanted to know the world of her mother and godmother.

She almost had herself convinced, would have managed it, except that Cub stayed so silent. He simply let her go through the process—another thing he'd learned from his father, he'd once told her. People might surrender to a superior argument, but they would fight for an idea they had reached themselves.

He was going to be a great king, she thought. He was already so wise.

Wiser than you, she told herself with an inward grimace.

"I can't go back, Cub."

"No. You're too angry. And," he added with some emphasis, "with right. This is, I think, indefensible. But even if it weren't, I am ever and always with you. As you have been with me."

And it was then that she realized she had come here not because the first available departure was coming here, but because Cub was here. He was who she always turned to when she was in an uproar.

This was what she had needed, she thought. This unconditional support, this complete understanding. No one knew her better than Cub. She doubted anyone ever would.

She settled back in, leaning against him as she watched the glowing embers of the fire. It could go a bit longer she thought, and still be hot enough to catch and flame when stirred, and fuel added. For a moment she could simply be here, far from the chaos her life had suddenly become.

"Do you suppose," she asked after a moment, "that we work so well because of who we are?"

"We're the only ones who truly understand what it is to be the children of heroes," he said.

Right now that wasn't a word she would apply to her father, but she didn't say so. Cub knew.

"I've never doubted their courage and valor."

"Except your father's when it came to facing his daughter's future. How does it feel, to know the greatest flashbow warrior of all time loves you so much his courage fails him?" Cub asked.

She hadn't thought of it that way. She hadn't been calm enough until now. The idea of her father's courage ever failing seemed ridiculous. And yet . . .

"How would you feel, Cub?" she asked. "What if one day you discovered you were not the prince, that your father had lied to you your entire life?"

"I can't imagine it," he said. "Perhaps your father is convinced the kind of fighting he has had to do will not be asked of the next warrior."

"Then he should have told me, for it would not matter."

"Contention valid again," he said. "I'm with you. You know that. But that does not mean I don't understand why your father did it."

"But you think it was wrong?" She needed this from him, for some reason she didn't quite understand.

"I know you. I know how strong you are. I think it was unnecessary."

It wasn't the blanket condemnation of her father she wanted just now, but it would do.

"Think of it no more now," he urged. "We will continue our adventure, and at worst have a pleasant, leisurely ramble through the woods, up this mountain."

"And at best find treasure?"

He laughed. "I'm afraid any treasure there might have been is probably long gone, looted by the Coalition. They wouldn't let a little thing like not being Graymist stop them. They've robbed every world they conquered of everything of value."

"Except Trios."

"Only because they never realized the greatest treasure Trios held was her people. When they failed to wipe them out, they sealed their own doom."

"Spoken like a true prince."

"Let's not think about that, either, now."

"Fair. We leave it all for this time. It will seem short enough."

"And we will have one last adventure," he said, sounding as if he were thinking of the countless others they'd had since they'd first toddled out beyond the gates of Triotia and into the world, adventurers together.

Chapter 6

FOR A MOMENT Lyon just stayed where he was, listening as she moved about. He was banking the fire, preparing for the night, while Shaina cleared a place for sleeping. She had inherited her mother's lovely voice, and it echoed even in the light, aimless air she seemed to be making up as she went. Once the fire was set for the night, she settled cross-legged before it and dug into her pack. She came out with a small brush and began to work it through her hair. He found himself studying how the strokes became longer as the glossy strands smoothed, and she reached a rhythm that was oddly pleasant to watch.

"I'm thinking my mother was right, back when she defied tradition and kept her hair short. And Rina, now."

She said it without looking at him, a fact for which he was thankful, since he'd been staring at her. Although he should have known she would sense it. Not much got by her.

As was fitting, for the next generation's flashbow warrior.

Just thinking it hit him like a blow all over again.

He tried to hide the chaos that was churning inside him. Since she had told him, he'd been haunted by images that made it hard to breathe. He only now realized just how much he had hoped that one day Shaina might wake to the fact that life had changed, that they had changed. He'd told himself he couldn't force her to see what she didn't want to see, that he couldn't make her feel what he wanted her to feel, what he felt. But neither could he change what he felt.

He'd come to Arellia for room to think, away from her, as much as anything. He needed some distance, and time to decide what to do about the simple fact that he wanted more from her. He wanted to be more to her. He spent half his time aching with the need to be more.

He'd understood her fear of losing what they had together as he began to assume his formal duties. But he'd hoped, with the examples of their parents before them, that she'd someday realize they didn't have to lose it at all. He'd told himself he had to give her time. That from Shaina, so stubborn about choosing her own path, it would be worth nothing unless she chose him freely, as their parents had chosen. Not because of some silly old predictions from people who wanted a legendary match between them, but because she wanted him. In the same way he wanted her—had wanted her, ever since the day he'd looked at this dearest of friends, who was everything he loved and admired and respected, and seen a woman, full-grown and beautiful.

It wasn't that he'd been blind; obviously, he'd seen the changes in his childhood companion as they'd grown, just as he'd seen his own. She'd even complained to him about the nuisances of it all. It was just that one day he'd caught himself admiring a slim waist, sleek skin, and curved hips he'd never really noticed before. Womanly hips, with a taut, rounded backside that, had it been on another woman, would have drawn his eyes long before.

But it wasn't another—it was Shaina. And so it had taken until that moment for his imagination to erupt with possibilities never before considered, possibilities that fired his senses.

But now that chance was gone, before it had ever flowered. Because as the flashbow warrior, she was tied to him in ways he'd never wished for. In ways she had no choice about. The biggest choice of all, who she would be, had been taken from her.

And one day, he himself might have to send her out to fight, to risk her life. Perhaps even send her to her death.

Needing to move, he walked down to the stream, thinking it had been a long time since he'd reduced life to the basics in this way—something he should do more often. He'd heard the stories often enough, usually from Glendar, of when his father had finally returned home after having been liberated by his mother, how the survivors of Trios had been living in caves, furnished only with what they had been able to salvage from the ruins. The planet, and especially the capital city of Triotia, still bore ugly scars from the war, but thanks to his father's guidance and his mother's seemingly endless energy, much had been restored.

What if one day you discovered you were not the prince?

Shaina's question echoed in his mind as he knelt to splash the cold, fresh water on his face. He couldn't conceive of his father lying in such a way, not as a man, nor as a king. And he truly could not imagine what it would feel like to find out his own father had hidden from him something of the same magnitude as her father had hidden from Shaina. He must think of this, of her pain, not his own shattered dreams.

He avoided the subject as he returned from his ablutions, letting her speak first.

"So, in the morning, what path shall we take?" she asked.

Not the one I'd hoped we would take, he thought, and firmly set aside the heated images that brought to mind.

"I've been trying to remember what I can of the old tales," he said. "Something about a cave below the crest, that opened to the west."

"And guarded by Arellian lions," she said.

"Which don't exist anymore," he felt compelled to point out.

"You're spoiling the fantasy, Cub."

"Sorry. I know that's usually your job."

She laughed, and in the light sound he sensed she had, for the moment at least, pushed her anger aside.

He rubbed at the still-tender spot behind his ear.

"Poor Cub," she said teasingly. And then, a note of concern coming into her voice, she asked, "You are all right, though? No dizziness, headache, odd vision?"

"No, mild, and no," he said. "I'm fine, beyond feeling more green than Triotian grass."

"You were here for the celebration, not expecting to get thugged at your first step," she said, coming to his defense as swiftly as she had teased him.

"But I should have been more wary. Large crowds, filled with many who started imbibing days ago, are always worth extra care."

"It is what you get if you insist on walking among them," she said. "But you would not be Lyon of Trios did you not."

He felt a small jolt of pleasure at her assessment. Shaina did not toss compliments about lightly.

"Glendar taught me well the lesson that our people must know us. And home on Trios, it is a joy. But I'm not sure it transfers well."

"You would have it no other way." She grimaced. "I may not know who *I* am, but I know you."

"Shaina—"

She waved him off, indicating she did not wish to go into it again. At least, not now. Because eventually, Lyon thought, they would have to. Her entire concept of her life, of the world and her place in it, had been shattered. It was going to take time and thought to deal with the debris. Not to mention the debris of his own shattered hopes.

"All right," he said. She threw him a grateful glance. "But eventually you will deal with it. One way or another."

"When I'm ready."

"I'm not certain one is ever ready to deal with something like this, but it can wait until it is less . . . raw."

She studied him for a moment, and then a smile slowly curved her mouth. "And that is why I know you will be a great king," she said. "You have your father's wisdom, and your mother's heart."

For a moment he was taken aback. This was more flattery than he'd ever had from her. Yet Shaina was nothing if not innately honest, to the point of bluntness. Flattery or no, she wouldn't say it if she didn't believe it.

THEY BOTH WOKE before dawn, ready to set out again.

Shaina stretched before saying, "So again I ask, what path?"

Lyon shrugged. "Since we are chasing but a legend, it hardly matters, I suppose, but the story says it faces west, so the west face."

"West it is," Shaina agreed. "And up."

"Down would be far too easy for such an adventure."

She flashed him the grin he'd been missing as she got up and headed for the stream to wash up. It was a perfect replica of her father's devilish grin, but calling upon some of that wisdom she credited him with, he didn't point it out. Once the comparison would have pleased her immensely. Now . . . Shaina may have inherited her father's grin and recklessness, but she had her mother's volatility.

You have your father's wisdom, and your mother's heart.

Her words came back to him, along with the look in her eyes when she'd said it. He hoped she was right. If she was, then he had a chance to become half the leader his father was.

Or perhaps not. Perhaps you had to go through something like what his father had gone through to be that kind of leader. He suspected only his mother knew the whole truth about what he had been subjected to. The bond between them was strong, unbreakable, and the rock upon which his own life had been built.

And in fact, what his mother had done, turning her back on her life and everything she had always known, leaving a career that had included medals and great acclaim, all to save the man she hadn't even known was a prince, was as courageous as any heroic action in battle. He respected her as much as he loved her, and that was a great deal.

Shaina emerged from the trees, hands in front of her. "I found some rockfowl eggs," she said. "I don't have a vessel to put them in, but I think that thin, flat rock there will heat enough to cook them."

"I have a few life bars left," he said.

"A meal fit for a prince, then," she teased. She was obviously in a better mood now. Or was simply doing as he'd suggested and not thinking about what had happened and why she was here at all.

He made his own visit to the stream to wash, and when he returned she had already begun the eggs, he suspected it was more to find out if her rock would work than from a desire to cook. It was working, and she was smiling.

"I just had to get it as hot as possible first, so the eggs started to cook right away and didn't run off the edges," she explained, clearly thinking it more a logistical exercise than a cooking chore.

"You should be in charge of the cooking, then," he said, knowing how she would react.

"You would subject yourself to that? You would starve in a week."

He laughed, glad to hear her usual bantering tone once more.

"I'm glad you're here," he finally told her when they'd finished the last of the eggs, garnished with some organics she had found growing on a small, protected ledge. And he meant it. Even with all the complications it had brought, even with the tangle of his emotions around her, her presence brought the balance back to his life.

"Then can you do something about these zipbugs?" she asked, swatting at one buzzing her ear. But she was smiling when she said it, and he knew his words had pleased her.

"I'll stir up the fire a bit, that should help."

He leaned forward and stirred the coals, then added another piece of wood. It flared up slightly, and the bugs retreated. He settled back, and finally brought up what had been on his mind since before he'd left Trios, in fact since the moment she'd announced she would not be present for his first official act. He thought he knew, but he wanted to hear it from her.

"I know you did not wish to come."

Her mouth tightened. For a moment he thought she would not answer. Finally, with a slight shrug, she said, "What I really wish is for it not to happen at all."

His brow furrowed. "The celebration?"

"Your part in it. Your official part. Because it's the end."

"End of what? Childhood, youth, carefree days?" For it did signal all of that, and he also was reluctant to see those halcyon days end. Yet he was eager to go on, to take his place as man and prince in the world he loved above all others.

"This." She gestured around the small encampment. "The days of racketing off on some adventure, no one's company but our own, responsible only for getting ourselves back in one piece, and convincing our parents we'd never really been in any danger, and . . . all that."

"There will still be times for this," he said. "Even my parents occasionally take their own moments. As do yours. Remember when we both stayed with Paraclon and my mother had to come get us?"

She laughed. "How could I forget? I swear, if we'd only had time to tweak the fuel formula a little more, that rocket would have launched."

"Instead of nearly blowing up Paraclon's lab?"

She waved away the destruction with a smile, but it faded as she looked at him.

"It's not really that, Cub."

She hesitated, which was enough unlike her that he focused on her completely, not speaking for fear she would retreat behind a mask of teasing and jokes. So had her father been, according to her mother, when he had first come home to Trios. Assuming he would be hated for his life as a skypirate, he had shown himself the contempt he expected from his people, wearing that same sort of mask.

"It's . . . us," she finally said. "It's the end of us I really fear. You will be busy with affairs of state, learning to be king."

"And you will be—"

He broke off suddenly, aware that whatever she might have planned for her life, whatever hopes and dreams she'd had, had been wiped away. She met his gaze, and he saw the acknowledgment there, both of what he'd thought, and that he'd stopped himself from saying it.

Silence spun out for a moment. He didn't know what else to say, and therefore resorted to the safety of saying nothing. And what could he say that didn't involve things she didn't wish to hear? That was pointless now, when he knew she had no choice about being tied to him, flashbow warrior to royal. If he'd known, perhaps he could have stopped his changing feelings early on. Her father had a great deal to answer for in this.

He waited, hoping the silence would move her to speak. But this was Shaina, who unlike many felt no need to fill the air with words.

"We must discuss it, eventually," he finally said.

"Yes."

"Then why not—"

He stopped abruptly when she threw up a hand for silence. She was suddenly tense in an entirely different way, and her gaze had taken on that distant look that told him she was sensing something beyond his reach.

They waited. He heard nothing, sensed nothing, but he trusted her instincts completely.

"Do you remember that old man who brought us that lovely brollet to roast?" she asked then, in a tone of nothing more than casual remembrance, as if the event had happened years ago, not mere hours. At the same time she turned her hand, moving her fingers in the gesture that told him to keep speaking. They'd developed the system of hand signals as children, to communicate without words in the presence of adults.

"I was just thinking of that myself," Lyon said, confirming that they were agreed someone or something was out there.

Shaina reached out to stir the fire unnecessarily, using the movement to surreptitiously draw her dagger. Lyon picked up his own, casually, as if he had no other concern than cleaning the blade to sheath it.

The ceremonial weapon was all he had. Dax had wanted him armed more completely, and his mother had agreed, but his father had had to accede to the fact that sending his son fully armed to an official ceremony with an ally seemed contrary. Diplomacy trumped caution in this case. Besides, there had been no trouble of note on Arellia in years.

Which didn't mean this world of "wonder and mystery," as the old man had called it, didn't have its own slimehogs. He hoped Shaina, who was under no such restrictions, was better equipped.

Almost on the thought, there was a rush of sound from all sides: crashing, and the snapping of branches. Four men broke through the underbrush and stepped out of the forest.

They were surrounded.

Chapter 7

RINA STOPPED at the end of the gangway and looked around. In the predawn gray, and from the elevation of the skyport, she could see the lights of the city of Galatin spread out before her. Just to her right were the city gates, behind her the broad river that formed the western boundary gleamed dark. To the east were the hills, and to the north the mountain, a weathered, ancient peak that looked down upon the city at its feet. Somewhere in the middle of it all was the square where the statue of Dax stood, and across from it the Council Building where the last stand had taken place.

That brought up painful memories she quashed—quickly from long practice, but never easily.

"Rina? Rina Carbray, is that you?"

She turned at the sound of the voice.

It took her a moment to place the man who had been walking past her; he had grown much in the years since the battle for Galatin. In fact, he had become rotund, both in body and face. Bratus Onslow had been a young major then, in charge of Galatin's defenses. And a bit in awe of her, once he realized she had indeed flown with Dax.

He wore a fancy suit now instead of a uniform, far too bright for her taste. But he'd obviously done well.

"Major Onslow, how are you?"

"It's 'Mayor' now," he said with pride. "But you may call me Bratus, of course."

So he was a speechmaker now, she thought as he shook her hand vigorously.

"How . . . perfect for you," she said, keeping her tone as level as she could.

"You look wonderful." She doubted that: she had slept on the transport, and had merely run her fingers through her hair and washed her face before they'd landed. "But then, Triotians are the most beautiful race, after all," Onslow said.

"Unless you're of the Coalition," she retorted, uncomfortable with the overblown flattery, "in which case we're the plague of the system."

"Along with Arellians," Bratus added proudly. "Come, there is a small place down the block, let me get you a warm brew. You are here early, the ceremony is not for days yet."

Somewhat sleepily she answered, "That's not why I'm here."

He frowned. "But they are coming, are they not? The royals and Minister Silverbrake and his mate?"

"They will all be here for the official ceremony. Prince Lyon is already here."

Bratus blinked, stopped walking. "He is? I saw nothing in the bulletins."

Rina smiled. "He came in quietly, a couple of days ago. He wished to see something of Arellia, and of the celebration, before he steps into his official role."

Bratus frowned. "But that's a breach of protocol. He should have been greeted properly, provided a guide for whatever sights he wished to see."

Bratus, Rina remembered suddenly, had always been a bit of a stickler for protocol. It had been hard on him when the battle for Galatin had gotten so ugly, so bloody, that protocol was shoveled. Apparently, in the years since the war, he had regained the attitude.

She started walking in the direction he indicated. It was as well, she could look away as the memories assailed her. Bratus wasn't the only one who had quailed at the task before them back then. Many had—and some simply ran, terrified. If it had not been for the courageous young captain who had stepped up when Major Onslow had broken, the battle for Galatin might have gone very differently.

She shook off the images in her head. Images of that man had haunted her for years, and somehow stopping herself from useless grieving had never gotten easier.

She made herself focus.

"You'll find Lyon an independent sort," she said, mentally marking Bratus off her list of people who might help her find him, and thus Shaina. For she was certain the queen was correct, that Dax's daughter had come here to unburden herself to her lifelong friend. She had watched the two grow up together, in fact had often found herself, still at a young age herself, their caretaker.

She hadn't minded. Shaina was Dax's, after all, and she would to this day lay down her life for him. Watching over his child had been little enough to ask, and of course being entrusted with the king's son had been an honor. It had been difficult at times to resist their rambunctious charm, and she had often found herself sucked into one of their adventures. There were still things kept between the three of them, things they had all agreed it was best their parents know nothing of.

"—hard to believe he could go unnoticed," Bratus was saying.

"There are many Triotians in the capital for the anniversary celebration."

Bratus's mouth twisted. "Along with most of our own population, I think. The onworld transport companies have been running double schedules, just trying to keep up. And the skyport is overcrowded."

"It would not be difficult to disappear into the throngs. Have you seen or heard anything of Dax's offspring?" she asked.

Bratus looked even more alarmed. "She too is here already? And told no one? This is just not correct."

Rina laughed. "Did you but know her, you would know that the word *correct* is not often used with her name. She is her father's daughter, with his spirit and recklessness. It is as well Prince Lyon possesses his father's charisma. It has gotten them out of more than one tricky situation."

Bratus frowned. "You believe they are together?"

"They were raised together. They are rarely apart for long."

Even as she said it, she thought of those days long ago, when the babies were tiny, having been born within a year of each other. There had been much teasing then that the two were destined, the final cementing of the ties between Trios and Arellia begun by both the Triotian king and the flashbow warrior taking bonded mates who were from their ally. But Trios did not believe in forcing such arrangements, and so such suggestions were quieted as the children grew old enough to understand.

She noticed, as they entered the small brew shop serving the strong, thick Arellian coffee the planet was famous for, that many looked up as they passed. She doubted any of them recognized her, so assumed the frowns and darting glances were aimed at Bratus. She nearly protested when, with a wave of his hand, a table was vacated by two men who were clearly not finished with their morning cups. But they left quickly, and she suppressed the urge.

"Where do you think they might be?" Bratus asked after a woman had hastened over to take their order.

She opened her mouth to reply, knowing they would likely be off in the countryside somewhere, exploring, as was their wont. Then she shut it without speaking as it occurred to her that Bratus was likely to send out an official search party, and announce to the gathered crowds that the prince and Dax's daughter were hiding among them. Neither Lyon nor Shaina would thank her for that, and she couldn't blame them.

She was saved from trying to answer by Bratus's sudden frown as he looked past her into the room. "Be warned," he said. "Tarkson is here."

"What?" Rina's breath caught in her throat.

"Tarkson. I caution you not to listen to his—"

"Tark is . . . alive?" she interrupted, her mind suddenly an odd combination of numbness and energy poised for explosion.

"Of course," Bratus said. "What—oh, I recall now. You had already gone back to Trios when he and his unit returned."

She was shaking, and didn't care that it was evident in her voice. She was glad they were already sitting, for she was certain she would have collapsed. "But we heard he—that they were all dead."

She had long refused to admit, had tried not to even remember how devastating that news had been. The dashing young captain had single-handedly kept the Arellian rebellion going with his daring raids and guerilla tactics. And he had made quite an impression on her youthful, impressionable self. Even Dax had spotted his skills early in the fight, and pulled him up to be his second in command, ruffling the feathers of some older members of the Arellian forces. But Dax was Dax, and no one was about to try to face him down.

"They were presumed so. That was why no rescue was attempted. It was really a shock," Bratus said, sounding as if he were reluctant to talk about it.

She wondered if he had been the one to decide not to send anyone into that pass to search for any survivors. It would be just like him. And the way he avoided her gaze made her think she was right.

"What happened?" she demanded.

"They held off an entire Coalition battalion for nearly two weeks. A handful of fighters against hundreds. The odds were impossible, there was no reason to believe they could have survived."

She knew then she was right. He had been the one who had abandoned them to die.

Alive. Tark was alive.

The words echoed in her mind in a careening loop. She remembered the moment when hope had died in her, when she'd finally had to accept the truth of his death. Some part of her had died in that moment as well, and she had never been the same.

"And yet they did? And escaped, right under those Coalition noses?"

"Yes," he said, clearly not happy with having to admit it.

She swallowed against the tightness in her chest. Fumbled for ordinary words in the face of the abrupt upending of her world. "Dax will be pleased to hear it. He, too, thought him dead."

And tried to comfort me when it was impossible.

"As long as he doesn't have to deal with him. Tarkson is much changed. Physically and otherwise."

And who would not be, after that? she wondered.

"It was a heroic act, I must admit. Earned him the promotion to commander before they retired him." He didn't sound happy about that, either, Rina noted. "Yet Tarkson wished no fanfare. The end was declared soon after they made it back, and he wanted only peace and quiet and time to heal."

"Heal?"

"He was grievously wounded. Nearly died after all."

Her stomach knotted up even tighter. She couldn't bear thinking of Tark being hurt so badly.

"I'm afraid it affected his mind. He does not speak much, at least not to me, but he has made some ridiculous claims of late. He has even been associating with that crazy Reyks woman."

Rina frowned. Tark had occasionally been called insanely reckless, but his mind had ever been quick, sharp, and admirable. "Reyks?"

"Pure troublemaker. She's usually to be found stirring up the masses with wild tales and predictions. Oh, dear. He has spotted you," Bratus said, sounding uncomfortable, and looking it even more.

"Or you?" she asked. His immediate blanching almost made her regret her query.

Almost.

And then he was there. She sensed him before she saw him. That, at least, had not changed.

"Rina."

His voice was deeper, rougher, but it still had the same effect. She took a deep breath to steady herself before she turned to look up at him as he came to a halt beside the table.

It was as well she had, for she forgot to breathe when she saw his face. For an instant it was as if her mind adjusted the image, trying to reconcile what she saw now with the memory she had of a face handsome to the point of beauty. Even warned, she wasn't prepared for it. A black patch covered his left eye. Had he lost it, in that lopsided battle? A crooked, white scar ran vertically up his cheek and reemerged above the patch, where it twisted his brow slightly before arrowing up into his hairline.

She saw her reaction register. Sensed he was adding her to what was no doubt a long list of people who found his appearance unpleasant. His tone, stark and flat, was in grim contrast to his flattering words. "Unlike some of us, you look wonderful. It is true, then, that Triotians live forever young?"

She stood up. Dax had always said if you can't defend, attack. So she said the first thing she could think of to change that reaction. "You truly are alive. All these years I thought you dead. You could have let me know, damn you."

His good eye blinked. "I—"

"All these years of mourning, for a man still alive," she spat out.

Something changed then, softened, in both his stance and his expression. "Mourning? You mourned me, little one?"

Is that how he saw her, still? True, she had been young when they'd met, but he hadn't been much older. And years had passed, and she was an adult now even by Triotian standards. And he . . . he looked as if he carried the full weight of every one of those years. The fire that had blazed in him was gone now, or banked so low it wasn't visible anymore. Her anger faded away.

"We were friends," she said, her heart aching at the thought of him broken. Of what he had been through. "Or I thought we were."

He reached out, cupped her cheek as he had the day he'd left on that ill-fated patrol. The last time she'd seen him alive.

"We were, little one. We were."

Abruptly, as if he'd only this instant realized what he'd done, he yanked his hand back. Rina stared at him, barely able to take it in. But it was true. All these years she'd thought him dust, yet here he stood. She nearly shivered under the impact.

"Join us," Bratus said, managing to hide his reluctance better this time.

Tark began to shake his head.

"Please," Rina said.

For a moment longer he hesitated. He was wearing, she finally noticed, the same battle-scarred leather coat he'd worn those long years ago, and what appeared to be the same battered boots. His clothes looked clean, but worn. And a bit loose, as if he'd lost weight.

At last he took the chair Bratus had indicated. He moved well enough, she thought. Not stiff or impaired. Perhaps the obvious had been his only injury. She wondered how long it had taken him to adapt to having the use of only one eye.

"We were just talking of the celebration, and the visit of the contingent from Trios."

Again Tark hesitated. Another change, she thought; the Tark of old was so sure of himself Dax had said he was barely on the right side of cocky—which of course had led to her making a pot-and-kettle comparison, which had made Dax grin. And the thought of Dax's grin reminded her of Shaina, and why she was here in the first place. She should be on about her task, but the shock of seeing Tark alive hadn't yet worn off.

And she couldn't keep her eyes off him.

"Dax is well?" Tark asked finally.

"He is." Family problems aside, she added silently. "He would be better had you bothered to tell him you'd been alive these many years."

"If that's what you wish to call it."

She noted the bitterness in his voice. And she didn't begrudge him. It was clear he had reason.

"You sound like my king once did," she said.

The single visible eye blinked again. "What?"

"Bitter. He was, in the beginning. But he is long past that now that Trios is becoming herself again, and thanks to the unfailing love of his queen."

"He is . . . fortunate in that."

"Yes. Shaylah is his true mate. Everyone can see it. And of course his son's birth was the final impetus that completely shifted his view to the future and away from the past."

Tark leaned back in his chair. "You have become rather wise, little one."

"It has been a long time. I would be quite a sad excuse for a Triotian if I'd learned nothing in all those years."

Bratus cleared his throat audibly. Rina guessed he wasn't happy at being left out of the conversation, especially after he'd unbent enough to ask Tark to join them.

"I'm glad to see you decided to join us for the celebration," he said to Tark. "I feared nothing would drag you back to the city."

"I would be on the opposite side of the planet, had I the choice," Tark said dryly, and Rina had the feeling he knew quite well Bratus's words were false.

"Will you not stay to see Dax when he arrives?" Rina asked.

And yet again he hesitated. Bratus took advantage of his silence.

"It will be a glorious event," he said directly to Rina, now not even looking at Tark. Perhaps he did find his appearance unpleasant. Bratus always had liked things in order, after all. "And when they arrive, you must tell them all not to believe any of the rumors flying about."

"Rumors?"

He laughed. "You know how it is. Anniversaries like this roll around, people start telling stories about the glorious battles, and then the watchers spring to life with their theories."

She smiled at him. "Still insisting it was all fakery, that it occurred only on cinefilm?"

"There are still those, as there always are," he said. "But now a new one has arisen. That the Coalition is coming back."

Rina's eyes widened. "Coming back?"

"Silly, isn't it, after all this time, that people still fear them so? They've given up, they'll never be back."

. . . the Coalition, or people like them, will never, ever give up, not really.

Califa's words, the words of the woman who had once been privy to the highest levels of the Coalition High Command, echoed in her head. They unsettled her even as Bratus laughed aloud.

But she was unsettled even more when she glanced at Tark.

He was not laughing; he was not even smiling.

Chapter 8

HE HURRIED ON through the dim light of dawn, eager now to reach his goal. The men he had hired should have contacted him by now, and he was angry that they had not. But he was almost to the old rundown building that was their lair, where his personal prey should be locked in a room by now, awaiting his doom. Everything he wanted was almost within his grasp. Vengeance and a triumphant return were so close he could almost taste them, even in this overcrowded, infested city.

They should have welcomed the Coalition, he thought, as he had often since his arrival. They imposed order, control—and this unruly mob certainly needed to be taught that. None of them knew their place. Especially the men he was here to see. It was chaos.

He did not knock. He was paying them, after all. The moment he stepped in and saw the two men sitting with full tankards despite the fact that the sun had not even fully risen, both apparently nursing headaches, he knew something was wrong. And the moment they looked up and met his gaze, he knew his plan had been foiled.

Fury exploded within him.

"Incompetents," he shouted. "Fools! He is but one!"

"Ease up now, man," the first man said. "He had help, you didn't tell us he'd like as have help."

"Three or four at least," the second man whined. "We was outnumbered."

He drew his weapon from within the folds of his cloak. The two men scurried backward like the Carelian muckrats they were.

"Hold, now!" the louder of the two cried. "You don't need to do that. The boss, the big man, he's handling this personally."

"You told me you were the boss." He hissed out the last word in his rage.

"Well, of our little district here," the man said placatingly. "But the big man, he's got a reputation to protect. He can't do business if people don't think he'll do what he says. He won't fail."

His hand twitched on the weapon, as if it wanted to fire of its own accord. He wasn't sure yet he wouldn't.

"This 'big man,'" he said, "where is he now?"

"He's already up on the mountain. Took three of his own gang men with him."

"What? Why?"

"He's got people, you know? They tell him things. And he found out that's where they headed."

His gaze sharpened. "They?"

The two men exchanged glances, looking almost panicked now. They had not meant to say that, it was clear.

"Uh . . . he picked up a woman," the first man said, sounding as he had looked.

"Yes," the second one chimed in, sounding oddly relieved. "After he . . . left here. Must have stopped by Akasen Court."

He knew the district. He'd found it shortly after his arrival, although it had taken longer to find an establishment that catered to his particular preferences. But the suggestion surprised him. Triotians were notoriously fastidious when it came to mating.

Not, he thought bitterly, that it had stopped their king and his vaunted flashbow warrior from mating with traitors. Even bonding with them, in that ridiculous ritual of a kind the civilized world had long left behind. All the more reason they needed to be destroyed, spreading such nonsense even beyond Trios.

He found his fury had ebbed at the thought. He would not kill them yet. This boss of theirs might get some idea of withholding what he needed if he returned to find his men slaughtered and spitted. So until he had his prize, he would restrain himself. He would, with what little patience he had left, wait to see if this big man would deliver. And if he did, then he would let him live.

In the end, however, these two would not survive breaking their word to him. He, too, had a reputation to protect. And rebuild. And this was only the beginning.

EVEN IN THE faint light of dawn on the mountain, it was clear all four men were armed, one with a small disrupter that had a singed, blackened barrel, looking as if it had been fired often. Which in itself was enough to make Lyon move cautiously, cataloging the man who held it in the "will definitely shoot" category.

The other three didn't look much kinder.

But the men didn't rush them. Not that they had to, armed and outnumbering them two to one, and coming up on them by surprise as they had.

"Well, well, look what we have here," the largest one said. He was carrying a cudgel that made the one that had left the lump on Lyon's head look like a child's rattle, and there was a full-size disrupter tucked into his belt. It didn't look as used as the other one. Perhaps he didn't have to shoot as often because he had the other man to do it for him, Lyon thought sourly.

"Ah, young lovers," said the man with the small disrupter, and his grin was not pleasant.

I wish, Lyon thought, but ignored the assumption and the lewd expression. Instead he was calculating possibilities, thinking of tactics, and of how they were going to be on the receiving end of a very large surprise if they assumed Shaina was a helpless female.

He saw her move on the edge of his vision. Her dagger was still at her feet, but she had moved slightly to mask it from the men in front of her. He kept his gaze fastened on the man who appeared to be the leader. And most of the brawn, judging by his size.

The man looked at her, rubbing his unshaven chin. "Well, aren't you a pretty one." The leer that accompanied the words made his thoughts clear.

Were this ordinary times, Shaina would have had a snappish comeback. But she was the daughter of Dax; in battle, tactics trumped temper. She put a hand to her throat, a delicate, feminine gesture. Her long, slender fingers moved, tugging at something.

And then she laughed. But it wasn't Shaina's happy, deep-throated laugh, it was a different thing, a light, floating laugh he'd never heard from her. Almost, impossibly, a giggle.

"My, you are a big one, aren't you?" she asked, now looking up at the man with a smile Lyon had also never seen before.

And only then did he realize that while her hand had been at her throat, she had tugged loose the collar of her shirt, and opened the first fastener. Even from here he could see the tops of her breasts, ripely curved. He could only imagine what the man was seeing, from his height above her. Anger shot through him, a possessive sort of blast that took the breath out of him.

She's mine, damn it! Get your filthy eyes off her.

"And who would you be?" asked the man, clearly intrigued and staring at her breasts more than her face. Oblivious to the fact that she was doing something further with the hem of her shirt, Lyon couldn't see what.

"Oh, I'm famous on Arellia. Just ask anyone in Akasen Court."

Lyon sucked in a breath as she named the district of Galatin that ran mostly to paid companions. He was a little surprised she even knew about it. And just the mention of it had clearly made the man put her in a certain category. Just as she obviously intended. Was she insane, planting such ideas in that brute's mind? Not that she had to—he wasn't fool enough to think he was the only man who would look at her and want.

"Well, now," the big man said. "What is it you're famous for?"

"I like them big," she said.

Lyon had to bite his tongue to keep from reacting. He tasted blood, but the pain was almost not enough as Shaina slowly got to her feet. She did it leaning slightly forward, assuring the man's eyes were fastened on her chest. And her knife was gone from where it had lain on the ground, and as she moved he could see the hilt at the small of her back, where she had tucked it into her leggings.

He'd told himself she was unaware of her own power, of her effect on him, that she was careless of the effect she had on other men—so he could afford to wait until she came around on her own.

She'd just blasted that to pieces.

She was using that power.

And it was working.

Belatedly, he glanced at the others. They were all watching her with an intense interest, as if they were anticipating a turn with her as well, and wondering how much would be left of her when their leader was finished. The focus had shifted entirely to Shaina. And he'd damned well better do something, and now, or the risk—the crazy, reckless risk—she was taking would be for nothing.

Fear for her tamped down his anger at her risky tactic. Making a sound of disgust, as if at the desertion of his companion, he turned away as though he didn't want to watch. Which was nothing less than true. But he used the motion to cover his true action, which was to pull the disrupter she had thankfully told him about from the side pocket of her pack. He flicked the control to just this side of lethal, hiding it behind the sleeve of his shirt.

As if she'd somehow sensed he had the weapon, Shaina began to move. She reached out with one hand, touching the big man's arm and trailing a finger down it as if measuring.

"Is it true, what they say?" She was purring again, Lyon thought. And then she was walking around the man, still trailing a finger over him as if she were taking his measure. "That the size of a man's hands shows the size of . . . other parts?"

Lyon's stomach churned as the big man laughed. She'd better be careful, or she'd unleash something she never expected. Then again, he'd never expected to hear such talk from the girl he'd thought of as such an innocent.

If I'd known, we would have had this out long ago.

"True indeed," the big man said. "Why do you think I have these?"

He held up hands the size of a normal man's head. Held them up away from his weapons. In the instant Lyon thought it, Shaina moved, swiftly. Lyon knew what she was going to do the moment she leapt—she'd practiced it on him countless times. She was on the man's back, had wrapped her booted legs around his waist. Her knife was at his throat in an instant.

The big man bellowed. Leave it to her to take on the big one and leave the others to him. He saw them gaping in shock. Realized he had only a second, maybe two before they recovered. And that Shaina was in his line of fire.

He dove to his right. Rolled. Came up firing. Two went down before the third spun and fired. Lyon felt a singe along his left shoulder. His own third shot went true, and the last man went down.

He whirled back to Shaina. The big man still hung onto his weapon, a full sized disrupter that looked as small as a pocket one in the man's huge hand.

And that weapon was aimed at Lyon. But Shaina's knife was at his throat, had already drawn blood. He clawed at her legs with his other hand, but could not dislodge her. Lyon had little doubt the man had been taken off guard by her speed, and startled by her strength.

"Get off me or I'll kill him."

The man snarled the words. Lyon imagined getting taken down by a girl a third his size was not on the man's list of things he wanted to be known for.

"Kill him and I'll cut your throat to the spine," Shaina said pleasantly.

Standoff. Lyon didn't move, kept his gaze fastened on the pair, his own disrupter aimed at center mass of his sizeable target. He slipped his thumb to the control lever, edged it back just slightly.

"Cub?"

"Anytime," he said casually, knowing what she was asking.

The big man's hand tightened on the weapon. Lyon was ready to jump to the side if he had to. She shifted her knife hand. The heavy, carved hilt dug into the side of the big man's neck. Her other hand flashed around to grab her own wrist. She yanked back, driving the hilt of the knife in her hand against the vital artery in the heavily muscled neck. Startled, the man's attention shifted. He staggered as she cut off the blood flow.

Lyon fired. Hit that center mass. The man went to his knees. Shaina jumped clear. The instant he knew she was safely away, he fired again. The man fell flat on his face.

It was over.

They got to their feet. Lyon surveyed the damage, the four unconscious men. And then he looked at Shaina, who was looking down at the big man. Her hair was tossed, falling forward and masking one jade eye. The damned shirt had pulled free of yet another fastener, baring an uncomfortable amount of curved, feminine flesh. He could see her bared stomach flex as she took in air, realized she was breathing fast.

He stared at her. What he'd felt up to now seemed nothing compared to this moment. It all crashed together, the longing he'd been fighting, the dreams that had been hampered by the reality of his destiny, and then shattered by the reality of hers.

She was the most alluring thing he'd ever seen, body, mind, soul, and spirit.

And he couldn't have her.

Chapter 9

"WHY," RINA ASKED conversationally, "is Bratus Onslow still alive?"

They had managed to get free of Bratus when he'd been called to some duty, and despite Tark's obvious reluctance she had convinced him to walk with her.

"Our illustrious mayor?" Tark's tone was sour. "Why would he not be? It is easy to stay that way when you hide from any true danger."

"Let me rephrase it. Why have you not slaughtered him for abandoning you and your men, for not even trying to send help?"

He shrugged, but his mouth was tight. "It was not unreasonable to assume us dead."

"It was not unreasonable to expect him to make certain, as any decent officer would!"

Tark gave her a sideways look that told her she had answered her own question with the word *decent*. She shoved down her anger at the pompous Onslow.

She studied him as they walked, to see if there were more changes than the patch and the scar, but he seemed to move with the same lean, easy grace as before. His hair was longer, falling in dark strands to his shoulders. She had just decided she liked it when a small group of revelers stopped, stared, and one called out her name. Startled, she waved, but urged Tark to keep moving.

"Did you think you wouldn't draw the attention of the crowd?" he asked. "You're remembered as well in Galatin. No one has forgotten you stood at Dax's side."

"As did you."

"I'm Arellian. This is my home. It was Trios who fought for her friends, when she was barely free of the Coalition yoke herself."

"Careful," she teased, "that sounded perilously close to admiration."

Once, the usually taciturn fighter would have laughed, but at that moment he simply looked grim. "What admiration I have goes to all who fought this battle." Warmth flooded her when he turned his head to look at her with his good eye and added, "Including you."

"I wish I had known," she said as they paused to sit on a bench in a pleasantly quiet spot on the far side of the Council Building. Somewhat hidden from the crowds out even at this early hour—or perhaps still out from last night—and with a few more capital officials to keep order, the small alcove was for the moment empty.

"Known what?"

"That you were alive. Hurt. I could have helped."

"Rina Carbray, nursemaid? I think not."

"I would have," she declared, stung by his biting tone.

"And I probably would have lost more than one eye's vision."

She drew back sharply. "But apparently you would have been entertained while doing so, since you seem to find me so amusing."

She saw the corner of his mouth twitch. His lips tightened. And she realized he was trying not to smile.

"That's the Rina I remember," he said.

"You baited me." It was more declaration than accusation, but she knew she was right.

"Better your temper than your pity, little one."

Something painful twisted inside her at his quiet words. "Pity? Is that what you think? You were always . . . the most un-pitiful creature. Although if you can't see the difference between pity and caring, then perhaps that's changed."

He went very still. "Caring?"

"It's what we Triotians do, you know, for our friends."

"Ah." He shrugged. "But as you see, I'm fine. Less optimal than I once was, but not quite useless."

"Did your injury affect your mind?"

He shrugged again. "Some would say so." He shot her a sideways glance. "It's only that pity that keeps them speaking to me at all."

"Oh? So the fact that you single-handedly saved this building we're sitting beside, and the life of every Arellian within it, including your highest leaders, has nothing to do with it?"

"That was long ago."

She waved toward the crowds even now dancing in the street on the other side of the row of trees. "Not so long that they aren't celebrating it."

"Any excuse for revelry."

Rina bit back the caustic response that leapt to her lips.

"Perhaps you have changed that much," she said instead. "The Bright Tarkson I remember had no time for self-pity, or those who indulged in it."

He winced, but she had the feeling it was more about her use of his much-hated first name than the gibe.

"There was a war to be won," was all he said.

"And now?"

"Now . . . I have no time for those who have forgotten what that war cost. Or why it was fought in the first place."

"And you think they have forgotten?"

"Our army has been depleted to below a bare minimum. They have old, failing equipment and weapons, or none at all. Nor does anyone seem to care. They seem to think we will never be called upon to fight again. Or they wish to ignore it, thinking one can negotiate with the likes of the Coalition."

She frowned. "Dare would never allow that on Trios."

"It would take someone of his strength to counter it. It is the nature of things, of people. And why history, if it does not actually repeat, at the least comes full circle again and again."

She studied him as he stared at the revelers just beyond the screen of trees and hedge. From this side, he looked as he always had, albeit more mature. Tough, strong-jawed, his face made up of uncompromising angles without a hint of softness. Yet when his blood had been high, and he'd come up with some impossible plan or tactic, he'd been the most alive, vital man she'd ever seen, next to Dax. Perhaps even more than Dax, since he'd not yet been tempered by pain and loss.

He was certainly tempered now, she thought. She hadn't imagined that bitter note that sometimes crept into his voice.

"You have become a philosopher, then?"

She almost got a genuine laugh from him at that. "Hardly."

"So you are . . . what? An old war steed who has no place any longer?"

He turned his head then. She sensed it wasn't just to look at her, but to remind her with the sight of the patch and the scar.

"Close enough. The old, especially."

"You're a mere five years older than I." And, she added inwardly, it had seemed a much greater gap when she had but seventeen years, when the decisive battle for Galatin had begun and she'd first met the reckless young captain whose courage was the talk of the war.

"As marked on the calendar, perhaps."

"If you're concerned about aging, you should move to Trios. There's evidence now that what gives us our long life is Trios herself, and the effect can extend to those not born there."

He seemed to ponder that before saying, "Are you sure it is wise to let that be known? You'll be overrun."

"I did not advertise it. I merely told you." Her mouth curved into a wry smile. "And since you apparently talk little to anyone, I think the information is safe enough."

That got her a second laugh, and it was a better one this time.

"You would be welcome there," she said. "Dax and King Darian would see to that, although all of our people know of you and would welcome you on their own accord."

"You Triotians," he said softly. "You always make your home sound like bliss."

"She is," Rina said simply. "And we treasure her even more now, since we almost lost her."

"The worst mistake the Coalition made was not exterminating every last one of you. And were it not for Corling's ego, wanting to humiliate your prince by enslaving him, Trios would still be the jewel of the Coalition crown."

"Yes," she said proudly. "But he left him alive, he failed to crush us, and he paid the ultimate price for his evil."

Tark's mouth twisted. "Executed by his own for his failure."

She wondered if Tark had become one of those warriors who could speak of nothing but the past, the battles they had been in. She wondered if he had no other life but that, and the thought was painful.

"Can you not look forward, now? You have certainly earned it."

He leaned forward, rested his elbows on his knees. Stared down at the stony path. Finally he spoke.

"Your people, the ones who did not see it when it began," he said, "were they not so intent on looking forward that they did not realize what was happening right then?"

It did not seem to be an answer to the question she had asked, but instead an opening to ask the one she had thus far held back.

"You did not find Bratus's stories of the Arellians who fear the Coalition's return amusing."

"I don't find anything about the Coalition, then or now, amusing."

"Nor do I. But they've been driven back to the far reaches."

"That's the common belief."

Uneasiness stirred within her. Tark was no fool, and if he thought there was substance to those rumors, it was not to be taken lightly. "But not yours?"

He didn't look at her. He merely shrugged. "Such ideas are not welcome, especially during this celebration."

She wasn't going to let him dodge this, it was too important. "You said you had other business to attend to."

He went very still. And did not answer.

"What?" she asked.

"Cannot even an old war steed have business of his own? Perhaps I ran out of lingberry liquor, or felt the need for a game of chaser."

"The only thing you ever gambled with was your life," she said dryly.

"Then perhaps I seek the company of a woman who can be paid enough to overlook my . . . deformity."

Pain stabbed through Rina, startling her with its sharpness. Words burst from her. "It is not a deformity, it is a badge of honor. A woman you would have to pay would not be worth your company."

His head came up. For a long moment he just looked at her before he said softly, "So fierce, little one. You have not lost your fire, I see."

"I defend my own," she said, her jaw set.

For an instant something flashed across his face, gone so quickly she could not be sure if it was pain . . . or longing.

"I am not your concern, Rina." He said it flatly, dismissively.

"I do not think you get to decide that, Commander Tarkson."

His mouth quirked upward at one corner. She had the feeling it was involuntary, that he had fought the reaction and failed to quell it.

"Captain," he corrected. "I do not believe one earns a promotion simply by surviving. And you have lost none of your fire, Rina Carbray. Or your loyalty. And you always had it to spare."

"Then trust me."

"Rina—"

"Or if not me, at least trust Dax. You know how he values you."

"He did, once."

"He still does. Dax does not forget."

"Did he ever tell you he once saved my life?"

She laughed, and he lifted a brow in surprise. "No. You did. He only speaks of the twice you saved his."

He blinked. "I never really did. I merely had his back, as his second in command should."

"And there is little Dax values more."

He looked thoughtful for a moment. Then, slowly, he asked, "And Dax . . . he still has the king's ear?"

"He does, as Defense Minister, but also as a brother. They are as one family, the royals and the Silverbrakes."

His voice went soft again, in that way that made her skin tingle oddly. "And you, Rina? What of you?"

"I am ever as welcome, as Dax's adopted ward. It is often forgotten that there is no blood between us."

"I am glad."

There was no doubting the sincerity of that, and it moved her that he would even be concerned about her life and happiness. Once it would have thrilled her beyond measure to have even that much of the daring Captain Tarkson's attention. She wasn't sure it still didn't.

"I thank you," she said. "But may we return to my question?"

For a moment longer he hesitated. It was unlike him, at least the Tark she had known, to be so uncertain. Decisiveness had ever been his hallmark. So this was either a measure of who he now was, or of his lack of conviction about the truth of whatever it was that had brought him here. Or perhaps some combination of both, she thought. Could any man go through what he had and not come out changed? She had evidence of that every day in Dax, in King Darian himself.

"Can you get me through to speak to Dax?"

She stared at him. "Have you heard nothing I've said? You could get access to Dax, or the king himself, without hesitation. You are not just remembered on Trios, Tark. You are revered."

He laughed, and this time it was a harsh sound with more than a little of that bitterness she'd heard before.

"You doubt me?"

"I wouldn't dare, little one," he said, his voice normal again.

"Then know you do not need me. Your name alone would get you an audience with anyone on the Triotian High Council."

"I'm not sure I agree with your first words, but I hope you are right about the last. There are things they should know."

So. He'd decided. She felt a rush of relief. Whatever it was, if it so nagged at Tark, it must be shared. He was a warrior, and his instincts had been ever true.

Only after that relief eased did she process what else he'd said.

Then know you do not need me.

I'm not sure I agree with your first words . . .

Her breath caught, and her head snapped around, but he was already on his feet and walking away.

Chapter 10

"ARE YOU INSANE?"

Cub's voice snapped out at her. Bit deep.

She finished securing the cord she'd used to truss up the big man, still unconscious and facedown in the dirt. Cub had found enough of it on one of the others to tie them all up. There hadn't even been much rush, since the disrupter strikes would keep them out for a good hour.

She straightened up and, finally, turned to face him.

"We're still alive, aren't we?"

"Only by sheer luck!"

"I prefer to think of it as good tactics in a hand-to-hand situation when outnumbered two to one."

It was an answer worthy of her father, she thought. And once more had to remind herself that she hated him. And loved him. It was an unsettling combination.

"You could have been killed."

"And we *would* have been killed, if we hadn't done something. Or worse, held for ransom, if they found out who we really were."

Cub stared at her. "Only you could think being held for ransom worse than being killed."

"You would prefer it?" she demanded, astounded at the idea.

"I would prefer to be alive to fight another day."

He snapped out the words. And she couldn't argue with them, not really.

"Contention valid," she conceded. But she refused to cede entirely. "But it worked."

"Do you even realize what you were risking from those men?"

"Of course I do. I'm not a child. But my mother told me there are certain kinds of men who go mindless at the sight of a female body. These seemed like the type."

She didn't add that she had never been certain it would work, that she could even do it. She had never in her life tried such a tactic, never thought of herself as the kind of woman who had such allure. But she had trusted her mother's words. And it had seemed, at the time, the only option open to her.

Cub was still staring at her. He looked clearly uncomfortable. Perhaps he thought she was a fool for trying it for the same reason she had had doubts she would succeed. She was tall, her body curved enough, but her face retained the childlike look of big eyes and upturned nose, and the combination struck her as singularly unappealing. She doubted she would ever be the kind of beauty her mother or godmother were.

"You shouldn't have risked yourself," he said finally, in an angry tone that stabbed deeper into her own uncertainty. Why was he so upset, when it had worked?

"And why not?" she demanded, her voice sharp with her own emotion. "I'm the next flashbow warrior. And the current one, my illustrious, lying father, is more than able to see to the well-being of Trios and her king and queen. The only thing left for me to take care of is you."

"I don't need you to—"

"You are the next king, are you not? It only follows my duty is to protect you."

"You are not the next flashbow warrior until you are accepted into training by the current one."

She wanted to clout him for pointing that out. "Then perhaps for the first time in history Trios will be without one, because my father has so decided. Or perhaps he'll just wait for the next one. Knowing him, he'll probably live to be two hundred anyway, and be the best man standing until the very end."

"Two hundred fifty, at least," he said so glumly she knew it was exaggerated for her benefit.

With an effort she reined in her temper. Somewhere in the back of her mind, she realized this was why they made a good team, she could jolt him out of his introspective calmness, and he could moderate her recklessness. But she never doubted his loyalty, and made sure he never doubted hers.

"Are you all right?" she asked, indicating his shoulder, thinking she should have asked sooner, except that he was moving fine and didn't appear to be in pain. And she had been too tangled up to think of anything but her own confusion, she thought, which in itself should tell her something.

"Yes. It barely brushed me."

"Good. What now?" she asked.

He glanced at the men lying unconscious in a tidy arrangement around what was left of their fire.

"When they come around, if they work together, they can eventually free themselves. I'm not sure they deserve any more consideration than that."

"Agreed," she said.

"We should leave some possibilities for them to ponder, just in case."

"Agreed," she repeated, glancing around, then pointing toward a large tree to her left. "I'll start a trail there. And another further up."

"I'll see what I can do to make them think they scared us and we headed back down the mountain."

She grinned. "You mean like sane people?"

"'Triotians never quit.'" He said it pompously, in perfect imitation of Ansul, their old tutor. She laughed, a little surprised at how relieved she was that he was back to himself.

"I wonder," he said, clearly thinking again. "I don't think they were simply robbers. They seemed more . . . specifically aimed."

"You mentioned a ransom."

He gave a slight shake of his head. "They didn't seem to recognize us."

"Perhaps they didn't react because they already knew who they were following?"

"But perhaps not specifically me. I mean, they may have been after me, but not necessarily the visiting prince." It warmed her somehow that he so completely separated the two. "And they did not recognize you."

"They might look past me because I look Arellian," she said. "It can't be coincidence that you've been set upon twice since you arrived here."

He grimaced. "I did think of that. But neither time did they seem to realize who I was."

"So they don't know. Which means . . . what?" she asked.

"I don't know. What do you think?"

"I think Triotians don't quit."

"Exactly."

She grinned at him suddenly; this was her Cub, adventurous and determined. "We trek on."

"We do."

RINA ADJUSTED the earpiece for the comlink. Were she just making a personal contact with Califa or Dax, she might have left it as originally set, but this did not seem something she should make public, and there were others here in the interplanetary comm center. For that reason she chose audio only; the appearance of Dax Silverbrake's face on a cinescreen would no doubt cause a stir.

Not to mention that what she was going to say could draw attention she would prefer to avoid.

"You have news already?" were Dax's first words after the connection was established. He sounded surprised, but then she hadn't been on Arellia for long.

"Not of the kind you mean, not yet."

He didn't miss the implication. "Then what kind?"

She glanced around. The others in the center were occupied with their own communications, and paid her no attention. As was her wont, she cut to the crux.

"Dax, Tark is alive."

Even over the vast distance, she heard him suck in a breath.

"Alive? But—"

She explained quickly, ending sadly: "It was by his choice, Dax. He was badly injured. He wished no pity from . . . any of us."

"Pity." Dax nearly snapped it out. "As if anyone who has seen him fight could ever feel pity for him."

Rina smiled to herself. She'd known what his reaction would be. Dax never changed, and she loved him all the more for that.

"Does he need help? We have better medical capabilities than Arellia."

"He would not, I fear, accept it."

"Still stubborn, then."

She laughed, barely refraining from making the old pot/kettle comparison again. Dax laughed in turn, as if he'd heard the words she hadn't spoken.

"Of course," she answered. "He appears healed well enough. But he is scarred, and has lost the vision in one eye."

She closed her own eyes as an image of him the first time she had seen him shot through her mind. Tall, rangy, full of an energy that rivaled even Dax's, his hair Arellian dark and his eyes a deep, cobalt blue. He'd been the most amazing creature she'd ever seen, other than Dax.

And she'd reacted to him in a way she'd never reacted to any male.

She'd spent a long time telling herself that it was only because he was the first male near to her own age she had encountered at length. There had been such change in her life since Dax had brought her home to Trios that simply adjusting had taken most of her energy, and most Triotians were focused mainly on holding the Coalition at bay. But when the rebellion on Arellia had begun, and they'd joined it, it had been almost like being back flying with Dax, ranging across the far reaches in those wild skypirate days. And Bright Tarkson had been the personification of that feeling.

When he'd been reported killed, it had been as traumatic for her as the many times she had feared Dax dead, but in a very different way. And it was that difference that had told her she had lost control of her silly feelings, and would pay the heavy price of grief. Grief mostly for something that had never really been, for possibilities lost.

"—otherwise?"

She snapped out of her reverie. "I'm sorry, what did you ask?"

"I asked if he seemed well otherwise."

"Physically, yes. He moves well enough, and if his vision gives him trouble, it is not obvious."

"Physically?"

She'd known he wouldn't miss that. Dax had spent too much of his life tortured by guilt and the past to take it lightly.

"Mentally . . . I'm not sure. He appears cynical, sharper, almost bitter."

"With reason, it would seem. I remember they did not even try a rescue."

"No."

Now that she was over the shock, she was thinking she should have been much less polite to Bratus. And she remembered all the times Dax had risked his ship, and his life for one of their own. As a skypirate he hadn't had many rules, but not leaving anyone behind was one of them, and it was unbreakable.

"His supposed commanding officer—who is the mayor now, revoltingly enough—simply looked at the odds and assumed. And was shocked when he and his men walked out of the northern pass weeks after they were left for dead."

Dax swore under his breath. "I know we must accept that other worlds do not hold life as dear, but that is a hard one, Rina. I would be surprised if he was not much changed."

"He does not quite trust anyone anymore," she said.

"I'm not sure I can blame him for that, either."

"Nor can I," she said. "But there is more. Something he feels you and King Dare should know."

"What?"

"I do not know."

There was a brief pause before he answered. "He has truly lost all faith, if he won't trust you. He was very fond of you."

That simply, he blasted rational thought right out of her mind. "He . . . was?"

"Quite. I had to warn him more than once of your youth and inexperience."

She smothered a gasp. "And who appointed you my guardian?"

"I did," he said, sounding utterly unruffled. "Who else was there?"

She felt torn. He was right, there had been no one else. And yet she couldn't help resenting that he'd interfered, that perhaps Tark had felt something of what she had felt, back then, and she had never known because of Dax.

She made herself focus on the reason for this contact.

"But he will tell you," she said.

"And Dare, I presume?"

"I don't think he expects that the king would grant him audience."

Dax let out an audible breath. "He needs to come to Trios, then. Perhaps he would realize that even if Arellia doesn't properly revere him, Trios does."

"I've told him he should come."

"And he said?"

"He dodged. He's gotten very adept at it."

"Hmm."

He didn't say it, but Rina knew Dax was remembering the old Tark, who had been direct to the point of bluntness and never hesitated to say what he thought, honestly.

Then she heard a voice in the background, recognized the deep, commanding voice of King Darian.

"Hold, Rina," Dax said, and the connection went silent for a moment as Dax and the king conversed. Quickly—Dax also had the knack of cutting to the core of matters—he was back. "Dare wishes to know, if Tark will not come here, if he requests us to come to Arellia earlier than planned. Will this matter require much time?"

"I do not know," she said. "It was effort enough to get him to agree that you should know. Perhaps you should command him, your majesty."

She heard Dare laugh. Acknowledged the absurdity of the simple fact that she, Rina Carbray, sole survivor of her family and onetime navigator on the most infamous skypirate vessel in the galaxy, could speak so to her king.

But then, kings of Trios were a different breed.

"I have no authority over outworlders," the king said, "nor do I wish it. Not, from what I know of him, that your Tark would listen anyway."

Your Tark . . .

She quashed the shiver the words gave her. "I will ask him."

There was a moment, and a brief exchange between them that she couldn't hear. Then Dax was back.

"The meeting of the High Council begins tomorrow," he said. "We cannot leave until it concludes. Dare asks if a holo conference would be sufficient. If so, he will divert a ship to Arellia."

The closed-circuit, carefully secured holo system would allow them to converse as if they were in the same room. But it was only available on Triotian vessels of the military fleet, and except by order of the Council or the king, used only in battle or defense situations. She'd have to arrange a shuttle to get them to the ship, so it could stay at a distance; even with the Pact in place, a Triotian military starship docking at the Port of Galatin would require asking for permission and giving answers she didn't want to have to provide, at least not yet.

"I will ask," she said again.

"Send a simple blast message," Dax said, "yes or no. If it's no to the holo conference, then we will be there as early as we can."

"Copy," Rina said.

The king's voice came through again. "And tell him, for all of Trios, that we are delighted he is alive. Enough to overcome our vexation that he did not tell us."

And that, she thought, she would tell Tark with pleasure.

Chapter 11

"YOU'RE GOING TO fall down this mountain if you don't quit looking over your shoulder all the time."

Shaina looked as if she wanted to stick her tongue out at him, as she often had as a child.

"Someone has to watch your back," she said.

"Let me worry about my back."

"You don't worry enough."

"You worry enough for both of us."

"Someone has to look out for the future king of Trios."

"That is so far into the future neither of us should be worrying about it."

It was thankfully so, he thought. His father was strong, and their best healers had said his time as a slave had only strengthened him, mentally and physically.

"But if that is what is behind these attacks on you, we'd best worry about it now." She had, he couldn't deny, a point. "Besides, I can't stop thinking . . ."

"Of what?" he asked when she stopped.

"How we were followed. Watched." She grimaced. "We should have been aware."

"That," he said dryly, "I can't argue with."

"*I* should have been aware. I should have sensed them."

He didn't bother to point out they'd been a bit distracted, because then he would have to admit he'd been distracted since before he'd even gotten here, that leaving home and her had done nothing to resolve his feelings. And her stunt with those men had only driven that new wanting home like a spike through his gut.

And then she said it herself, bitterly. "But I've been too wrapped up in . . . other things."

As, Lyon thought with an inward grimace, had he.

He fought the memory of a lithe, curved body displayed with purpose. Shaina, looking utterly, temptingly female, using that femininity to distract and tempt. With great success. And why not? The curves of hip and waist and breast, coupled with the tautness of a body he knew was a match for his in fitness, made for the perfect combination, in his view. Some men preferred the softness of a home-building woman, and he could see the appeal, but not for himself.

He was getting better at quashing it, with practice. And he'd had a lot more of that since they'd set out from the camp where they'd left the four men, trussed up like rockfowl. They might even be loose by now. And perhaps flailing about, trying to determine which of the trails they'd intentionally left to follow. It didn't matter; they were all false. They'd been trained by the best, and when they wished, they left no more trace of their passing than a whisperbird.

He flexed his arm, feeling the faint sting of where the disrupter fire had brushed his shoulder. That's what he should be thinking about.

But those images from that encounter tormented him in an entirely new way. It was one thing for him to be aching for her, quite another for lewd, brutal thuggers to be looking at her in that way.

For an instant he wished he could go back in time. His life had been so simple, so glorious, and he had never appreciated it enough. Despite his status he had been allowed to run free, if he kept up with his lessons with Freylan and Glendar and the other teachers. He'd been allowed the carefree childhood of other children, although simply by being witness to his parents' discussions at mealtimes, which often included his godparents, Shaina's parents, he was more aware than most of the cost of that freedom from care. His father was unrelenting in his vigilance, and his godfather the same. And neither his mother nor godmother were any less so; it was often Shaylah or Califa who came up with the new tactical or logistical ideas.

But still, it was not his direct concern, he had been allowed that freedom, and only when he ran a little too wild—usually at Shaina's urging—had his parents pulled him in a little.

If only he could go back, and freeze time.

If only is for children. Are you yet a child, son?

His father's words from long ago echoed in his head. As they so often did. It didn't help that whenever he spoke, it seemed worthy of being etched into Triotian marble.

But were he to be honest with himself, he would admit it was not so much that he wished to return to his childhood. He wished never to have to face the fact that his boon companion had turned into the kind of female who could turn men's heads away from their task simply by being. And that she was not his and now never could be.

An odd sort of sensation shot through him, reminiscent of what he felt when he touched Paraclon's lightning globe. Unable to stop himself, he paused on the upward track, turning to look at the woman keeping easy pace with him.

"What?" she asked, stopping as she nearly bumped into him.

She'd refastened the neck of her shirt, untied the knot, and let the bottom fall, covering her once more to below the waist. But that could do nothing to the picture he held in his mind.

"You're beautiful," he said, unable to stifle at least that much honesty.

She nearly rolled her eyes at him—he could see it. But for some reason, she stopped herself. Instead she looked him up and down, considering.

"And you are impossibly handsome, Cub."

Her voice was oddly soft, almost contemplative. It made him wonder if she'd once been as surprised as he had been, if she'd had that moment when she'd suddenly realized the companion she'd grown up with was no longer a boy.

And then she spoke again, in that same voice, and stunned him even further. "In some ways, you are even more handsome than your father, who is held to be the standard on Trios."

"I—" he began, then stopped, not knowing what to say to such a thing. He'd always thought of himself as an imperfect copy of an ideal. But Shaina thought the copy better than the original?

She was, perhaps, not unbiased, as close as they were, but . . . was it possible she wasn't as immune to him as she seemed? The fierceness of the hope that kicked through him nearly knocked the breath out of him. Maybe it wasn't that she didn't want him in the same way.

Maybe it was that she didn't want him that way *yet*.

"That, I suppose, is owed to your mother," Shaina went on. "Why should not the handsome king and beautiful queen of Trios have a most striking son?"

"And there are many who prefer the dark-haired Children of the Evening Star, such as your father," he said. "And your mother is a match for mine in beauty, so it is no surprise you are as well."

For a long moment she simply looked at him. And then, in a very different voice, she said, "It was a surprise to me. And not a welcome one."

That startled him. "Not welcome?"

"Do you think I wish to spend my life never knowing if a man cared one bit about who I really am, or if it was merely the structure of my body?"

He had never thought of it in quite that way, but he understood instantly. "No more than I wish to spend my life never being certain if what appeal I have is based on my real self, or my position as prince."

She blinked. Then smiled. Her grins were often warnings, but her smiles were like a sunrise, slow and warming.

"We're a pair, are we not?" she said.

"We always have been," he answered, not caring that his words revealed more than he wished her to know.

"We must not lose that. Promise me, Cub."

She sounded almost anxious, a most unusual tone for her. He stared at her. Could it be that it wasn't just the inevitable change in his responsibilities that had had her wound up? Could one reason for her unsettledness truly be that on some level she was starting to feel the same emotions and reactions he was? Hope, he realized, was a hard thing to quash once it arrived.

She's the next flashbow warrior. It cannot be.

"No matter what," she added, a fierce intensity in her voice

"No matter what," he agreed, meaning the words with all his heart even as he acknowledged they were a promise that might be impossible to keep.

He was still edgy about the changes to come. He was much more comfortable with a blade in his hand, or at the controls of a fighter, than giving speeches. The ceremony itself was simple enough, but it marked the beginning of his official life of service to Trios, and his life would never be the same again. He must focus on this, this first task of his office, and if he managed to do it without embarrassing himself or his home, he would count it well won.

This he could do. The fact that his hopes for a future with the woman who meant more to him than anyone in the world had been shattered was going to be much harder to deal with.

And for the first time, he was grateful he hadn't told her.

"COME EARLY? THEY would do that?"

Tark was staring at her as if in shock.

"I told you," she said, drawing on her always-limited supply of patience. "Do not underestimate their liking and respect for you."

"But—"

"Yes, the king and Dax would, were it not for the meeting of the High Council, be at your beck and call."

How had this man, who by rights should have been a bigger hero here than even Dax and Califa, been reduced to such uncertainty as to his own standing? He was, after all, the homegrown hero, the Arellian who had single-handedly saved the Council, their families, and the citizens who had sought refuge in the Council Building during the Battle of Galatin.

Were Arellians truly so small-minded as to be repelled by his disfigurement, and so would reject him? Shaylah and Califa certainly were not that way. Califa in particular was not, having, she said, learned the lesson the most difficult way, carrying scars of her own.

Or was it something more than appearances?

The sound of laughter drew her attention for a moment, to the large group coming into the dining hall. She kept her gaze on Tark, but watched them at the edge of her vision, wondering if she would get her answer when they saw him. Would they recoil at the sight of him?

He had heard them, but didn't look. In fact, he had stiffened slightly, and something like a wince flickered across his face. Was the sound of laughter, the presence of people without his shadows to carry, so painful to him? Or was it he who was painful to them, and he knew it?

Whichever it was, he didn't fit here, didn't blend; there was no carefree laughter coming from him, and she ached inside for him. But she sensed he wouldn't welcome that, and made herself get back to the matter at hand.

"Now," she said, needing to get a decision out of him, and needing it to be the right one, "will you agree? You know our holo system is secure."

One corner of his mouth twisted slightly. "As much as is anything."

"Yes," she admitted. "But more secure than anything based here."

"The king will really send a ship here just for this?"

"He trusts your judgment that much, yes," she said, giving him the answer to the question he hadn't asked. "It will be here tomorrow, unless you refuse him."

"He presumes much," Tark muttered.

"He is King Darian of Trios," she said simply.

He looked at her, his brow furrowed slightly. The band that held the patch had caught a strand of his hair, pressing it against his good eye, and he tugged it clear with a gesture that hinted at long practice.

"Your home is indeed a . . . different place."

"Yes."

His brow lifted as she left it at that. "No account of her history, her gloriousness, the miracle that is Trios?"

"Why?" she said with a shrug. "You already know."

Slowly, like dawn creeping over the mountains of her home, he smiled. And it warmed her just as that dawning did, only this went deeper, finding places she hadn't even realized were chilled.

"Ah, Rina," he said, and the sound of her name from him completed the warming. "Right to the crux. I'd forgotten how you truly are a woman of few words."

"As you have become a man of even fewer."

"I have little to say, and less that people want to hear."

It was an offhand, detached, almost throwaway comment, a gibe aimed at himself, and yet Rina sensed there was more truth in it than he cared to admit.

"That is their mistake."

He studied her for a long moment. "Tell me," he said, "what do you do on Trios, now? In peace?"

She laughed. "Peace? With Dax and Dare and their offspring? Were it not for Shaylah's calm and Califa's cool, I would know nothing of peace."

He looked as if she had given him more of an answer than she intended, just as he had earlier.

"You speak of your king and queen by their names, not titles."

Her chin came up. "By their request. They are my family, and consider themselves so."

"And any Triotian can obtain an audience with your king?"

"Yes."

"And any child need only approach to be able to speak to him?"

"That has ever been the tradition, yes." She had run through that limited store of patience. "And will stay our tradition. We fought too hard to get her back to let her slip away again."

"Then you are . . . prepared?"

She frowned. "For what?"

"For whatever may come."

She let out an exasperated sigh. "Dare is the most diligent and vigilant of leaders. Our forces are strong, our people trained, drilled, and reminded daily of how we were nearly destroyed. Yes, we are prepared."

She heard him take in a deep breath, then release it slowly. "Good."

"Tark. Tell me. What is it we need to be prepared for? This is more than a bad feeling for you."

He looked at her sharply. "What makes you think—?"

"I am not a fool," she snapped, cutting him off.

"No," he agreed, something different coming into his expression. "You are many things, Rina, but a fool is not and has never been one of them. Your life was too hard for that."

"My life," she said with determined emphasis, "taught me not to never trust, but how to pick wisely who I trust. I wish yours had done the same."

He winced. Lowered his gaze. "Teeth," he muttered.

"What?"

"You've grown teeth like a bark-hound."

"And you've grown a hide like a Carelian blowpig."

"Not so tough, I'm afraid," he said, not sounding insulted at all. And then, without warning, he stood up. "Let's get out of here. Too many people."

She glanced around at the dining hall. It wasn't even particularly crowded this afternoon; the midday meal was past, and those who had come in for sustenance had returned to the party in the street.

But Tark was already headed for the door.

And assuming she'd follow, like some sort of pet? Or perhaps more as a cloud of annoying zipbugs who wouldn't leave him alone? He seemed to react that way sometimes.

But he had assumed she would follow. Had he not wanted her to, would he not have just said his good-bye and left on his own?

She rose, grimacing inwardly. She'd never realized that her life with Dax, with all his secrets, would be preparation for dealing with the likes of Tark. She had learned to deal with Dax, had learned to read him, to sense his moods, and just how to bring him out of it when he got too far into the dark.

But Tark seemed even more lost, under all the sharp words and short temper. She had the feeling he had slipped so far into the dark it was blackness all around. And she wondered if anyone could pull him out.

Chapter 12

SHAINA DID NOT like this. And it wasn't just the terrain.

The path had become steeper, and strewn with rocks of an annoying size, too large to simply step over, but too small to need climbing. More than once Shaina muttered about simply shoving them down the mountainside, but subsided when Cub pointed out they had no idea where the rocks—and the landslide they would likely start—would end up. Or what—or who—they might endanger in the process.

"We're in no hurry," he had said the last time she had kicked at a large rock.

"I suppose it might put a damper on your first public appearance as the royal representative of Trios if you wiped out a large section of their main city," she had admitted grudgingly.

Had Shaina realized it would change things so much, she never would have tried that tactic back down the mountain. There had to have been another way, it was simply that she hadn't had time to think of it.

And now Cub was acting so strangely, barely even looking at her. He'd been angry, yes, that she'd risked herself. But it had all worked out—they had won. And now they were on guard. They would not be surprised again. She especially would see to that, by focusing that ability she had to sense threats, and never letting herself be so distracted again.

Yet Cub was silent. There was none of the usual banter, none of the far-ranging conversation they usually indulged in when off on an adventure alone. When they were younger they had, with the certainty of youth, solved all the problems of the galaxy in one way or another. From Daxelia to Zenox, they had sorted it all out, even though they occasionally had resorted to skipping a few of the galaxy's problems when there seemed to be no answer.

They'd once, years ago, asked Cub's father about those. He'd laughed and said that wiser men than he had been working on those problems for eons and had found no solutions. That some things must be left to future generations to solve, and perhaps they would be the ones to do so. He had turned serious when he'd added that the hardest thing to accept was that sometimes things would not be righted in your lifetime.

Leadership, they'd concluded then, was more complicated than they'd thought.

But Cub would manage. He had the right temperament, and the courage and intelligence needed. And he'd been trained by the best, learned from the best, and had long ago gained the kind of quiet confidence of a leader. So why this strange mood?

Perhaps he was ashamed of her, of what she'd done.

The thought hit her hard, sending a sort of hot and cold ripple through her that was unlike anything she'd ever felt before. She'd thought of it merely as a tactic, no different than any other diversion. Other ramifications had never occurred to her.

Until now.

She stewed over it as they paused for a midday meal, in a place chosen precisely because it would be very difficult for anyone to sneak up on them. Up against a rocky cliff that was high enough to make descending from above a complicated and dangerous affair, looking out over an unbroken expanse with little cover save a few trees ahead of them on the path, and with the rock of the cliff diffusing the smoke of their much smaller fire. They were shielded from view by the boulders that had over the years fallen from the cliff face; they felt they'd done what they could to prevent another incident.

And that had been the only discussion they'd had since they'd moved on from the scene of the attack. Which made her very uneasy.

She had never been one to dodge an unpleasant matter—except for her father—because dodging always seemed only to make it worse once the matter was finally, inevitably broached. Yet she was finding it hard to face this problem with Lyon directly, which only added to her restlessness. She got to her feet, planning to check the surroundings one more time, and to reach a decision on her approach by the time she got back.

"You just did that three minutes ago."

She whirled at the unexpected comment. "So? You think I want to go through that kind of confrontation again? Even in daylight?"

"Nor do I," he said. "But at least let us trade off watching, as we always do."

"We don't seem to be as we always were." She hadn't planned to say that, but there it was, out in the open, and she couldn't help but be glad.

It was a long, almost painful moment before he said quietly, "No, we do not."

He wouldn't even look at her now. So she'd been right.

"So you are ashamed of me. Of what I did down there."

His head came up sharply. "What?"

"It was truly all I could think of to do." She tried to keep her voice level, reasonable, but heard the plea that crept into it anyway. Not surprising, since the very fabric of her life seemed threatened. "Perhaps because my mother and I had just had the discussion of it."

"I'm not ashamed of you. How could you think that?"

"You've not looked at me or even spoken to me since—"

"If I'm ashamed of anyone, it's myself."

She blinked. "You? What have you to be ashamed of?"

"I should have spoken to you before now."

"Spoken to me?"

He drew in a deep breath. Before he said a word, she was sure she wasn't going to like it. She wanted more than ever to go back, to before, however childish the idea was.

"About you and I," Cub said.

"No," she said, "don't. Don't do this, don't go to that place we can never go back from."

"We are already there," he said softly. "Can you not see that?"

"Because you are male and I am female, we are doomed now to lose what we have?"

A different voice spoke. "Not lose. Change."

Shaina whirled, dagger already in her hand. As quickly, Cub had the disrupter and was on his feet, facing the man who had approached so silently out of the trees further up the path.

"Be at ease, children." It was the old man, Shaina realized. With the brollet. Theon Talberon. He must truly know this mountain well, to move so quietly. "Although perhaps children is not the right form of address at the moment."

"You," Cub said.

"We meet again," he said congenially. "I bring no meat this time, I'm afraid. But I do have something to tell you."

"We can start with an explanation of why you are here," Cub said, the disrupter never straying from its potential target. "Are you following us?"

"Actually, I was a bit ahead of you, so I could well ask the same."

He had come from that direction, Shaina thought. He must move at a more energetic pace than she'd expected. She shouldn't have judged him based on age and appearance alone—couldn't Glendar put them all to shame on rough trails?

"You have chosen your site well," the old man said. "It is good that you take care. Dangerous men abound."

"You think we would be careless twice?" Shaina asked.

"Thrice, in my case," Cub muttered, then stopped short, staring at the old man. "And just how did you know we encountered dangerous men?"

"I did not. I merely said they are about. And it would behoove you to stay wary, the Prince of Trios would be a valuable prize."

Cub glanced at her. She read his silent question and shrugged. Despite his surprise reappearance, the old man still seemed harmless enough. But she would keep her dagger within reach.

At last Cub lowered the disrupter. "Join us. We have rockfowl roasting."

"So I smelled," Theon said.

Gathered around the small fire, they ate, Shaina taking care to go slowly since there would be less now that they were sharing with the old man. Not that she begrudged it, he had shared his brollet with them, it was only right that the generosity be returned.

"So, are you closer to the treasure?" he said when they had finished.

"How would we know?" Shaina asked. They had been merely proceeding up the mountain, with no clear path planned. Cub had made the decisions when they had come to a choice of directions. Since she didn't really believe in this treasure it mattered not to her, so she had let him.

"The legends say the coffers are not simply the property of the Graymist clan, they are protected by them. The spirits are thick on this mountain, and they only bare their secrets to those who are of the blood."

"We've just been . . . wandering," Cub said, proving her earlier thought accurate.

"So you may think," Theon said. "But if the stories are to be believed, it is drawing you."

Cub frowned. "Are you saying the path we've chosen is not random?"

"You, of the Graymist line, have chosen it, have you not?"

"But I've felt no such pull as you describe."

"Or you have not yet, in your short time on Arellia, learned to recognize it."

Shaina managed not to scoff. He was an old man, and she'd been taught to respect her elders. And if he was indeed an old friend of Cub's mother's family, then he deserved it even more. But while she had enjoyed these tales of wonder and magic as a child, she was beyond childish things now.

"It has been an interesting trek," she said neutrally, "even if there are no riches at the end of it."

The old man smiled at her. "Oh, the Graymist treasure is said to be much more than just riches. It is said to hold the future."

"What does that mean?"

Theon laughed. "Full of such portent, is it not? And beyond my ken, I'm afraid. I'm just a simple painter."

Shaina found herself smiling back at the old man. Cub was smiling as well, as he spoke, "From what my mother said of that mural, you were far more than that."

Genuine appreciation glowed in Theon's eyes. "I thank you for that, Prince Lyon of Trios."

Cub's mouth quirked. "I'm not officially that until the ceremony. Call me Lyon."

"Ah, you have your mother's charm. I remember when, as a little girl, she captivated even the frosty old Coalition delegate who had come recruiting. It was he who years later approved her application to flight training."

Cub grimaced for a split second at the mention of their enemy, but then he smiled. "She told me of this. It pains her to speak of her time with the Coalition, but she so loves to fly."

"It was her dream, from tender years. The sunbird I painted was her choice. 'Twas her diminutive name."

Shaina had fallen silent, just listening to them talk. She saw the pleasure in Cub's face as he questioned and Theon answered, saw his delight in this unexpected view into his mother's past. That alone made this journey worth it.

And this was treasure enough for her.

Chapter 13

HE STARED AT the bodies of the men who had gone to retrieve his objective and failed yet again. But it would be their last failure. The big man had been the last to go down, but go down he had, on top of the bodies of his men. They were now simply a pile of rotting debris.

They had been thus even before he had killed them, he thought with a sniff of disgust. Four of them to take one, and they could not do it.

He would have to do this himself. No more trusting underlings. He had the most at stake—his entire future—so he would do it himself. He should have known better than to rely on Arellians anyway. Had they not been infected by that Triotian evil, and been the first to succumb?

He kicked aside the cudgel one man had dropped when he fell. Such crude weaponry should have been a warning of their inefficiency. He'd been too far removed from the early necessities of victory. It had been too long since he'd had to get his own hands dirty. But he would overcome that. He must.

He had come to Arellia searching for a chance, any chance, to regain his losses. He had no plan beyond that, had hoped merely for an opportunity to present itself, an opportunity to be of such aid to what was coming that they could no longer deny they needed him. Needed him back in his position of power.

And he had had this opportunity handed to him. It was a sign, it had to be, that he was to act upon it. Then perhaps even his old position might be beneath his status, if he was successful in this.

And so he must be. Everything hinged on it. So he must do it himself. Personally. Twice now hirelings had failed him. Yes, he must take matters into his own hands.

The more he thought about his new plan, the better the outcome became. To have done this, alone, and personally . . . they could not ignore that.

There could surely be no better way to assure his regained status in the Coalition than to hand Legion Command the son of the man who had defeated them.

"HAD I KNOWN you planned on crossing the continent, I would have rented an air rover," Rina said sourly.

"Tired, little one?" Tark asked, his tone mocking.

"No, just annoyed. You trek a couple of leagues out here into the countryside and expect me to simply follow, with no explanation."

"I need to get something."

"Out here?"

She looked around them. Arellia, she realized, was much less scarred than Trios. Arellia they had merely wanted to conquer. Trios they had wanted to rape and then destroy, along with her people. She wondered who among the cold-blooded Coalition had realized the true threat Trios or any of her survivors would be?

"Patience," he said.

"I can't believe I'm hearing that from you," she retorted.

He ignored that one, although she thought she saw one corner of his mouth twitch. "Why are you here so early? The anniversary celebration is not until week's end."

"A favor for Dax. A personal one. Where are we going?"

"Here," he said, gesturing ahead of them.

She looked. Frowned. Only when they had moved forward another few steps did she see the straight-line shape of a small roof, moss covered. It appeared to be on a small, ramshackle lean-to, not even a shed, built of wood so old and weathered it faded into near invisibility against the hillside. She could easily see walking right past it unless you knew it was here. And certainly anyone going by in an air rover or speeder would never even see it.

It also looked as if it would fall down at the slightest breeze.

"Welcome to my humble abode," Tark said when they reached it.

Rina barely managed to stifle a gasp. It looked no better, in fact even worse, up close. Surely he didn't mean it, the hero of the Battle of Galatin could not truly live in this dilapidated structure that couldn't be called a shelter even in its finest hour? Only three walls, offering little protection at all from wind or winter. And there was no sign anyone at all lived here, not even a place to sit, surely he didn't—

He stepped past a fallen board, and around a leaning timber that had apparently once been for support. Still stunned, Rina followed him into the shack. The thing was deeper than she'd expected, deeper than it looked from the outside. She looked back toward the outside, frowning as she confirmed they had come further than should be possible. She didn't doubt her assessment. It was what she did, after all, as an exact navigator. This was not that much different than looking at the distance and relationship between the stars in a system she'd committed to memory, and knowing if something was off.

She turned back to ask Tark another question he likely wouldn't answer.

He had disappeared.

For an instant she simply stared at the empty space where he had been standing beside the back wall of the structure, unable to comprehend what had happened.

She shook her head sharply, shaking off the impossible, so that she could begin to address the possible.

He'd been there, and now he wasn't. She looked down. The floor was dirt, packed hard. The wall to the left was blocked by rotting timbers, leaning perilously close to collapse. The wall to the right looked stronger, but only for now, as the pressure shifted by the pull to the left.

The third wall, the back wall, looked more solid. In fact, oddly solid, with boards that weren't eaten away into a network of empty holes held together only by the bits of wood that remained.

She moved closer, her eyes going over each board. And then she stepped back, staring at it from there, letting her eyes go slightly unfocused, as she did when committing a star pattern to memory.

And she saw it. It was subtle, even beyond subtle, but there was a pattern of breaks, of seams, that formed a vaguely rectangular shape.

A door.

It took her a moment longer to find the entry point, a spot on the upper right with the slightest of sheens to it, as if it had been touched often.

She reached up and pressed it.

Soundlessly it swung outward, stopping when the opening was less than two feet wide. She stepped through. Tark was standing on the other side. He reached up and pressed a spot on the opposite edge of the door. It swung shut, as soundlessly as it had opened.

She folded her arms across her chest. "Playing games?"

"Just seeing if you were still as smart as you used to be. Clearly, you are."

"Or perhaps you're not as smart as you think you are," she said sweetly.

He laughed. A real laugh this time, genuine and full. "That," he said, "is without a doubt true."

She found herself smiling, she couldn't help herself. And for a moment they were those young warriors again, barely more than children—wild, reckless, and heedless of their own mortality.

They had to be inside the hill itself, she thought, although it was too dark to see. A natural cave, or had he dug it out himself? And still the question persisted . . . why?

She heard his steps as he crossed the floor, and then light flooded the room. For an instant she stared at the source, a huntlight fastened high on the wall.

"How do you power that, way out here?"

Yet again he laughed, probably at the fact that of all things, that was her first question. And then he shook his head, as if surprised at his own laughter.

"There's a stream, not far up the hill. It spins a small turbine I . . . adapted."

Memories came flooding back, of battles fought not too far from here. Whatever was needed, from a clever, unexpected tactic to any mechanical device, it had been Tark they had turned to. Because he consistently came up with ideas no one else could or did. His brain was agile, and refused to be confined within the boundaries of mundane thought. And so many of the things he came up with others had scoffed at, saying they would never work.

Until he built them, and they did work.

It was silly, she told herself, but still she seized upon this evidence that the Tark she knew was still there, if buried beneath a façade of abrasiveness. And sillier still was the hope that flared within her. Hope for what?

She quelled it ruthlessly, turning to look around at last.

It was indeed a cave. A fairly large one, tall enough for even Tark to easily stand upright with room to spare. And a natural one, although she could see marks where he had altered things, widened a spot here, carved out a niche there. One clearly served as a hearth, embers glowed there even now. *How did he vent that?* she wondered. She would have to ask.

She turned slowly, seeing that there were two alcoves further back, on opposite sides of the main space. One looked to be for cooking, and one was masked off by a hanging drape. Sleeping area?

Out here, there was a rather oddly shaped curve of rock that rose up from the floor and was covered with cushions. She wondered if he'd dug it out, or had simply carved around it when he'd realized the shape of the rock would serve as a place to sit. The table before it looked solid enough, although a bit rough, as if he'd built it himself out of a tree chopped down with a hand ax.

It was quite habitable, she thought. Almost comfortable. Dry—and the fire no doubt would keep it so, in addition to providing warmth. And if his stream dried up in the summer so the huntlight was not powered, the fire would provide at least some light.

But most of all, she wanted to ask why he felt the need to hide where he lived. That dilapidated lean-to could be for nothing else but concealment. No casual observer, seeing that, would look any further.

At last she turned to face him. "You live here."

"Not the royal palace of Trios, is it?" A bit of that edge was back in his voice.

"The royal palace was not what it once was for some time," she answered mildly. "It was the last building to be rebuilt in Triotia."

"Your king's doing?"

"Our queen's choice. The king agreed. The people first."

He studied her for a long moment. The huntlight threw his face into sharp relief, and cast the injured side of his face into shadow. She could picture, then, what he would look like without the patch, and the scar. If he had come through unscathed, would his life be different? Or was it his own attitude that set him apart? Not that he didn't have every reason, but did his brusque manner keep people at a distance? Was that even, perhaps, his intent? Or was he simply a blatant reminder they could not ignore of a time they would all much prefer to forget?

She heard a faint beep, and Tark looked down at his left hand. She noticed then what he held, a small device with a gauge. It was giving some kind of readout, although she could not see what. But he began to move it, always watching that readout. The way he did it made her realize it had to be some sort of scanner.

And he was scanning her.

Her first instinct was to be irritated, but she reminded herself that Tark always had a good reason for what he did, even if it was clear to no one else at the time. And so she simply stood, waiting for him to be finished. Although she did cross her arms over her chest, letting her body language speak what her mouth was not. She knew he would not miss it, vision halved or not.

"You're clean," he finally said. He pressed a button, and the readout screen went blank.

"I assume," she said, her voice chilly, "you're not referring to the fact that I bathed this morning."

For an instant his face changed, and she almost expected him to make some teasing innuendo-laden comment. Instead he shrugged and turned away.

"You came via commercial transport, did you not?" he said, returning the scanning device to a shelf in a niche on the nearest wall.

"A cargo vessel, yes. It was the first departure."

"Not all who crew such vessels are of the same mind."

She drew back, her brow furrowed. "Meaning?"

"Some do not share our hatred of the Coalition," he said.

"We're aware some were left behind when the Coalition finally broke and ran. But that was long ago, surely they've all . . . either settled in now, or made their way back to the loving arms of Legion Command."

He seemed to hesitate for a moment before saying, "Or have come back with a new goal."

She blinked. "What?"

He turned back to face her then—this time standing so his face was in full light, the eye patch and scar fully revealed. *Intentionally?* she wondered.

Of course, she answered herself. This was Tark, after all.

"What?" she repeated, her voice soft as she sensed he was on the edge of either trusting her and explaining at last, or deciding he could never trust her as he once had.

Finally he spoke. "Of all people, you are most likely to see it."

"See what?"

"Sit," he said, gesturing at the stone bench. It did not seem wise to dispute him just now, when he was apparently going to talk, so she sat. And found the cushions surprisingly comfortable. Feathers?

"Picture our system," he said. "As you do for navigating."

She had no idea what he was getting at, but if it kept him talking she would humor him. She sat back, let her eyes go slightly unfocused, and brought up in her mind the three-dimensional chart she knew so well. It was the image of the holographic representation she was most familiar with. Not that she needed it, she knew this system so well, but if he wanted her to look before he would go on, then look she would.

"And?" she said, once the image was before her mind's eye, floating as if the actual holograph was being projected.

"Where do we know the closest Coalition outpost to be?"

"Sector Gamma 10," she said, without losing focus. "At least, the last I heard."

"And the next closest?"

"Clarion."

"And the third?"

She fought down irritation, wishing he would just get to the point.

"Beyond Zenox, we think."

"Yes. Now plot a course from each of those three, as if you were still flying with Dax. As if secrecy was paramount, and not running into anyone was crucial."

"Ice planet to asteroid to dead world, that kind of course, you mean?"

"Yes."

"A course to where?"

"Just make it as straight and direct as possible, with those parameters, into the center of our system."

"Our system?" Her voice rose incredulously. "They would not."

"Please, Rina. Just do it, and see where those three paths would all cross."

With a smothered sigh she did so. While in the closer view the paths she came up with, darting from uninhabited ice planets to asteroids large enough to hide behind, were far from straight, when viewed from the perspective of the entire system they were more direct. She set the first one in her memory, then turned to the second. She set that one, then went to the third.

And only then did she get the first inkling of why he was making her do this.

The paths from all the outposts crossed on the far side of Arellia's outer moon.

She snapped back to the room, to Tark watching her, the image of the star system vanishing from her mind's eye.

He spoke softly. "There are unmarked ships, gathering there. What kind we do not know."

"Then they could be freighters, transports."

"Yes," he agreed, but went on. "What is the biggest prize in the galaxy, the one the Coalition counted as its greatest gain, and in the end its greatest loss?"

"Trios," she said, her breath catching.

"And were you the Coalition, wanting to regain your glory and empire, what would be the ultimate symbol of triumph?"

"Retaking Trios," she said, staring at him now.

"And what would be the perfect platform, the perfect place from which to launch that effort? A place much easier to retake than Trios, with Dax and Dare to guard her?"

"Arellia," she whispered.

Chapter 14

IT WAS, HE THOUGHT, outrageous that he was forced to do this himself. Trekking through the mountains as if he were nothing more than a mere foot soldier. He who was once the pride of the Coalition, agreed by everyone to be the most likely to take the place of General Corling when he was promoted to Legion Command, as everyone was sure he would be, after his triumph on Trios.

And instead, the old man had turned fool, allowed himself to be outmaneuvered by a girl and a slave, and it had all slipped through his fingers. And Corling had taken his entire staff down with him. He himself had been forced to watch the general's execution, bloody, painful affair that it was. The man he had once admired so much had cried like an infant, turning into a begging, cowardly creature. It was a scene those he had conquered would no doubt love to have watched.

He allowed himself to dwell pleasurably for a moment on those many he had conquered. Those successes alone gave the lie to those who said that only his familial connection to the ground force supreme commander had saved his own life.

He continued climbing, hating how he stumbled gracelessly over stones in his path, and how the rough terrain was scraping his boots. He was certain he had been climbing for several hours, to the point of considering his time-piece broken when it had logged less than two. After a particularly bad lurch, he nearly smashed it upon the rock that had somehow gotten in his way.

"Eos damn them," he muttered again as the trail—if you could even call it that—made another turn and he saw that there was still no one in sight up ahead. How far ahead could they possibly be?

He trudged on, fighting for the icy calm he'd always held as his greatest strength. He had watched entire planets destroyed, watched thousands executed, with no more feeling than a stone. He would soon be liberated from this existence, now that he had taken things into his own hands.

"ARELLIA? YOU think they're coming here?" Rina repeated it, looking for some way to refute the conclusion Tark had led her to.

"Or are already here," he said. "It is the perfect base from which to take on Trios."

"But they are not able to do this, their forces were decimated."

"And they've had years to rebuild. Look at what Trios has done in that time."

"Exactly!" she said. "Trios now has everything in reality that Dare only bluffed them with before."

"Yes. Which is why they need Arellia. A full base here will give them more power to strike, more focus, better supply lines. And if they retake Trios, it will take the heart out of the rest of the system. Without Trios to lead, the others will simply give in."

She stared at him. It was impossible. It could not happen. Surely.

"But there's been no sign of movement, of a buildup," she said.

"I know."

He said it wearily, as if it were a question he'd answered often.

"Then why do you think this? Why has no alarm been raised?"

"There is nothing the powers here believe is proof."

She frowned. This was Tark. Tactically, he was never wrong. Yet they did not believe him?

Her breath caught as a possibility struck her. "This? Is this why you are . . . treated so?"

"They do not want to hear this," he said.

"And so they transfer their resistance to the messenger?"

"Something of that sort. My appearance only makes it easier."

She drew in a deep breath. "Tell me. All of it."

"I will, if you wish. But let me show you what I learned that brought me to the city."

"What?"

He turned, reaching for a handheld cine-unit. It was old, a little worse for wear, but apparently functional. The screen flickered, and then an image came into focus. It was of a cloaked man—tall, thin, dark. Tark pushed the button to play the clip forward. It was short, merely seconds, but at one point the hood of the cloak slipped back, and the man's face was revealed for a split second. Tark froze it, hit a couple of other keys on the device. The image enlarged, sharpened. He held it for her to see.

Her eyes widened. "Is that . . . ?"

"We think so. Mordred, in the flesh. Here, in Galatin. That was taken a week ago. And we have other clips, from other places across the system, all of men who look suspiciously like Coalition leaders, all out of uniform, and all in places of tactical value."

She looked away from the image, from the face so familiar even today to all of Trios's people, the image so often seen in the histories, the man who had ever stood at the madman General Corling's right hand. She turned her gaze back to Tark.

"Who," she asked, "is this 'we' you speak of?"

He let out a tight breath. "There are . . . some few who see. We have suspected for some time."

"Who? And why? What roused your suspicions?"

He was on his feet now, pacing. She remembered this, that he had always done his best thinking while in motion.

"We have . . . a network of sorts. Watchers. Several of us who fought the Coalition, who have kept in touch." He let out a harsh laugh. It grated, so different was it from the genuine laugh she'd heard before. "I used to laugh at the foolish old men who would do nothing but talk of the days past, nothing but days of glory and meaning long behind them. And now I'm one of them."

"You are many, many things Bright Tarkson, but foolish and old are not among them."

She'd used his full name intentionally, and it worked. He stopped mid-pace and turned his good eye on her. She gave him her sunniest smile.

"Thinking whether to thank me or clout me?"

"You do not want to know what I'm thinking," he muttered.

Then he shook his head sharply and continued his pacing and his explanation. "We are in different places. A sizeable group here on Arellia. Similar on Clarion. Smaller groups in Carelia, and on Darvis II. And a few scattered elsewhere throughout the system."

She waited. He was committed now; she knew he would tell her all if only she kept quiet and let him do it in his own way, in his own time. Finally he came to a halt before her.

"In the last few months we have all seen . . . men we recognize. Coalition leaders. Living among us. Each in a place they know well."

Rina drew back. "In all those places? You're sure?"

He nodded. "And they have two things in common. They have no apparent means of support—they do not work—yet they have coinage to spend, often to excess."

"And the second thing?"

"They have all been busy acquiring acquaintances with connections to the defenses of each place."

"Spies?"

"Or scouts."

The very idea nearly took her breath away. She had been so young when the *Evening Star* had come home to Trios. She remembered vividly the battles that had followed, what it had taken to finally rid Trios of the Coalition for good. And no sooner had they done it than word had come that Arellia had risen up, inspired by the example of their closest neighbor. . . .

"Rina?"

"I was remembering the speech the king gave, when we learned Arellia had declared open rebellion. Trios was war weary, there were so many dead to yet be found and mourned. We had little left in the way of weapons even to defend ourselves should they come back."

"And yet he sent us help."

"Trios sent you help," she corrected gently. "The king does not make that kind of decision by himself. Dare has always said a king of Trios must have the people's trust. And they must have his. Our people are not blind followers. The king must present them with the facts and let them decide." She shrugged. "He merely made the case, and the people decided."

"I've heard a recording of that speech," Tark said. "He did a bit more than make the case."

"Dare is very persuasive," she agreed. "He speaks from his heart, and his people know that what he says is what he truly believes."

"And so he sent us his vaunted flashbow warrior."

"Dax volunteered. He said Dare could not leave, he was needed at home."

"And Dax's mate?"

"She would never let him go without her. Even in battle, she is ever at his side, as Shaylah is by the king's."

"It helps that they are both warriors in their own right."

"Yes. They are. And would be again, if necessary. Perhaps even fiercer now that they have children to protect."

"I am glad to hear it. And that they protect you, as well."

"But I left childhood behind long ago," she said pointedly.

"I'm not sure you ever had a real childhood."

The gentleness in his tone startled her. "I didn't think you ever thought of such things."

"I have had too much time for thinking, since Arellia's victory." He grimaced. "At least, until recently."

And they were back to his incredible story patched together from grainy images, old memories, speculation, and a pattern no one else had seen. Did she believe it? That the Coalition was actually readying a return, preparing to start another war? How could she not take it seriously, when Tark obviously did?

"You believe this threat is real?" she asked.

"I do. As do the others."

"Are they believed, on their worlds?"

His mouth twisted. "About as I am here."

"But surely they cannot ignore the possibility."

"They seem to be doing a stellar job of just that," he said.

"Then they are fools."

His gaze came back to her face. "So quick to defend," he said softly.

"It shouldn't be necessary." Anger had crept into her voice, but she didn't try to temper it. He should know that someone, at least, had not forgotten that he was the truest kind of hero, that he had nearly died to save his people. "What else?" she demanded, sensing there was more.

For a moment he hesitated, looking at her, but finally he said, "I think . . . they may be planning to mark this anniversary in their own way."

Rina's eyes widened. "What are you saying?"

"Symbolism is important to them. I think they may have chosen this anniversary as the date for their invasion."

"That soon?"

"Yes. And Arellia is paying no attention."

"Dax and the king do not have their heads buried in snailstones."

"Then I will tell what I know. And hope they believe."

Rina's sense of urgency was doubled now. Much more than the relationship between an equally hotheaded father and daughter was at stake. The fate of their two worlds could be in the balance if Tark was right.

And when it came to war and battles and tactics, she had never known him to be wrong.

Chapter 15

LYON AWOKE ABRUPTLY. He had no idea what time it was, since he lacked Rina's internal clock that was as unerring as her navigation. For a moment the miasma of the dream clung to him. It had been a long time since he'd dreamed of that time, of living in a constant state of tension, his parents and godparents talking grimly of holding off a force so powerful it had swept through the galaxy virtually unopposed.

He raised up on one elbow, listening in the dawn quiet for any sign they had been found again. Shaina's bedroll lay tumbled and empty, and he guessed she was out on one of her countless scouting checks. He had never seen her more restless.

The thought brought back the other part of his dream. Shaina.

His memories of her from those days were so clear. She wasn't just woven into the fabric of his life, she was a thread without which it all fell apart. Even then, as a child, when fear seized so many, she had been fearless. Unwaveringly fearless, and confident Trios would triumph. They had his father to lead, and her father to fight, did they not?

But he'd seen how it consumed his father, how his every waking moment had been spent on the affairs of Trios, first holding off the expelled Coalition, then rebuilding and defending their world from recurrent attempts to retake her. He would, Lyon knew, do it unto death if necessary. And it was not long before the people of Trios realized that the infamous flashbow warrior turned skypirate they had once thought lost to them would do the same. In a much more reckless, breath-stealing way, but do it he would.

Shaina had, then and now, the same fearlessness, the same reckless daring as her father.

As the sun lifted that last fraction, and the golden light of dawn poured down over the mountain, he saw her. She was making her way back from the direction of the stream, her hair unbound, dark strands lifted by the slight breeze. She moved with the same easy stride as always, but it seemed different to him now. More graceful. With more sway.

She walked like a woman, he thought, and he had been a blind, utter fool not to have realized he could no more ignore that fact than he could stop breathing.

She paused, and turned to look up the mountain toward the rising sun. The golden light seemed to flow over her, and his breath caught. He knew he would always remember this image of her, bathed in the dawn's light, looking upward, onward. And he had little doubt this image would join the parade in his dreams, as so many others had last night.

He fought the stirrings inside him. Just because he'd awakened to her feminine appeal didn't change the fact that he'd always known her strength, and that she had that boundless courage.

Of course, until now, she hadn't known she was the new flashbow warrior.

The flashbow warrior. Another image flashed through his mind. A rare day of pleasure for their parents, when they had traveled to one of the few places on Trios left untouched by Coalition guns and explosives. Lake Geron, named for the ancient warrior, was nestled in a hidden valley—clear, blue, ringed by tall trees and edged by famous Triotian grass, soft and vivid green.

He'd marveled at it, and found it hard to believe when his parents explained that all of Trios had once been much like this, a place of pristine beauty. But then his father and godfather had begun to talk of the things they had done as children, the places they'd seen, when Trios had yet been unscarred by war.

And then they'd seen the kingbird, that majestic bird long feared destroyed, first soaring overhead, then diving in what Dax had said was a salute to his father.

"What is it, Cub?"

He'd let himself get lost in that memory. And on some level he realized that the fact that he had felt safe enough to do so was a sign of how much he trusted her; if there was someone around, she would know it. She had regained her focus—certainly better than he had—and that extra sense she had would not fail again.

"I was thinking of the time we went to Lake Geron," he said.

A softness came over her face as she lowered herself to sit cross-legged before embers of the fire they had, out of caution, let die down in the darkness when it might betray them. For a moment she said nothing as she stirred the coals and added a couple of pieces of wood that caught and flared quickly.

"That was a wonderful time," she said finally. "Over and above what we discovered there, I think it was the only time until the end of the war that I remember our parents actually relaxing. They actually laughed, and played games with us. And each other."

"They carried a heavy load."

"Yes. I've often wondered how they managed to set it down even for that long."

"They did it for us," Lyon said.

Shaina stopped stirring up the fire and looked at him. "Us?"

"I remember overhearing my mother tell my father she did not want us to grow up knowing only fear and fighting. That we needed to know there could be happiness and the love of family, too."

"You never told me that."

"I've only just remembered it now, thinking about that day."

He stopped, unwilling to speak of what had triggered the memory. She was still, he knew, very angry with her father, and he didn't want to poke at that particular zipbug nest. But the image that had come back to him, of Dax and his father swimming in a mock race, haunted him now in an entirely new way. For he had seen his godfather's bare torso, had seen the scars he carried, for the first time. Burns, disrupter marks, scars of the war. But most telling, the marks of a lash that crisscrossed his back. A whipping taken for Rina. They all knew the story of how he had allowed himself to be captured, and publicly flogged, just to find out what had happened to Rina's mother.

It was the kind of thing the flashbow warrior did.

And Shaina was the next in that unbroken line of protectors.

The possibilities that created practically exploded in his mind. What had already been a challenging future to face now seemed impossibly complex.

MORDRED ADJUSTED the viewing scope for the growing light. He'd finally caught up to them, but he didn't wish to get any closer and be seen. They had, he grudgingly admitted, picked a good spot for their camp. There was no way to approach without being seen, and the cliff behind them was far too high and steep to risk.

He scanned the area once more, but he was certain now they were alone. He shifted the scope back to his prey. He paused momentarily on the woman. She was attractive, much more than he would have expected from some paid companion picked up from Akasen Court. Not that she would appeal to him at all. No, she was a fully adult female, curved and shaped as such, far too adult for his tastes. He preferred them young and unformed.

And frightened. As this woman clearly was not.

In fact, she reminded him of someone, although he could not figure out who. But with her pale skin and dark hair she was clearly Arellian, so obviously the prince had just picked up a willing female for this journey.

If she was gambling on establishing some sort of connection to the Triotian prince, she had a big surprise coming, he thought. And then he discarded her as not worth any more of his time or speculation. He had simply spent too much time on this planet, and they had all begun to look alike to him.

He shifted his focus, zooming in now on the man. Bile rose in his throat. He looked just like his father, with the golden skin and hair of the Triotian, but there was something else about him that spoke clearly of the royal lineage. The tilt of the head, the strong body, the handsome face . . . oh, yes, he was his father's son. Even that air of royalty he so hated was there. It had seemed to him all Triotians had it, not simply the royal family. As if they thought—no, as if they knew—they were better, that their world and way of life were better.

Not that anyone truly believed the stories—that any Triotian would die to save another they didn't even know. No one individual was that important. Everyone knew that, yet the people of Trios clung to their old ideas, too stupid to realize the benefits the Coalition brought them.

He had been there when the then-prince Darian had been enslaved, had had the great pleasure of watching the implantation of the collar, and the even greater pleasure of watching the recalcitrant Triotian realize his days of independence were over, that never again would he be allowed to do anything not commanded by his owners, the Coalition that had destroyed his world.

Except they hadn't.

Yet another thing to lay at General Corling's door. He had sworn before Legion Command that Trios was finished, would never rise again, nor rally any others to rebellion. He had been wrong on both counts, and the man who filled the visual field in his scope now was living proof of that.

But that man could also give the Coalition incredible power, the power even to defeat the upstart Triotians without a shot. For if they truly believed in those outmoded ways, then would they not do anything to save the son of their king? Even surrender?

Pathetic. That's what they were. All this trumpeting of individuality. They were soft, in both mind and will. He doubted any of them would have the nerve to do what he had already done. The Coalition commander who had been sent here to Arellia in secret had been of high rank, an imposing and intimidating man.

But with his blustering he had also lacked the ability to fade into the background, and was in fact a poor choice to send to this most crucial target. He could have told them that, at Legion Command. He had done them a favor, really, by eliminating him mere hours after his own arrival. He wouldn't have gone unnoticed for long, not even among these drunken fools.

And of course it was to Mordred's own benefit. Once they realized their spy was dead, they would need someone else to rely on. And he would step in. Ready, and armed with priceless trophies.

He nearly laughed aloud, picturing his personal triumph. He, Ulic Mordred—the forgotten and disgraced—presenting this coveted prize to Legion Command. By Eos, it would be an exquisite thing.

But first, he must capture his prize. And he could not do it here, in the open. It would not do to assume the soft, royal offspring was helpless. He had escaped twice already, although not from the likes of Mordred himself. That rebel prince would learn that going against Ulic Mordred would be much different than fighting off some hapless street thuggers.

And that would be only the first of the many things this son of his worst enemy would learn.

Chapter 16

"IT IS VERY GOOD to see you alive, Commander Tarkson."

The holo images were vivid, clear, and made it seem as if they were indeed all in the same room together. The ship had arrived as promised, having already been on patrol halfway between Trios and Arellia. The queen's voice and expression were so full of warmth and sincerity that Rina smiled—and noted that Tark looked taken aback. It was a moment before he could speak.

"No longer commander, your majesty, but I thank you nevertheless."

It was a gracious answer. He had discarded any bitterness. In the face of such genuine caring, it would have been boorish, and she was glad to see he realized it. He may have isolated himself—or had it forced upon him—for some time, but at least he knew this was a time for civility. She hoped it was because he realized he was among friends here.

"And I thank you," Califa said.

Tark looked startled this time as he switched his gaze to Dax's mate.

"Two connections of mine, cousins of a sort, were in the Council Building during the Battle of Galatin. They are alive thanks to you." She grimaced. "Although they could have told me you had survived the war. I wish they had."

"It was my wish that they not," Tark said.

Rina saw their puzzled looks. She supposed you would have to see how he was treated here to understand that wish.

"Shall we get to business?" she suggested gently, wishing to spare him from any further explanation.

Tark nodded sharply, and plunged into his account, including the dire state of Arellian readiness. What few troops they had were rusty or untried, and led by those with either no experience or enough age on them to make true action difficult. He laid it out as he had once laid out wartime intelligence or battle plans: no emotion, simply facts. And presented that way, it all seemed a little sparse. It was Dax who stepped in then, prodding Tark for his take on what evidence he had. Tark gave it, although he clearly didn't expect his gut feeling to be taken seriously, just as it had not been on Arellia.

"You are certain of this?" Dare asked when he had finished.

Rina watched as Tark stared at the king. The protective walls were going back up swiftly.

"If you mean, sir, do I have proof I can show you, beyond these few blurry cinefilm captures, then no," Tark said, his tone flat now.

He and Dare had met only twice that she knew of. Once when Dare had flown in with Dax to assess the situation in the first days of the rebellion on Arellia, and offer what recommendations he could from what he had learned in the battle for Trios. Shaylah had accompanied him then, freely teaching the forces of her home planet all she knew of Coalition tactics—which was considerable; she had once been, after all, the most decorated pilot of Coalition Tactical Defense Wing 3.

The second meeting had been at the turning point of the battle, when Tark had flown with her to Triotia to urge the king to send more help. It was help Trios could ill afford—they were still rebuilding and focused on their own security—but when Dare had realized this was the man who had fought off a Coalition battalion during the siege of Galatin, that he was the one who had saved hundreds of innocent people who had taken refuge inside the Council Building, he had reconsidered. To his credit then, Dare had dismissed Tark's obvious youth and considered only the facts. She remembered how he had looked at her, not missing the fact that she stood at Tark's side, tacitly lending her support, for whatever it might be worth.

In the end, the king had sent his own protection detail, over the protests of his queen, Dax, and even Tark.

"*We ask only for help, your majesty, not that you sacrifice your own safety,*" *he had said.* "*You are crucial to sustaining the hopes of all of us.*"

"*And if I cannot look out for myself for a while, then I truly have become just a figure-head, and otherwise useless,*" *Dare had said, startling Tark, but making Dax grin.*

"*Contention valid,*" *Dax had said*—*that quickly acceding to the idea. The queen had been less quick, but in the end had withdrawn her protest.*

"*But be aware,*" *she had warned her mate,* "*that I have not forgotten how to fight, and I hereby appoint myself your protection until this is over.*"

"*You are the pilot who took out* The Wanderer *at seven to one odds against you,*" *Dare had said.* "*I would never think you had forgotten how to fight.*"

It had been on the flight back to Arellia that Tark had asked, with no small amount of awe in his voice, "*Was that true? It was your queen who defeated Cryon—one Rigel Starfighter against a Diaxin class cruiser with six fighters aboard?*"

"*It is,*" *Rina had said proudly.*

The young warrior had let out a low whistle. "*Your king has found a mate to match him.*"

"Tark," Dare said now, his voice surprisingly gentle as he used the informal address, "I did not ask if you had proof. I asked if you were certain."

Tark drew back slightly, and Rina saw him swallow. *Yes,* she thought fiercely, *he should be on Trios, where he would get the respect and honor he had earned.* Emotion welled up in her, and she moved to stand beside him, as she had before, years ago. Back then it had been more of a symbolic gesture, the king knew little of her, but listened as he did to all Triotians of blood or spirit. But now Dare knew her well, had taken her under his royal wing as part of his extended family, and she knew her support would mean something.

"I . . ." He began, but faltered when she joined him. "Very few believe it," he finally said. "Including the Council and our military leaders." His mouth twisted. "They think I'm looking for remembered glory."

Dax snorted inelegantly. "I fought alongside you those many weeks. You know better than most the high price of glory." He leaned forward, looking at Tark intently. "But is it what your gut tells you, Tark?"

Rina felt him take in a deep breath, as if to steady himself. And finally he said it. "Yes. And it tells me this anniversary is not a date they will ignore."

As if he had been only waiting for that, Dare nodded. He looked at Dax.

"I'll ready the *Evening Star*," Dax said. "It will take some time to recall her crew, but we will be there." With a glance and a nod at Califa, he was gone that quickly. Dare might have to wait for approval to send Triotian forces, but the flashbow warrior was his to command.

"Just like that?" Tark said, astonished. "What if I'm wrong, what if it is just some deranged unreality? My brain's been rattled a bit, if you hadn't noticed."

"And mine was not under my own control for a time," Dare said quietly.

Tark blinked. He seemed beyond words for the moment, so Rina spoke quickly. "Thank you, your majesty."

Dare's mouth quirked. "Your majesty? Now I know we're in trouble."

Shaylah was smothering a smile. "Be well, both of you," she said.

Both she and Dare looked at Califa. She gave a slight nod, which they returned. And then the king and queen were gone, their holograms vanished as quickly as they had arrived. As if the sudden cut in the power required to maintain the holograms had been a signal, a warning that departure was imminent came over the ship's speakers.

"Can you give us a moment?" Rina asked Tark, looking briefly at Califa's remaining hologram. "There should be water and something edible there," she added, gesturing toward the alcove off the projection room.

"Of course."

Rina knew what was coming, and answered before Califa had to ask. "I would say she's here, although I have little more proof than Tark has."

"I don't doubt it. Shaylah is right, she would go to Lyon. What have you learned?"

"Only that two people matching their description were seen heading up the old mountain. Noticed only because everyone else is on their way into town for the celebration. Which is," Rina added dryly, "apparently going to last forever."

Califa smiled. "We Arellians know a bit about merrymaking."

"So I see." She wasn't surprised at Califa's casual tone. While she was concerned about Shaina, she also knew her daughter could well take care of herself. She knew, because she had taught her.

"It is as well Dax will have something to distract him," Califa said. "He is brooding about Shaina."

"As well he should," Rina said.

"Indeed. I think he has realized the measure of his mistake. Although I bear some of the blame myself."

"You?"

"I should have pushed him harder to tell her."

"Because he responds so well to being pushed," Rina said dryly.

Califa laughed. "Yes. And you were the first to teach me that, my girl."

The old appellation, adopted long ago by the woman she'd come to think of as the closest thing to a mother she would ever have, made her smile.

"Will you come with him now?" she asked.

"A chance to fly on the *Evening Star* again? Of course." Califa paused, studying Rina rather intently. "And I want to meet your Tark."

. . . your Tark.

She didn't, Rina assured herself, mean it that way, in the way one spoke of lovers or mates. It only sounded—

"You care for him."

It wasn't really a question, but Rina doubted she would get away with not answering. "I . . . he is . . . he is a hero, and he is not being treated as he should be here."

"Because he is speaking things they do not wish to hear?"

"Yes, in part," she said. She almost went on about the apparently superficial tastes of too many Arellians before she caught herself. Califa, after all, was Arellian.

"And in the other part?"

"He is . . . difficult. Withdrawn. Has dark moods."

Califa chuckled. "Then you're the perfect one to deal with him. You handled Dax at his worst, better than anyone."

That Califa saw what she had only recently realized herself somehow heartened her.

"Is that why he is not held in the esteem he should be?" Califa asked.

"It is more that some here," she said carefully, "seem to hold his scars against him."

"Scars earned saving them from Coalition enslavement?"

In for a withal, in for it all, Rina thought and said it. "Yes. They seem to prefer their wounded heroes out of sight."

"Ignoring reality is what made them fall to the Coalition boot heel in the first place," Califa said. Sometimes, Rina thought, it was impossible to believe this woman had once been the pride of that same Coalition, so complete had been her repudiation of her past and all she had stood and fought for.

"Have I told you recently how much I admire you?" Rina asked impulsively.

Califa drew back for an instant. Then she smiled. "And I love you, my girl."

Rina matched her smile. Until Califa went on.

"Which leads me to ask again . . . your Tark. Just how much do you care?"

"He is . . . very important to me."

That, she thought, was nothing less than the truth. And was not cluttered by naming the emotions and feelings that tangled things up so. She heard a sound behind her, but Califa spoke again in that moment.

"That will do. For now. I understand this situation is . . . bigger, but you will keep trying to find Shaina?"

"Of course. Do you wish me to have her contact you?"

"She may not wish to speak to me, either." Califa had little talent for self-delusion—she often said she had spent it all in her time with the Coalition—and it made conversations like this easier. "Just make sure she is well. I leave anything else to your judgment."

With a nod, Califa's image vanished. Rina let out a breath. She turned. And came up short, nearly gasping aloud as she almost bumped into Tark.

That sound behind her, she thought.

The thought that followed that one did make her gasp.

He is very important to me. . . .

She had heard that sound, the sound she now knew had been Tark returning, almost as she had said those words. Had he heard her? Would he think she meant something other than she had intended?

Was she even sure herself that she hadn't meant more?

For a long moment silence stretched out between them. He was looking at her, searchingly. For an instant it seemed that impassive mask slipped, seemed as if there was a spark of the old Tark still there, just waiting to catch and burn anew. It took her a moment to recognize the sensation that welled up inside her as hope, hope that the real Tark, the warrior, the man who had so fascinated her in the crazed, frenzied days of the battle for Galatin, was still alive somewhere beneath the tough, battered exterior.

For his own sake, she told herself. Not because of any interest on her part.

"They are readying to depart."

Rina blinked. For a moment she had forgotten, truly forgotten they were on a ship.

"Oh."

"Will you be . . . staying aboard, to return to Trios?"

"Me?"

The brow above his undamaged eye lifted, making her realize how foolish she was sounding. She wondered, even more foolishly, if his injury made it impossible for him to lift both brows in that way he'd had, expressing volumes without saying a word.

"No," she said hastily. "I have . . . business on Arellia, still."

"Which I have interrupted."

"With good cause," she said.

He glanced over at the spot where the holograms had been. "They believed me."

He sounded surprised still. Annoyance spiked in her. Not at him, but at those who did not hold him dear enough. "I told you of the respect and trust you have on Trios."

"Yes. You did." His mouth curled at one corner. "Perhaps I should consider relocating more seriously."

"You would be welcome. And you would have no shortage of willing sponsors."

Being a sponsor on Trios was no small thing. Any outworlder must have one, and that sponsor did more than just vouch for the newcomer, they took responsibility, assuring they had not only useful skills, but the attitude and outlook that made Trios stand out from all other worlds.

"Including you?" Tark asked, and Rina couldn't help thinking there was more to his query than the almost teasing tone indicated.

"Of course I would sponsor you. Proudly."

Again, it was nothing less than the truth. And again, she dodged all thought that there might be more behind the instantaneous, sincere offer than just a desire to see this man treated with the esteem he had earned.

. . . your Tark.

That, she thought, was a fool's fantasy. And yet hope rose within her that he would even joke about coming to Trios. How she would love to have him there, for so many reasons. And what would she do? Could she ever reach him as deeply as she wished? Could she convince him his scars meant nothing but honor to her?

She could try, she thought. At least she could try. But even as she thought it, she realized the scars the world saw were likely nothing compared to the scars he bore inside.

Chapter 17

THEY WERE GONE.

Mordred swore, wishing a thousand fiery deaths upon the fates that continued to foil him. He had been so certain this time. He had followed them for hours, safely back, able to watch only through his scope. They were moving so slowly, as if they were on some festive leave, and it had infuriated him that he was having to move as slowly while he waited for the perfect ambush.

He had carefully calculated his approach and his tactics once they neared a likely ambush site, and had let himself feel some of the joy of his victory, just to whet his appetite.

Yet when he had emerged from the trees along the trail, so stealthily they could have never heard him coming, they had vanished. As if they had never been there, as if he had been following merely phantoms. As if this damnable mountain was enchanted. Or there truly was some omnipotent power who took a personal interest in protecting these bedamned Triotians.

But the woman was Arellian. And this was Arellia. Perhaps that was it, perhaps she knew this mountain, perhaps she knew of secret paths and hiding places. That had to be it, he thought. There was nothing supernatural about it, no mystical power who protected the likes of this Prince of Trios.

And he would be no prince when Mordred got through with him. As for the Arellian, while she was too womanly to appeal to his tastes, he supposed she was beautiful in a rakehell sort of way. There would be men enough at Legion Command who would thank him if he gifted her to them. Slaves were a luxury these days.

Of course, if she got in the way, she was quite expendable.

It still maddened him that he could not think who she reminded him of. It could not be any female he'd met, for he'd had no contact with Arellian women, and the two Arellian children who had assuaged that curling, slicing hunger that drove him in matters of the body hadn't survived the encounters.

But whoever she was, he would see that she regretted ever having anything to do with that spawn of a demon, no matter how much coin he had paid her. Or perhaps she was the sort for whom the title of *Prince* was enough for her to offer herself, sham though that title was. A lot of good that would do her—or him—when Trios was again conquered—and this time completely destroyed; he would not rest until he watched that piece of rock shattered into a quadrillion pieces and scattered out endlessly into space.

. . . no matter how much he had paid her.

His own thought echoed in his head. What if he hadn't paid her at all? What if there were something to this talk of treasure he had overheard in their silly nattering? He had dismissed the idea of some famous Arellian treasure hidden on this mountain as foolishness, some made-up adventure to add spice to the journey. He knew enough men who liked to play pointless games and pretend in sexual encounters.

But what if instead of an erotic game of the prince's making, she had lured him instead? Perhaps it had been she who had tempted him with stories of riches. What if she knew something, perhaps even where the treasure was? What if there really was something to the tale? What else would get a prince out of the city so close to the celebration? Surely Trios still needed money to rebuild. What prince wouldn't want to add to the royal treasury?

For a moment the tantalizing thought sent visions shooting through his mind. He savored the idea of capturing not only the hereditary prince of Trios, son of the man who had humiliated them, but a treasure stolen from the planet second on the list for annihilation.

He would let them lead him, he decided. Lead him to whatever they were searching for. And if it was truly a treasure, he would have that, too. And if it were merely a fool's errand, then he would still have the prince, as he had planned all along. There was simply no way he could lose.

Smiling, he renewed his search. He would find them again; they couldn't be far. And this time he would keep them in sight at all times. And then, his prize—or prizes—in hand, he would get off this bedamned, benighted mountain and begin his triumphant return.

"I'M NOT SURE this is necessary still, all this subterfuge," Lyon said. "There's been no sign for some time."

Shaina looked over her shoulder at him, then went back to laying a false trail at a right angle to the one they were actually taking. She finished bending—just short of breaking—one more branch of the bush at the side of the path. She let the heel of her right boot leave a faint print in the softer dirt at the edge of the trial. Then she straightened, and shrugged.

"I'm not sure it is not."

He had no counter for that bit of common sense, so he remained silent as she made her way back, stepping carefully so as not to destroy the picture she had created of someone having passed that way recently.

They walked on, he lost in his thoughts as she would occasionally pause to lay another false trail. But finally, when they came to a likely spot for a rest and some food, she stopped. She faced him, crossing her arms in front of her in a familiar way that sent a hum of warning through him. There was something to be said for knowing someone so well.

"What is wrong with you, Cub? You're past edgy, and it's more than just holdover from those thuggers."

He didn't try to deny it. It was all too true, and she knew him too well.

Besides, how could he ever explain to her? How could he ever tell her that the realization had little to do with thinking and everything to do with his newly awakened senses? To her, he was still that childhood companion, to be teased and pummeled, and kept close out of habit as much as desire.

And *desire* had been the wrong word to use, even in his thoughts. He was already having enough trouble keeping himself in check.

"Cub?"

She wasn't going to give up. But then, she never did. And he couldn't tell her the truth, that it was she herself who had him on edge. So on edge that he had left the planet to get away from her. And yet now here they were, and he knew deep down he was dealing with something explosive.

"Changes," he muttered.

"Oh." She sighed. "It always seemed so safely distant."

"Shaina," he began.

She held up a hand to stop him. "I don't want to hear it, Cub."

"Hear what?"

"Can you see the Prince of Trios taking off on rambles like this one?" she asked, an almost bitter note coming into her voice. "It will never be the same, and well you know it."

"It is already not the same."

Her gaze shot back to his face. "Don't say that. We were to have this one last adventure. It doesn't have to change yet."

"It already has," he said, determined not to backtrack now that he had begun. "I cannot pretend it hasn't."

"I'm still me," she protested.

"Yes. Which makes the beauty you have become even more compelling."

Something shifted in her expression, and for an instant he thought he saw a sort of longing there. An echo of what he himself was feeling. But it was gone immediately, and she dropped to sit on the large rock at the side of the path, as if her strength had given out.

But this was Shaina; her strength never failed her.

"What is this, Cub?" she asked, her voice so near to shaky it rattled him. "Have you taken to believing the old predictions?"

Oddly, until this moment when she'd spoken of it, he'd put it out of his mind. But her words brought it all back, the memories of the various adults who had watched over them as they played together as children, speaking of the potential union of the royal house of Trios with the house of Silverbrake. *Destiny* had been the word he'd heard most often.

He'd thought, as a child, they simply meant friendship. And the talk had stopped by the time he'd gotten old enough to understand. Rather abruptly, as if that talk had suddenly been banned.

And likely it had, he thought now, suddenly remembering something else he'd heard. Califa, speaking to his father.

They need to be free to make their own choices, Dare. No one knows better than you and I the pain of having that taken from you.

She had meant, of course, the one thing she and his father shared that his mother and Shaina's father did not. They both knew what it meant to be enslaved, your will subordinated, your entire being subjugated to someone else's will. They both knew what it meant to have no choice of your own. No wonder she had raised her daughter to be so determined to choose her own path.

He just hadn't realized exactly what choice she'd been referring to, then.

"I'm glad the talk stopped," she said.

"Thanks to your mother."

Her head came up then. "My mother?"

He told her then, of the memory he had of her mother and his father. "I think they banned such talk, at least from our presence."

"I wish they had done so sooner. I wish I'd never heard it."

"The idea is so distasteful to you, then?" He said it carefully, neutrally, wanting an honest answer from her. Better to know now, when he perhaps might be able to control his own response, if she found the idea and thinking of him in that way repellant rather than just unexpected.

"More frightening," she said, surprising him.

"You're never afraid," he said.

"What I am is contrary."

His mouth quirked. "And you suppose this to be news?"

"Quiet, skalworm," she said, but without much heat. "I meant only that I spend half my time coveting what my parents have together, and the other half wishing to forever avoid it."

Feeling it safe enough now, he sat down beside her. "An interesting conflict," he observed, still striving for that neutral tone. "I understand the coveting, I feel the same about my own parents, and the bond they share."

She gave him a sideways look, but at least did not push him off the rock into the dirt.

"Did you never fear it? Loving someone so much that their loss would destroy you?"

He had, in fact, thought of that. As a child, during the ongoing fight to keep Trios free of the Coalition, he'd early on realized the truth adults tried to hide, that anyone could be killed on any given day. Including his parents. Especially his parents since they were at the forefront of that battle, often putting themselves in the most danger.

But never both at once.

"I remember," he said softly, "the day I realized why my parents never went into battle together, even though I knew they wished it."

"Because they did not want you to lose both of them, should the worst happen."

"Yes. I knew even then that if that worst happened, they would prefer to go together. That one of them staying behind for my sake was, in fact, a sacrifice of sorts."

"Because that one would be facing life without the other. That's exactly it, Cub."

"But is it a price worth paying?"

Shaina shifted on the rock, now staring down the mountain, as if by looking they could return to where this journey had started.

"I don't know. I've had a taste of loss now, with my father, and I don't like it."

He opened his mouth to point out that her father still lived, and that they could repair the damage—and would, he was sure—but it didn't seem the right time. She was opening to him, and he did not wish to disrupt that.

"There are those who say you have no choice where you love," he said. "Not when it's that kind of love. Your parents, and mine, are proof of that."

She considered that. "If that is true . . . then it cannot be forced, can it?"

"No, I would think not."

"So we cannot make it happen, simply because of some old talk and the wishes of others."

He stifled a sigh. He'd been wrong to hope. To her he would always be Cub.

"No," he agreed. "It will only happen if it is meant to."

She grimaced, and he tried not to let it sting too much, but without much success. He wanted to ask her if she found nothing in him to make her even consider the possibility, but wasn't certain he cared to hear the answer, so held back the words.

"Truly meant," she said.

"Especially since we—" *you* "—are on guard."

"So if it were . . . to happen, it would be real, then," she said. "Not just the fruit of an idea planted long ago."

Something snapped back to life in him. Was she actually acknowledging the possibility? "Yes," he said, carefully. *Very real,* he thought.

He remembered again the moment it had struck him, back home on Trios. It had hit him so hard and so fast he had wondered if, on some level, he had been preparing this for longer than he knew. If the shock of realizing she had become a woman, and a beautiful one, had merely been the spark laid to the fuel he'd been piling up for a long time. Had it all been there, only awaiting that moment of realization?

He knew now it must have. It really hadn't been so quick at all. It had been building for years.

"We need to move on," she said, her tone brisk as she stood up. He wasn't sure if she meant physically, or move on from this morass of emotion.

Either way, he was in total agreement.

He stood, slung his pack over his shoulder once more, and strode up the trail.

Chapter 18

"WERE YOU NOT coming for the celebration yourself?"

Rina nibbled at the sweetstick she'd picked up at one of the street-side stalls along the main street of Galatin. She could hardly explain how little she had wanted to return to this place that so reminded her of his death.

"I had planned on coming when Dare and Shaylah did. Along with many others."

His mouth curved slightly upward. "It still strikes me odd, how Triotians interact with their king and queen so casually."

"It is the way of Trios. They rule by our choice."

"Yet it will be passed to their son."

"He will have his chance to rule, yes. But if he does not prove himself in his own right, if he loses the confidence of the people, he will also lose the crown."

"What would happen then?"

"It doesn't matter. I have no doubts Lyon will prove equal to the task," she said proudly. "His family has ruled by unanimous consent for centuries now. They would give their all—and have—for the Triotian people, and the people know it."

"Then your people do not hold the defeat by the Coalition in the first invasion against them?"

She wondered if there was something personal in the question, but answered only what he had asked.

"The Coalition did not come to simply defeat, or even to conquer Trios, they came to destroy her. No one could have defended against such vicious brutality."

She lost her appetite at the memory, and tossed the last bite of the sweetstick into a nearby trash atomizer.

"Besides," she went on, "King Galen, Dare's father, died defending and leading his people. In the very streets of Trios he led, no matter that the fight was hopeless."

"I heard what they did to him."

"They tried to destroy him. But they made him a martyr instead."

"Is it true Dax recovered the king's crown from the Coalition archives? That he actually broke in and stole it?"

"Yes. And brought it home."

She didn't mention his bit of vengeance, leaving one of the bolts for his famous flashbow in the royal circlet's place. That impulse had nearly cost him everything, including his life.

"He said he would ready the *Evening Star.* He still flies her?"

"Yes and no." She laughed at his expression. "He still flies the *Evening Star,* but she is not the old vessel I flew on with him. Dax and Paraclon and our engineer Larcos have built a new one, from a design by Dare himself. She is a remarkable ship."

"With an old name."

"An infamous old name," she said. "Dax says the infamy is half the battle won before he begins."

Tark smiled, one of the most genuine she'd seen from him yet, and it warmed her.

"Dax," he said, "is one of a kind."

"I'll not argue that one," Rina said, smiling back.

"I am glad he . . . found you."

She tried not to read anything into words that any friend might say. "And saved my sorry life?" She made herself grin. "So am I."

"You were so young, to have been through so much."

"And then Dax found me, and my life became one of the grandest adventures you could ever imagine."

She meant it. She had long ago put those painful early days behind her, only rarely thinking of that time of terror. And when she did it was only for comparison to her life now, because she loved the sense of wonder that filled her.

All of which she owed to Dax. And she had become distracted from her original mission here.

Almost on the thought, Tark said, "You said you were here to do a favor for Dax."

"Yes. And when I find Prince Lyon, I will accomplish that."

He gave her a sideways look. "So is that it? Has Trios lost track of her prince?"

She laughed. "Not Lyon. We knew he was coming. He wanted to see some of his mother's home world. And I think he wanted a few more days of freedom before the weight of office comes down upon him."

Tark shuddered visibly, and she wasn't sure if it was for effect or the thought truly was so abhorrent to him. "I cannot blame him for that."

"No desire to one day lead the Arellian council?" She had thought, once, that if the people of Arellia were wise, they would chose him someday. Never would they find a better leader, no matter his age.

Tark stared at her as if she had suggested he go interstellar without a ship. "There is no likelihood of that, ever, I promise you."

She studied him for a moment. "Then that is their loss."

He looked disconcerted, but quickly seemed to shrug it off. "If not the prince, then who is it you have lost track of?" To her surprise, he spoke her name. "Shaina?"

She should have known he wouldn't miss that, Rina thought. For a moment she hesitated. This was indeed personal for Dax, after all. But if she had trusted Tark enough to bring him to the king, surely he could be trusted with this.

"You know of her?"

"I know she is the prince's closest companion. They grew up together, did they not?"

"Quite literally," Rina said. "So you are not completely isolated."

He looked slightly embarrassed, which intrigued her. And when he spoke it was in a tone of reluctant admission.

"What news I seek is usually of Trios." That gladdened her. "You are here to find her?"

"Both of them, since I am sure they are together."

"Sent to rein in the children, Rina?" He gave a short laugh. "It seems just yesterday you were a child yourself, trapped in a battle when you should have been home playing."

"The *Evening Star* was long my home," she reminded him. "And I was no child. But if I was, so were you, being all of five years older than I. Have we not had this discussion before?"

"Countless times," he agreed softly. "It was my only defense, Rina."

Something about the way he said it made her breath catch. "Defense against what?"

He looked away. "Dax is worried about his daughter?"

For a moment she didn't want to accept the blatant change of subject. But she'd seen him shut down before, and knew she would get nowhere by prodding at him.

"They did not part under the best of terms." She left it at that; she did not think Dax would appreciate her telling the whole story, even to Tark.

"I can imagine. I still have trouble picturing Dax as a parent, especially of a girl."

"She is a woman now. Which only complicates matters further."

He looked back at her then. "It always does."

"Bark-hound," she said, without force. This was too much like their old days of teasing, and she was enjoying it. "It is men—in this case Dax—who complicate things. Shaina is eminently practical."

"Perhaps," he said quietly, "I wasn't speaking of Shaina."

And there it was again, that crazed swooping feeling, as if she had just dived off the cliff above Lake Geron, headed for the cool crystal water.

She tried to regroup, grasped for something sane to say. "Dax feels about all this celebratory fuss just as you do."

Tark grimaced. "You mean he would prefer to be somewhere else?"

"He would prefer a nice weekend at the ruins of Ossuary than to stand around with that statue."

He laughed. Each time was better, easier than the last, and she liked the fact that she was able to get that from him.

"Why do you not have your own?" she asked.

"My own what?"

"Statue." He blinked. "Don't look so surprised. You were as much a hero of this war as anyone. So why are you not up there next to Dax and Califa?"

"There was talk," he admitted with clear reluctance.

"But?"

"My parents did not approve. And they are still of some influence."

They were still alive, then. But puzzling. Rina frowned. "Did not approve of a tribute to their own son?"

"They do not approve of war."

She stared at him. "They preferred enslavement?"

"They thought we should have . . . negotiated."

"With the Coalition?" It burst from her incredulously. "Do they know no history?"

He shrugged. "As always, they believe what they choose to believe."

She waved a hand sharply, as if swiping at a zipbug. "I stand by my words. To have a son such as you and not be proud beyond measure is more than I can conceive of, and I've seen many cultures on many worlds."

For a moment he just stared at her, then he looked quickly away, downward, as if her words had moved him more than he wished to show. She hoped that was true.

"I heard, long ago, about the children of the king and the flashbow warrior," he said, in that tone she now knew meant he was changing the subject yet again. Something he'd apparently become expert at. "That they are . . . destined."

"That, I have found, depends upon the person you ask."

"How about the parties involved?" he asked, and they were back to wry humor once more.

"I think what is supposed to happen will happen. If they are left alone to discover their own path."

He looked at her then, steadily. "No wonder Dax sent you. They must feel close to you, since you're closer in age."

She wanted to protest, fiercely, and that startled her. Then she realized she only wanted him to stop painting her as so young. She was not, not any longer. She was a woman, yet it was as if he remembered only the youth she had been when they had met.

And she wondered why he seemed so determined to continue to see her that way.

She heard the midday strike of the bell. The original bell, which had been destroyed in the very first Coalition attack decades ago, had been replaced after the Arellian battle was won. The current one was a gift from Trios, etched with images of the two worlds and arcs between them to symbolize the bonds formed during the rebellion that had freed them. Tark had been the one to spark that rebellion, leading raid after raid against the Coalition forces left behind.

He stood suddenly. Instinctively, she rose with him.

"There's a meeting," he said.

"Of?"

"Those who see," he said.

She assumed he meant the watchers, those who saw what he saw in the suspicious presence of ranking members of the Coalition in various places in the system.

"Is there news?"

"I do not know. It was already planned. The current crowds provide a good way to remain unnoticed by those who fervently disagree." He studied her for a moment. "If you did not have other obligations, you could join us."

"Would I be welcome?"

"You are remembered among us, as well, Rina. And those who did not know you would only be wary until I explain it is you who secured the audience with King Dare."

His words pleased her. She hadn't thought about glory or reputation in those days of battle, only about the fight, but she was glad she hadn't been forgotten by those she'd fought alongside. It hit her suddenly, how deeply he must feel it, not just that he was not welcomed, but that his heroism had not only been forgotten but denied. And worse, not just by the people who knew no better, but by the people he had fought for and alongside. Anger stirred in her, so fierce she knew if she unleashed it, it would become fury.

"Then I would like to come."

"But you have your task here," he said.

She reined in her rage. "I will tend to that. It is important, but not burningly urgent."

She didn't add that she thought it might do Dax good to worry a bit longer. She would talk to Shaina, try to get through to her that what he had done had been out of immeasurable love, but that didn't mean she agreed with it. She knew he had wanted to protect his child, but Shaina was full-grown now, and as tough as she needed to be. And as reckless and hardheaded as her father, Rina thought with an inward smile. She could wait a bit.

"Then come," Tark said, "and we will find out if there is news."

She didn't hesitate or speak, she simply rose and followed, grateful he trusted her enough to ask her. Bright Tarkson's trust was not easily won, nor to be taken lightly. Then or now.

Chapter 19

"YOU WERE RIGHT. It was necessary."

Shaina turned at Cub's words. Night fell earlier here on the mountain, where the peaks cast their shadows, and one side of his face was thrown into sharp contrast by the angle of the afternoon sun. For an instant she almost didn't recognize him, the stark, chiseled angle of his face and jaw were so strong, so uncompromisingly male that it nearly stopped her breath.

It took her a moment to fend off all the things that she didn't want to think about yet, including the last thing he'd said to her before they'd started off again. It took a moment longer for her to recall his words and school her voice to evenness.

"Him, you mean? Behind us?" she asked finally. She had sensed their follower's presence a while ago, but had said nothing because he had stayed far enough back. She only knew because that was the kind of thing she always knew. Well, always knew as long as her head was straight. "Yes. Apparently he did not take the bait."

"Not it?"

"Yes."

"Close?"

"Back."

"Sightline?"

"Yes."

They fell into their personal shorthand way of conversing easily. That at least hadn't changed. It was just everything else that was shifting under her feet. And it wasn't just Cub reacting to her leap into using her womanhood as a tactic—it was her, too, looking at him differently. Seeing not the boy who had been her lifetime companion, but the man he had become.

"The old man, Theon?" he asked.

She tried to focus. "No. An unknown."

"More thuggers?"

"Only one. And he feels . . . different."

"Threat?"

She hesitated. Closed her eyes, reached out . . . "I can't be sure, he's too far back," she finally said, "but he's different." She shrugged to indicate she couldn't explain it any more than that. And rather than pressing her, Cub merely nodded, accepting. She hadn't realized until this moment how much she treasured that.

"Perhaps he's so far behind because he did take your bait."

"Perhaps."

Cub was never afraid to admit he'd been wrong, and he always found the best way to make up for it. But then, it happened rarely. At least, in comparison to she herself, who was always trying to make up for some scrape or other.

He looked ahead, scanning. Then he gestured to an outcropping of rock some distance away, a jagged prominence that jutted out, forcing the path to wrap around it. She nodded. It looked like a likely enough spot, giving a full field of view of the path both up and down the mountain. It was too early to stop for the night, but she didn't question him. Cub always had reason.

He started up the path ahead of her. She followed, watching his long, easy stride. She often heard him compared to the beautiful Arellian steeds, with their golden coat and flowing manes, and the extravagance of the estimation nearly always made her groan. And yet she couldn't deny the truth of it: he was beautiful, and as strong and graceful as they were. Only now she was focusing on that entirely too much. The flexing of fit muscle, the length of his stride, the way the slight breeze lifted the golden mane of his hair, so different from her own dark strands, seemed to be poking at her in a way she found most unsettling.

No. Annoying, that's what it was.

She'd always teased him when she heard girls giggling and whispering as they passed, giving him countless sideways looks, some shyly looking away, other, bolder ones smiling at him and waving, or even approaching. Everyone on Trios knew their prince on sight. While before he was officially invested with his title he was not required to follow the royal tradition of speaking to any citizen who wished it, he did so anyway. And it mattered not if they were young, female, and attractive, he gave the same courteous attention to men, to the old and gray, to all. She could not fault him there.

And what she felt at those times when the female was lovely and feminine in all the ways her rambunctious self was not, she told herself sternly, was not jealousy. Nor would she admit to satisfaction that he was no more than polite to them.

Her newly awakened feelings made the very thought of him linked with one of those simpering females, perhaps even bonded with one of them, churn her stomach. And she couldn't convince herself the feeling would pass.

She hated this. Why had everything had to get so tangled?

He led the way up a crumbled trail to the top of the rock outcropping. Even here he moved with grace and skill, as if born to it. She felt an odd sensation rising in her, and again felt as if her world had been tilted somehow. This was Cub, the one person she knew almost as well as she knew herself—why was she feeling so off balance?

Although their parents never spoke of the talk that had been rampant after they'd been born, there was always someone who could not resist teasing them about their destiny. Rina had once said, rather sourly, that there were advantages to the state of war, one being that no one had much time to dwell on such frivolous things. Somehow Rina always seemed to find the right thing to say.

And what would Rina have to say about this new bit of confusion? She'd confessed to Shaina that the kind of love between her parents, or the king and queen, frightened her a little. Shaina had laughed at the idea of the intrepid Rina afraid of anything. And Rina had laughed at herself when she'd added, "But it seems pointless to settle for anything less. And that's the paradox."

And it was those words that had crystallized Shaina's own feelings on the matter of mating and bonding. It was all a paradox, and ridiculously complicated. She couldn't imagine opening herself to anyone in the way that would require. She had her hidden places, secret thoughts and wishes no one else knew, nor would she wish them to know.

Except Cub. He knew it all. He always had. They had never hidden anything from each other.

And that way lay danger, thinking of him in connection with those other thoughts.

"Are you all right?"

Cub's almost sharp words snapped her out of her silly reverie. She realized he had topped the rock and was leaning back to offer his hand. She bit her tongue to prevent a snapped "I don't need any help" from escaping. He knew that. Often enough she was in the lead, and the one to do the same. He was only offering as first up, not because he thought she couldn't do it.

Saying nothing about his question, she took his hand and pulled herself up. His hold was solid, and his balance never wavered as she went up and over. She was thankful that he let it go and didn't ask her about her continually distracted state.

The rock gave them the view Cub had selected it for. High ground, with a sight line both up and down the trail for hundreds of yards. There was no sign of their follower, but Shaina knew he was still there. He could be simply another traveler, but that he was keeping out of sight bothered her.

"Are we staying?"

"For a bit," he said. "We can talk."

She grimaced inwardly, fearing he was going to bring up the strangeness that had sprung up between them.

He dropped down to sit on a smooth section of the rock, facing back the way they had come, pulled his knees up in front of him, and rested his elbows on them. Shaina chose not to comment on the fact that he had chosen the direction from which they were being followed for himself to watch. Instead she dropped down facing the other direction, close enough that they were able to lean their backs against each other. It meant they could not see each other's faces, but she wasn't sure that was not a good thing at the moment.

"I've been thinking," he said.

"When do you not?" she retorted. "You are always thinking."

"Yes," he answered, mildly given the snippiness of her answer. Which had the effect it always did, making her feel chagrin. She had merely been trying to avoid what she feared he wanted to speak of, not to mock him.

"You have your father's patience."

"Without which he would never have survived."

"I know that." She let out a sigh. "And I have none."

"I received a double measure, since my mother has it as well."

She couldn't help smiling at that. The queen indeed had it as well. Often it had been Shaylah she had turned to for deeper counsel, on things she didn't wish to discuss with her mother, things she needed a woman's view on. In fact, it had been Shaylah who had first called her beautiful, a declaration that had unsettled her more than pleased her.

"It is a good trait, patience," she said quietly, wishing to make amends. "Worthy of—and necessary for—a king."

"Just as courage and spirit are necessary for a warrior," he said, rather pointedly. "It's as well you have both in abundance."

Warrior. There was the other sore spot she'd been nursing. She wasn't sure which she wanted to talk about less. She stared up the mountain, where the shadows seemed to grow longer even as she looked.

"You have been thinking much yourself." His voice was quiet. She didn't bother to deny it, he knew her too well. In fact no one knew her as well as Cub.

"And it's annoying," she said dryly. "I don't know why you do it."

"For the same reason the kingbird flies. It is my nature."

He had that, too, she thought. That quiet sort of wisdom that didn't seem like much until he somehow understood the nature of something—or someone—better than anyone else. In that again, he had the best of both his parents, that thing that made them beloved of their people.

She had gradually become aware of the growing warmth on her back, where they touched. It was comforting, as any touch between friends, but other thoughts continued to intrude and disconcert her.

"I know sometimes you wish I would not think so much, and just do."

"And if you did," she said, "we would wind up in even more trouble than usual."

He laughed. She felt it through that connection between them before she even heard it.

"Honesty is, as always, another of your admirable traits." The laughter echoed in his words.

"There are those who would say I am excessively so."

"Then they have not come to treasure it as I have."

She didn't know what to say to that, only knew that his words again stirred those odd, unwanted feelings.

"Perhaps," Cub said, as casually as if he were merely making an observation about the clouds that were rolling in, "your own honesty is why you feel so strongly about your father's choice to hide your destiny."

"Call it what it is," she said sharply. "He lied. My entire life, he lied."

"Thank you for proving my point."

She wanted to clout him, but she would have to turn around to do it, and she still didn't want to face him. So she settled for an elbow to his back.

He laughed again. "Now that seems more familiar."

She couldn't help it, she laughed as well. Cub could always do that for her, restore good humor. And for some reason that made her realize the contradiction here, that someone supposedly so honest was avoiding confronting what she feared he wanted to discuss. She didn't like the feeling, didn't like being afraid of such a simple thing as spoken words. She made herself face it.

"What is it you wanted to talk about?"

"I've been thinking," he said again, and she resisted the urge to retort with the usual teasing. "Remembering, really, now that my head's clear after that thugger's blow."

Concern spiked through her. "Only now? We should have stopped, let you rest."

"No," he said. "It is better that we kept moving. And no fussing now, please, not when I've been so thankful you don't."

"Because I trust you to tell me if you're truly hurt."

"Thank you. And I would have, had I been. It has been an aggravation, nothing more."

She considered that, accepted it. For Cub was as honest with her, she thought. She had always just assumed that, but perhaps he was right, it was something to treasure.

"What is it you remembered?"

"Something one of them said, when they had me in that room. That they were waiting for 'the man with the coins' to arrive."

She sat up straight, whipped around to look at him. "What? When?"

He turned as well. Grimaced as he explained. "An instant before you bashed his partner with that rock. I didn't recall it until now."

"So someone paid them," she said. "And they did know who you were!"

"Not necessarily, they may have just had me pointed out to them as the target," he said. "But it seems someone did."

Fury rose in her—fast, fierce, and hot. In the first instant it was that her best friend had been targeted. But it was only a moment later that the bigger picture struck her. And the rage rose even higher.

"Someone who seeks to profit from capturing the Prince of Trios," she said grimly.

Cub sighed. The weary sound of it reminded her that the load he carried was so much heavier than hers, even with the weight of her father's deceptions.

"Let them try again," she said.

And there was nothing of recklessness in her words, only an intense, unmovable determination.

. . . the only thing left for me to take care of is you.

Her own words came back to her. And for the first time in her life she realized just how much more there was to being the flashbow warrior than simply a magical crossbow and some powerful, glowing bolts.

Chapter 20

"RAIN COMING IN," Rina observed as they walked.

Tark's mouth twisted slightly. "Indeed."

"It was merely an observation," she said, frowning.

"One I could have told you hours ago."

The frown deepened. "Hours ago it was sunny and clear."

"Except in my head," he muttered.

"Your head," she said sweetly, "is muddled by more than the weather."

To her surprise, he laughed. And not to her surprise, she felt that warmth again, that she had caused it.

"Indeed," he said again.

"Your head hurts when the weather changes, truly?" she asked.

He hesitated, as if loath to admit to even this pain.

"Not hurts, exactly," he said finally. "More a . . . tightness. And only with coming rain."

She glanced at the clouds still building, about to crest the mountains and roll down toward them. "An hour, I'd guess, maybe two."

"Feels about right."

She looked back at him. There was a slight furrow between his brows, which only emphasized the twisted scar above his patched eye. An outward sign of that tightness, she guessed. She should have noticed that before.

"Does it remain?"

"Only until the rain actually begins."

"Handy, then," she said.

He gave her a wry, sideways look. "In the nature of a weather prediction, yes."

"Enough warning to get under cover," she said. "Assuming one has the sense."

"Was that a general observation, or a personal assessment?"

His tone was a bit prickly, and she realized her words could have seemed aimed at him.

"I've been accused of a lack of sense more than once," she said with a purposeful grin at him.

Tark stopped dead in his tracks. He stared at her, his gaze no less intense than it had ever been when he'd had two good eyes. She wasn't sure what she'd said to cause it, only knew that the power of that stare unsettled her.

And then she remembered. That day, long ago, at the height of the battle for the Council Building, the deciding clash in the Battle of Galatin, when he had been the one to accuse her of that lack of sense.

If I can get to Dax, he will come!

You cannot.

I can, if I go to the kitchens and out the back.

We are surrounded. You'll never make it.

I can do it.

Have sense, Rina! For once. Their blood is up and if you are caught, they'll show no mercy. They would rape and torture any female, but a woman as beautiful as you would be a rare treat for them. What they would do to you . . .

It hit her now much as it had then, the simple fact that in that moment, no matter how he denied it, he'd seen her as a woman. And a beautiful one.

She'd never had any illusions about her appearance, in fact had cultivated the lost waif look, the short, tousled hair that made her eyes seem huge. That and her slight stature had often allowed her to be dismissed as a child, and when flying with Dax it had more than once saved her life. Even after Dax had brought her home, she had stayed the same, defiantly. It had taken all her energy just to adjust to her new life, to learn anew about the home she'd nearly forgotten in the years since she'd been gone. Dax had tried, speaking to her of her home world often, but nothing compared to actually being there.

And when she was older, she had ignored those few Triotian males who had the nerve to approach the ward of the flashbow warrior. By the time the Triotian resistance and their success had sparked an echoing rebellion on Arellia, she had been old enough to insist on joining the force sent by Dare to assist, and her navigation skills were ever worth having.

And it was then that she met the man who changed everything.

When Tark had said those words that day, something basic and primal had shifted in her. It had been a revelation. And it had unleashed all the unchildlike thoughts she'd been fighting, thoughts that had begun the moment she'd set eyes on the tall, rangy Arellian fighter.

"I made it, that day," she said softly.

"Only by sheer luck." The line of his mouth tightened. "And you disobeyed a direct order. I told you not to go."

"My only *orders* back then came from Dax," she pointed out. "I was with you by my choice."

For an instant something flickered in his gaze, something hot that flashed and was gone so quickly she couldn't name it. And didn't dare speculate.

He turned away suddenly, as if aware he'd revealed . . . something.

"If we do not hurry, we will be very wet when we arrive," he said gruffly.

They picked up the pace, stopping only once when a young boy darted out of a building right in front of them, followed by an older woman screeching at him. He didn't even look at them, merely dodged around them and kept running. The old woman glared at them, as if she'd expected them to stop the boy.

Muttering about the doom this younger generation was leading them toward, she walked back inside and slammed the door.

True to Tark's prediction, the skies opened up just as they reached the rear door to an establishment that had, from her view in the darkened, trash-strewn alley, little to recommend it.

"Nice place."

"We avoid notice as much as we can. Some dislike what we say enough to take action if they knew where we met."

For a long moment they stood in the downpour, until a small cutout in the heavy wooden door, at about eye level, slid open. A pair of Arellian blue eyes peered out, these a lighter shade than Tark's deep, dark, midnight blue.

"Been waiting on you," a raspy voice snarled out, stirring further memories from years ago. "But who's this? You've actually brought a woman? I didn't know you even knew any, anymore."

She placed him then. "How quickly you forget, Crim."

The eyes narrowed, then widened. "Rina? Rina Carbray, is it truly you?"

"Whereas I have no doubt it is you. I'd recognize that voice and nasty mood anywhere."

The door swung open. The man standing just inside stared at her. He had been old when she'd known him, during the war here, when he'd been Tark's good right hand. To be truthful, he didn't look all that much older now. A bit more hunched over, a bit more grizzled, but his perpetually aggrieved expression hadn't changed at all.

That is, until now. To her amazement, the old man smiled, revealing a row of teeth still notable for the crookedness of those in the front.

"Well, now, you've changed, child! You went and grew up on us."

"I was grown up before," she pointed out.

"Not like this," the old man said with a laugh. His gaze slid to Tark. "So, you two have finally found each other again."

There was an instant of silence that seemed electric to her. And then Tark reached out and gave the old man a gentle nudge on the shoulder. "Will you make us stand here in the rain, Crim?"

The old man let out a sound that was half laugh, half cough. The cough didn't sound good, and Rina frowned at the old man's back as he led the way inside the building.

"Is he well?" she whispered as they followed.

Tark shook his head. "He's never been the same since that disrupter blast he took."

"Yet he's one of you? I would think he would be among those who want to believe it could never happen again."

"What we want to believe does not change the truth."

He said it harshly, and she realized belatedly that no one would have more reason to want to believe it was over and done forever than Tark. The battle for his home had cost him more than many, but she had the sense yet again that deep down, he would have preferred to have joined those who had lost all in the fight.

The room was dark, shadowed. The only light came from a few sconces on the walls, and those were live flames. The room got warmer as they stepped further inside, and she saw a fire also burning on a stone hearth on the far wall. Was there no power to this place, then? Was that part of avoiding the notice of those around them?

Tark had spoken true, she realized; more than one person present recognized her, and she saw a few more she knew as well. Some looked much the same, some much the worse for the time passed. A couple of them, as Tark, bore visible, although lesser scars, or moved in ways that spoke of scars hidden. All looked weary, but none more than him.

And they all, other than some smiles and hails when they saw her, looked grim. It was all the more marked when compared to the revelry and celebration taking place outside, mere yards from here.

"Why have you brought her here? We have things to discuss."

The voice came out of the shadows, demanding, authoritative. It sounded familiar, but when she turned to look she could see only a shadowy shape sitting in the corner, just out of the light cast by the fire.

She felt a hand at her back, Tark's hand. She was a stranger to them, so she'd expected some resistance to her presence. At the same time Tark's silent support moved her, stirring something deep inside. Or perhaps it was simply that she was entranced by the warmth of his touch. In fact, she was barely able to resist the urge to lean into that touch, to turn just slightly, move near enough that they would touch even more. And that this was neither the time nor the place—if there would ever be either—didn't do much to alleviate the urge.

"She fought with us," Tark said sharply. "Stood beside us when the days were darkest. She has the right."

"So did Onslow," the voice came back, dry and bitter. "Now look at him."

"I'd rather not," Rina said. "Hard though that is for him to believe, I'm certain."

There was a startled laugh from the shadows, echoed by more than one around the room.

"Ease up," Crim called out. "I remember the girl. She did well, stood fast. And if Tark vouches for her now, that's enough for me."

A rumble of assent went around the room. Here, at least, Tark had the respect he had earned.

"You would all do well to be hospitable," Tark said. "She has given us something we would be hard pressed to obtain otherwise."

"And what's that?" The voice sounded a bit less harsh.

"The ear of King Darian. And Dax."

The room went silent.

The figure in the shadows rose. Rina smothered a gasp as the face came into the light. Kateri.

She had never met the old woman who stood there, but she knew the face. Everyone who had spent any time on Arellia knew of her. The woman with the uncanny vision, who had sounded the warning, years upon years ago, before the first incursion of the Coalition—had sounded the warning and been ignored.

That she was here, among the watchers, gave them credence. "I am Kateri Reyks," the woman said to Rina, almost imperiously.

Reyks was her surname? Bratus's mention of a crazy woman named Reyks flashed back to her. Had he been referring to Kateri? It must be, she thought.

"This is true?" the woman asked, looking from Rina to Tark. "The king himself?"

"I spoke to him not two hours past," Tark said.

"And did he tell you you were a fool?"

"He did not."

"He would not," Rina said, irked. "Unlike the people of your world, he does not forget heroes."

Tark tried to hush her, but she crossed her arms in front of her and stared at the woman. Kateri might be a legend to Arellians, but Rina was Triotian, and she wasn't overly fond of how this world treated the people they should revere. And she let it show.

"Harsh words," the woman said, holding her gaze. Rina had the feeling she was being inspected inside and out, as if the legendary predictor indeed could read into even the darkest places.

"I would think you of all people would appreciate being listened to," she retorted.

Kateri laughed, unexpectedly hearty. "Well said, girl. Welcome to our alarmist cabal."

"Is that what they call you?"

"Among other things," Crim said as he moved around the room, offering drink to those present. Water, it appeared; this was quite literally a sober gathering.

"Tell me," Kateri said, switching her gaze back to Tark. "You actually spoke to King Darian?"

He nodded.

"You spoke of our . . . concerns?"

"The king appreciates straight talking. I told him what we believe."

"And that we have little of what most would call proof?"

"Yes."

"And?"

The room went silent once more, as if every one of them were holding their breath. Waiting.

"Dax is coming back to Arellia," Tark said.

"But we knew this," Kateri said. "He's coming for the ceremony."

Tark shook his head. "He's coming sooner. As soon as he gathers his crew."

"And," Rina added, knowing no one who had fought here would have forgotten the starship that had saved them, "he's coming in the *Evening Star*."

"Then he comes to fight?" The voice rang out from the back of the room, and set off a burst of chatter.

"He comes to stand with you," Rina said. "As he did before. If a fight comes, he will not shy away."

"It will come," Kateri said bleakly.

Rina studied the famous face. She would have thought the woman's accurate predictions of the first Coalition conquering would have won the woman acceptance, but apparently the willingness to deny reality was stronger than she'd ever realized.

"And they pay you no more heed than before," Rina said softly. "It is they who are the fools."

Unexpectedly, the woman looked at Tark then, and smiled. "You've chosen well. I approve."

Rina blinked, drew back slightly. She looked at Tark, just in time to see him turn away, shaking his head. But he said nothing. And Kateri only continued to smile at him.

"But there is little time," Kateri said then. "We must plan."

Chapter 21

"YOU KNOW THIS is crazy."

He looked at Shaina as she spoke. It was safe enough, now, now that they were having a serious discussion about what they should do. Except . . . she was up now, pacing the small, flat area of the rock, even in the light rain that had begun. And he found himself watching her again, watching the pure grace of her movements, how beautifully she was put together.

He shook it off. It wasn't getting any easier. The irony was that he doubted it would have even if she had stayed safely behind on Trios.

"Convinced now it's only a legend, a myth?" he asked. "I won't deny Arellia is ripe with them."

She finally stopped, came back, and sat down again. He knew their follower was still safely distant, so that wasn't the source of her restlessness.

"In some quarters, Trios was long thought of as a mythical place that did not really exist," she said.

"Then you think the treasure is real?"

She lifted a brow at him. "I was merely making an observation, Cub, not assessing validity."

He managed to keep his grin directed inward. This was more like it. This was their old way, speaking of esoteric things, teasing and jabbing at each other with humor.

"Whoever hired those thuggers must not have been pleased," she said, changing the subject. "They weren't exactly the best at the job."

"I think they just hadn't counted on you," he said, giving her her due.

She threw him a smile, and blasted to crumbs all his thoughts about being safely back in their old ways.

"But," she said, "that doesn't explain who's behind us now. I don't think it's them again, and it's not Theon."

He was still reeling from the impact of that smile. It was a potent warning. He simply could not be with her like this and fend off these feelings. The longer this went on, the more he realized he wanted everything from her, or nothing. And explaining that was going to be one of the most difficult things he would ever do.

"Then maybe," he said quickly, grasping at anything, at the first thing that popped into his head to say, "we should go back and ask whoever it is for the explanation."

Shaina blinked. "You mean go confront who's following us? Why, Cub, that's an idea worthy of . . . me."

He couldn't deny that. And couldn't help grinning at her. "Exactly what you'd do, were it up to you. Isn't it?"

"Exactly. I don't like being followed," she said.

"Then perhaps we should turn the tables."

"Perhaps we should."

WHY COULDN'T they talk a little louder?

Mordred crouched in the shadow of the large boulder, the closest he dare get to them, straining to hear.

He was getting mightily tired of skulking after these two, out in the open, without any comforts. He would have been better prepared, had he known they would climb so high. But he'd assumed this trek had been some whim, and that they would give up when it got rough. The woman especially; the whores of Akasen Court were not known for toughness, and inventiveness was usually left to their customers.

And yet they had picked the perfect spots each time they had stopped, places where he'd been unable to get close without being spotted. And that annoyed him. Trios might have temporarily defeated the Coalition, but they'd only been lucky, not good.

"We will take you down, Darian," he muttered into the growing darkness. "Your head will be on a pike at the gates of Triotia, just as your father's was." He stared at the couple atop the rock. "And your son's beside it. Perhaps I'll add that skypirate as well. What a fitting ally for such as you, *Wolf*."

He felt better using the slave's name.

He wondered when they would start moving again. Soon, surely. It would be dark on this accursed mountain in a few hours, and he didn't relish spending another night huddled in the cold. But it would be even colder up on that rock; the wind was picking up, so even they wouldn't be foolish enough to stay up there.

Even as he thought it, they moved, and he felt a spark of satisfaction at his judgment. It turned to annoyance when they dropped down over the far side of that rocky promontory they'd been perched on, and out of his sight. He could not see from here which way they were going, and he dare not emerge from his hiding place too quickly. They had not spotted him yet, and he intended to keep it that way until they had led him to their goal. The only thing better than handing the Sovereign the prince's head would be to hand him a pile of treasure along with it.

But if this turned out to be nothing more than a fanciful story, he would settle for the just the head. And the destruction of Trios.

He allowed himself the small pleasure of picturing that planet's destruction. The famous world would be blown into fragments too small to even walk upon, and the seat of rebellion destroyed completely and for all time. He still had a few friends in the High Command, so he knew the Coalition had the capability, but only used it to rid themselves of planets—and people—that no longer served any useful purpose for them. Only planets that had been scoured of all things of any use, and provided what slaves were of any use. But in the case of Trios, they might make an exception.

He leaned forward, peering into the growing gloom of twilight. He should be able to see them by now, if they were back on the path up the mountain. But there was no sign of movement. Were they on the other side, perhaps making camp early? He himself was weary, and this was hardly the kind of activity he would have expected from a spoiled prince. And again the thought pricked him, that perhaps this prince was not as spoiled and soft as he had assumed.

More time passed with no sign. Perhaps he should look about himself, determine where he would settle for the night. Or perhaps he should work his way ahead of them; the higher they went the fewer choices of direction were open, and they seemed to have settled on this path. Perhaps he could even find this legendary treasure first. That thought made him smile.

He pondered that idea as he continued to watch.

They had to be settled in for the night. Perhaps they were out of food. He himself was running low, as he had not expected this to take so long. But then, he was no scavenger; he was above eating such things as they did. Why, they even hunted for their food, an idea that disgusted him.

But then he realized that such activity was perhaps what Trios had been reduced to by the Coalition, and the thought warmed him.

He leaned forward farther, risking being spotted. He still saw no sign of movement. He didn't think they could have made it to the trees beyond the outcropping without him seeing them, and they had no reason to veer into the forest on either side of the path, so they had to be hunkered down on the far side of that rock. Although it made little sense, given that the wind was coming from above and would make such a spot a chilly proposition.

Perhaps they weren't as clever as he was thinking they might be, after all. Perhaps they were just possessed of that dumb luck Triotians seemed blessed with. He liked that idea. They were nothing special. They were merely lucky. They were—

"Looking for something?" a cheerful voice called out.

They were behind him.

Chapter 22

SHE WAS, RINA thought, in a difficult place.

She had come here with a purpose. A purpose she was little closer to accomplishing than when she had first landed. She knew only that a couple matching Lyon and Shaina's descriptions had headed up the mountain. An adventure into the mountains was exactly like something they would do. At home their wanderings were far-reaching.

But now she had another purpose, and it loomed even larger than her initial goal. While nothing was more important to her than her family, she couldn't deny the simple fact that if the watchers were right, storm clouds were once more gathering. Were, perhaps, imminent.

She sat now in silence, listening to the reports from various places, made with grim certainty by those gathered in the gloomy room. They had used the gathering of tens of thousands for the celebration as cover, coming in from worlds across the sector once owned by the ruling Coalition. They pretended to be merely revelers, although Rina had her doubts as to how effective that pretense was, given the unrelenting bleakness of their expressions.

From what she observed, it was clear Tark was second only to Kateri herself in influence. And first in strategy; using the celebration as cover had been his idea, and had allowed them all to gather unnoticed.

She wondered fleetingly what would happen if they disagreed, but the thought vanished as the reports ended with a man from Clarion reporting the sighting of one of the Sovereign's personal advisors, a man responsible for the running of Ossuary on Daxelia, the pit of Hades for slaves deemed too uncontrollable for use. The place where Dare, then known only as Wolf, had ended up, near death, to be saved only by the stubborn courage of the woman now his mate and queen.

In the end, the consensus was unwavering, and unanimous. The Coalition was coming back.

Rina had no illusions about what the goal would be this time. The Coalition did not take defeat graciously, and took embarrassment even less graciously. They would destroy Trios, Rina knew. And this time there would be nothing left to rebuild, nor anyone to do it. Rumors heard through the telerian, that underground network of communication, of a Coalition device that harnessed the very power of the sun and could reduce planets to splinters, had made all of Trios even more grateful for the endless power supply for their sensors and weapons. Thanks to the discovery old King Galen, Dare's father, had made—and to Lyon and Shaina for finding the pieces of the puzzle—Dare had been able to order the long-range scanners at full power day and night. They would have warning and options.

If such a device existed, she had no doubts the Coalition would use it. Trios must be crushed to rubble at all costs, if what the watchers suspected was true, and the Coalition was on the path to return to power. Her instincts told her it was true.

The shadow of war was looming. Again.

Her priorities were clear.

MORDRED FROZE. How had they done it? How had they moved so silently?

He resisted the urge to turn. He could not reveal his face, he was too well known. Especially on Trios, where they blamed him, as well as that idiot Corling, for the death of King Galen. He pulled his hooded cloak tighter around him, both to conceal his face and to cover his movement as he pulled his disrupter from his belt. He wanted to present the prince alive, but if necessary, his head would do.

"What is it you're after?"

The voice rang out again. They were still in the trees behind him, he guessed, so turning around would do him no good; he wouldn't be able to see them while he himself would be fully exposed. He smothered a curse, angry at himself for underestimating his prey. Or the luck of Triotians. The woman he dismissed. He would deal with her later. Right now his mind was racing.

The whelp had asked what he was after, so this princeling had no idea who followed him.

"A pleasant ramble up the mountain," he said, adopting the rather drawn-out, provincial tones of an Arellian. His face was hidden—they couldn't see his eyes weren't blue.

"Why aren't you in town for the party?" the woman asked.

He barely managed to stifle a sniff of disdain that the whore would even speak to him. To *him*!

"I will be, when the real party begins."

It was all he could do not to laugh at his own clever remark, but he schooled his expression to bland ignorance, so as not to betray there was more than one meaning in the words.

"Why are you following us?" the woman demanded, and her tone required even more restraint on his part. Were she close enough to strike down, he wasn't sure he could stop himself.

"I merely follow a path. You do not own the mountain."

"Don't be so sure of that," the woman said, and he heard the tinge of laughter in her voice. It infuriated him.

"Very well," he said, putting on the most affronted tone he could manage. It was not difficult. "I shall choose another path. Be on your way, and I will be on mine."

He turned and started to the east, all his attention focused to his right, where they were still concealed in the trees. *Cowards*, he thought. Not enough nerve to come out and face him.

That he had not wanted them to was beside the point.

"YOU SHOULD have let me take him," Shaina grumbled as they followed from a distance, to assure the man was indeed taking a different path.

"And do what?" Cub asked.

"Roll him down the mountain?" she suggested, half meaning it.

"Feeling bloodthirsty?"

"At least we would have seen his face, to be on guard."

"It is enough that he knows we know he's there."

She grimaced. "Do you believe him? That he was just out for a ramble?"

"Do you?" he countered. "You're the one with that flashbow sense."

She blinked. Stared. Then felt silly for not having put that together herself, that the ability she had always had to sense such things as people silently following, or the nature of a threat, was part of being the flashbow warrior.

Yet another thing to hate her father for keeping from her.

She shook her head sharply, made herself answer his question.

"I don't know." She cast about for an answer that would make sense, then shrugged. "There was just something about him."

"Yes. There was. And . . ."

"What?" she asked when he trailed off.

"There was something familiar about him."

"But that hood shadowed his face."

"Yes, but I feel as if I've heard that voice before."

"Perhaps down in Galatin?"

"I don't think so. I don't think it was in person."

"A recording?"

"Perhaps. But I can't place it."

They followed the man until he was well along the eastern path. When he stopped and went calmly about the business of making camp, they stopped as well, watching. They pulled back, well out of earshot, and crouched in the shelter of a huge, old groundsweeper tree.

"If he knows we're following, he seems unconcerned," Cub said.

"Or that's what he wants," she suggested, her mouth twisting downward at one corner.

"You're such a pessimist."

"Realist, you mean."

For a long moment Cub just looked at her before saying gently, "Do not let what happened with your father turn you sour, Shaina."

"I have not changed."

"But you have. And I miss your moments of sweetness."

"Sweetness?" she scoffed. "Me?"

"Yes," he said. "You have them. You used to have them more."

"Most would laugh themselves sick at that idea."

"Then I'm lucky, if you save them just for me."

She stared at him for a long, silent moment. Everything she'd been feeling welled up anew inside her. It seemed to force out words she otherwise never would have said.

"Always for you," she whispered.

"Shay," he said, his voice as hushed as hers as he whispered the childhood name he'd not spoken since she'd declared herself too mature for such things, even as she continued to call him Cub. Hearing it now, his voice sounding like this, made her feel as if all pretense had been stripped way.

When he leaned toward her, she wanted to shout "No!" but perversely that word wouldn't come. Nor could she seem to move, even as her body tensed and her breath stopped in her throat.

Her last thought before his lips reached hers was "Inevitable."

And then he was kissing her, and all thought was seared away.

Chapter 23

DARKNESS HAD FULLY fallen, but it seemed to have no effect on the revelers. They were determined to get their fill of this week of endless celebration, and it made progress through the crowded streets difficult.

"At this rate it will take until dawn to get to the skyport," Rina muttered, dodging a reeling celebrant who had clearly imbibed too much lingberry, but seemed intent only on drinking more.

"You're leaving?" Tark asked.

He sounded . . . something, Rina thought. Since he usually betrayed no emotion at all, it was hard to tell what. He hadn't always been that way. When she'd first met him, she'd been drawn by the reckless joy he took in living—something that, coupled with sheer courage, made him a fearsome warrior. He'd reminded her of Dax in that. He still did, but now it was a Dax of grimmer moments, when he'd been on trial for his actions and thought his fate sealed, when he expected nothing less than death by order of the king.

She couldn't imagine what it was like to live feeling that way constantly.

"No," she said. "Not leaving. I have a room at the billet there."

"Not in town?"

"Amid this chaos? No, thank you. Besides, everything is full."

"The Council Building has quarters."

"For visiting dignitaries," she said with a laugh.

He shrugged. "It is by tradition also open to all who fought there."

She stopped amid a gap in the crowd. A half step later he stopped as well, and turned to look at her with that lifted brow.

It amazed her that the revelers, even drunk as many of them were, could be so oblivious to the simple fact that the man who more than any other had made this celebration possible was standing in their midst.

"Then why are you not there?" she demanded.

Again he shrugged. He looked toward the large white building visible in the distance even in the dark. "If pressed, I suppose they would make room. But I make them uncomfortable, which in turn makes for unpleasantness. But you would be welcomed."

"I clearly have a different definition of welcome. Mine includes all that matter to me."

His head snapped around with a sharpness that betrayed him. She met his gaze levelly. If he did not know he mattered to her by now, it was time he did. That he mattered more than most, and in a most different way, was something she herself wasn't quite ready to face.

"Besides," she said when she realized he was not going to speak, "I'm not here officially. Yet."

"If they find who you gather with," he said, his tone dry now, "you might not be so welcome."

"Then I've made the right choice, haven't I?"

Only after she'd said it did she realize there could be two interpretations of her words. But again something flashed in his gaze, that same heat she'd seen outside the meeting room, and she bit back an explanation that she'd only meant her choice of rooming options. But it made no difference, again the look vanished in an instant, leaving her wondering if she'd really seen it at all. And when he started walking again, apparently not caring if she followed or not, she was sure she'd been mistaken.

She caught up with him, spoke as if her internal foolishness had never happened. "Besides, I wish to stop at the comm center at the skyport to send a message."

He gave her a sideways glance. "To Trios?"

"Yes."

"About what we learned tonight?"

"Yes."

"To the king?"

"Yes."

He was silent for a moment. "You have suddenly become fond of one-word answers."

"Yes." His mouth twitched. She couldn't help it, she laughed. "Now you know what it is like trying to converse with you."

"I spoke at length tonight," he protested. "And," he added, "I speak to you."

A warmth flooded her all out of proportion to the simple words. She fought against betraying herself; he would not welcome it, she thought.

"Yes," she said again, only this time it was an effort to make it sound casual, level.

He grimaced, whether at her single-word answer again or at the thought he then expressed, she didn't know. "We did not learn anything we did not already know tonight, merely more of it. More sightings of more high-level Coalition strategists in more places."

"Names they will know were in that room tonight. Dax especially. People he fought alongside here. Although your name was enough, it will lend even more credence when Dare takes it to the Council of Elders."

He still didn't seem comfortable with the thought that his name was of such renown on a planet not even his. Surely he could not prefer the way he was treated here?

"It is this council that will decide? Not the king?"

"They decide together. Each has the power to say no, although it rarely happens that they disagree. Except perhaps on method, not on what needs to be done. Not," she added, "that those disagreements don't get a little . . . hearty."

They threaded their way through a knot of carousers gathered at the base of Dax's statue. Some were still upright and staggering about, more were sitting on the statue's base, lifting their mugs of lingberry, and a group of about four were singing, or trying to. It was a bawdy song about Dax from his skypirate days, one she hadn't heard in many years.

She gave them a glance, and grinned.

"Drunkenness amuses you?"

"When it is born of celebration, yes," she said. "When it is to avoid truth, no."

To her surprise he winced. "Some wish mightily to avoid reality."

She wondered if there was too personal a note in that observation. "And some have every reason. You, for example."

He let out a weary breath. "I tried, for a time. But whenever I stopped reality was still there. It seemed a pointless—and expensive—exercise."

She ached for him, but knew he would not want to hear that. Tark would want no one feeling sorry for him, although what she felt was so much more than that, so much more complicated.

So complicated she couldn't fathom it out herself. At least not when there was so much else at hand.

"Besides, that song takes me back," she said. "I was merely wishing I had my vidcom unit on me, I would like to send a shot of that to Dax."

Tark looked back over his shoulder at the revelers they'd now worked their way past. "How much of those . . . exploits they sing of are true?"

"More than he would ever tell me, I'm sure," she said with a grin. "I was of very tender years in those days, after all. But I think he would laugh to hear it again now."

One corner of his mouth quirked upward. "I have a feeling he would consider it the best use of that statue, as well."

She laughed, startled by the observation and the fact that he'd made it. "You're right. He would."

He was silent until they reached the interplanetary center. And then, unexpectedly, he stopped and faced her.

"You love him, don't you."

It did not sound like a question, as it should not for something so self-evident. "Of course I do. I adore him. He saved my life, over and over. I loved him when he could not love himself. I love him still, and will forever. I would die for him, if need be."

He lowered his gaze, as if her answer was too much. She didn't care, it was all true. When he spoke again, it was softly, as he avoided looking at her. "Yet he bonded with a Coalition hero."

"Califa was that, yes. That is why they understand each other so well, she knows much of hating yourself. She—" She broke off suddenly as the true meaning of his words struck her. "You think I love Dax in that way? God save me, I'm not that foolish!"

Or maybe I am, she thought as she stared at this man who had bedeviled her thoughts all the years she'd thought him dead, and tenfold more now that she knew he was alive.

His mouth twitched. "Careful. He is the hero of the week here."

She snorted inelegantly, a habit picked up from the crew of the *Evening Star* long ago, and never quite shed.

"Dax is a brother to me. At times even a father. An annoying one." She hesitated to say more, ask more, then realized she was hesitating, and wondered when she'd become so cautious. With the memories of those bolder days stirring, she leapt. "Why would you ask such a thing?"

He looked startled. He lowered his gaze once more, and she wondered in turn when the intrepid Bright Tarkson had become so hesitant.

"Perhaps I'm worried about your happiness," he muttered.

"Perhaps," she said with some sharpness, "you should worry about your own."

His mouth twisted as a sour chuckle escaped him. "Not something that I aspire to any longer."

"Then what did we fight for, if not every man's right to find his path to his own happiness?"

That brought his head up sharply. He opened his mouth to speak, then halted. For a moment he just looked at her, and when he finally answered she was almost certain it was not what he had originally been going to say.

"Apparently we fought only to have to do it all over again."

"As Califa would say, the most precious things require considerable maintenance. So we do it again."

And she realized with her own words that she had accepted it. What she had heard tonight, and the people she had heard it from, made it impossible to ignore. All the denial taking place in the streets of Galatin and all over Arellia this week couldn't make it go away.

She wished they were wrong, all of them, wished she herself was wrong for believing them. For believing Tark.

But she knew she wasn't. Just as she knew he wasn't wrong. He might be battered and scarred and not the same man he'd once been, but his deep-down instincts had never failed, and she knew they were not failing now. What she did not know was what to do next.

She looked at the man beside her, remembered the tactical session before the Battle of Galatin, when he and Dax had huddled over the projections of the city, planning, mapping, strategizing. Remembered the reckless, powerful energy and determination that had somehow overflowed to them all. They had been determined to take the city back. And take it they had.

He should not have to fight again. Ever. He had paid so much, given so much to this world that didn't appreciate it as they should. Yet here he was, trying to sound the alarm even though those fools would not listen. And when the time came, as she was sure now it would, he would fight again.

A chill swept through her as another reality struck.

This time, she very much feared he would see to it that he did not survive.

Chapter 24

"WHAT IF THEY decide against it?"

Dax was pacing the outer council chambers restlessly. He had run all the way from the palace to the skyport and back again this morning, yet he still felt as if he would fly apart from the unspent edginess building inside him. He was ready to go, his crew had arrived, the *Evening Star* was ready. He had only delayed to find out the results of this emergency session, and whether he and his crew would be going this alone.

It was taking too long. Things of state always and ever took too long. If Trios herself were under attack, there would be no delay, but it was Arellia. And there was, so far, no attack, just a lot of suspicion.

Would it be enough for that robed assembly?

As if she had read his thoughts, Califa spoke. "Dare is speaking, is he not? He has yet to fail to persuade them to his view, whatever the issue."

"But this is bigger. It will take more to convince them. We have had relative peace for years now."

"Thankfully." She glanced toward the closed double doors. "But they know Arellia would be the prime base for attacking Trios. Surely they will not allow the Coalition to gain a foothold there again."

"I hope not," he said grimly, turning to cross the white Triotian marble floor once again.

"Do you truly think they would fall prey to the same thinking that allowed Trios to fall before?"

"'Too much peace softens,'" he said.

"Geron."

"Yes."

"I know you are concerned when you begin to quote ancient Triotian warriors."

Dax stopped in his pacing and turned to look at his mate. They had been through so much, each of them alone and then together. She had come to love Trios as her own. In the way of many who were here by choice, she loved with more fervor even than some born here. She had thrown herself into learning about her new home as fiercely as she had once fought for their enemy.

"I love you," he said suddenly, warming at how she, once the careless, cool, and uncaring Major Califa Claxton, colored as he declared it.

"And I you," she said softly. "And if it comes to it, I will fight beside you again, Dax Silverbrake."

He frowned. "I—"

"Do not even say it. Nothing you can speak would stop me."

He drew in a long breath as he looked at this woman who was his mate in all things. They had had their rough times over the years, they were both so independent and had led such different lives that it had been inevitable. But the bond between them had yet grown continually stronger.

"And what," he said softly, "makes you think I would venture into any battle without the premier tactician in any system at my side?"

She smiled then, and that heated combination of pride, gratitude, and pure, deep love shot through him. Spiced with a jolt of the lust she never ceased to rouse in him, it had him wondering just how long they might have before the council rendered the decision.

"And what of the next flashbow warrior?"

The question drove the breath out of him as if she'd hit him with that driving fist of hers, something that had happened occasionally in the beginning, as they'd struggled to find their way together.

"No," he said instantly, instinctively.

"Hmm." Her voice was carefully even. "Our daughter is showing her father what it is like to live with one so stubborn."

He let out the breath he'd been holding since the moment she'd planted the idea of Shaina actually fighting. The thought of the current state of his relationship—if there was one left—with his daughter brought tightness to his chest once more. And with that unerring sense of hers, Califa knew it.

"It will be fine, in the end," she said quietly. "She will forgive you, and you will be . . . not as you were, perhaps, when she was a child, but as adults who love and respect each other."

"Not encouraging," he muttered.

"Did you wish to keep her a child forever?"

"Yes," he said, knowing even as he admitted it the foolishness of it.

"Then it will be the only thing you ever fail at," she said.

"I feel as if I have already failed her."

"I doubt there is a parent alive who has not felt so."

"You're saying it is part of the process?"

"I'm saying it's part of loving so fiercely."

He turned then, came back to her. Reached for her. She went into his embrace as if she were a whisperbird coming home.

"You do not want her to risk herself, to be in danger, to be hurt," she said against his chest. "Perhaps you should think more of what you do want for her."

"I know what I want for her," he said, his voice low and rough as he tightened his arms around her. "This. This is what I want for her."

She made a low sound as she snuggled closer. "My skypirate. You always find the right words, eventually."

He sighed. "Except with our daughter, it seems. Or she would be here now, instead of scarpering around the mountains of Arellia."

"It is as well she is," Califa said. "If what Tark suspects is correct."

"You doubt it is?"

"No. I never chanced to meet him during that campaign, but I know you trust him."

"Implicitly. Other than you, there is no one I would rather have at my side—or my back—in a fight."

"Being severely wounded and abandoned, left for dead by his own people, could have an effect on someone's thinking."

"I've considered that. But Rina believes him"

Califa was silent for a long moment. Too long.

"What?"

She hesitated, as if considering what to say. "She . . . cares for him."

"I think she is fuming on his behalf, over the way he has been treated." Dax's mouth twisted. "I'm not happy with your home world myself on that score."

"Nor am I," she agreed. "But I think it is something more."

"It was, then." He leaned back to look at her. "They fought side by side, at Galatin. They got on well, from the moment they met. A little too well."

"As you've said. You also said she was too young for anything more, then."

His brow furrowed. "Yes, I felt she was. Her life was so . . . different, she had no experience in such things."

"But why did that even occur to you?"

"Because there was a zap between them. Everyone saw it . . ." Belatedly, he got there. And sighed. "You think it's still there."

"I know it is. I asked her. She did not deny it." She looked thoughtful. "I have always sensed she was angry, and sometimes unbearably sad, after he was reported dead. I think she never got over grieving for him."

"Perhaps she was merely remembering a youthful passion."

"All I know is, had I met you when I did, or ten, twenty, thirty years later, it would be the same. And if I lost you, my aching over it would never end."

She said it so simply, as if there could be no doubt, and as always, she managed to turn his insides to something molten and urgent. But noise from inside the chamber, the sounds of a vote being taken, brought him back sharply to the matter at hand.

"If they vote no, what will you do?"

"I will still go," he said. "Even if I go alone."

"Your crew would never allow that. They would stand by you if you announced you were flying into Hades. As would I." She said it simply, without reservation, and he knew she meant it. Yes, this was what he wished for his girl.

"Then we will go."

"Some on the council would not be happy."

"That also would not be new," he said. "When I was Shaina's age, they were fuming at me more often than not."

She smiled. It still amazed him that this woman found such joy in his history, when others preferred to ignore what it had been.

"The flashbow warrior is the king's to command."

"Yes. He needs no approval for that. And I would go for Lyon. It would not be unexpected for me to be there to protect the heir, after all."

"If they vote no, then they are not convinced there is anything to protect him from."

"That," he said flatly, "is not their decision to make. When it comes to protecting Dare and his, the decision is mine."

"As it was your decision not to tell Shaina of her destiny?"

He stiffened. He knew she had never been happy about that decision, but she had accepted it was his to make. She never jabbed at him in the way of someone who could not let an issue rest, so he knew she meant it to make him think.

"And I would make it again," he said.

She tightened her arms, pulling him even closer. "It gives me great pain to see the two people I love most at such odds. But I understand." She sighed audibly. "You two are so very alike. Intractable, determined, short of restraint."

"I—"

Noise from the council chambers saved him from making a denial he didn't even believe himself. They broke apart, turning toward the chamber entrance. The heavy double doors swung open, and Dare strode out. He was clad today, for this speech, in the royal garb he eschewed most other times. And not just the black shirt embroidered precisely with the royal crest in golden thread that matched his hair, and the belt with the gold buckle that was also the crest, along with the ceremonial sword that had been handed down in Dare's family for generations. But he'd gone full royal and added the cloak, the rich, full sweep of black velvet lined in shining silk, trimmed as well with the golden royal crest. It fell nearly to his heels, and made him look undeniably regal as it swirled with his long strides.

"Who could deny him?" Califa asked.

"He does know how to move them," Dax muttered.

Dare spotted them and changed direction. This man who was a brother to him looked every inch the king, Dax thought. Califa was right, who could deny him?

No one, apparently, because he came to a halt before them and said simply, "Go. We will follow."

Chapter 25

"WE SHOULD go back."

Lyon looked at her, although he didn't meet her gaze, as she had been avoiding his for some time now. It was not like her to want to retreat. At least, not from any physical threat or danger. But this was different. Very different.

Everything was different, now.

And he realized that her words could easily apply to something other than this expedition they were on.

"We are chasing a legend that likely has no basis in reality. A treasure that probably doesn't even exist."

Again he felt the subtext but wasn't ready to face that conversation, so he let her finish her point.

"If they're after you, if they somehow know you are the prince and mean you harm, it would be easier to hide in the crowds."

"From whom? The thuggers? Sir Pompous in the fancy cloak? Some new, unknown adversary?" Hiding from a threat had never been in her nature. Was she already taking on the mien of the flashbow warrior, suppressing her own instincts for the protection of a royal? He shifted uneasily before countering, "Any of those threats is easier to defend against here, where we have the high ground."

She didn't respond. And the other unspoken matter lay between them, as potent and present as if it were a living, physical thing. Did she think returning to the city would solve that problem? They would eventually have this out—city or mountain. He'd see to that now that he realized she wasn't hiding from a threat. She was running from him. From the promise that lay between them.

He resorted to her own tactic of diversion, trying to put her off balance. "Do you think your father does not know what he has done?"

"He does now."

"Can you truly hate him for it?" he asked. "Who would know better what you are facing? The rest of us know only the glory, he knows the danger, the blood, the pain, the weariness. What father would not want to protect his child from that as long as possible?"

"If you're going to defend him, I'll find my own way down."

Her voice was sharp. He'd gotten to her, but not enough.

"Is that really why you want to run?" he finally said.

Finally, he'd stiffened her. "I don't run." But she still did not look at him. "What would you call it?"

"I would call it ending a fool's trek. I would call it seeing sense. I would call it not chasing an Arellian dragon."

"Shaina Silverbrake, urging sense. This day may go down in the annals."

That earned him a sideways glance. And he saw there, in her face, in even that brief glimpse, the truth of what he had suspected.

The memory of what had happened between them, of the fire that had flared even as the sun was setting, was even still hot enough to scorch. His body fired to the memory almost as fiercely as it had to the feel of her lips beneath his.

"It wouldn't change anything," he said, his voice as rough as he was feeling inside. "Even if we were to turn around and go back."

"Because," she said, "everything has already been changed. It seems that I've lied to myself as much as my father ever has."

She sounded so lost, so forlorn, it tore at him. "Shay—"

She didn't react to the revived nickname. "We're well and truly lost now, Cub. We must choose and either choice may cost us what we have."

"Are you angry at me?"

She sighed. It had the same sad quality as her voice, and caused that same tightening in his gut.

"No," she said at last. "I'm angry that it was so . . . much."

He couldn't help the flood of relief that welled up in him. "Yes. Yes, it was."

He hadn't thought he was alone in that rush of sensation, the fierceness of it, the near-overpowering urgency. Had it been anyone else, and since they were not on Trios, it might have gone beyond a few searing, soaring kisses and caresses. But the strictures of Triotian culture were strong in both of them. Between them they had somehow found the power to stop, even if it had felt oddly wrong, as if stopping were the mistake.

To him, it was the mistake. But if she didn't feel that way, it meant nothing. He struggled to find words to make her see, make her realize. But then remembered this was Shaina, and she did best when allowed to reach the conclusion on her own. So he could only guide her, not tell her.

"Do you remember when Fleuren left us?" he asked after a moment.

She looked at him then, clearly puzzled. "Of course."

"Do you remember how devastated we both were?" It was nothing less than true; the elder woman Dax had rescued and brought home had been their stern yet benevolent guardian and teacher from birth. She had, Shaina's mother had told them, appointed herself from the moment Califa found herself pregnant, delighted to have at last found a way to pay Dax back some small amount of the debt she felt she owed him. But when her own family, nearly destroyed by the Coalition, had begun to increase itself, she had withdrawn to tend to her own.

"And then Ansul came," he said.

Shaina smiled. The crusty old tutor who had taught both their fathers had annoyed them at first. He'd been strict, demanding, and they'd spent many fruitless hours trying to best him in one way or another. They had never succeeded. "If you really think you two can come up with any scheme, any mischief Dax or Dare didn't try before you, you're mistaken," he'd told them.

And yet he'd continued, almost encouraging them, and it wasn't until much later they had finally realized he'd been teaching them all along. Tactics, preparation, execution, they learned all of it in those efforts to outsmart him.

"And it was extraordinary, was it not?" he asked, looking steadily at her.

"Yes. It was . . . wonderful."

He stayed silent then, just watching her. Watching her face, that expressive, beautiful face. He saw when she got there. Her eyes widened.

"You're saying this is like that?"

"I'm saying that when we thought we'd lost everything, it was only a passage to something even better. We didn't have to forget one way of life to experience something new. To make something new."

For a long, silent moment she looked at him. In her face, her eyes, those jade green eyes that were a direct gift from her father, he saw the same sort of turmoil he himself was feeling.

"Think about this, Shaina. Who is your father's best friend?"

Her brow furrowed. "Your father."

He shook his head. "His very best friend, confidant, the one person he could not survive without."

She got it then. "My mother."

"Yes. As my mother is my father's."

"Your point?"

He smiled at her, and for an instant he let it show, the longing, the need, the possibilities. "They didn't lose their friendship."

She drew back slightly. Something in her expression changed. He saw the same tangle of conflicting emotions, of fear and anticipation, of resistance, but now also eagerness. It was the eagerness that nearly undid him. When he realized that as reluctant as she was she still felt an eagerness to explore what had sparked between them, he knew it was time.

"We're not children anymore, Shay. And I can't go on pretending we are. We have to decide where we are going, and if we are going together."

"What are you saying?"

"That my lifetime friend and companion, my cohort, my accomplice, my abettor, is no longer the impish child who was my partner in all things, but a woman. A beautiful, intelligent, compelling woman. I'm saying I want more than this, I want—"

"Good eventide, children!"

Shaina was on her feet, dagger drawn, in a split second. He barely managed to stay his own hand when the old man stepped out of the shadows.

"You risk much, old man," Shaina said. "We're a bit on edge."

"These paths are more traveled than usual these past days," the old man agreed.

"We don't care for being surprised." Shaina was frowning at the man, but Lyon noticed she'd sheathed her dagger.

"You've made that effectively clear," Theon said, sounding almost proud of them.

"And yet here you are," Lyon observed, earning a grin and a hearty laugh from the old man.

"Indeed. I find myself drawn to an unexpected and pleasant link to my past. Something I think you may be feeling yourself?"

"A bit, yes," Lyon said.

"'Tis natural," Theon said. "Our futures rise out of our heritage. And a large portion of yours is here, Lyon of Trios, son of Graymist. And if the legends hold true, it will determine your future, and the future of far more than walk this world now."

"And what has this treasure of yours to do with all that grandiosity?" Shaina asked. "Gold is gold, is it not? Worth killing for to those who have nothing else, worth less than nothing to those who prize other things."

The old man's gaze fastened on her then. He studied her for a long moment. "One of the things I prize," the old man said at last, "is perspicacity. For one so young, you have a great deal."

To Lyon's surprise Shaina colored slightly. She was pleased, he could see that. Theon's eyes flicked from her to him and then back again. A smile curved his mouth, and when he glanced back once more, Lyon saw a sparkle in the depths of dark eyes.

"I see things have changed with you," he said, including both of them with a wave of his hand.

He had overheard them, Lyon thought uncomfortably. He glanced at Shaina, whose color had deepened.

"People," Theon said, very gently, "are vastly resistant to change. It requires effort, moving on and through. Given their way, they would live in a never-changing world. You two must have faith that while some changes are for the worse, and some for the better, some few changes are for glory."

"Will you stop speaking in riddles, Theon?"

Shaina sounded tense, and Lyon guessed she was embarrassed, but Theon merely smiled. "Riddles. You remind me. My brain is not as quick as it once was, so forgive me for taking time to remember the prophecy correctly."

"Prophecy?" Cub asked.

"About the treasure." His voice changed, took on a deeper timbre. *"For Graymist of pure heart and mind, the cavern of the waterfall shall open when the two halves are joined, when what is destined is completed."*

"Well, that's nonsensical enough," Shaina said.

"Prophecies are by nature, are they not?" Theon said, smiling. "I heard the tales many times, while I worked in your mother's house," he said to Lyon. "They say the real treasure hidden in that cave is not the gold, but the Graymist Orb."

This was a new addition to the tale, Lyon thought. "The what?"

"The Orb, a rounded crystal of no good whatsoever except to one of Graymist blood. For a true child of Graymist, the Orb has the power to warn that rightful possessor of the presence of enemies, to tell truth from lie, and it has the power to heal."

"And would it be warning of lies right now?" Shaina asked, in that sweet tone that Lyon knew too well was a warning of its own. She didn't care for being embarrassed, and she was already in an internal uproar.

Theon merely laughed delightedly. "If you find the Orb, the tales say it will change history."

"How? What are we to do with your magical rock?" Shaina asked, her tone more amused now.

"A little respect, please. It does not do to laugh at destiny."

Shaina laughed in turn at the last word.

"Off with you then," Theon said.

"Continue on tonight?" Shaina asked, clearly startled now.

"You have the moon to light your way."

Lyon saw Shaina glance at the night sky. He shifted restlessly himself. The old man's words of destiny seemed to have infused him with a sense of urgency, a sense of having to do just that, move on, now, not waste any more time.

The pull, he realized. The pull old Theon had spoken of. He'd been right, he'd been feeling it for some time now, he just hadn't recognized it. Or it had been swamped by that other pull, toward Shaina.

It made no sense, given he'd never even thought of this supposed treasure for years, but there it was, growing more undeniable with every breath.

He looked at Shaina. Her arched brows were furrowed as she looked at him.

"Cub?"

"I feel it," he admitted. "Just as he said. I feel I have to go on. Now."

She held his gaze for a moment. Then she lifted a shoulder in a half shrug.

"Let's go then," she said. Just that easily, she was with him. As always.

He turned to Theon. "Are you going on?"

"Perhaps, after some rest. I may see you yet again."

"Do. I would like to hear more of my mother as child."

Theon smiled. "And I would like to hear of her as queen."

Lyon nodded. He didn't quite understand what this sensation was, only that it was growing stronger. He was still trying to analyze it as they started up the moonlit trail.

Chapter 26

"DO YOU ALWAYS answer a knock with a dagger in your hand?"

Rina had reached the hidden cave late. Too late to be polite, since the crescent moon had already risen, but she'd gone nevertheless. And in the moment before her eyes adjusted to the deeper darkness of his doorway, all she could see was the glint of Clarion steel in his hand.

"Few know of this place. And there are those who would be happier if I vanished."

For a moment pleasure at being one of the few who knew mattered more. But she didn't doubt what he'd said. Resistance was high to the very hint that war might be starting all over again. And the delusional among the populace transferred that feeling to the messenger.

He stepped aside and let her in through the hidden door. The large room was in darkness.

"If I woke you, I'm sorry."

"I don't sleep much."

She supposed it was a negation, but she felt even worse if he didn't sleep well and she'd disturbed him. In the darkness she heard, rather than saw, him move toward the back, and then the huntlight flooded the room.

She'd awakened him, all right. His hair was a dark tangle, as if already his night had been restless. He wore sleep leggings and a light shirt open at the throat. She realized abruptly that he had changed, physically, more than she'd realized, aside from his injury. He was still lean, rangy, but his shoulders and chest had broadened from the younger man she'd known, his arms grown more muscled. And he—

Her thoughts stopped short as her wandering—and admittedly appreciative—gaze stopped at his face.

No eye patch.

His head snapped around, away. "Sorry," he muttered.

He turned, took a step toward the sleeping alcove, no doubt where the concealing patch was.

"No. Don't."

He froze. "My face," he said tightly, "is not something you want to look upon in the light."

"And who are you to decide that for me?"

His head snapped back around. She took advantage, studied the scar that twisted its way from his cheekbone to his hairline.

It was both better and worse than she'd expected. Better, because there was no glimpse of a damaged, blind eye, the scar had sealed his lids shut. Worse because it was a thick, jagged thing, a ridge of tissue that twisted and pulled even as it spoke of a grievous injury healed.

"Pretty, isn't it?" he said.

She couldn't speak. When he did again, his tone was sour, and oddly disappointed.

"I would never have thought you one of those."

"Those?"

"Those with the peculiar fascination with the gruesome."

She smothered a gasp at the harshness of both voice and accusation. She drew herself up and faced him head on.

"Bright Tarkson, you are a fool." She bit the words out, sharp and nearly as harsh as his own.

His good eye blinked. "I've been told that before."

"You are a fool if you think I feel anything but pain at what happened to you, if you think I do nothing less than ache inside at the thought of what you had to endure."

"I—"

"Did I wish to see? Yes. But only because I was hopeful it could be helped, if seen to properly. Battlefield wounds never heal as they could, especially when no help is at hand. Nelcar, our medical officer from the old days on the *Star*, could always work wonders if someone was hurt, even in the field. And now, with full equipment and time to work slowly, he does even more."

"It would take more than a wonder." The words were as sour, but the heat was gone from his tone.

"Nelcar is very good. But even if he can do nothing, that scar is still a mark of honor, of courage."

"More of ineffectiveness."

She scoffed. "Oh, yes, that too, because the vaunted Captain Tarkson must of course be able to deal with one hundred to one odds, must he not? There were five of you against an entire troop of Coalition forces, but nevertheless, you were ineffective to not have walked away without a mark."

"I meant I should have seen it was a trap. Dax would have. And he would have won."

"Won?" She stared at him. "*Won?* Against hundreds of the Coalition's best—you came out of that canyon alive, and your men with you, and you think you did not win?"

"I—"

"Dax prized his crew above all else. They are the one thing that was irreplaceable to him."

She hadn't even realized she'd moved, that she'd stepped forward even closer in her need to get through to him. But now she was there, bare inches away from him, meeting his gaze, refusing to avoid the sight of the twisted scar.

"You were irreplaceable," she finished, hating how her voice broke on the word, but unable to help it. "To all of us. When we thought you dead . . ."

Her voice trailed off. The memories of that time were too painful to voice, even now.

"I would have thought you would have forgotten by the next battle."

"Then you are indeed a fool. I could—" She caught herself. "We could never forget you. And we never did."

He studied her for a moment. Facing her, she realized. Letting her see the reality he lived with. The patch covered the worst of it, and she wondered if he wore it for others, or himself. Perhaps both; keeping them from staring would make his own life easier, surely.

"So fierce," he said softly. "You needn't spend your concern on me."

"I'll spend it where I please."

"What if I don't want it?"

"Then reject it. As you do all others. It will not change how I feel."

For a long moment there was silence, and she didn't think he was even breathing. But he didn't look away, didn't step back, and that alone seemed to freeze her in place, unable to move.

"And if I did want it?"

The words sounded pained, forced, as if he had fought them and lost. And suddenly, as clearly as one of the star maps filed away in her head, everything snapped into focus.

"Then concern would be only the beginning," she said softly.

"Rina."

Her name was all he said, but the way he said it told her he understood.

"That," she said, lifting a hand to his scarred face, trying not to react when he winced and pulled back involuntarily, "means less than nothing to me. This"—she touched the other side of his head at his temple, tapping to indicate the mind inside—"and this"—she lowered her hand and gave a single, gentle tap to his chest, over his heart—"are all that matter."

He caught her hand in his, startling her. He pressed her hand flat against his chest, and she thought the heat of him would sear her fingers.

"You cannot want this."

"That is not your decision," she said, although breath to speak seemed in short supply at the moment.

"You are too good for the likes of me."

"Funny, I always thought the same of you."

"I'm merely that broken-down war steed."

"And I flew with the most infamous skypirate ever known."

"You're too young."

"That mattered then. Not now. Besides, my youth ended the day my family was slaughtered by the Coalition."

The mention of the conquerors reminded her of why she was here in the first place. She hesitated—she did not want to interrupt this, but the choice was taken from her. He seemed to see or sense the change.

"Ah. So there is a reason you're here in the night, other than to plague me with impossible dreams."

She pulled back and glared at him, hands on her hips. "The only steed you resemble just now is an Omegan cart horse. That discussion will continue," she said.

"I am warned." His voice was a pained combination of weariness and longing. She seized on the latter, tucking it away in her tight chest, next to the hope that had sprung in her when he'd said, "*And if I did want it?*"

"There is something I came to tell you. I received word from Dax. Dare spoke and the council has voted."

He went very still. "And?"

"Dax is coming now. With the *Evening Star* fully armed. And Trios is preparing backup forces to follow, if he calls for them. Dare will lead them."

He let out a long, harsh breath.

"Your king must be quite convincing."

"He is. He is both loved and respected, the kind of man who would be a leader anywhere, royal blood or no."

He nodded slowly. "I just hope he does not come to regret it."

"Dare—and Dax—would rather mobilize a hundred times unnecessarily than not be ready the one time it was necessary."

"It is coming, Rina."

"I agree. Although I sometimes wonder why you would fight for this world that has turned against you."

"I fight the Coalition. The place is secondary."

She reached out once more, cupped his cheek below the scar. "And you will not be alone."

She felt a tremor go through him—and vowed in that moment that this gallant man who had borne so much would someday find the ease he deserved.

Chapter 27

SHAINA PAUSED once more to study the path ahead. She led because there was only the one path now, all others had faded away once they'd left the spot where the old man had caught up with them.

This was crazy, trying this mountain in nothing but the stark light of the moon. And all this talk of treasure and magical crystals was crazier still. But if Cub said the pull was that strong . . .

She shook her head, sharply, as if that would rid it of the fanciful thoughts Theon seemed to bring on. It was all his mystical talk and riddles, she thought. That and the darkness caused such silliness.

The darkness caused other silliness as well. An uncomfortable kind.

His touch, his kisses had seared her to her very soul. Childlike notions seemed burned away, leaving her only with the thoughts of a woman. A woman who had suddenly realized that the person dearest and closest to her was also a man who fired her blood in a way she had never thought possible. She had thought herself immune, and had silently discounted her mother's promise that one day she would meet the man she could not walk away from.

She had never imagined that man would be the one person she had never wanted to walk away from since the day she had been born.

"Don't you think this is all rather strange?" she asked, grasping for distraction.

"I think this is Arellia," he said simply. "Home to myths and legends and magical ideas."

"Do you believe in them? Is that why you wished to go on this quest in the first place?"

He let out a long sigh. "Maybe I just wished to avoid the inevitable a little longer. I've trained for this all my life, yet I find myself wishing I could simply be a fighter. It seems simpler, somehow, than the governmental side."

"Cleaner, perhaps," Shaina said with a grin. "But you worry needlessly. I know you. I know your mind and your heart. I have faith in you and always will."

"As long as I have that, I will muddle through," he said.

Her heart wrenched oddly in her chest at the simple declaration. All he needed was her faith in him? She could think of nothing to say that would not circle them back to that thing now between them that she did not wish to acknowledge.

Cub looked up the mountain, up the pathway lit by that odd silver light. "As for this quest, it may be as simple as not wishing to quit when I feel we are so close."

"It is truly that strong, this feeling you have?"

"All I know is I feel we are drawing very close."

She supposed it was no odder than her own ability to sense approaching threats, that sense she was unable to explain in any logical terms.

"You mean you are," she said. "You're the Graymist."

"Yes," Cub said, almost absently, as he stared up the mountain. The path they were on curved sharply right up ahead, and they could not see anything beyond that from here.

"I do not like this."

Cub looked back. "You sense something else?"

"Not in the way you mean. I just do not like this idea of being pulled."

"You do not like feeling you have no choice," he said.

He knew her so well. There was that, too, she thought. What would it be like to be with, as man and woman, someone who knew her mind, her heart, as Cub did? He knew what moved her, what she wished for, what she feared, what she scorned. And she knew the same about him. There would be no learning period for them, when mates had to learn each other's ways, except—

She cut off the hot, sensuous vision that flashed into her mind, but between one breath and the next, her blood had heated to near boiling. Why was she even thinking of that one place where they had yet to learn everything about each other? Why was she even thinking about them together in that way at all?

"Whatever you just thought," Cub said, his voice oddly husky, "I would give much to know it."

Just the idea of admitting what she'd thought overwhelmed her. "Are we moving on, or are we not?" she snapped out.

He frowned in the silver light, at her sharp tone no doubt. "I'm as unsettled as you are. No need to sting." He turned and started up the path.

Even this, he understood, she thought as she followed. And it struck her suddenly, the thought that if she were to be joined with someone, in that unbreakable Triotian bonding that was forever and beyond, who better than her Cub, who knew her so very well?

That simply, everything changed in her mind. What had seemed impossible now seemed imperative, for how could it ever be anyone else? And how hideous would it be to stand by and watch him with someone else?

And no matter how much going along with old wishes of people she didn't even know went against her nature, she had to live with the simple, undeniable fact that no man she had ever known had made her feel the way Cub had with one simple kiss.

At least they were, as usual, in this together. For feeling like this if he did not would be the most impossible of all.

THAT DAMNED moonlight. It kept him back too far; he could not hear them. It had taken him too long to relocate them, after he'd had to change his route. It rankled that they had gotten behind him; that the woman had spoken to him in that insolent tone—that the whore had spoken to him at all—still rankled. The entire time he had worked his way back to them he had regretted not simply taking them then and there. This treasure they searched for was merely a legend, and he was beginning to feel he was truly on a fool's errand, following them as if they would lead him to something worth all this effort.

True, the prince was more important. Riches might buy his own life after killing the Coalition's advance scout, but not the life he wanted, back in good graces, back in power. Riches would merely stop them from killing him. And there was no promise for how long; Coalition memories were long and their hatred implacable.

But the king's son would buy him everything he dreamed.

But he must have patience. The Coalition had waited a long time, and so must he. He could ruin everything by indulging in his need to hurry. And indulging in need was what had brought down that fool Corling.

So he would wait. And follow. And when they were distracted by the treasure, or by the realization it had never existed, he would make his move. He would kill the woman and take the prince, and his future would be assured. And it would be soon. He had gleaned from those few who dared remain his ally that the move was imminent. The Coalition was already gathering, and would be on the wing again soon, and this time they would obliterate any opposition regardless of the assets that would be destroyed in that cleansing. They would not make the mistake of leaving anyone on Arellia and, most particularly, Trios alive to mount another rebellion. This time they would die to the last man, woman, and child.

They were moving again, up the path. Their every move was painted for him with that silver light, but it also forced him to hang back, out of sight. Only when the path curved to the right, around the flank of the mountain, did he dare pick up his pace.

He kept close to the rocks, moving from shadow to shadow as he followed the bend in the narrow track. He moved slowly despite his impatience; he did not want them to spot him this time. With infinite care he worked his way around that curve, pausing to listen carefully before peeking around for a glimpse of the path ahead. They kept moving, as if they hadn't a care in the world. They clearly had no idea he was behind them this time.

He was still congratulating himself on his stealth and cleverness when he peeked around the next outcropping of stone and brush. The path straightened up ahead, and he could see it in that cursed light for some distance. He blinked, squinted, his brain refusing to accept what his eyes were telling him.

The path was empty.

They had vanished.

Chapter 28

SHAINA DIDN'T question him when he suddenly veered off the path and dove through the trees on the right—she merely followed. Even when she'd thought him wrong—a rare enough occurrence that he should likely prize her unwavering trust more as well—if he was determined, she would follow. Someone, she'd always said, had to protect his back.

He wondered if on some subconscious level she had known—had sensed—that protecting him would fall to her. His mind recoiled at the thought. He'd always known it was the job of the flashbow warrior to protect the royal family, but when he'd thought of it, he'd always thought of Dax. It was part of the tradition over the centuries, and he'd never questioned it.

Until now, when he realized that the next flashbow warrior, the one who might one day have to die to protect him, was Shaina.

That she would do it even now was not at issue—as he would for her without hesitation, if it came to that. His discomfort was over the idea that it would one day be her responsibility. That it would be expected because she would be the flashbow warrior, not simply because of who she was, and who he was to her.

That she would have no choice. He knew how having no choice made her feel.

That she didn't want to discuss it right now had been made quite clear. And he understood that as well, although it was not like her to sidestep an issue.

A heavy branch whacked his chest, nearly took him off his feet, and he made himself focus on the task at hand. He pushed through the thick stand of trees. He couldn't explain the pull that had made him change direction, but he could not deny it was there.

Something snapped. He stopped short midstride. For a moment he thought the tingling sensation was from the memory of that kiss. But then he realized it was something outside, something that had begun at his skin and shot through him.

He heard an odd, muffled sound from behind him. He whirled, hand on the disrupter they had agreed whoever was in the lead would carry. He heard the sound again, faintly, like a distant cry.

Yet Shaina was there, barely ten feet behind him.

She was darting back and forth, looking, searching. For what? And why was she looking past him even as she called out his name? And it was too distant, too far, that cry. It sounded as if it were coming from halfway back down the mountain. He started back, running toward her. Felt that tingling sensation again.

She stopped dead in front of him, looking as if he had materialized out of the moonlit air.

"You're all right," she said, eying him warily. There was something odd in her voice, a touch of something he didn't recognize.

"Yes. What happened? Did you see something, hear something?"

Her brows rose. "You disappeared."

He blinked. "I what?"

"One moment you were pushing aside that large branch, the next you were . . . gone."

It was still there, that odd undertone, and he suddenly realized what it was. Something he had never heard from her before. Fear. And since she seemed incapable of fearing for herself, he had to assume it was for him. He added that to the growing heap of things they had to address, later.

"Shay—"

"I was right behind you. And then you were gone."

It made no sense, but he couldn't doubt she meant what she'd said. He wondered if it had something to do with that strange sensation he'd felt twice now.

"Well, come." He turned to retrace his steps upward, taking her hand. The oddness, and her distress, had rattled him more than he cared to admit. "I think I've found something."

He felt the sensation again, although less this time.

Shaina muttered something under her breath—he suspected one of those unladylike words she wasn't supposed to say. She rubbed a hand down her arm, and he realized she must be feeling the same thing he had, that sharp snap, followed by that odd tingling sensation running over her skin.

Then she seemed to forget that. They both stared for a long moment. He was aware for the first time that they were in what, in daylight and in normal circumstances, would probably be a pleasant mountain meadow, half-ringed by a semicircle of the mountain itself. To one side was a narrow waterfall, its rushing sound a soothing, natural counterpoint to the oddity of what had just happened.

Shaina looked around as well, then turned to look back the way they had come. She frowned. Studied . . . something, he couldn't tell what. She moved then, taking a step back down the path. Then another.

She reached out. Something in the very air sparked, snapped, and she jerked her hand back with a cry.

He covered the distance in two long strides. He collided with her. They steadied each other, barely managing to keep their feet. There was a split second when their gazes connected, when he knew they were both acknowledging things yet to face, but in this instant there was something immediate to deal with.

"What is it? Are you hurt?"

She looked at her fingers, which he could see were reddened.

"It . . . burns."

Thoroughly puzzled now, he lifted a hand. He felt the same tingling sensation, but nothing more. Shaina lifted her own hand again, and the spark flashed again, and she yanked it back.

"Enough of that," he said sharply.

He knelt down, picked up a fist-sized rock. Tossed it down the trail.

The air sparked again. And the rock bounced back and landed at their feet. Lyon's brow furrowed.

"That's not the main thing," she said. "You . . . vanished. The moment you went past this, you weren't there. And I couldn't see this meadow, the waterfall, none of it. There were just trees."

He blinked. "Wait," he said. He walked down until he felt the sting. Took one more step, then turned back.

"Can you see me?"

"Yes," she said, "but you sound muffled."

"As do you." He came back.

"I don't understand. When I was down there, when you went past that point, I could no longer see you. Nor any of this," she said, gesturing toward the meadow. "But you can?"

He nodded.

"And once past it, I apparently cannot go back. But you can."

Lyon drew back slightly, thinking. He turned, searching the area around them. All looked normal, natural. He looked at Shaina, who was watching him.

"I think . . . maybe . . . take my hand."

She did, although she was still frowning. He started walking back down the hill once more. She came, but when they neared the spot, the screen or whatever it was, she held back, hardly surprising after what had happened when she'd merely brushed it.

"Trust me," he said.

Immediately she stopped resisting. He felt a tug inside at her instant trust. Her hand in his, they walked through the screen.

She stopped on the other side, staring at him, then back the way they had come. Keeping her hand in his, he led her back.

"So . . . I can come through, but only if we are together?"

"Touching, I think," he said.

He looked back toward the meadow and waterfall he could see as clearly as if there were no barrier at all. Yet she could see none of it.

"'The spirits are thick on this mountain, and they only bare their secrets to those who are of the blood,'" he quoted the old man softly.

"Home to myths and legend and magical ideas indeed," she muttered.

He took her hand and once more they walked through the barrier. He stopped, and stared. "The waterfall."

"What about the—"

Her words broke off and he saw her remember the old man's words.

"Just as he described," she whispered.

"Yes."

He walked to the edge of the pool at the base of the falls, where the water gathered before spilling over and continuing down the mountain. Shaina joined him, stood beside him staring at the misty fall of water. It dropped a great distance, widening from a narrow stream at the top to a wide cloud of spray at the bottom, where the fall hit a boulder taller than both of them. The huge rock was split, as if the soft spray had been some sort of giant's hammer, cleaving it nearly in two.

"'The cavern of the waterfall shall open when the two halves have joined. . . .'"

He was barely aware of having said it aloud until Shaina responded.

"We're supposed to join the two halves of that rock? How? Either half must weigh more than the ceremonial stone."

"I don't know," he said. "I'm not even sure that's what it means."

She studied the rock. "It does make sense, if you accept that any of it makes sense. Do you suppose . . . the cave is behind it?"

"It is not uncommon, a cave behind a waterfall. There is one at Lake Geron, remember?"

"Are you even sure this is the place?"

He glanced at her, gave a half shrug. "Yes. Do not ask me how, but I am sure."

"Well, then." She shrugged off her pack and looked around. "I think over there is the best place to set up camp."

And just like that she accepted his word. His Shaina, of most logical and practical mind, asked for nothing more from him than his own certainty. Odd, how he was thinking so much of loyalty and constancy since they'd been on this mountain. Before, he had always taken her presence, even with all her flash and fire, for granted. He should not have. For even now, when the weight of her own future had to be pressing down on her, she was with him in all ways.

Except one . . .

His traitorous mind answered his own words with resounding emphasis. And that swiftly, the ache rose in him anew, until he despaired of containing it. He had thought, a couple of times on the trail when he had turned to look at her, that her face had betrayed a similar heat. But he could not be sure.

Better to be thinking of how they were to be moving the two halves of this real rock, he told himself.

"—the boundary."

He snapped out of his frustrating reverie. "What?"

"I said we should see if that . . . barrier, whatever it is, is still in place, and check the boundary of it."

He nodded. "Good plan."

They returned to the spot, found the mysterious visual and auditory obstruction still in place. They separated and went in opposite directions, testing, until they had reached opposite sides of the waterfall and had determined that the barrier enclosed the entire area from the trees to the precipice the waterfall tumbled over, although they could not tell how far up it went. What they could tell was that anything within that perimeter was both invisible and unheard from the outside, by her and they guessed by anyone not Graymist.

"Do we trust it?" she asked.

"I feel we can," he said slowly, "though again I could not tell you why."

"It fits with the rest of this insanity," she suggested.

There was wry humor in her tone, and he felt a spark of that admiration again. No matter what life threw at her, Shaina would always cope.

They set up in the place she had suggested, falling into old, familiar ways. He built the small fire they had decided to risk, since Shaina lacked the knack—or the patience—for it, while she gathered wood for fuel. A little food, and perhaps even some sleep in the hours remaining before dawn, then in the light of day they would examine the rock. Perhaps some way they had missed in the fading moonlight would be obvious then.

He only wished the rest of their path would become obvious as well.

Chapter 29

"IT'S TRUE, THEN?" Hurcon asked.

Dax looked at the burly Omegan, short, stout, and thickly muscled as most from his world were, thanks to the heavy gravity of the huge planet.

"What is?" he asked as the man slung his bag onto his old bunk. He was the last to arrive, recalled from his home. The call had been voluntary for all offworlders, but every one of them had responded immediately.

"Rox said the Coalition is gathering again."

"We have a very reliable source. Heard you nothing on Omega?"

"Rumors, nothing more," Hurcon said. "Although the whisperings did seem more active than usual."

"Were they being taken seriously?"

"By some. Others called them crazy." Hurcon looked up at him. "Your source is not, I gather?"

"He is not." Hurcon had been with them, in the battle for Galatin, so he would understand, Dax thought. "It's Bright Tarkson."

The Omegan's eyes widened, and he let out a low whistle. "Reliable indeed," he said. Then he frowned. "But I thought he was dead."

"We all did. Rina found him alive shortly after she arrived on Arellia."

"Well that bedamned bark-hound," Hurcon exclaimed. "He could have let us know. I've regretted his loss for an age now."

"As have we all," Dax said with a grin. "But I decided to forgive him, since he was still alive after all."

Hurcon grinned back. "I will still give him a load of snailstones when I see him." He arched a brow, an expression that looked exaggerated on his broad, squarish face. "And Rina found him, did she?"

"Yes."

"And he is the one who put out this alarm?"

Dax nodded. He didn't explain further, curiously waiting to see the old warrior's reaction.

"Then it's in the vault," he said with certainty. "I'll make ready for departure."

Again Dax nodded, but this time with satisfaction. His men had not forgotten Tark either, and his word, his instincts, were as gold for them.

He left the crew to their preparations, and went up the narrow stairway behind him. For a long moment he stood at the top in silence. He thought of the old *Evening Star*, and the glory days of flying her. This new incarnation was stronger, swifter, and even better armed. And soon Califa would join him, and it would be a taste of that glory anew.

He couldn't deny he felt a growing thrum of excitement. He stepped forward. He was on the bridge, most of his old crew was now here, supplemented by Triotian volunteers he'd barely had to ask for. The word had gone out, and they'd been lined up at the skyport doors within hours.

The skypirate would fly again.

"I SHOULD LET you return to your sleep."

Rina said it more because it seemed polite than because she wanted to leave. If she had her way, she would stay forever in his company. And the thought no longer frightened her; it merely helped her to understand. For years she had watched Dax and Califa, and even the king and queen, with a sense of puzzlement. That they loved, fiercely, was without doubt. She even understood why, since she admired all four of them more than anyone she had ever known—it only made sense that they would feel the same, and the shift from that to their kind of love was not so hard to fathom.

She just couldn't picture it for herself. For there had never been a man she had even begun to feel that way about.

Save one. And she was with him now.

They had been seated for some time on his cushioned stone bench before the fire he had stirred back to full flame. She had asked him for a more detailed assessment of the defense situation on Arellia. His answers weren't promising, but she knew they were honest. There were a few hundred, perhaps, who truly believed in the coming threat. A few thousand, perhaps, who would respond quickly when it came. The rest had convinced themselves the Coalition was forever beaten, and had let themselves lapse into a lazy, unconcerned existence.

"I will not sleep now," he said in answer to her suggestion she leave him to his rest.

"I should have waited until morning," she said, regretting even more that she had disrupted his sleep, since it seemed he got far too little. She wondered how much of her poor choice had been rooted in her desire to simply see him again. She felt as if she were floundering in uncharted stars. Even an exact navigator was of no use in unknown reaches.

"No," he answered quickly. "It was good news. At least, as good as any can be, if I am right."

"You are," she said.

He looked at her then, straight on. He'd donned the patch, and she had to admit it made a difference. She wondered how long it had taken him to get used to seeing that twisted scar on his own face. Perhaps he had yet to get used to it. Perhaps the patch truly was as much for himself as for the sensibilities of others.

Could she get used to it? Could she ever look at that ridge of thickened, distorted tissue without thinking of how he had once appeared, young and strong and impossibly handsome?

"You put a lot of trust in my instincts."

"I always have. I always will." She grimaced. "Well, except for the one that told you to keep the fact of your survival hidden."

"Rina, I—"

She waved a hand, cutting him off. "I understand. I merely wish you had felt you could trust me. Us," she corrected quickly, her cheeks heating enough that she was grateful he had turned off the too-bright huntlight.

He looked away, toward the fire. She wondered what he did not wish her to see. "I never doubted I could trust you," he said softly. "But I did not want your pity."

"Of all the things I feel for you, pity is completely absent."

He went very still. Without looking at her, he spoke again, in that same low voice. "Were I a bigger fool than I am, I would ask what those things are."

She forgot to breathe. She felt as if she were standing on the precipice of the Rift of Rycross, that yawning gap that Coalition explosions had caused in the floor of the Valley of Rycross, southwest of Triotia. She gathered her breath and her nerve, and answered him.

"Since you are no kind of fool, I think you already know the answer."

"Rina—"

"If you do not wish to hear it, say so and I will leave now."

"It is not that I do not wish it."

"Then what?"

"I am . . . afraid of it."

She was astonished at words she would never have thought to hear from him. "You? You fear nothing."

"I fear you," he said.

"Why?" she whispered. "I cannot hurt you anymore than you have already been hurt."

He laughed, but it was a low, harsh, painful sound. "You could tear me apart," he said. "You have ever had that power."

"Me?" She nearly gaped at him.

He finally looked away from the fire. He faced her straight on, and the strain in his face told her it had taken more strength than she ever would have expected.

"You have been, more often than not, the memory that has kept me going. Not memories of victories, or final triumph, but the knowledge that a universe that still had you in it was worth staying in."

The admission that he had considered not staying, that he might well have turned that dagger he'd met her with on himself, tore at her, set up an ache inside that she didn't think she could bear.

"And I," she answered hoarsely, "have been railing at that same universe for all these years, for letting you die."

"Rina—"

"I have been angry for all that time. I could not even think of you without crying. I could not forget you, no matter how many times Dax or Califa told me I had to let go."

"They . . . knew?"

"That I was furious with fate? Yes. It is hard to hide when you've lost the only person who ever made you feel you were capable of their kind of love."

He jerked as if she'd struck him. Looked away again. "Be careful where you tread, little one."

"I know exactly where I walk. It is up to you to decide if I am welcome."

And odd sort of tremor went visibly through him. "You cannot want this."

"Do not tell me what I cannot want, Bright Tarkson. You think there were no males on Trios who had interest in mating with me?"

He made a low sound, a sort of snorting chuckle. "I had not heard that all men on Trios were blind and stupid, no."

The words warmed her, but she didn't stop to savor them. It was too important to get this out and said. "And yet I wanted none of them. Could give none of them my heart. Because I had already given it away, the first moment I saw you."

He took in a deep, shuddering breath. "A girlish infatuation. And even were it not, I am clearly no longer the man you saw that day. You cling to a memory, and it no longer exists no matter how you wish it did."

"And yet that memory sits before me."

He turned back then. Reached up and yanked off the eye patch. Faced her straight on. "This is what sits before you."

She leapt to her feet. With a tremendous effort she spoke carefully. "Does it pain you?"

"What?"

She gestured at the scar. "Does it hurt, even now?"

"No."

"Good," she said flatly.

She slapped him. Hard.

He uncoiled with the same fierce grace she had always remembered, and was on his feet in a split second. Unlike most would, he did not put a hand to the cheek she had struck. Perhaps he was inured to the pain of such a small jolt, or perhaps not only skin and tissue had been damaged by the wound, perhaps nerves had been cut, numbed. She let her anger overwhelm the pain that thought caused.

"Good," she snapped. "If you're going to insult me again, Arellian, you should do it on your feet."

"Insult you?" He sounded astonished.

"You dare to accuse me of being so small-minded, so silly and foolish as to hold that scar against you? You truly think it matters one snailstone to me, beyond the pain it caused you?"

He was staring at her, as if stunned. She didn't care. It was as if a dam within her had been breached, and she could no more stop the flow now than she had been able to stop thinking of him all these years.

"You believe my thoughts so trifling that I would find you less the man I knew because of some small change in your appearance? A change acquired in the most heroic of acts?"

"Rina," he said, his voice tight, strained.

"Because if you do, then perhaps you are right. I cannot want this. Cannot want a man who thinks so little of me."

For a long silent moment he simply stood there, staring at her. She could hear his breathing, for it was coming in short, audible pants. Whatever else, he was not taking this lightly, and that gave her hope. He drew in a longer breath before he spoke again.

"I think more of you than anyone I have ever known." His mouth twisted. "And I mean that in all senses. Which is why I know you deserve more than—"

"Stop. I don't wish to strike you again."

"You caught me by surprise. You might not find it so easy again."

"I would not expect to. So I would find another way."

"As you always have, little one."

His voice had gone quiet. And something had changed in his gaze, shifted somehow, as if he were seeing possibilities instead of hopelessness.

"I know," she said, softly now, "that Dax gave you warning, when we first met."

His mouth twisted. "Warning? He threatened to remove whatever body part I might touch you with."

She couldn't help but laugh; it was so very Dax. "He worried overmuch."

"And likely still does."

"I am far from a child any longer, even by Triotian standards, and he is no longer my guardian. Are you saying you fear him still?"

"Any rational person would. And I doubt he has removed himself from the position of guardian, no matter what your laws say."

"So is he to be your excuse?"

To his credit, he did not pretend to misunderstand. "Now you insult me."

She shrugged. "If that is what it requires."

It was a long moment before he said roughly, "Be very sure, Rina. Be very sure this is what you want. Because it has been a very, very long time, and I can make no promises about holding back. Or stopping, if you change your mind."

Her breath caught, and heat of a kind she'd never known slammed through her at the blunt words. "It may have been a long time for you, but for me it has been . . . forever."

He blinked. "Forev—You mean you've not . . . ever?"

"How could I? I'm Triotian, we bond for life. Casual mating is not our way. And the only man I ever wanted in that way I thought dead."

He grabbed her arms, held her in place. His gaze shifted upward, as if in some sort of mute appeal. She heard him, barely, mutter an oath under his breath. And when he looked at her again, she saw in his gaze the same sort of searing heat he fired in her. Joy slammed through her; it was returned, this glorious, terrifying tangle of emotion.

"War is coming, perhaps worse than before. I cannot promise you tomorrow now any more than I could then."

"All the more reason," she whispered. "Do not leave me with only wishes and imaginings this time."

He groaned. "You've always been the only one with the power to break me," he rasped out.

And then she was in his arms, his mouth was on hers, and her entire body was singing with the rightness of it.

At last.

Chapter 30

"YOU'RE CERTAIN?"

"Saw them m'self," the man said, tipping back his mug to drain the last of the brew. He didn't seem to mind the cheapness of it, Mordred thought. It was the effect he was after, not the taste. Of course these rustic sorts had little refinement; they wouldn't know good wine or food were it set before them.

"When?"

"Not three days ago. Captain of that cargo ship I grabbed passage on said I was imagining things, but I was back where they could be seen, not like him, up front."

"How many?"

"Least twenty ships."

He took another long swallow. Wiped his mouth on his already filthy sleeve. Mordred barely managed not to recoil in his distaste.

"Couple really big ones." The man shuddered visibly. "Even bigger than during the rebellion. I was here then, you know."

"Were you?" Mordred asked, his voice tight with excitement at the realization the invasion was indeed imminent.

He had, after impossibly losing all sign of that infuriating pair, retraced his path to this inn halfway back down the mountain. He needed food and rest, although he was sure it was only because he'd been on the move for so long now.

And he had, by some overdue turn of luck, heard of the garrulous drunk who had migrated here because those in town had wearied of hearing his tale of a fleet of ships amassing beyond Arellia's outer moon. It had been a welcome bit of information amid all the nonsense these people seemed to favor, so absurd it was all he could do not to visibly roll his eyes in disgust.

But he had found the man who had told them the latest tale, one they seemed to find more impossible than the silly myths and fantasies they accepted so readily. And he had resigned himself to staying at it until he got what he needed.

He tried to shrug off his distaste at having to glean information in this way, but it lingered. That he, once the pride and future of the Coalition, had to bribe a drunk with more brew to learn what he should have been privy to all along was an insult. He told himself it was no different than being a spy, when odious methods were necessary to achieve the goal. Gathering information could be a nasty business, but it was necessary.

Somewhat mollified, he plied the man with more brew, scorning the local libation himself. He suspected it was concocted in some dirty vat in a back room, and he longed for the days when nothing but the finest wines and foods had graced his table.

When the man's head thudded to the rough-hewn table for the third time, Mordred knew he had gained all the worthwhile knowledge the addled drunk had. He rose, ordered the innkeeper to prepare a bundle of food and drink for him, to be picked up at first light, and retired to his rented room for a few hours' well-deserved sleep.

THE SKY WAS lighter, Shaina decided. Dawn was, if not near, at least coming. Finally.

She had slept little, when he had had the watch they now kept. And what sleep she had managed, had been full of unsettling dreams. Not, as she would have expected, of following threats or even an old man's silliness. No, her dreams this night turned to a hidden, unknowable future, the one person she trusted above all others, and childhood speculation by others that went against everything she believed about freedom and self-determination. Just because some old wishes still rolled around in the elders' minds didn't mean it was real, true, or destined.

Besides, she had always assumed it had been invented to please their parents. It was only natural that a union between their houses would be welcomed.

And then she and Cub had come along, conveniently male and female—despite the fact that never before in Triotian history had the firstborn of the flashbow warrior been female—and only whetted the Triotian appetite for what seemed to them the perfect match.

She stared at the sky, which still seemed the same as before, thinking. So she was the first female offspring. The flashbow ability had never been hereditary before, either.

The anger that had driven her to jump that first transport, to get herself as far away from her father as she could, was still there. But now it was a cooler thing, not the boiling rage that had erupted. She was calmer now. Soon she might even be able to think about it without losing all logic.

Not, she thought, that he deserved it.

Perhaps she'd been mistaken about the closeness of the dawn. The sky was no lighter than when she had first opened her eyes. Perhaps she had been awake so long it had just seemed that it must be near.

She had sensed, more than once, that Cub was as restless as she. And yet she did not speak to him in the darkness, as she typically would have. It seemed too dangerous, as if the quiet night would take the discussion places she was not ready to go.

So you avoid thinking of your father, and talking to Cub, because you are afraid. When did you become such a coward?

Her thoughts were harsh, unforgiving. *And true*, she told herself sternly.

"Shay?"

She went still. Barely breathed. She hadn't heard him stir. "What?"

"Just making sure you were awake."

His tone was clearly teasing, but she was so edgy she snapped anyway. "It's my watch, of course I am."

"And barbed, I see."

Only the fact that the sharp retort that leapt to her lips would prove him right stopped her from saying it.

"Wishing you had stayed home now?" he asked.

Just that easily he deflated her irritation, for the answer to that was clear. She turned her head, was barely able to make out his shape in the darkness. He, too, sat up, drawing his knees up to rest his elbows across them. She crossed her legs before her, leaning forward to rest her chin on her propped hands.

"No," she said. "I could not stay. I was too angry."

"But it has cooled a bit now? It's as well, then. You might have said something . . . irrevocable."

Her mouth tightened. "You don't consider 'I hate you and never want to speak to you again' irrevocable?"

"In the face of the love your father has for you? No."

His words bit deep. "And what part of love does a lie of that magnitude represent?"

"The part that fears losing that love. The part that says a father's task is to protect that which he loves. The part that has seen enough of the trickery of life to know that no one is ever completely safe."

She turned her head, studied him for a moment, completing in her mind's eye the image of what she could not see in the darkness. She could see the long, lean shape of him, could see even the faint light gleaming on his golden hair, could see the sheen of skin and the shape of jaw, brow, nose. Her memory filled in the shadows with every detail of the face she'd grown up with, the face she'd seen change from the soft, round innocence of childhood to the sharper, promising leanness of youth, to the solid strength of manhood.

"You truly have your father's knack for the right words at the right moment," she said.

"It is easier to see all sides when you are a step back," he said. But she saw the flash of his teeth, and knew he had smiled. Odd, she thought, how they were both so much like their fathers, and yet their relationship with each was so different.

Or it was now. She had ever been as close to her own father as Cub was to his. Until it had all been shattered between one breath and the next.

And she had come, as always, to the one person she knew would understand.

"It seems I'm ever coming to you with my troubles," she said, her voice as quiet as the night. "Tell me, Cub, do you never tire of soothing me?"

"I worry. Worry that your temper and recklessness will one day cost you too much. But tire? No, I don't."

His words stilled her. Something deep inside shifted, changed. She had never, in all their years growing up together, realized he worried about her. Oh, she knew he did when they were in a rough spot, when one of their larks had skirted the edge of danger a little too closely, but she had always thought the worry began there and ended when they were safely through it.

"I never meant to worry you."

"Your fearlessness worries us all, Shay. We wish you would be more careful. For the sake of those who love you."

For the sake of those who love you.

If you can't tell the difference between a man who's tamed and one who's curbing himself out of love, then you have much yet to learn, my sweet. Your father is far from tamed. And he will ever be so.

Her mother's words came back to her in a single rush, as if a cinefilm was playing in her head. Could those words apply to her, as well?

Somehow, she had never thought of it in just that way. She had always accepted that her impulsiveness carried a price, but she had always thought herself the only one to pay it. Now, with Cub's quiet words, she realized that when others loved you, what you did cost them as well. And she felt a fool for not realizing it sooner, and for thinking she was grown when she had in fact been in this way still a child.

No wonder her father felt she still needed protecting.

Chapter 31

ON SOME LEVEL Rina was aware she was sleeping, had that odd feeling as if she were swimming toward the surface from the bottom of a very deep lake. Some part of her resisted, for the depths were warm and comforting and she wished to stay. Forever, perhaps. She had no desire to surface, to open her eyes and face the world. She wanted nothing more than to stay, right here, safe and sheltered in the arms of—

She jolted awake.

Tark.

Heat flooded her, not the heat of embarrassment at waking naked in his arms, in his bed, but a glorious, delicious heat, remembering the night and what they had found in the quiet hours.

Hours that hadn't stayed quiet for long, as again and again they had come together, she crying out his name, he gasping out hers.

She had finally seen the redoubtable Bright Tarkson brought down, and in the most intimate of ways. And she had done it. He was sleeping even now, so deeply she thought that this once, he might not wake as he always had, alert, on guard, and ready for any threat.

She moved slowly, wanting, no, needing to look at him. He was but a faint outline in the alcove's darkness, lightened only by the slight glow from the banked fire in the cave, but she needed no more. Had she not carried his image in her mind for years? And the changes in that image were part of what she saw now. There were more scars than the one that sealed his eye. His lean, hard body was marked with them, dagger bite here, a burn from a laser pistol there, and what looked like a spray of shrapnel over his back.

She had learned each during the night, turning each into a marker, a point on which to linger, to caress, until he was arching to her hands, her lips. She had done her best, with her limited knowledge, to drive him mad, until at last he took it out of her hands and joined them.

He had held back much longer than he had warned her.

And it had been more glorious than she had ever imagined.

"Regretting your mad bargain?"

She had been so lost in her heated reverie she did not even realize he had awakened until he spoke.

"Regretting so many lost years," she whispered. "I'm sorry if I woke you."

He made a sound, low and rueful. "Deeper than I've slept in all those years. The world could have ended, and I doubt I would have known."

"Good."

"It was your doing."

"Good," she repeated. "Do you feel rested?"

"I feel . . ." His voice trailed off. Then, his voice touched with puzzlement, he said, "I'm not certain how I feel."

"I was hoping for rested. Or at least recovered."

He moved then, away, and she was struck with a sudden fear that he would pull back now, that he would retreat behind that harsh exterior, hiding from her once again. She reached for him, pulled him closer.

"Running from this is not among your choices," she said, her tone edgy with that fear. "Between us, there is no hiding now."

"You didn't warn me of that."

He sounded nothing more than rueful again, and his body relaxed, so she took heart.

"When you take on a Triotian, it is part of that bargain."

He was silent for a long moment, but he made no further move to pull away from her. "Dax once explained to me that Triotians do not normally mate outside of bonding."

She wondered if that had been while Dax had been threatening him with bodily harm if he touched her, but merely said, "Yes."

"But we aren't . . ."

"It matters not." She hesitated, knowing what she wanted to tell him, but her usual boldness failing her for a moment.

"You are so proud—rightfully—of being Triotian, yet you discard this primary tenet?"

Had he sounded in the least critical, she probably would have taken advantage of their intimate position and applied her knee to a very vulnerable part of him. But he sounded merely puzzled—and she had plans for those parts—so she did not.

She knew he was not Triotian, and that offworlders sometimes found the ancient bonding custom quaint, or too restrictive. It had been abandoned as such in many quarters, but it was inborn in Triotians. They were known for it.

And yet Califa and the queen were both Arellian, and they had bonded with their mates as thoroughly as any native born. Perhaps it was something about Trios herself that changed people.

All the more reason, she thought, to convince him to come back with her. Selfish, yes. But there it was, and she couldn't deny it.

Nor could she deny him the truth.

"It doesn't matter," she said, plunging ahead, "because my heart was lost to you years ago. My mind has ever held you close. And bonding is as much of the heart and mind as it is of formal ceremony."

He went very still. "Are you saying you feel we are . . . bonded?"

"That is for you to decide. It can only be mutual. Especially with a non-Triotian."

"But—"

"I am saying I will never be bonded to another, for I do not have what is required to give. It is all already yours."

She felt a shudder go through him. Gladdened by this proof that he was not unmoved, she lifted her head and kissed, as she had before, that thick ridge of tissue, that a badge of honor in her eyes. He had tried to turn away the first time, but she had refused to let him, had repeated the move again and again until she felt he was convinced it did not repulse her, but rather reminded her of all the reasons she was here with him.

This time he did not pull his scarred face away, but he whispered, "Rina, I don't deserve—"

"If you finish that idiotic and unwise statement, I will have to forgo my plans and send my knee a handsbreadth upward. Hard."

He froze. She nearly laughed. The hovering darkness outside the cave, the turmoil that was approaching, seemed distant, at least for the moment. And it was a moment she wanted to seize, to treasure, for when that chaos arrived she might never have another chance.

"I would prefer you did not," he said. "I had fears enough I would not be able to function."

She hadn't realized that. There had been one scar on his upper thigh, perilously close to what would have been her knee's target. But since he had already been aroused to full measure, it had not occurred to her that there might have been doubts.

Since it was already proven he was more than functional, she only smiled. "You cannot say I didn't warn you this time."

"I suppose Dax taught you that?"

"And more," she said cheerfully. "I can dismember a man in the most painful way."

"Dare I hope that was not the plan you spoke of?"

She did laugh then, and let into it all the joy bubbling up anew inside her. She had meant what she'd said, there was no hiding now, and it went for her as well as for him.

"Eos." His voice was nearly a growl, the oath sounding as if it had been ripped from him.

And then he moved, rolling on top of her, pinning her. She welcomed him, relished the solid weight of him, gloried in the sudden, surging readiness of his body, and how it betrayed a need she, for now at least, would let herself believe was only for her.

He, too, had learned in the night. Her scars were no match for his, Dax had been too effective in protecting her. But he had learned every part of her, learned how and where to touch. His hands traced the paths anew, and then his mouth. Her face, her lips, down the side of her throat. Lingering at the hollow of her throat, as if he were savoring the beat of her pulse there. As perhaps he was, since he was the one who had set it to racing.

And then he was at her breasts, kissing, caressing. She arched up to him, begging silently for him to hurry.

He stopped. She whimpered.

His voice was harsh when he spoke. "I was not gentle with you when I should have been, that first time. I could not."

It had hurt, she couldn't deny that, but she hadn't cared. She hadn't cared about anything except him, and having him take her where no man ever had. Because only he could.

"You warned me. Now please—"

He laid a finger over her lips, hushing her. "You gave me a gift without price. The least I can do is show you how much I treasure it. Will treasure it. Until my last breath, Rina."

With that he began again, slowly, teasing, tormenting. He brushed his fingers over her lightly, then harder, teased her nipples into aching tightness, and then, at last, lowered his dark head and suckled her. She cried out at the slam of sensation that made her body fairly ripple under his mouth.

She opened for him, wanting more than anything that connection, that joining, wanting him to become part of her once more, so close she could, in those glorious moments, believe this would never end. But still he waited, until she was writhing beneath him, beyond words but still pleading with her every movement. She had feared this would never happen, and now that it had she let down all barriers, for this had ever been and forever would be the only man who was worth such a baring of mind, body, and soul.

Some part of her reasoning mind insisted it could not be as she remembered. Nothing could be. Her memory had to have embroidered upon it, made it hotter and fiercer in memory than in reality. But when at last he gave in, when he slid forward, flesh into slick, ready flesh, when he made that sweet, driving invasion, her body clenched around him with a fierceness that made her cry out even as he groaned low and deep. And she knew it had been real, and beyond even her memory's ability to embellish.

He had driven her so close she felt her body gathering even before he began to move again. One stroke, two, three, and she was flying, his name on her lips as an explosion swept over her. Before, he had gone with her, but he kept his promise and held back, barely letting her crest and ebb before starting anew.

"Tark—"

"Hush, little one," he said, even as he moved within her, "this is as it should have been the first time."

It was impossible, she couldn't, she simply couldn't, and yet she felt the tension building again. He changed the pace, the angle, until she thought she would die from the growing pressure. She savored every stroke of his body, reveled in the simple fact that it was him, that he was here, not years dead and gone, but very, very alive.

She slid her hands down his back, feeling rather than seeing the sheen of moisture on his body. She felt the muscles flex, tighten as she urged him to move faster, harder. He let out a hoarse, guttural sound and did just that. In the instant before she felt her body shatter, she heard her own name as if it had been ripped from his throat, and he shuddered violently, crushing her against him as if he feared she would somehow vanish.

For a long time after their breathing had slowed, they lay silent. A shiver went through her as she wondered if this was all they would ever have, this stolen night, if the threat from outside might in turn steal this from them. He reached for the roughly woven blanket and pulled it over them, and she burrowed against him as if he were the only source of warmth and safety in her world.

She wasn't sure he was not. For the first time in her life, she wanted to hide, to run, to stay huddled in this darkened cave, hanging on to this man, letting what would happen outside happen, wanted to ignore the reality she knew was coming.

She wanted to ignore the fact she had learned very early in her life, that fate sometimes had a vicious, nasty sense of irony. And that thinking Tark dead for so long, finding him alive and discovering this unparalleled joy, and then losing him for real and forever, would be just the sort of thing to be expected.

Chapter 32

"IT'S THERE."

Lyon wasn't sure how he was so certain, but he was. They stood beside the small pool, looking up at the misty spray, sparkling in the morning light. The mysterious barrier had apparently held, and they had had a peaceful night.

"Behind the fall?" Shaina asked.

"Yes."

"All right."

He glanced at her. "You don't want to ask how I'm so sure?"

"Do you know?"

"Not in any way I can explain."

She shrugged. "Why I didn't ask."

Lyon couldn't stop himself from smiling. "You're handling this rather well."

"And you accept that I can sense things you can't. Why is this different?"

"It's not, I suppose," he said.

He turned back to study the waterfall. It wasn't particularly wide, coming as it did from a narrow notch in the cliff above, but the volume of water was impressive, and the chaotic swirling in the pool below rather forbidding. The large boulder that had split blocked the bottom of the fall from their view.

. . . the cavern of the waterfall shall open when the two halves are joined.

He walked closer, leaned as far as he could, but still could not see behind the broken rock. There was nothing for it but to climb it, he thought, eying warily the surface that was wet with spray from the falling water.

"If we had climbing rope, it might be easier to come down from above," Shaina said.

He didn't react to the fact that she had seemingly read his mind; after all, it was a regular occurrence, and only the fact that it went both ways allowed him to be at ease with it.

He glanced upward, considering her words even though they were decidedly short on any rope or line strong enough for climbing. He quickly spotted what had likely inspired the thought, a bare stretch of the cliff alongside the falls, where a quick, easy descent could be made if you had the line, could get up there, and find something big or heavy enough to secure the rope to.

"Even if we combined what's in our packs, I don't think it would be enough," he said.

She sighed. "I know. I was just trying to avoid climbing that wet rock."

"You don't have to climb it," he pointed out. "The old man said—"

"Graymist, I know. But if you think I'm letting you tackle that alone, you're crazier than he is. You'll end up shedding some of that Graymist blood."

He grinned. "Wouldn't be the first time."

"Doesn't mean you need to court it."

He lifted a brow at her. "What's this? You, favoring caution?"

She lowered her gaze. "Maybe I don't want to be responsible for bloodying the heir to the throne of Trios."

"You wouldn't be responsible, Shay."

Her head came up then. She looked at him steadily. "Yes. I would."

He studied her eyes, those jade green eyes he knew so well. "Does it feel wrong to you?" he asked, not even sure where the words rose from. He searched for the words to explain what he meant, but as usual she grasped what he hadn't said.

"Us?"

He nodded.

She drew in a deep breath. "Not in the way I think you mean, but I keep thinking of what you said. About a passage to something even better."

"I cannot guarantee that I am right."

"Life has no guarantees, isn't that what your father always says?"

"Yes."

"My mother always adds, 'Except that what you expect rarely happens, and what you don't expect often does.'" There was a long pause before she spoke again, and in keeping with her mother's words, it was something he hadn't expected. "I'm not a coward."

He stared at her. "Of course you're not a coward. Shay, you're the farthest thing from it."

"Then why am I so afraid?"

His mind was racing, searching for the right thing to say, because he sensed whatever he spoke would be crucial.

"Maybe," he said slowly, "because what we have is so precious. And you fear that we will lose that."

"What if we do?"

"Our parents did not. Besides, you've never feared what-ifs before."

"I've never thought of losing what I treasure most before."

Her words, so earnestly and honestly spoken, warmed him more than the rising sun ever could. He reached out and cupped her cheek, looked at her familiar, beloved face. She tilted her head back, and just slightly turned to rest her cheek against his palm. And in that instant he could no more have stopped himself than he could have stopped the waterfall beside them with a wave of his hand.

He lowered his head. Nuzzled her cheek. And at last found her lips with his.

Fire blasted through him. As if that first kiss had been but a primer, and his body had since learned, the spark caught, burned, exploded.

It was hot. It was fierce. It was flooding him with feelings he'd never known. And knowledge he'd never had, of life, of love, of the why of it. And of the future.

And most of all, of inevitability.

Chapter 33

RESISTING DID not even enter Shaina's mind. Some part of her realized there was no point. He swept away her doubts, her fears, as if they had never existed. Or as if compared to what was happening now, they didn't matter.

They didn't lose their friendship. . . .

He hadn't had to remind her of that, the thought had been tumbling inside her since he'd pointed out that simple fact.

She should have known, she thought. She should have realized long ago. She had only two options. Be with Cub, or be alone. She trusted only Cub to see beyond the physical to her heart and soul. The very idea of being with anyone else was absurd. She should have seen that long before now. Should have realized that the fact that others wanted it as well didn't make it any less her choice.

He deepened the kiss, and a hunger unlike anything she'd ever imagined possible seized her. Her body fairly sang with the rightness of it, and she wondered why she had ever doubted that this, that they were meant to be. This was it, the moment she'd feared, as if she'd somehow known how fierce, how consuming, it would be. But she feared nothing now—she was beyond that, far beyond. It was as if a wall she hadn't even realized was there, as that invisible barrier around this meadow, had been blasted away. The future, their future, together, seemed spread bright and clear before her.

She spared a split second to take joy in the certainty that he was feeling it too; they were both of Triotian blood as much as Arellian, and to them bonding was real and true and forever.

That joy spread, until it practically bubbled up out of her. When he at last paused, whispering her name, she could do nothing more than cling to him, nearly shouting, "Yes. Yes!"

"You're certain?"

"Beyond certain."

She went down to the ground, letting her weight pull him down with her. The grass was not as soft nor as green as the famed Triotian carpet, but it would do. For this, the very rocks would do, for what was beneath her mattered nothing next to the man above her.

She knew without asking that this was as new to him as it was to her. Such was Triotian culture. Besides, not only had she always known where he was, he had also told her of his few forays into experimenting—usually carelessly, as a man who had tried sips of various brews and discovered he liked none of them—although he was too well-bred to name names. She couldn't blame him for those, not when they practically lined the paths he walked with velvet.

She had once wondered aloud why he took none of them. He had given her a crooked grin and answered, "Maybe I'm waiting for you to join them."

"You'll be old and gray before that will happen, half-wit."

The memories flashed through her mind in an instant. She felt the odd need to acknowledge this, now. She reached up, cupped his face. Her words were statement, not question. "It truly was destined, wasn't it."

"Of course," he said easily, and kissed her again.

She knew little of this, beyond the basics once explained to her as a girl by her mother in a session she'd mostly ignored because what did a mother know of it? That her mother obviously knew a great deal or she herself would not be here was something that had only come to her later.

There was fumbling, a bit of awkwardness, but none of it shook the sense of destiny, that the inexorable journey toward this had indeed been inevitable. It was only the physical they didn't know. Their hearts, their minds, all else was work long done. They knew each other as few did. They had only to focus on the moment, the now.

Any lingering resistance, born of stubbornness, was seared away by the heat of his mouth, his body, and when the fumbling with clothing was done and they were bare to the sun in each other arms, it felt so right she couldn't wait another moment.

"Now, Lyon," she whispered, opening her body to him.

He froze even amid caressing her until she could barely breathe. "You never call me that."

"And so now I do. As you call me Shay."

He seemed, as always, to understand. He kissed her, even more deeply this time, and she let go of all restraint and kissed him back with every bit of heat and fierceness she was feeling. He let out a sound much like his namesake, low and rumbling. Then again his hands were stroking her, while his mouth trailed down her throat. He cupped her breasts, lifted them for his lips. She arched in delighted shock at the way her body fairly rippled in response, an almost violent clenching of every muscle. Uncontrollable.

But there was no need for control. Not here, not now, not with him. Her hands slid over him, stroking, urging. From this moment, that beautiful golden body was hers, forever, and she wanted to start that journey with an urgency she couldn't mask.

It hurt, in that first moment of his body joining hers, but the strange feel of it distracted her. And then he was there, and the sound of his low groan was enough to make her body clench anew.

She breathed her earlier thought. "Forever."

He settled deeper into her. "Yes. How long we've waited. How long it will be ours."

The rough words arrowed through to the last protected corner of her heart, and she gave him that as well, as she had given him everything else, and always would.

It was wild, and a bit mad as the unbearable tension built with his every move. He drove hard, as if overtaken by the same frenzied need that had filled her. She arched to meet him, clinging to him even as he slammed into her. All the years of waiting, when she hadn't even known what she was waiting for, culminated in the moment when her body hit the peak, when fire and emotion and need and drive all exploded at once, and her entire being seemed to clench around him. He gasped even as she cried out, unable to hold back.

She felt the hot pulse of him inside her. Her name burst from him in a voice she'd never heard before. The world seemed to spin, even to rumble beneath them. If it were to fly apart at this moment she wouldn't care, for they had achieved this and there could be nothing more.

At last it ebbed. She waited, cradling him, savoring his quickened breath, his hammering heart as evidence he'd been on the same soaring flight she had. Not that she needed evidence, she knew as well as she knew the color of his eyes and that small scar on his right shoulder, that he had.

She wished they could stay like this, lying quietly in the sunlight, bare to a world that in this moment seemed without shadow, without threat. That they would have to speak of this, she knew, but not yet, she pled silently, not yet.

Long moments spun out, and she was momentarily glad she did not have Rina's internal clock; she wanted time to stop, just as it was now. She stroked his back, fingertips tracing the line of lean, strong muscle. Her other hand touched his hair, fingers threading through the golden strands, letting them slip through her fingers. It was said a mating between a golden Triotian and a dark one such as she, one of those known as the Children of the Evening Star, could produce either, although the golden coloring was more the norm. She wondered what—

She snapped out of her musings with a start. Was she truly thinking of such things? How had she gone from resisting this with all her might to pondering a future with a child?

As if her jump had transmitted to him through their connected bodies, he slowly, almost lazily lifted his head, as if he were indeed the fabled golden Arellian lion, bestirring himself after a nap in the sun.

Or after a fierce mating with his lioness.

Something new, something different glowed in his deep blue eyes. And she could have sworn he was fighting a smile when he said, "How much does it provoke you that they were right?"

She blinked. Tried to brush away the lingering fog of pleasure. "What?"

"The ones who wished this upon us."

She nearly gaped at him. Of all the things he could have said. . . . But the moment she thought about it, a rueful smile curved her lips. He knew her so well.

"I know how little you like being given no choice. You've been fighting it your entire life."

"And you have not? You have always had less choice than I." The still new realization hit her. "Or," she amended, "at least you did."

"Now we're even," he said.

He lowered his head and kissed her, this time a light, gentle caress that nevertheless sent a tingle through her.

"I should have known," she said with a small sigh.

"I think I did," he said. "On some level. It's why I . . . dallied now and then, a few kisses, but this"—he shifted, pressing his body against hers—"this was only for you."

She was torn between kissing him and demanding to know who had been the recipient of those kisses, although she suspected Glendar's great-niece, who had made no secret that she greatly admired her prince.

Sorry, Avalyn. He's mine. He has always been mine, and now he is in every way.

"I was not so wise." Her voice was quiet. "Yet I dreaded losing you to your future more than anything."

"You are my future, Shay." He ducked his head, pressing his lips to the spot where her pulse beat in her throat. "And I'm glad you waited for me."

"It is the Triotian way."

"And you—we—are half-Arellian."

"Perhaps that's why it happened here."

He smiled as if he liked that. "It is not a bad place, this home of our mothers," he said, glancing around.

He froze. He was staring over his shoulder, and she could not see at what. She was loath to surrender the connection between them, but something about his reaction made it imperative. She moved to sit up, and he shifted to let her, but slowly, as if transfixed by whatever had caught his attention.

She wondered if she should dive for her weapons, if their follower had returned, or if—

She saw it then. Her eyes widened. For a moment she forgot to breathe.

It had not been just a flight of fancy, a by-product of consuming pleasure when she had felt the ground beneath them rumble.

It had.

The split boulder had moved. Had rolled apart, as if moved by an unseen hand with the power to move mountains.

For Graymist of pure heart and mind, the cavern of the waterfall shall open when the two halves are joined, when what is destined is completed.

The old man's words echoed in her head.

It hadn't been the rock he'd been speaking of.

It had been them.

"We're the halves," Lyon whispered.

She rose to her knees, staying close to him yet staring at the impossibility before them.

A breeze caught the spray of the waterfall at the base, which they could now see. And there was no mistaking the dark opening behind it.

Chapter 34

"DO YOU KNOW of a private place in the forest, or on your mountain here?" Rina asked with a vague wave upward as she took another sip of the dark, powerful morning brew in her mug. Even weakened with water, as Tark had done for her before handing it over with the explanation that he'd gotten used to the more potent strain of the beans it was produced from, it was more than she was accustomed to, and she guessed a small amount would go a long way.

He stopped his restless pacing—the man never seemed to be still if he was on his feet—and turned to look at her. "A private place?"

"Somewhere no one would stumble across."

He considered for a moment. "I know of a few, yes."

"Good."

He tilted his head slightly, brows furrowed. "Are you thinking of a meeting place? For the watchers?"

"I am thinking," she said, her gaze fastened on him, "of the pleasure of mating with you in the sunlight."

For an instant he just stared at her. And then, abruptly, as if his legs had given out, he dropped to the stone bench. In the glow of the huntlight he'd turned on when they had at last left his bed, she saw with satisfaction the tinge of color beneath the sun-toughened skin.

"Mating with me," he said harshly, "is something better kept in darkness."

"If I thought that, it never would have happened at all," she said. "Why is it so hard to believe I find you beautiful?"

He laughed, and it sounded even harsher than his voice had. "I do not have a mirror, but the faces of the people who see me serve as well."

"Perhaps," she said, her tone intentionally mild, "it is your glowering expression they fear."

He made a sound, a low, unintelligible sort of grunt that nearly made her laugh. She had heard this sound from Dax, from Dare, even from Lyon when they were uncertain of their ground with their women.

"You are, after all," she went on, "the man who laid waste to an entire battalion of Coalition troops. When you go about looking as if you'd like to do the same to them, anyone would be wary."

"You weren't."

"But I am notoriously stubborn," she said blithely.

"That," he said, his mouth quirking, "you are."

"And I," she added, putting all she had of sincerity into her voice, "have adored you since the first moment I laid eyes on you. No mark, no scar could change that."

"Rina, I—"

She was thankful when an odd knocking sound cut him off; she did not want to hear that while she might be Triotian, he was not. True, but she had Califa and Shaylah as examples of offworlders who had accepted bonding.

Belatedly she realized the knock had come in an odd rhythmic series, rapid, then slower.

"A signal, I assume?" she asked as he rose.

He nodded. "One of us."

He crossed to the hidden door. She stole the moment to watch with enjoyment; he had not put on his shirt—because she was wearing it—and she found the sight of his muscled back and shoulders, brushed by dark strands of the hair she had not so long ago had her fingers buried in, a much more potent brew than that in her mug.

As Tark reached to open the door, it occurred to her that her own skimpy attire at the moment might be a reason for concern. Quickly she darted back to the sleeping alcove and grabbed up her own clothing, reluctantly surrendering the worn yet comforting shirt she had pulled from his body last night.

She dressed hurriedly, wondering if she should stay here, hidden, if Tark would be embarrassed if her presence were revealed. She discarded the idea almost instantly. Not only would she not hide her feelings from him, she would hide them from no one else, either. Besides, anything worth the trek out here was something she wanted to hear.

She stepped back into the main room. One of the men she'd seen at the meeting was the first thing she spotted. His face was knotted with worry. Crim followed. And then she heard a female voice. She took another step into the room and saw Kateri, somehow still managing to look imperious even in a slightly frayed cloak.

The woman might be old, but her eyes were quick and clear. She spotted Rina the moment she moved. A gray brow rose, and that penetrating gaze flicked to Tark for an instant, but it was followed by a slight nod. And, Rina thought, a fleeting smile that looked almost as one of approval. And it warmed her, not for herself, but for the simple idea that someone cared enough about him to be concerned.

She glanced at Tark, half-afraid she would see embarrassment in his face. But she saw only a new grimness, and wondered what news Kateri had brought.

"Good morning," Rina said respectfully.

"'Tis well you're here," Kateri said, her voice brusque. "We received word this morning that what appeared to be a Coalition flagship was spotted leaving Darvis II two days ago. Our informant states it jumped to light speed almost immediately."

Rina sucked in a breath, her mind racing, doing the navigation in her head, the calculations. "It could be here by tomorrow, if they're any good."

Kateri nodded, and the approval was more definite this time. "We're sending a scout up, to monitor the rally point where the other ships are holding."

"You have a ship capable of reaching the far side of the outer moon?" Rina asked, surprised. From what Tark had told her, what ships Arellia had not decommissioned were in no shape to venture that far.

"No." To Rina's surprise, Kateri gave her a wink as she added, "But we have one capable of low orbit equipped with a Paraclon-modified scope."

Rina grinned at the mention of the eccentric but brilliant Triotian inventor. The old man had come up with a rather bizarre-looking arrangement of mirrors and hinges and beam enhancers that enabled his telescopes to, in effect, see around corners.

"Tark?" Kateri said.

He was, of course, pacing. He turned then, and Rina stared at him. Gone was the brooding, shadowed man she'd first seen when she'd arrived. Gone even was the intense but tender lover of last night. This was Captain Bright Tarkson, before the token promotion, the man who had been the pride of the Arellian operations force, the daring tactician, the fierce warrior who had held twice against impossible odds.

"We have little time," he said. "If this is true, and I have no doubt that it is, then our assessment was correct. The battle is imminent."

"You think they will strike on the anniversary?" Kateri asked.

"They are much about the significance, the symbolism of such things," Crim said. "And the people will be in the streets, even more than now."

"Easy targets," Tark agreed. "And yet . . ."

"What?"

Kateri's demeanor was one of respect, as if she knew she was now dealing with that warrior. Rina liked her even more for that.

"They might realize we would expect that," he said.

"And thus strike at a different time?"

"When we are off guard."

"Do we know which of their strategists survived?" Rina asked.

Tark glanced at her, and one corner of his mouth turned up slightly in approval. She felt a burst of heat within, so fierce she feared it must show in her face.

"We know Brakely is still with them," he said, his voice suddenly husky, as if he had indeed seen her response.

She fought to keep her voice even. "Then if he is in charge, anything could happen."

Tark nodded. "He is half the reason the Coalition was able to spread as far as they did. He is brilliant, and unpredictable."

"And trained by Califa Claxton," Rina said with some dread. "And if Mordred is truly here, if he is somehow back in the Coalition fold—"

She stopped as Kateri held up a hand. "We have news on this as well. One of ours swears he saw Mordred last night. Off in a corner in a taproom, plying a drunk with more drink." Her mouth tightened. "The drunk was Hared."

Rina knew from the groan that went around that this mattered more than just the confirmation of the presence of one of the Coalition's most infamous officers. Tark saw her expression and explained.

"He is not one of us, but is the one who first spotted the gathering of ships."

She frowned. "Does he have some other knowledge in addition to that?"

Kateri shook her head. "We know he has a weakness for drink, and it loosens his tongue. We've kept away from him."

"Then why would Mordred care? He would know already, would he not, about the presence of the ships?"

Tark went still. "Unless he did not."

"But if he is back with the Coalition, then . . ." Rina's words trailed off as his meaning registered. "You think he did not know, that he is still in disgrace?"

"And he hopes to use the coming battle to somehow regain his place?" Kateri asked. "It would fit what I know of him."

"And I," Tark agreed. "He always had a very high opinion of himself."

Unlike you, whose isn't high enough.

Rina shook it off, now was not the time. "This man from the inn who reported, he's reliable?"

"Yes. We have used the Mountaintop Inn for our meetings, when we needed to be far away from prying eyes in town," Kateri said.

Rina went still. "Mountaintop?"

"It's not really at the top," Kateri explained. "Only halfway, but it's the highest place there is."

"Mordred is on the mountain?" Her voice was low, tight. Tark, who had begun pacing again, stopped at the sound of it. She saw him get there.

"Dax's daughter," he said, in a tone that echoed her own. "And the prince."

"What better way to buy his way back to power?" She leapt up, began to gather her things.

"Are you saying," Kateri asked, "that the Prince of Trios is already here? And that he is on the mountain? With the flashbow warrior's daughter?"

"Yes," Tark said, sparing her the need to answer.

Rina asked, her tone clipped now, "Can someone show me the path to this inn?"

"I will take you," Tark said.

"You will be needed here," Kateri said.

"I need only the location," Rina said, not wanting him to be torn between his duty and her job here, which she had obviously not taken seriously enough.

"I will go with you," Tark insisted, then turned to face Kateri. "If those two are taken, this could end before it begins, and not in our favor. Do we really want the son of our closest, best, and right now only ally taken on our soil, when we could have stopped it?"

"It might make them fight all the harder," Kateri observed. Anger flared in Rina, and all her newfound liking for the woman nearly vanished in that moment.

"If Triotians fight, they fight to the fullest measure, whether it be for themselves or a friend. That you would even consider letting the rightful Prince of Trios be captured, because you think it will spur them on, is—"

"—Coalition thinking," Tark said, putting a gentle hand on her arm, restraining her. She bit back the considerably more severe words that had been on her lips.

"My apologies," Kateri said, with a nod to Rina. "I am too long used to being alone in this battle. I cannot make my own people see the truth, the danger, the need to prepare. I forgot Triotians are a different breed."

"Indeed they are," Tark said, so softly she knew it was intended for her ears only.

Kateri reached into the folds of her cloak. "Take this," she said, holding a small comm unit out to him. Rina knew they, along with weapons, were scarce. "At the inn you will be at the very edge of its range, but we should be able to get something through if the situation here changes."

He nodded, and took the device.

"Want my blaster?" old Crim asked Tark, holding out the oversized pistol.

"Tempting though it is," Tark said, eyeing the battered weapon that appeared held together with a few twists of wire, "you may need it more here. My own weapons will do."

He turned then, vanishing into the sleeping alcove. Rina allowed herself a moment of sweet memory of last night, of dreams fulfilled, of long-denied passion, and the glory of life where she had once thought there was only death. And then he came back, wearing the shirt she'd taken off, which gave her a hot sort of thrill again, deep inside, in the places only he had ever touched. He wore the familiar, battle-scarred leather coat and boots. The lethally sharp dagger was sheathed at his waist, and a disrupter was tucked into his belt. He had a small pack slung over one shoulder, the long gun she remembered over the other.

He was once more the fierce fighter of her memories, the man who had saved more lives than anyone could count with the willingness to lay down his own.

And now he was going to risk it again, for her. For all his talk of hostages, which was, she had to admit, based in truth, she knew deep down he was going as much for her as for Lyon, or the daughter of the man he called friend.

Without a word he took a place by her side. With nothing more than a nod, which got him one in turn from Kateri, he led the way to the disguised door.

To save her family, Bright Tarkson was doing what he had never wanted to do again. He was going to war.

And for all she knew, he could be walking into another ambush.

Chapter 35

DAX SAT AT THE command station, allowing himself a last moment to remember the times spent in this chair on the original *Evening Star.* Those days had been wild, reckless, and no doubt insane. But they had also been invigorating—exhilarating, and he'd felt utterly alive.

But then, war was also all of those things. Perhaps anything that teetered on the sharp edge of death on a regular basis was.

Trios had held off the Coalition for many years, thanks to the eternal vigilance of Dare and his council. But outside the group that knew at what cost even relative peace came, did anyone realize? Had the people, now that a new generation had come to adulthood, forgotten the price paid?

He'd been surprised when Dare had ordered the cornerstone of the old Council Hall, all that remained of the old building, to remain as it was, battered and cracked, with the words "Not Beaten" carved into it by some unknown, bloodied hand after the city had fallen.

His own instinct would have been to clear away and rebuild as soon as possible. But Dare had prevailed. The building had been rebuilt, defiantly bigger than before, but the cornerstone of the old one remained. More people passed that marker every day than anything else in Triotia, Dare had said, and he didn't want them to ever be able to forget what their laxity had cost. And the more Dax thought about it, the more he saw the sense in it and agreed.

And that, he thought now, not without wryness, was the difference between the skypirate and the flashbow warrior. Thinking.

They were well clear of guided Triotian airspace now, and the crew who had been clattering around amidships, settling in, were headed to their stations. With an inward grin he stood up as Rox, his longtime first mate, entered the bridge. They grinned at each other; it felt much like days past. Yet there was the awareness of change, of time. He felt a qualm. Qantar was gone. And Roxton was not Triotian, and the years that had passed had aged him. Gray predominated at his temples, and he didn't move quite as quickly as he had. But his mind was as sharp as ever, and Dax wouldn't have anyone else in his place as first mate.

"You look exactly as you always did, cap'n," Rox said, as if he'd read his thoughts. There were darker aspects to being one of the longest-lived races around, Dax thought.

"Bedamned Triotians, never do get old, do they?"

Dax whirled, and his grin returned as Larcos, the *Star's* resident engineer, scavenger, and brilliant inventor strode in. He, too, had aged a bit, but he'd been younger to start and so it wasn't quite as stark. Nelcar, the medical officer and the youngest of his original crew save Rina, was close on his heels.

"Larc," he said as he shook his hand, then turned to the other man. "Nelcar, didn't really expect you." It was true—the man was a fixture in Triotian medical circles these days, and much in demand.

"As if I'd miss the chance to fly with you again. Is it true, Rina is already there?" Nelcar asked. He'd always had a soft spot for their young navigator. But then, they all had.

"Yes," Dax said. "With Tark."

Nelcar's grin returned. "I heard he was alive. Good for her."

"Couldn't pick a better man," Larc added.

"Now all she needs is for you"—Rox thumped him on the chest—"to stay out of their way."

"She was little more than a child then," he protested.

"And she's years a woman now," Larc pointed out. "And we'll need Tark's knowledge of Arellia before this is over."

"Not to mention those crazy tactics of his." Rox grinned. "No wonder you two got along, he was as crazy as you."

Dax didn't—couldn't—deny either. The combination had been a large part of why the Battle of Galatin had ended the way it had.

"He is much changed," he warned.

"And who would not be, what he went through?" Hurcon had lumbered up to them, sparing a nod of greeting to his old crewmates. "I'd like to get my hands on the throat of the coward who refused to send aid."

"Wouldn't we all," Larc said.

The muttered assent ran through them all; even Nelcar, whose instincts were to heal, looked suitably grim.

"And yet he survived," Dax said. "And walked out of those mountains with most of his men with him. Carrying one of them, in fact."

"A feat worthy of a certain skypirate we once knew," Rox said.

Dax looked at them, his throat tight. They'd been through much together. Some of the crew might be grayer, some off to new, different lives, but when he'd put out the call, they'd all come.

He turned away for a moment, thinking he'd become soft himself, and not about to let his crew see the sheen of moisture in his eyes. He grabbed up the bottle of lingberry liquor he'd retrieved from the galley.

"A toast," he said, his voice tight, "to Qantar."

The one member of the bridge crew absent, the man who had been older than all of them when he'd flown on the *Evening Star*, had died last year, shortly after Dax had flown him home to Zenox. Qantar's entire family had been murdered there by the heavy hand of the Coalition, and his last wish had been to rejoin them. Dax had known that while the man had been glad to live to see the Coalition ousted, he'd also been only half alive since that day Corling and Mordred had slaughtered every man, woman, and child in his small town.

"To Qantar," they echoed with every swig as they passed the bottle around just as they often had after a successful raid.

Dax took the bottle back when Larc handed it to him. He set the cork back in place with a solid slap. Then he looked at them.

"We just now received a report from Tark that there is a Coalition flag-ship on the way. I won't insult you by saying this now will likely turn into something ugly, I know that you all suspected that. But as always, I will neither force nor expect any man to go along on a mission he does not feel right about. Now is your moment to withdraw, with no hard thoughts held against you. A shuttle will take you back."

Not a man spoke, they merely held his gaze levelly, except for Hurcon, who snorted with audible disdain at the very idea.

"All right, then," Dax said. "We fly."

They went to work as if they had never stopped. Rina's navigation station was empty, but she'd join them once they reached Arellia. In the meantime Califa would handle it, when she finished overseeing the weapons and ammunition stowage. The chatter among the crew, raucous and usually insulting, started up as if the intervening years had never been. Dax smiled inwardly as he listened.

The *Evening Star* would fly—and if necessary fight—again.

IN THE END, IT was so simple it seemed impossible. They got a bit wet slipping behind the waterfall, but once in the cave it was dry. Strangely dry, Lyon thought. The spray from the falls should have kept it fairly damp.

"There are tunnels," Lyon said as he peered into the darkness.

"Of course there are," Shay retorted somewhat resignedly.

He smothered a smile at her tone, and decided not to point out just now that they appeared to have slipped right back into the old, teasing ways. For all they had gained—and the memory of those golden hours in the sun would never leave him—they had not lost this, not as she had feared.

"Shall we go about this in an orderly manner, or just take a wild guess?" he asked.

"We've already tossed reason to the wind, why stop now?"

He laughed.

She glared at him.

Yes, things were back to normal. She'd made her decision in that meadow, and she wouldn't backtrack. No fluttery, embarrassed afterthoughts for his Shay.

And he knew he wouldn't have it any other way.

"All right, then." He looked at the back of the cave, at the three openings that appeared to be tunnels. He had no idea how far they might go. For all he knew, they came out on the far side of the mountain. Or didn't come out at all. Or both.

On impulse he gestured to the opening on the right. "Let's try that one."

"You're the Graymist," she said, and started that way.

He spared a moment to grin inwardly, thinking of all the things he loved about her. Why had they fought this for so long? Simply in rebellion against the idea that their destiny had been chosen for them? If so, this day had shown them it was a small price to pay for what they'd discovered, for the joy their union had brought them.

"Coming, Your Highness?"

He must have been standing there longer than he'd thought, if she'd dragged out the title to prod him with. With a laugh he let escape this time, he followed her. They walked into the tunnel.

And less than a minute later, they had found it.

Shaina stared at the large niche halfway up the wall of the dead end of the tunnel, then slowly turned to look at him.

The gold gleamed, seeming to capture every bit of what little light there was. A chalice here, a stack of plates, and a large, ancient-looking leather pouch from which spilled coins too many to even estimate a total.

And in the center of the display of riches sat a rather plain-looking object, a roughly hewn wooden stand in which sat a small sphere. Barely the size of his fist, it looked like glass, except that it did not seem to reflect its surroundings. The gold should have gleamed in the polished surface, but instead the orb swirled with the colors of oil upon still water.

Lyon felt drawn to it, pulled in a way much stronger than that urge to pick this of all the tunnels. He took a step forward, ignoring the gold piled before him, and focusing on the ball, the Graymist Orb. Odd, he would have expected something more ornate, something other than the simple wooden holder that looked as if it had been made out of wood scraps found on the forest floor. Perhaps it had been, for all he knew.

He reached out, touched the sphere. It flashed sun-bright, and he instinctively jerked his hand back. The brilliant light gradually subsided, until the orb emitted a barely perceptible but steady glow.

"I think you woke it up," Shaina said, her tone a mix of wariness and jest.

He studied it for a moment, watched for any changes, but the odd glow stayed steady. Slowly he reached out again. At his touch the light flared again, although not as blinding as that first flash. He pulled his hand back again, slowly this time, and just as slowly the orb subsided to that steady, faint glow.

Again he studied it. Shay stayed quiet, letting him think. She might not have his need to understand how everything worked—she settled for it working as it was supposed to—but she accepted it, even admitted it was sometimes useful, and a good balance for her more impulsive nature.

"You try it," he finally said.

She blinked. "What?"

"Touch it. I'm curious to know if it reacts to any touch."

Her mouth quirked. "Feeling special, Graymist?"

He smiled outwardly this time at this return to their normalcy. He would never be in danger of losing his humility, he thought. And could there be any more necessary quality in a king?

"If I were, it's ever your job to disabuse me of that notion," he said.

She colored slightly, she who was rarely embarrassed, and he wondered if she had had, as he just had, a vision of the future unrolling before them, of the partnership that would someday lead a world.

But she reached out and touched the orb. It flared, but not as brightly, and the light faded more quickly when she removed her hand.

"So . . . what does that mean?" she asked. "It responds to anyone, but a Graymist most of all?"

"Perhaps," he said, in a tone of great concentration, "it simply likes me better."

Her head turned; he could feel her gaze, and couldn't stop himself from grinning. He knew her so well, he saw a teasing retort coming. But then her face changed, softened somehow, and when she smiled every memory of those fiery, sweet moments in the sunlit meadow slammed into him, so powerful he wanted to take her to the ground right here and now and begin it all over again.

"It might," she said softly. "I certainly do."

He realized suddenly there was something he had forgotten. Something he had never said, since their world—and apparently the physical world around them—had been changed by that passionate encounter.

They rarely put their feelings for each other into words. It was a given, and they both knew it. But that had been when they had been lifetime friends and companions. Now they were mated, and the words took on a whole new meaning.

"I love you, Shay," he said quietly, putting every bit of emotion and need and gratitude and certainty in that unrolling future into the simple words.

She gave him no quick response. Instead, her expression became very solemn. And he knew she had heard everything he had tried to say. Of course she did, she understood him better than anyone.

"And I—"

Her words broke off as a low, somehow disturbing hum filled the air. They both turned to stare at the apparent source in time to see the orb change color, shifting to a dark, almost purplish blue, the color of a nasty bruise.

. . . the Orb has the power to warn that rightful possessor of the presence of enemies.

"Warning?" Shay whispered, clearly remembering the old man's words as he had.

"I don't know. Do you sense anything?"

She shook her head. "Nothing. Perhaps the screen blocks that, as well."

The color grew brighter. For an instant he hesitated, then reached out for the sphere. The moment his fingers touched the surface he could feel the pulses as if they were more than just light. And just as quickly he knew.

"Yes. Warning."

Gaze fastened on the cave entrance, she pulled the disrupter from her belt while he slipped the orb into an inside pocket of his jacket.

"The screen," she said. "Perhaps it will stop them."

"I don't think we can count on that. There may be a way through we haven't discovered yet."

She looked around. He could see her mind racing. "You have the orb?"

"Yes," he said.

Interesting that that was her first thought, that she had apparently accepted the old man's words, that it was the orb that was the true treasure.

"Do you know if it is more than one? Our four friends returning?"

He reached into his pocket and touched the orb again. Wrapped his fingers around it, wondering if that would make whatever signal the thing was sending clearer. Instinctively he closed his eyes.

"No. Just one," he said. "Still beyond the screen. Approaching the meadow."

Something flared in her eyes. He realized she was angry at the thought of that meadow, where they had first come together in that way that connected them for life, being invaded by whoever their pursuer was.

"It must be the other one," he said. "The man in the cloak."

"Are you guessing, or did that fancy rock tell you?"

"Guessing. Unless it is yet another, a new one."

"Too crowded on this mountain if it is."

She bent, grabbed a handful of the golden coins. She scattered them across the cave floor, in a path pointing toward the cave entrance.

"We can hide in the far tunnel, the gold will draw him," she said. "He'll see the treasure and be distracted by all that shine."

He looked, calculating the distance, the angles. "That outcropping," he said, pointing. "The way it sticks out, we won't be able to get a clear shot until he's clear of it."

"We? You mean you. He'll only be in view a couple of seconds, if he dives for that treasure. You're a better shot with a disrupter."

He flashed her a grin. "I am, though I never thought to hear you admit it."

"There are lots of things I never thought to admit."

Memories kicked through him again, heated images, and he doubted at this moment if he could hit a target if it stopped a foot in front of him. "And we will speak of those things," he said, his voice rough.

"Yes, Lyon, we will. But later," she said.

He was startled by her use of his name even now. Those golden moments in the meadow had transformed more than he'd realized, if he was no longer Cub to her at all. *About time*, he thought.

They moved then, quickly, and found a spot in the tunnel that was almost across from the one that held the gold. They wouldn't be able to see the newcomer until he was practically at the niche, so his first, probably only shot was going to have to count. He noticed the faint gleam reflected from the first few coins she'd scattered. They would be visible easily from the entrance, once the intruder looked that way. He also realized that light from outside would make their quarry cast a shadow; they might not be able to see him, but they would know at least some of his movements by that.

"He's past the screen," Lyon said suddenly.

"Yes. I can sense him now." Her hand tightened around her disrupter. "And definitely a threat."

They waited in silence for several minutes, and Lyon guessed she was also picturing how long a slow, wary traverse of the distance from the screen to the cave would take. This man took even longer, so he was either uncertain, or very cautious.

The silhouette that eventually appeared in the light from outside the entrance made it clear it was the man in the cloak. He looked around, then moved quietly toward the far edge of the cave wall, quickly slipping into shadow. Had they not known he was coming, he could have gotten alarmingly close. The simple fact that this man had had the strength of mind to ignore the evidence of his eyes and go through the screen, risking a serious burn, or was clever enough to find a different way, warned Lyon he was not to be taken lightly.

He heard the faintest of sounds, as if the cloth of the cloak had caught on rough stone. Then nothing. A long moment passed, and then the shadow was back in the middle of the cave, elongated, then suddenly shorter, as if he'd crouched down. Lyon knew he had spotted the first of the coins Shay had scattered. Brilliant, his woman was. A warrior worthy of the flashbow. He tried not to think of the danger that position would put her in. They were the greatest fighters in existence, but they were not invincible. More than one flashbow warrior had died protecting Trios or her royal family. How did his father do it, send the man who was his brother in all ways but blood out to quite possibly die?

He pushed the thoughts aside to focus on the immediate threat. They stayed frozen, barely breathing, making no sound that might betray their presence. The cloaked man stayed still as well, and Lyon knew he was listening. After what seemed an eon, he finally moved. Even as a shadow, it was clear he reached out and picked up one of the coins. Then another, and another, following the path Shay had left.

And then the shadow grew tall again, as he straightened to stand before the tunnel that held the niche where the gold lay. He leaned forward, and for an instant Lyon could see him, just as the man reached up and pushed the cloak's hood back, and it slipped off his head. Then he moved back, the instant gone far too quickly for a shot. But the lingering image of the face was seared into Lyon's brain.

His breath stopped in his throat. He felt Shay stiffen beside him—knew she had seen what he had. The same images, from old cinefilms and captures embedded in history texts, had probably flashed into her mind. She knew that the man before them was the man who had helped the infamous General Corling nearly destroy their world.

Mordred.

Rising star of the Coalition, disgraced by his commander's failure to crush the rebellion begun on Trios that had spread to the entire system and resulted in a humiliating defeat.

Mordred, who had promised to return.

Mordred, who had sworn vengeance on Trios and every Triotian left alive.

Once again, in a single moment, everything had changed.

Chapter 36

"TELL ME OF YOUR prince and Dax's daughter."

Rina glanced at Tark. They were pressing hard, moving at a speed that made talking a bit difficult. "Do you truly wish to know, or are you merely looking for distraction from this hike?"

"Would you shove me down this mountain if I said both?"

She nearly stopped in her tracks. Had the man actually made a joke? The old Tark had been full of them, using a dry wit and a flair for seeing the ridiculous to defuse many a tense situation. She had thought this Tark scoured of any sense of humor.

She made herself keep the smile that threatened inside, but it was difficult, for she could not help but feel she had aided him in finding this bit of the man he had once been. That in the indescribable sweetness of the night just past, he had found that not all his hope and joy had been destroyed. And if it were true, if she had given him that, she could live on it the rest of her life if she had to.

And now who's full of grim?

She shook it off, telling herself expecting fate to play one of its nasty tricks was tantamount to inviting it.

"That is a valid option," she said lightly, winning a faint smile.

"It wouldn't take much," he said wryly. "My vision sometimes throws off my balance."

She had wondered—he seemed so unaffected by the loss. But she should have known he, being Tark, simply refused to give in to it. And she was heartened that he would even admit it to her.

"But I am curious," he said in answer to her original question. "About Darian's son, and even more about Dax's child. It seems almost retaliation for fate to give him a daughter."

Rina laughed. "Oh, indeed. I think he panicked a little when he realized it. When he first found out Califa was pregnant, Dare told him he hoped it was a girl because it would serve him right."

He gave her a look that seemed oddly wistful. "I am glad you have such a family."

In that moment she renewed her determination to get him to Trios, where she knew he already had the kind of love and respect that abounded for the royals and the Silverbrakes. They would accept him for the hero he was, for what he had done, how hard he had fought. And her family would expand to include him; they would accept him as hers, if she wished.

She just wasn't sure he ever would.

It would just take him time to learn, she told herself. She wanted him for herself, for always, but she wanted him healed even more.

She turned her mind toward answering him. Perhaps hearing of such normalcy on Trios might help him along the journey he was only beginning.

"Lyon is intelligent, curious, and kind. But he is also tough of mind and will. He will be a fair ruler, and if need be a brave warrior."

"And the girl?"

Rina grinned. She could not help it. "She is the handful Dare wished upon Dax. Clever as a snowfox, and twice as quick. Adventurous to the point of reckless. And fearless."

"In other words, she is Dax all over again."

Her grin widened. "Exactly."

He smiled back, fully this time, warming her. "There was talk, when they were born . . ."

She nodded. "Of course Shaina will fight it. She does not take well to the idea it is destined, even though it's clear she loves him."

"Perhaps she thinks of him as a brother."

"I think she tells herself so. A way to protect against her true feelings."

"It's been done," he said, his voice taking on a neutral tone that somehow managed to sound pointed. "Sometimes you must use what defenses you have."

Little one. He'd called her that from the first moment, and it had irked her for a very long time, until she had come to care enough to forgive him that and more. Was he saying that had been for the same reason? To defend against his feelings? It seemed so.

"You truly thought of me as a child, then."

"I had to." He stopped walking. Turned to face her. "Because if I didn't, what happened last night would have happened then. I would have taken you, and used the threat of war and death to persuade myself it was acceptable. And I had no right." He lowered his gaze. "I have no right now."

She reached up, brushed the back of her fingers over his cheek, his jaw. "You have the right," she said softly, "because I gave it to you."

"And I fear you will regret it."

She chose her words carefully. "I see, now that I am older, that had you not had such restraint—"

"And Dax glaring daggers at me," he said dryly.

"That as well," she said, allowing a smile but continuing intently. "But had you not had such restraint, and then word had come as it did, that you were dead . . . I could not have borne it."

"Rina—"

"I know this," she said, forging on, "because I could not bear it now. So whatever comes, you had better make bedamned certain you stay alive, Commander Tarkson."

His gaze slid back to her face. Slowly, almost tentatively, as if he were still uncertain he had the right, he reached out to cup her cheek. "You humble me, Rina."

"I hope not," she answered. "You're already far too humble."

He smiled. "I believe I have an idea where Dax's daughter trained her spirit."

"I tried," she said sweetly.

He laughed, and she reveled in it. Just as she had reveled, more fiercely and intensely than she'd ever thought possible, in his touch, his body, his strength last night. There was, perhaps, nothing like giving tenderness and, yes, love, to a man who had known little of either.

They walked on, the path becoming ever steeper and the landscape wilder as they went. They reached the inn at a point when Rina was ready for a cool drink.

"Good placement," she said as they walked to the door beneath the swinging sign with a weathered carving of the mountaintop above them.

"Yes. It has been here an age, because of that. This mountain has many a tale told, of secrets and treasure and magic."

"I can see where all of that would intrigue my escapees. On Trios we are much more literal."

He smiled at her term for them. "Let us see what we can find out," he said as he pulled the door open.

"I KNEW IT."

Shaina heard Mordred's harsh whisper as she watched the man's shadow. From the glimpse she'd gotten of the actual man, he had not aged well. Of course, he was not Triotian, but still. . . . His hair was straggly, looked none too clean, and was oddly dark, as if he kept it so artificially. His ears, preternaturally large and protuberant, poked through the lank strands. His skin was still that same sickly white she remembered from her studies; it almost glowed in the dim light of the cave. The contrast was reminiscent of things found hiding under rocks, away from the light, and she suppressed an instinctive shudder.

The man's hair had also looked singed on one side. She remembered how merely touching the screen had burned her fingers. Going through that screen wasn't simple for anyone who was not Graymist.

Or was not with one.

She gave an inward, ironic grimace at how quickly she had slid from the world of logic and reason into the mist of magic.

They watched that shadow as the man moved ever closer to the niche, picking up the rest of the coins as he went. Most were Arellian novals, but she'd noticed a few Carelian ducas and even a couple of Romerian withals, those rarest and most valuable of all coins.

Shaina held her breath. Once he spotted the niche with the full treasure—minus the orb Lyon had—he should hasten forward. And for one brief moment between the outcropping and the other tunnel opening, they would have a shot.

They waited. He gathered coins. They watched the distorted shape of the shadow as he moved forward, following the golden trail she had laid. Five more steps, and he would see the niche, she thought. That would be their moment, when he was so distracted by the riches that he would be paying little heed to his surroundings. He would rush forward and into their line of fire.

Three more. Two. One. And there. He saw it now, he had to.

He stopped. Her hand tightened on her weapon. Lyon was the best, but a little redundancy never hurt.

Mordred didn't react. She frowned. He was standing in front of a pile of gold, silver, and gems, and he didn't even lean in for a closer look. Instead he stood there as if the niche held nothing more interesting than curlbugs and muckrats.

The top of the shadow moved, as if he were looking down at his hand and at the coins he had gathered from the main cave. Then he looked around again. He turned his back on the treasure and walked back the way he'd come, fully into the shelter of that outcropping of rock that blocked their line of fire.

For an instant she forgot to breathe. He had picked up the coins eagerly enough, why had he not gone forward to gather the even more valuable trove right in front of him?

There was only one answer she could think of. The answer that had been gnawing at her since the moment she'd realized their follower was Mordred. She hadn't really put it into words, but now here it was, undeniable.

He wasn't after treasure. At least not of the gold and jewels kind.

He was after Lyon.

The realization sent a shock through her. To Hades with this, she was going to take Mordred out, right now. She'd have surprise on her side if she rushed him—it would be enough. And Lyon would be safe, which was her job. In more ways than one.

Lyon must have sensed her tension as she readied herself for an attack. He held her back. And just his touch brought back sanity, as quickly as it had robbed her of it in the meadow. Her fury faded, and her tactical mind re-emerged.

They watched that damned shadow as Mordred turned again, and walked into the tunnel next to the one that held the niche. They had not yet explored the others, since Lyon had uncannily known exactly where to go, so they had no idea how deep they went.

What they did know was that the Coalition was ever thorough. Hadn't her father pounded that home to her countless times, with the king's help? Mordred might not be of the Coalition any longer, but some habits were hard to break.

She silently counted down the seconds as they waited. Every part of her wanted to put an end to this now, but she also knew the value of knowing your enemy.

It's not just knowing your enemy's weaknesses, Shaina. It's knowing their strengths, and how to use them against him.

Her father's words echoed in her head. And she reminded herself again that all her fury at him did not negate the validity of his lessons. And that had been one he had hammered her with.

If she was right, and Mordred was after a bigger treasure than a mere pile of gold, she had a duty to fulfill. She would have done it anyway, because it was Lyon, and he was the prince.

Now he was her life, her future, her very heart, and she would die to protect him and do it without hesitation. Of course there was a problem. As sure as she was of that, she was also sure he would do the same for her. And that could not be allowed to happen. If it came down to it, he was more important than her. He, of course, would argue that, but it didn't change the fact.

Lyon touched her arm. She saw in his posture he was ready to move at last, and wondered if the orb had somehow told him Mordred was on his way back. Her own sensing told her only he was here, not how close. She saw Lyon make a gesture toward the tunnel the man was in, then another with both hands, moving apart. She nodded.

They moved. Split up, taking positions, one on each side of the tunnel entrance. Shaina leaned forward slightly, straining to hear any trace of footsteps from the tunnel. She heard nothing but the muted rush of the falls outside.

"Close," Lyon whispered.

"Yes." The smug voice came from behind them. "I am."

They whirled, staring at the man approaching from the tunnel they just vacated, the man who had somehow turned their own tactic against them and gotten behind them. A full-sized disrupter was trained on them, and a frighteningly well-used laser pistol was tucked into the man's belt.

He laughed, no doubt at their expressions. They'd been taken like fools. They'd gotten self-sure with their earlier success. Of course, they hadn't realized then they were dealing with Mordred himself.

"Did you really think I didn't know you were in here?"

A sick sort of anger bubbled in Shaina, most of it aimed at herself. It was her job to protect the prince, no matter that she hadn't known it until a few days ago, or that it wasn't official or known. She clearly had much left to learn.

And now it appeared she never would.

But Lyon would, she promised silently. Whatever else, he would survive. He must return to Trios, go home to their people. She would see to that, whatever the cost.

"Point of curiosity," Lyon said, as casually as if asking after the weather, "just how did you get from here"—he gestured at the tunnel entrance they had so uselessly surrounded—"to there?"

"If you had taken the time to do a proper reconnaissance, you would have realized the tunnels intersect."

Shaina groaned inwardly. He was right, and that only fired her self-anger further. It had never occurred to her, or to Lyon; they had assumed the tunnels led somewhere or nowhere, to a goal or to distract from the treasure. It had never occurred to them that Mordred would be able to double back from some spot where the tunnels joined. This man had been famous for his efficiency. That much of it had been in the extermination of resistance did not escape her now.

"Contention valid," Lyon said, still in that same easy tone.

Either the words or that tone seemed to irk Mordred. "If you were Coalition trained, you would know better."

Shaina thought swiftly. If he merely wanted them dead, he would have killed them on the spot. So he had something else in mind. She could think of only one thing, and that was something that she could not allow to happen.

Keep his attention on you. Away from Lyon.

"Coalition," she said, as if the term was unfamiliar. "Isn't that that old band of miscreants who were driven out of the entire sector eons ago?"

Color flared in the pale skin.

"No," Lyon said warningly. She glanced at him, saw in his eyes the knowledge of what she was doing, trying to provoke Mordred into coming after her to save him.

She shrugged. "Nothing to me if he wants to long for the old days, like all old men do."

"You will be speaking differently soon, whore," Mordred hissed, "when you have a collar around your neck and learn your manners."

Shaina didn't have to look at Lyon to see his reaction—she could feel it, coming off him in waves. He knew too well the depth of that threat. Most people grew up thinking the phrase "worse than death" to be nonsensical, for what could be worse than dying? But Lyon knew what it meant, and so did she. Her mother and his father had taught them well.

She steadied herself. "In order for there to be Coalition slaves, there has to be a functioning Coalition, does there not?"

"You will soon learn how well we function." He looked at Lyon. "You most of all will learn. Triotian scum. You will pay for your father's crimes."

She hadn't really had any doubts, but this confirmation that Mordred indeed knew exactly who Lyon was still made Shaina's throat tighten.

"And I shall watch with enjoyment when the Sovereign separates your head from your body himself."

So he meant to take Lyon alive, Shaina thought. She could not let this happen. It would not happen. If she couldn't provoke him to an attack, perhaps she could convince him she wasn't worth killing. If he intended to hand Lyon over, he'd have to get him there first, and if she was free, she could see that that never happened. As long as he thought her merely a strumpet from Akasen Court, and no danger to him, she had a chance.

She just had to hope Lyon would understand.

"You don't need me at all, then," she said, as casually as if she hadn't just been poking a slimehog with a stick. She shoved her disrupter in her belt, but left it armed.

"Another step and I'll fry you where you stand."

"She's no danger to you," Lyon said. "She's merely a paid companion."

She let out a breath as he played along. "See? You have your main prize and all that gold, you don't need to bother yourself with a whore."

"So quickly you desert him," Mordred said scornfully. "No matter. You show me where he hid it, and I may spare you."

Her brows lowered. Hid it? When just minutes ago he'd been standing before it?

"Hid it?" Lyon echoed her thought. But then he went on, making no sense at all. "We never even found it, how could we hide it?"

"If you had not found the main treasure, you would not have left those coins as they were," Mordred said. "You would have gathered them up unless they were superseded by something of even more value. Something you found, and moved. You will tell me where."

Shaina was beyond puzzled. None of this conversation made sense. The treasure was practically within sight from where they now stood, yet Lyon was pretending it wasn't there. Pretending Mordred couldn't see it, as clear as if it were under the Trios sun.

Couldn't see it.

Was it possible? Could Mordred truly not see what was in fact right before him? Could the treasure be screened as the meadow had been? But if that were true, why had she been able to see it? She was with Lyon, but they hadn't been touching, as they'd had to be for her to get through the screen.

"I cannot tell you what I don't know. We found those coins, nothing more. Someone apparently got here before all of us."

Mordred was too focused on Lyon, Shaina thought. "Perhaps ages ago," she said. "Perhaps even your precious Coalition, before we chased them off like scalded blowpigs."

"Enough! I have wasted precious time chasing you around this be-damned mountain. I must be back by tonight, so you will tell me *now*."

Tonight? What was happening tonight? she wondered. This was all starting to feel very ominous, in a much bigger sense than simply their own dangerous situation.

Whatever made a man like Mordred feel urgency did not bode well. For anyone.

Chapter 37

THE MAN WAS still a machine, Rina thought. She wasn't hard pressed to keep up with him, but she was feeling the effort. Living so far away from everything had a side effect she hadn't considered: extra exercise. But then, this was also the man who had walked miles out of the mountains, horribly wounded, carrying one of his men every step of the way.

Not that she didn't appreciate his fast pace. She was feeling a sense of urgency herself, coupled with a bit of guilt that she hadn't pursued her original task of finding Shaina. The fact that both Dax and Califa had agreed the new turn of events took precedence didn't ease her mind at the moment. Not when Mordred, the right hand of the Butcher of Trios, walked this mountain with Shaina and Lyon.

Not when he walked this or any other world.

The innkeeper had described Mordred as a pale-skinned skalworm of a man, and shown them the direction he had gone. He had not seen anyone answering the description of Shaina or Lyon, although a man from the bar said he had seen two people yesterday, from a distance, heading up the mountain. He had told them where, and since it fit with what they knew from the trail they had thus far traversed, they had continued that direction.

"We will find them."

Had it not been for that urgency, Tark's quiet words, uttered without a trace of breathlessness, might have been annoying. She was going to have to add some mountain work to her regimen when she got home. They had been pushing hard, no casual ramble this. Shaina and Lyon had been on the mountain three days, and while they were likely moving much slower, they still had a lot of distance to make up. Even at triple time, they would be lucky to catch up with them before well into darkness.

And Mordred could be anywhere.

"Yes," she answered. "We will."

"You have said they are smart, and clever. The campsite they chose at the base of the cliff indicates they are also careful."

"Or aware someone else is here. Shaina has a . . . sense of such things. And they have been well trained, by the best."

"Including you."

She smiled. "I taught them of navigation, orientation and such. But mostly I'm afraid I taught them mischief."

He laughed. And it warmed her yet again, more so now that it was coming more often. "And what a joy that must have been for them, taught by one of Dax's own crew. For who would know better all kinds of mischief?"

She gave him a sideways look. "And what kind did you learn?"

He gave a one-shouldered shrug. "According to my parents, my mischief was not being like them, and wanting to learn those same weapons and tactics."

"I'm sorry," she said, regretting having asked. But she had wanted some glimpse into his past, some sense of who he'd been before he'd become who he was. "Some people cannot deal with reality, and turn a blind eye—"

She broke off, realizing that hadn't been the best choice of words. He gave her a sideways glance as they negotiated a narrow turning on the path.

"Don't alter your language for my sake, Rina. I do not take offense at the truth."

"Would that more would listen to it," she said.

His laugh this time held a tinge of bitterness. "I have an inkling of how Kateri must feel, shouting into the wind, having the people you are trying to warn deny there is any danger."

"They will learn soon enough," she said, her voice nearly as grim as his.

They had reached a stretch of path strewn with boulders of an annoying size, too small to block them, too large to simply step over. Times such as this she rued her relatively short stature. While it had helped her often, allowing her to be dismissed as no threat, at times like this it was a nuisance.

At the largest he reached back and offered her help. Normally she would have declined, but time was of the essence here, so she took his hand. He pulled her up with an ease that spoke of his strength. She wondered how many never looked past his obvious injury to see that he was still the same powerful warrior he had always been. In a way, she supposed, it was a similar sort of camouflage as her size, allowing people to dismiss at their own peril. Although anyone who looked at the man was a fool if they didn't see the danger there.

She had seen it. And had rushed in anyway.

She let go of his hand, afraid he would somehow sense the stream of memories that had flooded her. Memories of that that powerful body moving over her, beneath her, within her. Memories of the pleasure they had found, and his stunned surprise at the force of it.

She saw him flex the hand she had released, as if it were tingling just as hers was from the brief contact. With an effort she forced herself to concentrate on their progress. She wished either Shaina or Lyon had a communicator, but when they were off on these rambles, being out of touch was one of the things they treasured. For all their love of her, and the many times she had joined them on their treks at home, she knew that they were complete, with only each other. That they considered her welcome in their private world had never failed to touch her.

She wondered when they would realize they were meant for each other in all ways. *Soon*, she thought.

I wish you both the kind of bliss I have found.

She sent the thought out on the breeze, and then laughed at her own whimsy. Something about this place seemed to give rise to such silliness. And she set her mind to thinking of all the tales she'd heard since she'd arrived.

It was better than thinking of other things. Such as the fact that while Lyon and Shaina might be destined to be together forever, she had no promise she and Tark would last beyond this day.

THEY WERE TRAPPED here. They could do nothing, not while they were hemmed in by the cave walls. It was foolish enough, Lyon thought, that they had not explored, that they had not scouted the territory before getting distracted by the fact that they had found what they hadn't really believed existed. They couldn't trust that a dash for one of the tunnels would save them when they did not know where they led. They knew from Mordred that they intersected; perhaps that's as far as they went, perhaps it was only a useless half circle that began and ended in the same place.

They had to get out of here to have even the slightest chance, and he had no idea how to manage that.

"You will tell me, you know."

Mordred said it easily, with full confidence. A confidence he backed up by using his free hand to pull the laser pistol from his belt. He flicked the power switch, and a small yellow light atop the weapon came on. When it turned blue, Lyon knew, it would be ready. A fiendish weapon, it easily carved away pieces of flesh, cauterizing the wounds as it went to prevent bleeding and prolong the agony. Compared to it, a disrupter on full was a blessing, a quick death.

Lyon had never been afraid of physical risk, had grown up tackling the elements and geography. But in fighting, his early training had been in controlled conditions. Even if told to press him hard, his instructors were always aware of who he was and loath to injure him, so he'd been glad of the chance to later test his mettle in a couple of Coalition skirmishes and come away unscathed.

Only his father, or Dax, ever pushed him beyond the limit, and it was from their teaching that he bore what scars he had. Well, except for the one on his shoulder. That was courtesy of Shay, who as a child had jumped him from a tree as he passed under, laughingly explaining after the bleeding had been staunched, Neuskin applied, and he'd been pronounced fine, that not all enemies were polite enough to give warning.

She had always kept him on his toes, he thought now. And he knew what she was doing. She was trying to keep the man's attention on her. And while the man thought her merely a paid companion, it would work, at least until he became annoyed with her jabs enough to eliminate her because of that same assumption.

And once he threatened her, Lyon knew he would inevitably betray how much—how very much—she meant to him. And Mordred would realize he had the perfect weapon at hand. Either way, Shay seemed the most likely first victim. And no matter how much she would want it that way—and he had realized that despite the late discovery she was indeed flashbow warrior material to the bone—he would never let that happen. It was a conundrum, and he wasn't having much luck figuring a way out of it.

"But," Mordred said, with enough apparent pleasure at the prospect of torture that Lyon's stomach turned, "where to start?"

Shay continued her reckless taunting. "I'd say your shriveled manhood, but I'd guess it's already been removed."

He wanted to yell at her to stop it, but knew it would hand Mordred the one weapon he could not fight. He could use one of those magic screens just now, or whatever it was that prevented Mordred from seeing the gold. He wondered why the man hadn't considered the possibility, after he'd had to walk through the screen outside the meadow. Or perhaps it had failed? Or shut down somehow, once they'd made it past? But then wouldn't the one in here have failed as well, once they'd found the treasure? Perhaps—

It hit him then. A possibility. Not much of one, but all they had.

With an effort he quashed the anger that had flared in him the moment he'd realized who they were facing. Lyon had wanted nothing more in that moment than to smash this disgusting being like the skalworm he was.

But now, he had to convince the man otherwise. Convince him that he was cowed, afraid. With his likely opinion of anyone outside the Coalition, it shouldn't be hard. And he had his fear for Shay to draw upon.

"Just put that thing away, will you?" he said, letting a bit of that fear into his voice.

Mordred's attention switched back to him.

"I see you're familiar with this weapon."

Lyon tried to put fear into his expression, tried to eye the pistol as if it were a giant jumpspider, fangs glistening with venom.

"Then you know what it can do," Mordred said, his voice disturbingly gentle. "And I'm quite expert in its use, I can assure you."

It was an effort to hide the flare of anger. He knew too well of the man's expertise. Many Triotians had died, more had been maimed by this man and his favorite up-close weapon.

"Please," he said, putting a quaver into his voice. "Just put it away."

He felt Shaina staring at him. Had to hope she would stay quiet. That she would realize he had a plan, however feeble it was.

"Ready to talk?"

"I . . . you have to promise you won't hurt us."

The almost whimpering plea sickened him, but he could see from Mordred's face it was no more than he'd expected. The flash of pleasure he saw in the man's eyes sickened him even more.

Shaina moved. *Hold, Shay. Please, just hold a bit longer.*

He wished he could just send the thought to her unspoken. Now that would be a useful bit of magic.

She went still again, and for an instant he wondered.

"Tell me what I want, and I'll put this away," Mordred said, gesturing with the pistol whose light was now glowing a blue even deeper than the warning of the orb. The orb it now seemed more imperative to keep out of his hands than all the gold of the Graymist treasure.

The treasure that might save them yet.

"I . . . there was too much. To carry, I mean," he said, with the air of someone stumbling hastily through a desperate explanation. "In one trip. We were just coming back for the coins we dropped when you arrived."

That, he guessed, was the kind of greed a man like Mordred would understand. He knew he'd been right when a small, somehow evil-looking smile curved the man's mouth as he lowered the weapon slightly. "That's more like it. Now tell me where you put it."

"I can't."

The laser pistol snapped up, trained on him again.

"No, no," Lyon threw his hands up. "I just meant I can't tell you. I'm not very good with directions. But I can show you."

Again the man took the confusion and expressed cowardice and idiocy as only to be expected. No wonder the rebellion—and its success—had astonished the Coalition, if this is what they thought of everyone outside their own horde.

It had been their downfall.

And this time, it had gotten them out of the cave.

They walked into the sunlight, and Lyon drew in a deep breath. They had a chance now. They had room, cover, and there were two of them and only one of him. Together, they always had a chance. He glanced at Shay.

I love you, he thought fiercely, in the same way he had in the cave.

It was silly, it had been merely coincidence back there that she had stilled just as he had silently begged her to hold. But he did it anyway.

She winked at him.

Only when Mordred jabbed at him with the disrupter he'd thankfully switched to shock level, did he realize he'd stopped dead.

It was worth a try, he thought.

Run. Get away.

This time, he got an answer. It formed in his mind as if he were thinking it himself, only he knew he was not.

Not a chance.

In a split second, he simply accepted that it was all part of the whole, the destiny, amplified by the power of their mating, the establishment of the unbreakable bond. He had no time now to marvel at this new connection between them.

Right now he had to focus on keeping Shay alive. Mordred wanted him alive, but he had no reason to wish her so.

For now he had to stop wondering what else was going on, what it was that made it so imperative for Mordred to be back in Galatin, the scene of one of the greatest battles of the rebellion, by tonight.

Somehow he didn't think it was for tomorrow's celebration.

Chapter 38

THE KING'S SPAWN was supercilious and impudent, just as he had expected, unable to comprehend the full depth of his current situation. He would see that that changed soon, Mordred thought as they emerged into the meadow below.

It occurred to him that perhaps this was some kind of trick, to lure him outside in an effort to escape, or perhaps even turn on him despite his weapons and the fact that he had disarmed them. He doubted either of them had courage enough for that, however. Certainly not the woman.

It was she who was most annoying him, however. Not simply because of her insolence, her outrageous remarks, but because something about her continued to niggle at him. Before now, he'd shrugged it off, had assumed he had seen her in the brothel that catered to all tastes, including his own. He paid little attention to grown women, but he was naturally observant and thought he had probably noticed her without realizing.

But now that he was closer, it began to tug at him anew, as if there was something about her he was missing. Something important. It was not a feeling he enjoyed.

In fact, he was enjoying nothing about this except the fact that he had accomplished his goal and captured the son of Trios. He hated everything else about this world, almost as much as he hated Trios itself. The two places were so closely allied as to be one now, with their ridiculous Mutual Interest Pact, and the fact that the two most powerful men on Trios mated with Arellian women. He snorted. That absurd bonding ritual, as if there was something different, something more about their pairing than the simple, physical act.

He realized suddenly they were nearing that fiendish barrier, whatever it was that guarded this meadow. Had he not been so certain this was the way they had come, he never would have found this place. They had been there one moment, vanished the next, even their footprints. But he was certain. Slowly, he had moved forward, watching only his own feet as if he half expected them to disappear as well.

The sizzle of that unseen barrier had knocked him flat. He'd used his disrupter on it, set on low for fear of rebound. It had failed to break down the barrier, but the invisible force had scattered the weapon's energy along the curve, illuminating a sort of bubble over the entire place. That had inspired the idea of using the laser pistol to carve a hole. It had worked, although the hole closed back up quickly, so quickly that it had singed his hair and his left hand as he dashed through. He had wondered for a brief moment how his quarry had gotten through, but didn't let it stop him. He had been so close he couldn't bear to wait any longer.

And now, he had his prize. The key to everything was in his possession.

He should just kill the woman, he thought. She was a nuisance. Even though she had settled into silence at last, something about her mere presence irritated him. He glanced at her, although he kept his disrupter trained on the boy prince. It niggled at him again, that feeling he'd missed something.

He suddenly realized they were almost to that blasted barrier. "Stop!"

The two obeyed. At least they realized who was in charge, Mordred thought.

"Enough of this. Where is it?"

"It's right over there," the prince said, gesturing rather vaguely toward the trees.

Mordred eyed him suspiciously. "How did you get past the barrier?"

"Same way you did."

Fury spiked in him. Did this Triotian take him for a fool? "You dare lie to me? You have no laser pistol."

The prince met his gaze. Odd, he'd thought Triotians all had green eyes, but this one's were blue. A legacy from his mixed parentage, he supposed.

At last, it struck him. The niggling became a full-blown explosion in his mind. He whirled to look at the woman. The structure of her face, her impudent grin, her arrogance . . . her eyes.

Eyes the color of jade. Eyes he had seen before.

The eyes of the man who had orchestrated their defeat, their ouster from this wretched planet.

Dax.

"You're his," he breathed in shock. "You're the spawn of that devil with the flashbow!"

She met his gaze with an infuriating ease, not a trace of fear or even trepidation in her face. It was so clear now, he cursed himself for not having realized before who she was. He had faced her father in the last battle for Galatin. The damned man had blasted Corling's own ship out of the sky with that rattletrap converted cargo ship of his. He and the general had fortunately been on the ground at the time. He had never seen Corling so enraged, and he had thought ever after that that had caused his downfall. The rebellion on Arellia had been Corling's last chance at redemption, and his fury at the loss of his ship to a former skypirate had clouded his judgment.

Mordred had spotted Dax later, on the ground, and had nearly taken the man out himself. Would have, had Corling not insisted they continue the siege of the Council Building. A fruitless effort, Mordred could have told him. Whoever was inside, coordinating the defenses, was clearly a pure fighter. A tactician of no small talent. And fearless. Only later had he learned the man was one Captain Tarkson, a young Arellian, amazingly. And clearly a much better warrior than Corling himself.

That had been his real mistake. He should have relieved Corling of his command. The troops would have followed him, he was sure of it.

"Reminiscing?" the woman asked, her tone so sweet as to be sickly.

He gave a sharp shake of his head. He had no time to give to shock. And it was dawning upon him that his triumph had just been magnified. Bringing the Sovereign the Prince of Trios was one thing, but add the daughter of the man who had driven them from their stronghold on Arellia? He would sit at the leader's right hand, become his closest confidant, with more stature than he had ever dared hope!

"My father drove you off this planet once, don't think he won't do it again."

The woman's snide tone sliced through his pleasant vision like a laser pistol through cinefilm. He snarled a vicious curse at her.

"Or maybe," she said easily, as if merely discussing the weather, "I shall do it for him."

His fury broke loose. He raised the disrupter to her. His finger tightened on the trigger.

Something hit him. Hard, fierce, square in the back. He staggered. Went down. The prince, on top of him. How had he worked up the nerve?

He twisted, trying to raise the disrupter. His foe pressed him back with shocking power, so hard he could barely breathe. Where had such strength come from? He fired his weapon, even knowing it would go wild, hoping the shock of a disrupter fired so close would terrify this princeling. And yet he never lessened his grip, never even flinched as the weapon went off bare inches from his head. The blast hit the screen, sizzling along the curve, lighting it up.

The prince struck him in the face. His ears rang. He was as much stunned by the power of it as by the actual effects of the blow. And another blow, even stronger. He clawed back, flailing, uncertain if he was doing any damage. For the first time he thought he might have underestimated things. He might have to settle for bringing in the man's body. Again he tried to maneuver the disrupter.

Something hit him in the gut, hard. The woman. She had kicked him. Fury raged through him. Why couldn't he simply shake off this vermin? He struck out with one hand, hoping to draw his prey into releasing his weapon hand. The man didn't even wince. He absorbed the blow as if it were no more than a tap.

This was impossible. Next to himself, Mordred, this princeling was nothing, a foolish relic of a more foolish tradition. These rebels had merely been lucky, and aided by the assignment of fools like Corling to crush them. And yet this one had him down. Rolling in the dirt like a common foot soldier.

The woman, the spawn of that piece of galactic trash, kicked him again, a fierce, solid blow to the belly.

Rage swept him. Enabled him to land a sold blow this time. And a second. And he took great pleasure in the blood that now flowed from his adversary's lip and nose. It had been a long time since he'd fought on such personal terms. He preferred the distance and scale of large bombs and torpedoes. But there was a certain satisfaction in this. Especially now that he had freed the hand that held his weapon.

And then the woman struck again. She kicked the disrupter out of his hand with even more force. The weapon went flying. It hit that invisible barrier, sizzled and popped. It fell back, blackened and useless.

In the moment when he himself would have gone in for the kill, the prince released him. He grabbed the woman, and pushed her through the barrier, despite her protest. The surprise of seeing her go through it without even a spark immobilized Mordred for an instant. And in that instant the prince followed, just as unscathed.

Mordred scrambled to his feet, bellowing his wrath. He ran at the barrier. Screamed as it seared him. He drew back, reaching for the laser pistol at his waist, ready to cut a hole in that infernal screen. In that instant an arm shot back through the barrier, yanked the weapon clear of his belt, then pushed hard against his chest.

He fell back. Stumbled. Realized what had happened. That he was unarmed and trapped.

On his knees, he howled. It seemed to echo back at him from the barrier, and his own rage filled his ears.

"THAT WAS *MORDRED*, and you left him alive."

Lyon looked at her, and his voice held that same deceptive calm it had in the cave. He seemed oblivious to the blood trickling from his nose and lip, and she used her own sleeve to mop at it.

"Did I?" he asked mildly.

She stopped. Her gaze narrowed. "Didn't you?"

In answer, he merely held up one hand.

She stared at what he held. The laser pistol Mordred had threatened them with.

"That's what you reached back to grab?"

He nodded.

"But why—" She cut herself off as the memory of Mordred's words came to her. "That's how he got through."

He nodded again. And the true brilliance of what Lyon had done struck her.

"Did you know he couldn't get back out either, without it?"

"I wasn't sure until the disrupter hit it and bounced back."

"And that quickly you decided on this course?"

He shrugged. "He will singe himself to pieces, bit by bit, trying. He will die slowly, painfully. And a short distance from the treasure he sought, without ever knowing. A more fitting end than a clean death for such as he, is it not?"

She flung her arms around him. She was prouder of him in this moment than she had ever been. He held her, grinning. She looked up at him. Opened her mouth to speak the words she hadn't gotten to finish when Mordred had interrupted them.

An explosion echoed up the mountain. For the second time in this day, the ground shook beneath them.

They both turned. A pillar of smoke arose from below.

Another explosion. More smoke. And then more of each.

Galatin. Under attack.

Neither hesitated. They ran toward the battle.

Chapter 39

"YOU HAVE TO go back."

It nearly ripped her heart out to say the words. Rina wanted nothing more than for him to stay with her, to stay safe, away from the chaos that had erupted below. They could not see from here; their view was blocked by trees and the rock of the mountain itself, but she knew the sounds too well. Soon clouds of smoke would rise, and likely already citizens had fallen. Galatin was, once more, under attack.

Tark had given, given, and then given more to this world, near unto his life, and they despised him for it. To ask him to give again, when he was battered and scorned, was beyond the pale.

And yet she knew she must. She had spent enough time now around the palace, had been on the edges of discussions of the council, and most of all had heard the king and queen's impassioned discussions with Dax and Califa, and she knew that Trios would fight, just as they had when Arellia had first followed them in rebellion against the yoke of tyranny.

And if her world fought, she must fight. And since she could not, not until she completed her true mission, she must do the only thing she could. Galatin must hold until assistance arrived. Tark was their best, perhaps only hope. She must release Arellia's finest warrior to do what he had to. No matter that it left her bleeding inside.

"They will hold," he said, then amended it. "For a while. We must find the prince. And Dax's daughter."

"I will find them." Rina's mouth tightened as she looked up the mountain. They were close now—they had to be, they were near the summit. "As I should have done before now."

The sound of explosions continued. She could feel the ripple of them under her feet.

"You were . . . distracted. For my part in that, I am sorry."

Her head snapped around. "Don't you dare say that. I am not sorry. I could never be sorry."

"I was speaking," he said with deceptive mildness, "of getting you involved with the watchers."

"Oh." Abashed, her temper ebbed. "You still must go. The attack has begun."

"This is more important just now." She nearly gaped at him. Had Tark, the warrior down to his soul, truly just said that? "Did you really think I could regret what has happened between us? It may be foolish, it may be the wrong choice for you, but Eos, Rina, it—and you—are the most extraordinary thing that has ever happened to me."

"And that is unforgiveable. On Trios you will find things are much different."

He drew back slightly. In reaction to her assumption that he would be going to Trios?

Or to her assumption he would still be alive to go anywhere?

"You listen to me, Bright Tarkson, I mean what I said. You come back. If you get yourself killed I will make your ghost miserable for eternity."

He blinked. Then, unexpectedly, he grinned. "So if I die, you're going to haunt me? Backward, is it not?"

She didn't care how ridiculous it had sounded. It was a small price to pay for that grin.

Another explosion, the largest yet, echoed up the mountain. Regretfully, she knew they could no longer stand here and talk of what she most wanted to speak of. And as much as she wished he would not go, she knew he would, so it might as well be now, in the beginning, before the Coalition made it impossible for him to even get there to fight.

"You must go," she repeated. "They need you."

"And I," he said slowly, "need you."

From this man, it was a stunning admission. Both of his own feelings, and perhaps more importantly, his right to them. It was a small step, but it was a step, and for now it would have to do.

"I will stay alive, Rina. We have much to discuss, you and I."

He grabbed her then. Pulled her hard against him, and kissed her. The heat that exploded between them obliterated, for a moment, even the sound of the attack.

And then he was gone. Since she had told him to go, feeling so bereft seemed silly, but there it was.

She took heart from the knowledge that the hero of Galatin would fight again, and the Coalition had a big surprise coming.

SHAINA THREW out a hand as she skidded to a stop, halting their headlong race down the mountain.

"There is someone approaching."

Lyon came to a halt beside her. "Danger? Or someone fleeing the attack?"

"I don't think so." She didn't clarify which, so he assumed the no was for both possibilities. She glanced at him. "Check your shiny rock."

He grinned at her, suppressing a wince as the action tugged at his sore mouth and nose. He pulled the orb out of his pocket. It appeared as before—cool, with that odd sheen on the surface. No dull, bluish pulse. "It agrees."

"But it might be wise to see them before they see us, even so," she said.

He agreed, and they stepped off the path and back into the trees, where they could see but not be seen.

"Be nice to know what the real range is on that thing," she observed as they crouched behind the low branches of a tall groundsweeper tree.

"When there is no screen involved? Yes." He looked down the mountain. A spiral of smoke was visible even above the trees now. They had made rapid progress now that they were going downhill. "We may learn that soon."

"If it reacted as it did to one man, it's going to burn a hole in your pocket before we ever get to Galatin."

"I may wish for an off switch, with enemies all around," he agreed. "We should have a plan. Just wading in without one isn't going to be much help."

Their first instinct had been to hasten back to Galatin, and they had set off at a run. The first thing that occurred to him was to make their way to the Council Building, where the last great battle for Galatin had taken place, but once they got closer, circumstances might dictate differently.

"Let's deal with whoever this is first," she said. "Then we'll figure out—"

She broke off suddenly as a figure darted quickly from the cover of one boulder to another, taking care even though the battle was far below.

"What in Hades?" she whispered.

"I don't know," Lyon answered, his mind racing at this sudden, unexpected appearance. He looked at Shaina, whose brow was furrowed. She shifted her gaze down the path. It appeared empty, not a flicker of movement.

"Might as well let her know we're here," he said.

Shaina nodded. She lifted two fingers to her lips and let out the piercing whistle that, to his lifetime annoyance, he had never been able to match.

"You didn't need to be so loud, I'm right here."

Shaina whirled, and Lyon's head snapped around as a petite female with a short cap of Triotian blonde hair stepped out from behind the large rock barely fifteen feet away.

"You've lost none of your stealth, I see," Lyon said with a wry grin.

Shaina, a little to his surprise, ran to her, enveloping the woman they'd thought of as both sister and aunt in a welcoming hug. He supposed it had something to do with the way she'd left things on Trios. He followed, giving Rina a hug of his own. She had ever been there for them, and was the bridge between them and his or Shaina's parents, on those occasions when one was needed.

"Did he send you?" Shaina asked.

"Not exactly," Rina answered. "He was coming after you himself, but I thought it might be less . . . volatile if I came instead. Your mother agreed. He surrendered." Rina grinned. "She's the only one who can consistently beat him at anything."

Lyon was glad to see Shaina smiling widely despite it all. He took her hand and squeezed it in support. She looked at him, her gaze lingering for a moment, and that smile curved her lips, that soft, gentle smile that was so unlike the wild, reckless companion he had always known.

"Well, well," Rina said, crossing her arms before her as she studied them both. "So it finally happened."

Shaina sucked in a breath and lowered her eyes, and Lyon thought he saw a tinge of color in her cheeks. His cool, unflappable Shay, self-conscious?

"Is it so obvious?" he asked.

"To one who loves you both and knows you well? Yes."

Shaina looked up then. "We have so much to tell you."

"I'm sure. But—"

"There's a battle on," Lyon said. "And we need to get there."

"Yes. So I suggest we get moving. I don't know what the status is down there, so we'd better be on watch for Coalition scouts or patrols on the way."

"We'll have warning."

Rina glanced at Shaina. "No, even more warning," she said. "He's got a fancy rock now."

Rina blinked. Shifted her gaze to Lyon.

"It's a long story," he said.

After a moment she nodded. "And I have one for you as well. But for now, we need to go."

There was really no way to talk as they headed down; the path wasn't really wide enough for two, let alone three. So they focused on a quick pace, and as the explosions from below picked up in intensity and frequency, they picked up speed. They went on and on, covering ground quickly, steadily. Moving at three times the pace they had on the ascent, he thought they just might make it to the bottom by nightfall.

Which could be either benefit or detriment, he thought leaping to dodge a rock. Darkness would hide them, but make it harder to see what was going on. And now the explosions had lessened, and knowing why became crucial.

He pondered possibilities as they went, trusting his body to handle the job of getting there. He was feeling the same way he did when his blood was up and he was racing across some forbidding obstacle at home. As if he couldn't put a foot wrong, and if he did, he would recover, or even convert the misstep into further momentum. Everything was working, and he was starting to feel as if he could run straight down this mountain without pause when Shaina, in the lead, threw up a hand and stopped.

They skidded to a halt. They had nearly reached the outcropping of rock they had climbed to gain a field of view downward when Mordred—although they hadn't known then it was him—had been behind them.

"Someone is here," she whispered as he and Rina came up beside her.

This time Lyon checked the orb immediately. It was unchanged. Not an enemy then. He spared a brief moment to wonder how he had come to so trust it after one experience. What if the warning about Mordred had been its last, or its only? What if it only worked inside the screen? What did he know of it? Perhaps it was calibrated somehow, and would warn only of great dangers and pass over lesser ones, such as someone outnumbered three to one. Did it even know they were no longer alone?

More likely the question should be are you insane, wondering that about a "fancy rock?"

Even just thinking the words Shaina teasingly used warmed him. And then something brought him sharply out of his ill-timed musing. A man stepped out from behind that outcropping of rock.

Lyon stared. He heard Shaina gasp in shock.

"But you're supposed to be dead!" she exclaimed.

Indeed, Lyon thought. But there could be no doubt—he'd seen the pictures, watched the cinefilms too often to mistake him. Without the eye patch, yes, but there was still no doubt.

"Bright Tarkson," he breathed, awe echoing in his voice.

The man looked startled. And, oddly, Rina was looking at them with the same kind of pride she had always shown when they'd done something particularly clever.

And then she was looking at the man, the hero of Galatin, a man they had never expected to ever see in the flesh.

"I told you," Rina said to him.

Chapter 40

"WELL, WELL," SHAINA said, crossing her arms, purposely mimicking Rina's reaction to them.

She realized now how obvious it must have been, simply because it was just as obvious here. The electricity between this woman, who was so much a part of their lives, and the man they'd known only from history, the vaunted hero of the siege of Galatin, one of the few men her father and the king spoke of in tones of utter awe and respect, was palpable.

They had been but small children when her parents—and Rina—had gone to stand with the Arellians, but the memories were vivid still. That Rina had met Tark—he was so famous on Trios only the one name was necessary—during the Battle of Galatin years ago was well known. Shaina herself, along with Lyon, had grown up hearing tales of his courage, his fierceness, his brilliant tactics. Tales told with sadness at his heroic death, still and ever fighting.

But Shaina had never realized that for Rina it might have been more than that.

So was this what had been behind that touch of sadness she had always sensed in Rina? Had she found her one true mate and then thought him lost to her forever? And since he was obviously not, as they all had thought, dead, why had he not communicated with her? How had she found him now?

She shook her head sharply; she was starting to sound like Lyon, ever questioning, analyzing. Maybe what had erupted to life between them had simply made her overaware of such things. Or curious about things she had always put off wondering about.

"So you're the one," Lyon said. "I always knew there was someone she was missing."

Tarkson looked oddly uncomfortable. Which made no sense to her. The man had faced down horrific odds and won, why would he be—

"Why did you let everyone think you dead?" she demanded. "Why did you let Rina think you dead?"

"Shaina, he had his reasons, now—"

"I know, I know." She glanced at the woman she loved as if she were blood. "He's the Hero of Galatin and I should be polite, but when have I ever been when someone I love is hurting?"

"Never," Lyon said in that mild tone that always somehow soothed her.

"You hold nothing back when it is someone you love."

She wasn't sure he'd intended it, but images of that precious, golden time in the sun swept through her mind in a rush. It was so powerful she could almost feel it all again, their bodies joined, the joy flooding her and wiping away any lingering resistance to the destiny of it with the sweet knowledge this was right, meant, and as it should be.

"I—" Tark's voice broke slightly as he spoke for the first time. He cleared his throat and tried again. "I am glad she had you."

"I love you both, but this is not the time," Rina said. "Hold it until we are all home again."

So, he was coming home with her, Shaina thought. Or at least, Rina thought he was; she had caught a flicker in his visible eye that made her think he wasn't quite sure. She sized him up anew, this time not as the historic figure she'd learned so much of, or even as the man her father had such admiration for, but as the man Rina obviously loved.

She could certainly see why. He was the kind of man who would stand out in any throng. His hair was as dark as Lyon's was golden, as dark as her father's even, although shorter. He was as tall as Lyon, and despite being noticeably older, was as lean, and looked even tougher. Or rougher. His unshaven jaw was strong, his gaze steady. The eye patch detracted little, in her view. In fact, it added to the air of toughness, made it clear this was a man who would let nothing short of death stop him.

She was sorry he had been so damaged, but that he had survived it spoke to her of strength and courage. And made the stories about him even more believable. Bright Tarkson, the hero of Galatin, here in the flesh. This was truly becoming a memorable trek.

"I didn't expect to catch up to you," Rina said to Tark then.

"This is a good spot to do some reconnaissance," he said. "The city is masked from here down. And the first wave appears to have ebbed."

"Knowing them, the first demand for surrender has already been made," Rina said. "What have you seen?"

"It appears they have not changed their tactics. Starting with lots of firepower from their ships to soften things up. I don't think they'll dare send fighters, not over Galatin itself, they know of our defenses."

"And then wave after wave on foot?" Rina asked. "As before?"

"That would be my guess."

"Where will they put them on the ground?" Lyon asked.

Tark turned his head. "There are a few possibilities . . . Your Highness."

Lyon quickly shook his head. "I require no such address from the hero of Galatin," he said firmly. "Call me Lyon."

Again Shaina saw surprise in the man's expression. And somehow sensed it was at more than Lyon's unpretentious request. Belatedly she realized she had dispensed with all proprieties when she'd blurted out her earlier question.

"I," Shaina said with a wide smile, "am just Shaina."

Tark shifted his gaze to her. And somehow it softened, although it seemed hard to credit in such a strong face. "You are very like him," he said quietly.

However she felt about her father just now didn't matter. Not in front of this man. Not when he spoke with such admiration and respect. "To my pride, and occasional dismay," she said.

Tark smiled. It changed his entire appearance, and she saw in that moment the dashing, bold warrior Rina must have known all those years ago. She felt Rina's look, and gave a one-shoulder shrug. Her anger at her father seemed rather pointless now. As perhaps it had been all along.

"He deserves nothing less," Tark said. And she saw in his expression a touch of humor, and knew that he meant the dismay as well as the pride.

"Indeed he does," she said wryly.

Lyon had been watching them, smiling. But now he scanned the sky. "They're staying safely distant. No sign of small fighters in the air."

Tark nodded. "I'm sure they haven't forgotten we have fusion cannons protecting the city, thanks to your father." His mouth twisted. "Although I doubt they've been manned in some time. We can only hope someone in Galatin still knows how to use them."

Shaina looked at him curiously. "You don't know?"

"I . . . have been out of the city for a long time."

Something flashed between he and Rina, and Shaina saw both pain and a touch of anger in Rina's face. There was obviously more to this, but she doubted they would discuss it now.

"What is the status, in the city?" Lyon asked. "Are they prepared?"

"Some few are. Most are not. They would rather believe this day would never come."

"Did they have no sign this was coming? Enough Coalition ships for a planetary attack would be hard not to notice," Shaina said.

"Unless you were determined not to," Rina said, her tone sour. "Most of Arellia seemed focused entirely on this party that's been going on for days now."

"I'm surprised they didn't hold until the anniversary," Lyon said. "They care so much for symbolism."

"We believe that was the original plan," Tark said with a nod, and Shaina thought she saw approval in his gaze. But not surprise. He looked like a man whose expectations had been met.

My Lyon will exceed them, sir, you will see.

Even in her thoughts she accorded him the esteem he deserved, so often had she heard her father speak of him with respect, and sadness at his death.

"Does my father know you are alive?" she asked suddenly.

Tark blinked at the sudden, unconnected question.

"He knows," Rina said softly.

"Good," Shaina said. "It will gladden him."

Tark lowered his gaze, as if even this embarrassed him. Rina smiled at her. "Why did they change to today?" she asked.

Tark looked at her once more. "We think because they realized that if we spotted them, we would expect it that day." He let out a disgusted sigh. He looked down the mountain toward the spirals of smoke, fading in the wind, now, in this lull. "They give us too much credit. Had they known how ill-prepared Arellia would be, they would have sent a smaller force sooner and still won."

Lyon frowned. "Did your people think they were gone forever?"

When Tark did not speak, or even look at them, Rina explained quickly. The evidence ignored, the resistance to the idea, and to the people who tried to sound the warning. Including, Shaina guessed, Tark. How could they have ignored this man, of all men?

"Do you think they are attacking elsewhere, other planets in the sector as well?"

"It would not surprise me," he said, turning back to them. "They have been gone for a long time, enough time to rebuild and advance their weapons and ships and other capabilities."

"And a simultaneous return across the sector would be just the kind of audacity I would expect from them," Rina said. "They've done it before, in other sectors."

"Yes. Corling was a genius at that much."

Shaina nearly jumped. "Mordred," she exclaimed.

"Yes," Lyon said.

Rina looked from one to the other. "That is why I left Galatin amid all this to find you, we learned he was on the mountain with you."

"He still is," Lyon said.

Shaina laughed, she couldn't help herself. "Thanks to my clever Lyon."

They explained as best they could, given the peculiar nature of what had happened. Rina was as literally minded as she herself was, and when they finished she looked doubtful. Shaina couldn't blame her.

"Believe me, I understand," she said. "Had I not seen it all for myself, I would not believe it."

"You're Graymist," Tark said to Lyon. He, Shaina noticed, did not look as skeptical.

"Yes. My mother."

"I grew up hearing such tales. The Graymist treasure was supposed to be on this mountain."

Lyon glanced at her. She nodded. "It is," he said.

Tark's brow rose. "You found it?"

"Yes."

"And left it?"

"Escaping seemed the wiser course," Lyon said matter-of-factly. "And it is safe enough in the cave." He didn't, she noted, explain about the screen there, it had been enough to try to explain believably the screen that protected the meadow—which now held Mordred prisoner.

"We will need the whole of the story," Rina said. "But I think we should take advantage of this lull while it is still on."

"Of course," Lyon said. "We should not have spent so much time here."

"Some things," Rina said quietly, turning her head to look at Tark, "deserve time, even if stolen."

Shaina glanced at Lyon. Tried that odd trick again. *He's hers*, she sent.

And so he is ours. It came back even more clearly than before; this apparently got better with practice.

"When will they start again?" Shaina asked.

"Nightfall, I think," Tark said.

Rina nodded. "It is a familiar tactic. War is more terrifying at night, in the darkness."

"Then we had best hurry," Lyon said, "if we are to learn the lay of things."

They started down the mountain once more. Nightfall would come soon enough, and with it the lethal coil-gun fire would return. Unless, of course, Arellia surrendered immediately, on first demand.

That could not happen. Not only for Arellia's sake, but for Trios. There could be no better gathering place for an assault on Trios than this closest planet. And Shaina was certain this time the Coalition would not make the same mistake. They would leave no Triotian alive to spark a new rebellion across the sector. They would leave no Trios.

A grim determination rose in her. Arellia must fight.

And they must hold.

Chapter 41

THERE WAS AN odd crackling sound as they passed the Mountaintop Inn—without stopping this time. It took Rina a moment to realize it must be the communicator Kateri had given Tark.

"Hold," she said to Lyon and Shaina as he pulled it out. The transmission was garbled, broken. He walked a few paces away, and tried again. She could not hear, but apparently the communication was better there. He held the small device up to his ear and listened quietly for too long a time for her comfort.

When he came back to them, his expression was grim.

"The barrage was effective. Too effective. Crim thinks they have some new kind of guided torpedoes, capable of changing direction after launch multiple times."

"They have been busy," Rina said.

"While Arellia has grown soft, and complacent," Tark muttered. He seemed to shake it off. "Our meeting place in town was destroyed, along with most of the western district."

"Were they there? Are they all right?"

"They were, but got out in time."

"Was it specific?"

"To them? She doesn't think so. They seem to have just picked a district to obliterate."

"To show they could?" Lyon asked.

Tark nodded. "To try for that immediate surrender. It is their way, to destroy district by district."

"What else?" Rina asked.

"There are rumors of a new model of coil gun," Tark said. "Small enough to be carried by two men."

They truly have been busy, Rina thought. Something that powerful and portable could be a daunting weapon.

"How would they power it?" Lyon asked.

"Reports are it takes another two to carry the power source. And a large enough level spot to place it."

"So they're not going to sneak it up on you," Shaina put in. "At least, not near town, where the land is all flat."

"Might not be much help, depending on its range," Lyon said.

For a moment Tark just looked them, his gaze shifting from Shaina to Lyon and back. *Assessing*, Rina thought. And judging by his expression, a little surprised but pleased.

"Obviously Trios has not gone soft in these years," he said.

"My father would not allow it," Lyon said. "He never lets them forget how near we came to losing everything we hold dear. Triotians are ever ready to fight."

"And my father makes sure they know how," Shaina added.

Rina smiled at her. For all her anger, Shaina was still honest and clear-sighted. She would never deny who her father was or what he'd accomplished.

Rina saw Tark's sharp nod. Acceptance, approval, and, she thought, a touch of a salute to both men who were not yet here.

"Dax will be here soon," she said. "And now, Dare will follow."

"Yes," Lyon agreed, "he will. In full force."

"They must hold until he arrives," Shaina said. "Will they? Can they?"

"I do not know," Tark said, sounding as uncertain as the words.

"They will hold," Rina said. "Once the hero of Galatin returns to rally them."

THE FLOOD OF refugees began before they got down to the flat. The mountain seemed a likely place to escape the next round, and people, mostly women with children, were hastening there. They were too frightened to even notice the four headed against the tide, except to occasionally shout to them that they should turn around, get out, not head into the chaos.

"You have a secondary meeting place, for the watchers?" Rina asked.

"Yes," Tark said, and something in the wry twist of his mouth told her.

"Your dwelling?"

"Yes. They will be there if they are able to get there."

Neither Lyon nor Shaina questioned when they left the main road. They exchanged glances, but it was clear neither of them was about to question the decisions of Commander Tarkson in war. Pride filled Rina, pride in them, in him. She wished more than anything that Tark would not have to do this. But she knew he would because he must, because it was who he truly was, and she loved him all the more for it.

They reached the ramshackle shed, and she saw Lyon and Shaina both grin when the hidden door swung open.

There were fewer of them there this time. Kateri was giving instructions, assigning those who remained to different districts, and Rina guessed that was where the others were already. For she had no doubt all of the watchers would fight, even those who were reluctant. It took courage to go against the common stream of thought as they had.

Kateri had turned the moment the door opened.

"You heard the battle begin?" she asked Tark.

Tark said nothing, just stood aside to let Lyon and Shaina step into the circle of light cast by the huntlight. The older woman's eyes narrowed as her gaze fastened on Lyon, and then Shaina. She'd known who they'd gone after, but seeing the resemblance in person was always startling. Thanks to his parent's protectiveness, there were not that many images of Lyon allowed beyond Trios, but he looked enough like his father for anyone who had seen Dare to guess, and Shaina looked even more like Dax.

Rina heard whispers running around the room. She heard "Trios" and "Dax" more than once, and knew others had realized. She turned to the two subjects of the stir.

"This is Kateri Reyks," she said to Lyon and Shaina. "She is the leader of the watchers, the only ones on Arellia with the wisdom and heart to see this coming. She has been the clarion call of a truth no one wanted to hear."

She turned then to the woman, who was smiling now. In the short time she'd known her, Rina had never seen Kateri smile so widely.

"I introduce you to Prince Lyon of Trios." A buzz of sound went around the cave as those who had not guessed his identity realized who was among them. "And," she added, "Shaina Silverbrake."

The sound erupted then, chatter, even cheers, continuing until Kateri raised a hand for silence.

"We have just received," she said slowly, "our best weapon."

And so it begins, Rina thought.

THE SMELL OF smoke was strong. Lyon's eyes stung as they made their way against the growing tide of terrified people, all seemingly intent on getting out of Galatin. Kateri and Crim had come with them; the others had scattered to their prearranged points to assess both damage and atmosphere among the people.

"Fools," Crim muttered. "As if there is any escaping this."

"They are afraid," Tark said.

"And a hundred times more blind with two eyes than you are with one," Crim said. The man did not wince, Lyon noticed, a measure either of his acceptance of his circumstance or his respect for the speaker. Or both. There was much to admire about this man, he thought.

"Some are not running," Lyon observed as they reached the square. There was a large cluster, fifty, perhaps more, near the statue. The argument was fierce, and even from several feet away Lyon could hear that these few at least did not want to abandon their city.

"Too few," Shaina said.

"Five times what Tark had at the Council Building," Rina said.

Lyon turned to look at her, and couldn't help but smile. Rina was so fierce only about her own, those she loved, which told him all he needed to know. It was as well he was impressed with the man.

"But we had Dax and the *Evening Star* above, then," Tark said.

"He is coming," Lyon said, glancing up at the statue of his godfather. Somehow, in cast metal, the resemblance between him and Shaina seemed even more marked.

"But not soon enough," Crim said grimly.

"But," Kateri said, "we have Dax's daughter here now."

Shaina blinked. "And what good will that do?"

"They will rally to you." She glanced at Tark. "Despite their willing blindness, with Tark at your side they will rally. Not all Arellians are fools and cowards."

"We," Lyon said mildly, "would hardly be the ones to argue that, given that we sprang from two of the smartest and bravest, and stand here with three more."

Kateri smiled widely. "I see you have your father's gift for speech."

"And calm," Tark said with a wry quirk of his mouth.

"Which makes his anger all the more fearsome when roused," Rina said.

"And your father?" Kateri asked Shaina.

Shaina gave a shrug. "He is the best flashbow warrior Trios has ever known," she said simply.

"So far," Lyon said quietly, letting her see the pride he felt that she had justified his faith that she would be able to set aside her anger when faced with something bigger than them all. Shaina flushed, looked away. But she was smiling.

For a moment none of them spoke, and in that silence Lyon realized the tenor of the sounds from the group near the statue had changed. The mutterings punctuated with occasional angry or frightened exclamations had changed to an excited sort of buzz. And when he looked toward them, he saw the entire group was staring at them.

"Now, Tark," Kateri said.

"I am no speaker—"

"You must. They must see you willing to stand once more." She turned to Shaina. "And you must join him."

"Me?" Shaina was so startled she nearly yelped it, something that happened so rarely Lyon wished they were in a position for him to enjoy it.

"Now," Kateri insisted. "The base of the statue."

"But I'm no warrior, not like my father."

"Have you not realized," Lyon said softly, "that he has prepared you for this, every day of your life, even if he kept from you your true destiny?"

Her gaze met his. "My job is to protect you," she said.

With an effort he fought back the thoughts of what dangers that could put her in. And realized he had never appreciated enough the partnerships both his parents and godparents had built together, how hard it was to let the one you loved beyond all others do what they must.

"And what better way to protect me than to drive the Coalition back from here?" he asked in a tone of calm reason he supposed was much like his father's.

The crowd of people was pointing now, and he heard Dax's name repeated, along with Tark's. One man called out to Shaina, "You! You are Dax's daughter!"

"You are," Lyon said to her. "Now show them."

He sensed her reluctance as clearly as he could see the same emotion on Tark's face. The two exchanged a long glance, and finally, they almost simultaneously nodded.

Shaina leapt up on the base of the statue of her father. Tark followed.

"Yes, I am the daughter of Dax Silverbrake, the flashbow warrior of Trios," she said loudly. The crowd's milling stilled, and at her ringing cry even some of those fleeing paused, turned, stared. "And he, as he did before, is coming to aid those who will fight for their homes, for their world. Will you make him regret it?"

"You are with her, Tark?" The question was shouted from the crowd.

For a moment Tark said nothing. Lyon wondered what was going through his mind as he looked out at the people who had scorned him once they no longer needed him. He would be within his rights to turn his back on them, now that they needed him again.

But he did not. For that, Lyon thought, was not what heroes were made of.

"I will stand with the daughter of my greatest ally. And friend."

Shaina, looking so much like the man immortalized larger than life and towering above her, let her voice ring out even more strongly, the note of challenge unmistakable. "And I will stand with the man my father and my world reveres, the hero of Galatin."

Cheers erupted. Even in these few minutes the crowd had grown. Lyon saw people gesturing, urging others to join in. He saw communicators in use, as people called others. Perhaps, he thought, they had merely been bewildered, dazed by the attack.

The crowd seemed to multiply with every moment. He should have known, Lyon thought. The planet that had produced the likes of his mother, and Shaina's, couldn't be populated with nothing but frightened brollets. Although he suspected they would encounter a few of those when they tried to rally the leadership that was, according to their scouts, holed up in the Council Building once more.

If necessary, they would do without those whose expertise ran to talk instead of action. It would make it more difficult, but nothing about war was easy, as his father had so often said.

Many might run, but many would stand. They would be untrained, and need strong leadership, but they would fight. He could only hope there would be enough of them.

And that they could hold long enough.

Chapter 42

THE LIGHT HAD begun to fade when they finally left the now-crowded square. There were at best a couple of hours until nightfall. Places that had been full of revelers now were full of those fleeing, belongings stuffed into any available carrier, vehicles ranging from sleek airspeeders to rovers full of dozens, to even children's air scooters, clogging the streets that had been the scene of a never-ending party just hours ago.

But as their party passed, people stopped, stared.

As it had been at the base of the statue, Rina heard people calling Dax's name.

And Tark's.

"Are we fighting?" someone called out.

"We are," Tark answered. "With or without them," he added, jerking a thumb toward the Council Building.

Rina was gladdened by the cheer that rose, and by the number that abandoned their flight to follow.

The debate was in full force as they entered the chamber. The upper and lower galleries were packed with citizens. Down on the council floor shouting, most often simultaneously, was the most prevalent means of communication. From what Rina could decipher, the question wasn't whether to surrender, but who would actually do it.

"Cowards," Crim muttered.

"They did not want this fight," Tark said.

"Nor did you," Rina said to him. "And yet you are here."

"More fool I."

Before Rina could respond to that, there was a lull in the vociferous discussion. And into that lull Kateri walked, head up, eying them all as she went.

"Such brave souls, we Arellians!" she proclaimed loudly. The room fell silent in shock as all recognized the woman who had warned them again and again this was coming. "We do not gather to discuss how to repel this unprovoked attack, we do not gather to discuss how best to defeat this enemy whose evil we know too well. We gather instead to decide who shall announce our cowardly capitulation."

There was a stir in the room, a shuffling. But there was no denial. How could there be? Rina thought.

"I care not that you would not listen," Kateri said, as if she had read their thoughts. "But I care that you will not fight."

"We are not prepared," someone called out.

"I could remind you who is at fault for that, but there is no time for blame now."

"We cannot withstand this!" The high-pitched, querulous cry came from one of the men on the council floor.

Rina recognized the voice immediately. Beside her, Tark's head snapped around as he searched for the speaker. When he spotted the man, he muttered, "I thought so."

And then he moved. He strode onto the council floor as if he owned it. As, indeed, he once had.

"I recall you saying the same thing once before, Bratus. You were wrong then, too."

A gasp went around the chamber.

"Tark."

"It's Tark."

"Tark is with us."

His name was repeated from all quarters, in tones of awe now, as if this man were somehow different from the man they had scorned for so long.

"You were the first to cut and run then. I see you have grown no braver since."

A wave of barely suppressed snickering went around the room. *How on earth had he managed to get himself chosen mayor?* she wondered.

Tark turned then, looked at the officials gathered. Shrugged dismissively, then lifted his gaze to the galleries above.

"Is this what you wish, people of Arellia?" he called out. "To surrender without even a token resistance?"

The "No!" that echoed around that room was nothing less than a roar.

"You," Tark said, his head still lifted, "I will fight for." He lowered his gaze back to the politicians gathered. "You, can go to Hades."

The cheers that erupted threatened to take off the roof as surely as Coalition cannon fire. Tark strode off the floor, coming back to her. Rina felt her eyes sting with moisture as pride in this man filled her anew.

"People of Arellia!" Kateri shouted. "You must decide. Cravenly surrender, or push this"—she glanced at the fuming council with disgust—"deadwood aside and do what should be done. But before you decide, there is something you should know. We do not fight alone."

She looked toward them. Toward Lyon, Rina realized. For an instant she wanted to take his arm, reassure him as if he were the boy she'd known. But Lyon wasn't a child who needed her encouragement. Even since he had left Trios, only a matter of days, he was changed. He and Shaina both. They were no longer the unproven heirs who had left Triotia such a short time ago.

And he rose to the challenge now. He walked toward Kateri as if he wore the royal cape, his bearing making the humble clothing and lack of royal insignia—save the ring now back on his finger—irrelevant.

"I give you Prince Lyon of Trios!" Kateri exclaimed.

The murmur that went around then was quieter, more assessing. They had known Lyon was coming, so there was no surprise, but he had their attention nevertheless.

Lyon didn't waste any time. Nor did he waste his breath on the now-chastened men before him. As had Tark, he addressed the people in the galleries, the citizens. "Trios will honor the Pact," he said. "Help is already on the way. My father is readying even more. We will stand with Arellia, as we have before. But you must stand."

To Rina's surprise, Shaina moved suddenly. She strode out onto the council floor much as Lyon had, confident, determined, as if her success in the square had inspired her. A gasp of recognition went around the gallery. They clearly had recognized the daughter who looked so much like the father.

"And in case you have forgotten, people of Galatin, how Trios answers a call for help," Shaina called out to them, "that help will be led by my father!"

Shouts went around the room.

"Dax!"

"We have the daughter of Dax with us!"

"I am with you," she said, "as is my father and my king. We will fight with you. But we will not fight *for* you."

It was not, perhaps, the most politic thing to say, Rina thought. But politics seemed suddenly out of place here in this chamber usually full of it.

Someone called out from the upper gallery.

"We have Tark, the Prince of Trios, and the daughter of the flashbow warrior! We cannot lose!"

And the noise as the crowd rose to their feet, shouting, cheering, was deafening. Kateri had been right, it seemed, when she had said they had their best weapon now. The three of them, Tark, Lyon, and Shaina, had turned the tide. She had no doubts now.

Arellia would fight.

Chapter 43

"GO," TARK ORDERED.

Shaina watched as the young man, barely more than a boy, nodded and ran out. Seconds later they heard the sound of the air speeder as it shot down the street. He was the last of the messengers sent to get word to the citizens that had already fled the city that the climate had changed, that Galatin at least was going to make it a fight. They could only hope that some would take heart and return to join them.

Lyon stood on one side of the table. She took advantage of the moment to study him—and remembered the brief conversation they'd had on the way down the mountain.

Did you really hear my thoughts?

Yes. And you mine?

Yes.

This could get . . . interesting.

It was all they'd had time for, but she knew they would explore it more later. That it had begun after the meadow did not surprise her. She was beginning to think that nothing that happened in this bewitched place would surprise her. She wondered if it would continue once they got home.

If they got home.

She looked around the tactical room once more. It was full, but it was a small room. There weren't enough here to take on the Coalition. Were they on Trios, there would be no doubt. If the king put out a call such as this, everyone, able-bodied or no, would respond. And she realized that even she, who had been raised to love her home above all others, did not fully appreciate the wonder that was her world.

There were others she recognized from her studies of that time, and from the tales told by Rina and her father. Mainly Ardek, an older man who had been the medic during the first Battle of Galatin. She remembered Rina saying he had been efficient and steady, had kept the thrice-wounded Tark on his feet, and she was glad to see him standing among those who would fight.

Shaina fought the urge to pace nervously. The light was fading rapidly, and she knew it would begin at any moment. Kateri stood to one side, watching, saying little. Shaina wondered if she felt a bit lost, now that her goal of stirring the population to resistance had finally been achieved.

"I wonder if they really expected a complete surrender so quickly."

Shaina mused aloud.

"They have gotten it before," Rina said.

"Often enough that it is usually their first tactic," Tark said.

"They will come back ruthlessly," Kateri warned, stirred to speech at last. "What happened this afternoon was merely a testing."

Tark nodded. "But they will not come in planning total destruction. They need some things intact, as a base."

To go after Trios. He didn't say the words, but he didn't have to. She knew it, Lyon knew it, as did Rina.

And she knew as soon as darkness fell it would begin, and they'd had little time to plan. But Tark knew not just this building but the town and the surrounding area for miles, and he knew it well. And he had, it was clear, been thinking of this since he had become convinced the return of the Coalition was certain, because his commands were quick and decisive.

"I've set sentries here, here, and here," Tark said, making marks on the map spread before them in the basement of the council chambers. It had served him as a command center in the last battle for Galatin, although it had clearly been ignored since then. "They will watch for any activity, ship landings, or other movement."

Lyon was studying the map. Then he looked at the projection hovering above the table, Arellia and her three moons, with the positions of the Coalition vessels marked behind the outer one.

"Were it me," he said thoughtfully, "I would come in from dark side to dark side."

Tark shifted his gaze to Lyon. "As would I. Your father taught you well."

"As did hers," Lyon said, giving Shaina a wink. She felt her cheeks heat, she who was not easily discomfited.

"And if it were you," she said hastily to Tark, "where would you choose to put down those troops?"

"It would depend on the size of my force. And the method of insertion."

"I don't think the Coalition has ever gone in for subtlety," Lyon said.

Tark gave him another approving glance. "No, they have not."

"A mother ship and transports, then?" Lyon asked.

"Assuming the mere sight of them arriving in such force will hasten the surrender?" Shaina added.

Tark leaned back slightly, looking at them, then at Rina. "You were right. They are everything you said they were."

Shaina glanced at Lyon, saw in his face the same sort of pride she was feeling. That this man, of all men, thought them worthy to be at his side now was praise unmatched.

"I would put them down there," Tark said, pointing to a large and apparently empty plain on the other side of the mountain they had so recently descended. "There is a pass into the city here"—he pointed to the north-east—"wide enough for a large force."

Shaina studied the hologram intently, then looked at Rina.

"The spot where we met you," she said.

Understanding the clipped query, Rina leaned forward slightly. Her navigation skills were not limited to space, Shaina knew, and in a split second she pointed to a spot on the image of the mountain, about halfway up.

Both Lyon and Tark waited silently for her to go on. She felt an odd sort of pressure—self-doubt—something she was not used to. There were many things she was not used to happening to her of late. But here she was, and she had little choice but to plunge ahead.

"Is there any place to cut them off?"

Tark frowned. "Only if you could get there before them." He pointed to a spot halfway around the flank of the mountain, where the pass narrowed. "But they would be well past that point by the time we could get around the mountain from here."

"What if we didn't go around?"

She heard Lyon's breath catch. "Of course," he said.

"We aren't even sure it goes through," Shaina cautioned.

"Might."

"Mordred." The man was likely still alive, she thought, unless he had sizzled himself trying to get through the screen.

"Yes."

"Still worth it."

"Who?" was his only answer.

"Me."

"Needed here."

"You as well."

They had reached an impasse. And only then was she aware that Tark was staring at them.

"Welcome to their world," Rina said dryly.

Tark gave a shake of his head. But for a moment, he grinned. It changed his entire countenance, gave it a rakish sort of dash, and Shaina guessed they had had another glimpse of the man Rina had first met.

"Are you saying," he said then, "that you found a way?"

"A tunnel. Inside the cave," Shaina said. Then she added ruefully, "We should have checked. It went deeper than we explored."

Lyon grimaced. Rina's gaze sharpened. "Is that how Mordred came upon you unaware?"

"We were foolish," Lyon admitted. "And we did not know it was him, then."

"And you did not know this was coming," Tark said, to Shaina's surprise. "I will go and—"

"No." Kateri cut him off. Tark shifted his gaze to her. "Whatever the

Coalition plans for outside the city, they will send their prime force here. They know they must take Galatin to take Arellia."

"Contention valid," Tark agreed.

"The battle here will be fierce. You must stay."

"You would have me hide?"

"Far from it. You must lead. Visibly. With the supreme confidence of the Captain Tarkson who held this city once before."

Tark grimaced. Shaina wondered fleetingly if she would one day look back at her younger self the same way, with a ruefulness about that blissfully ignorant youthful confidence she had come here with. She had learned much these past few days, most of all how much she had yet to learn.

"They will stand with you now, Tark," the older woman said. "They needed the three of you to begin, but it is you they need here now. They may not wish to remember, but it is your name they know, you who are one of them, you who saved Galatin before."

Rina smiled at the woman's words, then drew the conversation back to tactics. "Will it not take too much time to get there, when we don't know if this tunnel indeed cuts through the mountain to the other side?"

"I heard talk Bratus has an air rover," Crim said with a snort. "Keeping it hidden for his own escape."

"That would get there quickly enough," Shaina said. "I'll take it."

"I will," Lyon countered.

"But—"

"You may be a better fighter, but I'm a better pilot. And I need no laser pistol."

She opened her mouth to protest, but his steady gaze held her back. It was, she knew, nothing less than the truth.

"All right," she said. "You fly. But I'm going."

Once more Tark gave them a look of approval. Her father had always said half of victory was going with your strengths, the other half knowing your weaknesses. She supposed he had taught that to Tark as well.

"Take the north road. I will give you what cover I can and draw their fire to the south, near the gates."

"That will be all we need," Shaina said. "We can check the plain as well, for any sign it's been scouted or prepared."

Tark nodded. "We will prepare a force to move upon your report," he said. "I have a feeling there is more transport available. I doubt Bratus is the only one among those cravens hiding a means of escape."

"And then we fight," Kateri said with satisfaction.

"We do," Tark said.

Chapter 44

"THEY'VE TAKEN my mansion," Bratus said, his voice at a high pitch that told Rina the man was terrified. Not that there wasn't reason, but he could at least try to hide it a little better. He was the mayor, after all. "The clock tower scout says they are setting up a command post there."

"Good," Tark said bluntly.

"Yes," Rina said. Tark wasn't given to explaining, but she saw those gathered exchanging glances and thought it might be wise in this instance. "I doubt they planned on needing one. They realize now this will not be an easy sweep, ended quickly. They thought to march over us. Now they now better." She glanced at the man beside her. "And I suspect, by now, they know they face Tark."

Tark looked startled. But the stir shifted to one of renewed confidence.

"He beat them before," Crim said gruffly. "He will do so again."

"But there are too many, they will kill us all—"

Tark cut off the mayor—and the man who had left him to die—with a sharp gesture. "If I don't kill you first," he warned. Bratus made a sound that reminded Rina of nothing less than a muckrat, and scrambled into the outer room much like that same creature.

The others grinned; the mayor was no favorite with any left in the room, although she doubted they realized Tark had even more reason to hate him.

Rina wondered if Tark even realized what his mere presence did here. They might have turned away from him, avoided him as a painful reminder of a time they wished to forget, but now that it was here again, they turned to the man who had saved them before as if he were their savior.

You don't deserve him.

The thought was uncharitable, perhaps even vengeful, but she didn't care at the moment.

"The cellar," a young-sounding voice came from across the table, near where Ardek, their former medic, stood.

Tark's head came up as the older men around the table, some from the council, those who had stood for resistance, hushed the speaker. Those who had advised immediate surrender were, at Tark's orders, locked in the closet, where, he had said, they could continue to hide from reality.

"Let him speak," Tark said.

The boy came forward, head up, refusing to be cowed. He was only a boy, but he reminded her of Tark nevertheless. He had the same fierceness, the same determination, the same air of a crackling intelligence and fire. She wondered if Tark saw it too, was reminded of the youth he'd been the first time he'd been asked to hold this place.

"Rayden, is it?" Tark asked.

The young man nodded.

"What cellar? I thought there were none in Galatin."

"Because it gets wet, I know. But there is one."

Tark set down the holo controller he'd been holding. "Go on."

"My friends and I found it, one night, when we were behind the brewer—"

He stopped suddenly, glancing at the elders warily, looking for a moment nothing more than a mischievous child.

"So you're the one who broke in and stole my lingberry liquor," Wystan, who had run the distillery before becoming their armorer, said.

"We were exploring," the boy protested. "We just happened across the vat."

"And it likely made you sick," Wystan said. "It was nowhere near ready."

The boy grimaced at the memory. The others laughed then. And Rina suddenly realized she had seen this boy before. The night they had gone to the meeting of the watchers, he had darted out of that building, the old woman screaming after him. He clearly hadn't curbed his wandering habits.

"The cellar," Tark prompted, "where is it?"

Rina had already guessed, and she thought Tark probably had too, but he wasn't going to deprive the boy of his moment. She loved him all the more for that.

"Under the mayor's house. Under the kitchen. It's full of wine and spirits."

"Well, that fits," Crim said dryly.

"I have been in that kitchen," Wystan said. "There was no door except to the state room that I saw."

"Get him back in here," Tark ordered, and three men instantly sprang to do his bidding. The mayor was protesting vigorously, as if he thought he was being brought back so that Tark could make good on his threat.

"Your cellar," Tark said as the man cowered before him.

The man gave him a blank look. "What? I have no—"

"Do not try my patience. How do you access it?"

The mayor glanced around, saw nothing of support, and answered weakly. "There is a hidden door, behind a cupboard. And a hatchway outside, for deliveries, but only the taproom keeper knows of it."

"Afraid the masses might raid your wine, Bratus?" Crim said in disgust.

Tark turned back, and knelt to put himself at eye level with the child. "And you know where this outside entrance is?"

The boy nodded. "But it's covered up with rubble now. From the explosions."

Rina could almost feel Tark's mind racing, yet he kept his focus on the boy, who was practically glowing that he had his full attention.

"And you have an idea about that?" Tark asked.

Again the boy nodded, excitedly this time. "I think those skalworms don't even know it's there."

Tark nodded, giving the boy a slow smile that lit the young face with pride. The boy cared nothing for Tark's scar, knew only that he was the hero of Galatin and it was the most exciting thing in his young life to be acknowledged by him. Rina could have hugged him. Or both of them.

"The best way to deal with the Coalition beast is to take the head," Tark said. "They are lost without it."

"And that head will be in the mayor's mansion," Rina said. "Taking the best for himself, because that is what they do."

"Yes. Wystan, I need every bit of nitron you can spare, and then a little more. Fused and ready. Crim, you're with me," Tark said, his tone brisk. He looked at the men across the table. "I'll need one more, if there's anyone willing from your ranks."

Bratus Onslow, Rina noticed, cringed backward. She nearly laughed at him. Would have, aloud, were the situation not so grim. This was, after all, the man who had left Tark to die in the mountains. Were it up to her, he would not be allowed to breathe the same air. In truth, if it were up to her, he would not be allowed to breathe.

"I'm with you," she said.

He turned to look at her. Shook his head. "You must stay. You will be in charge here during this mission."

Her hackles went up instantly. But before she could speak, he put a hand on her arm and took her aside.

"It is not to protect you," he said quietly, so the others would not hear, "although I will not deny that is my strongest desire. But someone will need to rally them, should we not succeed. You were at my side in that first battle for Galatin, long ago, and you fought with Dax. They will follow you."

She hated it, but saw the sense of it. She thought of telling him she should go in his place and he stay here for those same reasons, but she knew it wasn't in him. She knew this man down to the bone, and he would never keep himself safe while sending others into danger.

And she did not allow herself to think about the grim truth buried in that phrase, "should we not succeed." That if they did not, it would mean he was dead. In truth, this time.

But there would be no moving him, she could see it in his expression, in the set of his jaw. "You will come back. I am not about to lose you again," she ordered, her own jaw set.

He stared at her for a moment. "You will be fine, I want you to believe that. Better perhaps, if I don't—"

"Looking for another slap? You once said what we want to believe does not change the truth. And you know the truth, Bright Tarkson."

For a moment she let it all shine in her eyes, her face. She saw it register, even as she saw his doubt. She would wipe that doubt away, she thought. She would find the way to prove to him that he was not just more than worthy of her complete love, that he already had it.

She saw him take in a deep breath. He opened his mouth then closed it again, as if he could find no words. Since this was neither the time nor the place, she would take that as sign enough.

The chatter in the room was rising, and they turned back to the others.

"I'll go," Rayden said eagerly running up to them.

Tark looked at the boy. "I will need you to show us this entrance. But then you must come back," he said. When the boy looked crestfallen, he added with a gesture at her. "She will need a lieutenant. I think you have earned that."

Put in that light, the boy perked up.

"I am an old man," Ardek said, "but my grandson here shames me." Rina's glance flicked from the old man to the boy; she hadn't realized they were related. Rayden stood taller as he went on. "I have not stood by you as I should have, but I would join you, if you'll have me."

Tark met the man's gaze across the holo table. "You held fast in the last battle for Galatin, Ardek. I would be honored to have you again."

"The honor is mine," the old man said with a slight bow of his head.

She silently thanked the old man as Tark nodded in turn. He picked up his weapons from the table behind him. Then he turned back to Rina. For a moment he simply looked at her, as if to commit her to memory.

The reality that she could indeed lose him so soon after finding him again struck her anew. Ignoring the others, she stretched up and kissed him. And this time there was no hesitation in him as he kissed her back, fiercely. Claim, declaration, and maybe good-bye were all tangled in that single kiss, and it left her shaken when at last he ended it.

His good eye closed for a moment. She saw him draw in a deep breath.

He turned to the boy.

"Rayden, lead on."

The boy whirled and ran.

"And we," Crim said with a grimace as he picked up his own long gun, "shall endeavor to keep up."

Tark grinned at the man, and suddenly it was as if it were all those years ago. He looked to her in that moment as young and daring—and fool-hardy—as he had then, and the eye patch merely underscored the demeanor.

The hero of Galatin was back.

DAX LET OUT a string of curses he hadn't uttered in an age.

He paced the bridge of the *Evening Star*, every muscle tense. They had been enjoying being in flight again when word had come that Tark's guesses had been all too accurate, and the Coalition attack had begun. Even ever-cool Califa had let out a curse worthy of her past days.

And somewhere on Arellia were three of the people they loved most. Including the daughter Dax was terrified he would lose before they had the chance to mend the breach between them.

"She will be fine."

His mate's soft, husky voice came from behind him, as her hand came to rest on his shoulder. Her touch, her very presence soothed him like nothing else, but this was the worst thing they had faced since the tribunal when they had first made it back to Trios.

"You are so calm," he said.

"Because worrying will not get us there any faster."

"Well, something should," he muttered. He crossed to the control console and slapped at the intercom link.

"Larc!"

"I'm trying, Captain. If I divert power from any more systems, it will take time to get them back on line."

"Then we'll do without them."

"Er . . . life support?"

"Narrow it to the bridge and you. Everybody's at those stations already anyway."

"What about weapons? They'll have to charge back up—"

"Then we'll fight with hand weapons. None of it will matter if we don't get there before the Coalition wipes them out." Frustrated rage had made his voice sharp, almost vicious. "Sorry, Larc."

"We love them too, Dax," the engineer said, forgoing the rank.

"I know."

"Comm coming in!" Rox called out.

Dax turned to look at his first mate. "Arellia?"

The grizzled veteran shook his head. "The king, Captain."

Dax nodded. Rox hit a switch, and Dare's voice echoed across the bridge.

"We're airborne with a full squadron. The second is fueling now, and the third assembling. What we have left will remain here, on alert, in case the Coalition is planning a second attack on Trios."

"Good." He opened his mouth to ask if there was any news from Arellia, but stopped himself, realizing Dare would tell him if there were.

"We're getting bits and pieces. Latest credible information on the Coalition forces is on its way in a burst file. It looks bad, but not insurmountable."

"If we can damned well get there," Dax muttered.

"Dax?"

The queen's voice came through then, and Dax braced himself. "Here."

"We got a hand keyed-in burst message from Rina. She found them."

"Then they're together?"

"They were. It's from some time ago. She was still on the mountain, so it had to be relayed."

Something in Shaylah's voice warned him. "And?"

"They were heading back to the city. Quickly."

It hit him like a blow. "Because the attack had begun."

"Yes. They should be there now."

He swore, a particularly pungent oath. Then collected himself. "Sorry. That wasn't aimed at you."

"I assumed," Shaylah said.

For a queen, she was a damned good sport, he thought, not for the first time.

As a mother, she had to be as worried as he was.

"We're locking down to emergency systems only," he said. "Diverting all power to the engines. We'll be out of touch."

"Understood." It was Dare again this time. "Tark is holding Galatin. And he will hold until you get there. He must."

"He will," Dax said, meaning it. If it was possible, Tark would do it. "We'll be there before dawn. Somehow."

"If anyone can, you and the *Evening Star* can. Dax?"

"Here."

There was a pause before Dare said, in a voice Dax had not heard in a long time, "Never mind. You know."

Dax swallowed tightly. "Yes. I do."

For a long moment after they signed off, Dax stood, staring out the viewport into the vastness outside. For years he lived in this world, on this ship's forerunner, living the crazed life of a skypirate, taking wild chances, risking everything with the slimmest chance of victory, sometimes an even slimmer chance of survival. He'd grown more cautious since. Being responsible for the protection of Trios—and becoming a parent—had accomplished what nothing else had.

But there was no such thing as caution now. Everything he held dear was at stake, and there would be no holding back.

Chapter 45

RINA PACED THE floor. Her internal clock told her they had been gone less than an hour, but still she was restless.

The council had retreated, apparently content once more with sitting back and letting Tark do their fighting. Some she forgave, they were old, tired. Others she knew had fought the last time to save their city, and she gave them some leeway as well. But the others, the younger, strong ones who seemed either bewildered or afraid or simply unwilling, she had little patience for and had thrown out of the room.

Rayden, who had come back as Tark had ordered, although clearly reluctantly, she asked to stay.

"You're the only sensible and brave one among them," she told him after the room had cleared.

The boy straightened proudly. "What shall I do?"

"First, report. Was there any trouble?"

He shook his head, an expression of wonder coming over his face. "Nobody heard a thing, even when they moved the rubble. Tark can move like a whisperbird."

"He can," she agreed.

"And after I showed them the steps up into the house, he lifted me back up out of the cellar like I was no heavier than a perla."

"And a perla you are, Rayden. Amid snailstones."

The boy grinned. "They're going to do it. I know they are."

"If it can be done, Tark will do it."

The boy studied her for a moment. "Is it true you flew with Dax? When he was a skypirate?"

"I did."

That earned her widened eyes and an awed expression.

"And you fought with him, and with Tark here, before I was even born?"

"That too," she agreed with a smile at his innocent wonderment. She doubted there would be much innocence left on Arellia when this was over. But she was silently thankful to this boy's parents—or perhaps his grandfather—for teaching him what so many others here chose to ignore.

"No wonder Tark picked you."

She blinked. "What?"

"You're both heroes. You should be together."

She studied the boy in turn. "Did he . . . say something to you?"

Rayden drew himself up proudly. "That he was trusting me. That I would be guarding the most important thing in his life. The only person he loves."

Had there been a chair handy she would have collapsed into it. Instead she had to lean on the table when her knees suddenly seemed reluctant to hold.

Leave it to Tark, she thought. Only he could manage to deliver a declaration of love, and the first one at that, in the middle of a war and through a child.

She would make him pay for that one. She buried all thought of the danger he was in, refused to even acknowledge any longer that he might not return from this foray. Instead she focused on just how she would make him pay.

And how she would wring that declaration from him face-to-face.

When it came, the explosion rocked the Council Building even though the mayor's home was at least two blocks away.

She heard shouts—some laced with fear, others triumph—coming from the chamber outside, where those who sheltered here were gathered. She wondered if any of them would find the courage to fight now. Perhaps. If she had learned nothing else from her skypirate days with Dax, it was that there was a vast array of types spread across the galaxy, from coward to hero. It did seem, she thought rather sourly, that there were many more of the former than the latter.

But Kateri was with them, and speaking. Rallying them in her own way, so perhaps they would hold. They all knew now she had been right all along, and it gave her credence with them. Or should.

Rina resumed her pacing as the minutes ticked past. And then it began. The communicator crackled nonstop with reports from districts all over the city.

"They're retreating!"

"They just stopped!"

"They scattered, going all directions!"

"It's as if they don't know what to do."

Rina looked at Rayden. The boy looked back at her. He was quick to realize.

"They did it!" he yelped. "It's like Tark said, they're lost without someone thinking for them."

She winked at him. "Indeed, Lieutenant."

He whooped, and ran around the room in high spirits he couldn't contain.

"And," Rina added, grinning as she watched, "let's not forget your part in this. They couldn't have done it without you."

That brought on another noisy circuit. She wouldn't be completely happy until Tark was back, safe, but this was very, very sweet.

The noise outside was increasing. Kateri had a communicator out there, so they had heard as well.

The door to the tactical room crept φpen.

"Is it true?" the mayor squeaked. "They've done it? It worked?"

"It did. The Coalition troops are panicking, running scared. You know something about that, don't you, Bratus?"

The man flushed. "I am a man of peace now, not war."

She looked at him. Her mouth twisted into a sour half smile. She wondered how he had managed to get to this position after Tark's survival and return had shown him for what he was, a coward who would abandon those he was responsible for. It wouldn't surprise her at all if he was not responsible for a lot of the ill-treatment Tark had borne.

"You're not a friend of the senior Tarksons, by chance, are you?"

"What?"

"Never mind," she said.

"My home," he began.

The whining in his voice grated, and Rina whirled on him. "I hope it's a pile of rubble."

"Come, you skalworm," Kateri said from behind the man. She glanced at Rina and winked as she pushed the man back into the other room.

"Tell them all to stay in place," Rina said to her. "This retreat will only be temporary, until they regroup and are assigned another commander."

Kateri withdrew. Rina resumed her pacing. That the mission had been successful she couldn't doubt, the results were still spitting out of the speakers. What she did not know yet was at what cost.

The retreat would be, as she'd told Kateri, temporary. She had to hope Lyon and Shaina truly had a way to entrap those reinforcements.

The door burst open this time, unlike Bratus's timid approach. Rina's heart jumped as Tark strode into the room. She had a brief moment of concern when she saw his left arm was bloodied, but it vanished in the moment he swept her up in a strong embrace.

"They're running like scalded slimehogs, and sounding about the same," he said.

"I heard," she said. "Every quarter of the city is reporting it."

He kissed her then, so fiercely she wished they were alone back in his cave. So fiercely she thought her knees would not hold her. And then they didn't, and she was sagging against him even as she kissed him back.

"You're hurt," she said, trying to think through the haze of heat and pleasure he so easily stirred in her. "Bleeding."

"Not mine," he said, and kissed her again. But at last he seemed to realize they had an audience. A young one.

He turned to the boy.

"Rayden," he said. "It is your grandfather who needs tending."

The boy's eyes widened.

"It is but a scratch," Tark said quickly. "He got it taking down a guard who tried to stop us. You should be very proud."

The boy's face lit up, and he scampered out into the chamber in search of his grandfather.

"However proud he is, it is nothing next to how proud I am," Rina said.

Tark turned back to her. And she saw in his expression the truth of what Rayden had told her.

"Rina," he said, and stopped, as if he couldn't find the words. He even looked a little pale. She nearly smiled at the thought that this warrior who faced death again and again without quailing was shaken now. "I can make you no promise. This is war."

"You are free from that need until this is over," she told him.

He reached for her then, and for this moment she let herself settle into his arms as if they had all the time in the world.

"You've held Galatin once again, Bright Tarkson."

He grimaced at the name, but said only, "For now."

"And you will hold as long as necessary."

"I will," he said. "But I hope Dax gets here soon anyway."

"He will. And the king will not be far behind."

"Then we have a chance."

She hugged him, ignoring the battle for the moment, thinking only that finally those words applied to them as well.

Chapter 46

"THEY HELD," ROX exclaimed as the report over the slightly hissing connection ended. "The Coalition Ground Commander and half his staff are done for. The rest are scrambling madly."

"Tark," Dax said simply, but inwardly he was grinning.

"That boy is a fighter," Hurcon said, a smile curving his heavy, Omegan face.

"Indeed he is," Califa said, her voice oddly soft.

"I'm guessing his name is right alongside yours on the Coalition nightmare list," Larcos said with a grin.

"Leave it to Tark to blow up their commander within hours of the first attack," Rox said. He looked at Dax then. "There will be a lull, while they regroup."

"Yes." He saw in Rox's eyes that the man knew what was coming. His first mate knew him well, after all these years.

"Once we were within range, I knew you wouldn't be able to wait," Rox said.

Dax turned to Larcos.

"It's ready," the engineer said before he even had to ask. "Armed, fueled, Galatin coordinates locked."

"Am I so predictable?"

"Predictably reckless and insane, yes," Larc said easily.

"She's the fastest, most maneuverable thing we've ever built, Larc. And with the screening, she's practically invisible."

"Uh-huh. And it's still the Coalition."

"For now," Dax said with a grin.

He looked at Califa. He saw the worry in her eyes, but also the steadiness of her gaze. "You must do what you must," she said simply.

He kissed her then, fervently, thankfully. She had never asked him to be anything other than what he was, and he loved her all the more for that.

He turned to head back to the fighter bay. Nelcar, their medical officer, who had so far remained silent, spoke quietly as he passed.

"Bring them back safely, Dax."

Dax felt his throat tighten. Many years had passed since they had flown together as the most feared skypirates in the system. But these men would ever back him, and they loved Rina and Shaina as if they were their own.

"I will," he swore. He looked back over his shoulder at Rox. "Let Tark know I'm coming, or he'll likely blast me out of the sky."

"Copy that," Rox said with a laugh that all of them echoed.

At last, Dax thought as he raced down the gangway to where the sleek, wedge-shaped fighter sat ready and waiting. He was finally doing something. Even if Shaina still hated him, she would be alive. He didn't care just now if she threw stones at him, as long as she was there to do it.

"WHERE DO YOU suppose he went?" Shaina looked around warily for any sign of Mordred.

"No idea." Lyon scanned the meadow. And found himself glad he saw nothing; he did not want the image of Mordred here etched into his mind. Not here, where they had first discovered that acceding to your destiny could be the most glorious thing on any world.

"I half expected to find him toasted, from throwing himself at the screen."

"He did not rise to his position by being a fool," Lyon said, his tongue instinctively testing the sore spot on his lip; it was better, but still tender enough to be a reminder. "But I do wonder how he escaped. If he did."

"The screen," she said. "I barely felt it at all when we passed. And I could see through it, some at least."

"Perhaps it's weakened." Lyon turned. He picked up a stone and tossed it back the way they had come. There was a snap and a flash as it hit and bounced back. "Apparently not."

"Odd," she muttered. She turned back to look up toward the caves. Then, suddenly, she looked back toward the screen.

"What?" he asked.

She shook her head. "Nothing," she muttered. "We should go."

He nodded. "He could be hiding up in the cave, or one of the tunnels."

"Perhaps he finally saw the treasure."

"We will soon know."

"The orb!" she said suddenly.

He'd almost forgotten. He reached into his pocket, pulled it out. It was only faintly dark, like a bruise beginning to fade.

"What does that mean?" she asked.

"Distance? Dead or dying? No longer a threat? I don't know."

"Bedamned thing should have come with instructions."

He couldn't help grinning at her tone. That his ever practical and literal-minded Shaina had accepted the stone had properties they could not explain was occasion enough, but that she accepted it enough to joke was even more amazing.

"Reason enough to be on guard," he said as he put it back. "Let's go."

They had left the rover, hidden as best they could, outside the screen. It might have gone through with Lyon at the controls, but they hadn't wanted to risk a transport that might be badly needed later.

Neither of them spoke as they crossed the meadow, although Lyon felt a slow pulse of heat begin in him as they passed the spot where they had come together for the first time. He gave Shaina a quick glance, and saw by the slight color in her cheeks that she was not immune. They had so much to learn of this, so much left to explore; he wished for nothing more than the chance to revisit that wondrous place again right now.

But they could not. They had a job to do, and even a moment stolen for themselves was impossible.

They entered the cave cautiously, taking care to make no noise, and pausing to listen often. No sound reached them. They worked their way around the cave. It seemed empty, but they stayed silent, not risking it. They took a quick glance at the niche, which still held the treasure, sans the orb. He saw her brow furrow, but she said nothing aloud or otherwise.

But there was a brief, silent discussion about whether to split up and check the two caves, or stay together.

Time, Shaina sent him.

Safety, he sent back, trying to hide that it was her he was worried about. Were it someone else, splitting up would be the logical course.

It didn't work.

Right now, I'm a scout, she sent.

A scout. Not his mate. He let out a compressed breath. She was right, of course. This was too big to let anything interfere with what had to be done. He would just have to trust she could hold her own. And in reality, he would have before. It was only what had changed between them that had changed his outlook.

Then go, he sent.

He would have sworn that what she sent back was a kiss.

As it turned out, the split was a minor point. The first cave on the left, the one she took, indeed curved to meet the second several hundred yards in, about a half a mile, he guessed. But the middle tunnel kept going. And going.

They moved as quickly as they dared, ever watchful to the rear this time, and pausing to listen. They used only the faintest light setting on the flarelight from the rover, just enough to get past any hazards on the tunnel floor. They went on and on, the cave twisting deep into the mountain, until he thought perhaps it might indeed go all the way. It was narrow, however, and would accommodate only three, maybe four fighters abreast, fewer in spots. That could cause a bottleneck, but perhaps the wider spots they encountered would balance that.

They had gone what seemed like miles. The air was stale, but breathable. The darkness was total, and the faint beam vanished mere feet ahead of them.

They continued on. And on. He did not know the exact diameter of this ancient peak, and the tunnel was not straight, but it seemed as if—

On the thought, they hit a dead end. There was no warning, no shrinking of the tunnel's dimensions; the tunnel simply ended in a nearly flat wall of rock.

He ran the flarelight's beam over the surface. Then he upped the setting a notch and got a clearer view. It made no difference—it appeared to be solid rock.

"Of course," Shaina muttered, running her hands over the seemingly impenetrable wall, searching for a weakness. She found nothing. "Perfect. And us without a single bit of nitron."

"That would probably bring the whole thing down on us," Lyon said, tacitly agreeing with her that they hadn't been followed, this time at least.

"Disrupter?"

"I think it would take more power than we have."

"Too bad we can't get the rover in here. Those side guns might do it."

"But we don't know how far we need to go."

"I'd swear we walked the breadth of this mountain. It can't be that far to break through."

"Far enough, in solid rock."

Shaina sighed. She curled her hand and hit the wall with the side of her fist. "What we need," she muttered, "is my father and his blessed bow."

"Indeed," Lyon said carefully, watching her for any sign of the old anger. He saw none, but didn't know if it meant she had gotten past it, or it had merely been overshadowed by the urgency of the situation. "Let's send Rina the coordinates. Perhaps she can extrapolate how far we are from the outside."

Shaina glanced around at the suddenly heavier-seeming walls. "If we can even get it through to her."

"If not voice, then by burst. If not burst, then I will make note and we will head back until we can."

"My ever-patient Lyon," she said softly.

Her use of his name, the possessiveness in her words, and the huskiness of her voice fired a vivid image in his mind, of moments when he was buried inside her and far from patient.

"Not always," he said.

She reached out, took his hand. The jolt he felt told him she was thinking the same thing; and the wonder of what they had found, when they had thought there was no more to learn about each other, nearly swamped him.

It took all his self-control to dig out his locater and take a simple reading.

Chapter 47

RINA GRINNED AT the roar that went up the moment the sleek little fighter dropped out of a cloud. She'd last seen it in the air on the final test flight. Dax had planned to unveil it at the ceremony, she knew.

The ceremony that would have been today, she realized.

The gathered crowd knew it was Dax. Somehow word had gotten out from the moment Rox had sent the message. She had little doubt the Coalition knew it as well; the message had not been encoded. And that, too, was Dax. He knew well enough the effect his name would have. And that his presence would make even the Coalition tread carefully—especially knowing that where Dax was, the ship that had wreaked havoc on them both here and on Trios was close at hand. If they knew of the new version of the *Evening Star*, they'd be even more worried.

The fighter slowed, pivoted in place and, narrowly missing the pile of shattered stone that was all that was left of the fence, dropped neatly into the courtyard of the Council Building.

"I see he's lost none of his flair," Tark said dryly.

She glanced at him. He gave her a sideways look in turn. One corner of his mouth curved upward, and she knew he was looking forward to this.

The hatch opened, and the roar went up anew as Dax stepped out. To the gathered Arellians he looked much as he had all those years ago: tall, strong, dark hair lifting in the breeze. He was even dressed the same, loose white shirt tucked into dark leggings, the knee-high boots, one holding a lethal dagger, the other the powerful bolts in small pockets stitched along the top.

He reached back into the small fighter and pulled something out by a heavy strap, then slung it across his back.

The flashbow. Everyone on Arellia would recognize the sleek, silver weapon, she thought.

The shouts came wildly as Dax scanned the throng.

"The flashbow!"

"Dax!"

"Skypirate!"

He gave them a wave, which raised the sound level a bit more, but his eyes never stopped searching.

He found them. Rina saw him register her presence with a smile, but then his gaze shifted to the man beside her. For a moment he went very still, as if he hadn't really believed it until now. A huge, joyous grin formed, and he leapt easily down from the fighter. He crossed the distance between them at a run.

It began as a handshake, but Dax bent his arm and pulled Tark toward him, to clap him soundly on the back. After an instant's hesitation, Tark returned the gesture, as close as two fighting men would get to a public embrace, Rina guessed with a wide smile.

"You son of a skalworm, I should fry you right here for letting me think you dead all these years."

Tark looked slightly embarrassed. "It seemed a good idea at the time."

"Well, it wasn't," Dax said. He released him, but held him with a steady gaze. "You were the one true regret we were never able to let go of."

Tark lowered his gaze, clearly self-conscious about the heartfelt emotion. He would learn, Rina thought. When she brought him home to Trios, he would learn.

"So," Dax went on, "it's a bedamned good thing you changed your mind."

Tark flicked a glance at her. "I've come to think differently."

Dax released him then, and turned to her. He leaned in, cupped her face, and planted a kiss on her forehead. "That's my girl." Then he looked at Tark and grinned again. "Or at least, she was. Somehow I think that's changed."

"Everything has changed," Tark answered. He squeezed her hand as he said it, and from that small gesture her heart soared.

"Show me where we are," he said. "Same place?"

Tark nodded. He glanced back at the sleek fighter. "You sure you want to leave it in the open? They'll be back as soon as they regroup."

Dax grinned. He reached into his pocket and brought out a small device with two glowing buttons on it. "Leave what?" he said as he clicked the blue one.

The fighter vanished. There was nothing there but the rubble from the fence.

Tark stared. Rina grinned.

"I see Larc got the veiling perfected," she said.

"He did indeed."

Tark's mouth curved into a smile. "He is still with you?"

"They all are, save Qantar. We lost him last year."

Tark nodded, signaling he remembered the man. "I recall thinking that he had died inside a lot longer ago."

Dax smiled sadly then. "Yes. But he recovered some joy, and passed peacefully where his family had died. He was content."

"A simple but powerful goal," Rina said, looking at Tark. Above all, she wished him content. And she would have it, she vowed.

Much of the crowd followed them, entranced by Dax's arrival in the flesh, and tried to cram into the outer room. She couldn't blame them. Dax and Tark to fight together again was history being written as they breathed. But only the men Tark trusted—and Rayden—were allowed into the tactical room.

Dax strode to the table and studied it silently for a moment. The flat maps, the holo projection, the logs.

"Nice move, taking out the command post before they even got comfortable."

"Head of the snake," Tark said. "And it was thanks to Rayden. He is the one who knew of the cellar that gave us access."

Dax smiled at the boy, who gaped back, speechless.

"Good job," Dax said.

The boy drew himself up proudly then. "I knew it would work."

Dax's gaze softened. "You remind me of my girl. That was always her answer after some crazed escapade."

Tark shifted uncomfortably then. "Your daughter," he began.

When Dax shifted his gaze back, Rina stepped in and quickly spoke. "She would not hear no, Dax. Lyon was going, and she was with him, no matter what anyone said."

"Going?"

"I know the irony. I came here to check on her welfare, and then let her venture out in the middle of a battle to scout for us."

"Rina," Dax said gently, "this is war. We all must do what we can. Besides, my worry was more . . . personal. Where are they?"

Tark quickly explained about the tunnels. He left it to Rina to explain about the rest. And while Dax accepted the part about the invisible screen—after seeing how well Larc's veiling worked, she supposed that was not a big jump—the bit about the treasure and the orb made his brows raise.

"Time for that later," Tark suggested.

"Yes," Dax said. "We must—"

The door opened. Kateri stood there. She scanned the room, her gaze stopping on Dax and Tark and Rina. Something warm and pleased came into her usual weary expression. Rina understood both. She had been proven right at last, but the cost had already been high. The last count she had heard, casualties, mostly civilian, had been in the hundreds.

"I have word. The mother ship has been sighted by our scout ship. They are coming."

"Direction?" Tark demanded.

"Not committed yet, but either to the plain as you suspected, or the highlands beyond."

"The highlands make no sense," Tark said. "Brakely is not stupid. He would know massing there would cost them too much in time and gain them little in stealth."

"Hard to hide a Coalition-sized army," Dax agreed easily. His blood was up—Rina could see it. The flashbow warrior was ready for a fight as much as the skypirate ever had been.

"There is more," Kateri said. "There is a second contingent. Nearly as large, judging by the number of ships."

"Headed straight here," Tark said flatly.

"Yes."

"You knew they would not take what you did here lightly," Dax said.

"Yes," Tark said.

"You've made them very angry, my friend. Again."

"Yes," he repeated with satisfaction.

Dax grinned. "And they are dividing their forces because of it."

Tark looked at him then, his old rakish grin forming. Rina saw the nod of salute Dax gave him. Her love and admiration for these two men tightened her throat.

"Your communicator is blinking," Kateri said, pointing to Rina.

She looked down at her belt, saw the red light flashing. The sound of the alert must have been lost in the noise of Dax's arrival. She unclipped it, read the burst message.

"It's from Lyon," she said.

The room went silent. She read the short message, the numbers. Some of the men stirred, but fell silent when Tark lifted a hand, his gaze fastened on her. Dax seemed to note this, a faint smile on his lips.

She stared at the holo projection. Walked to the end of the table to stare at the far side of the old mountain, and at the gridlines that hovered faintly in the air. She looked at the numbers Lyon had sent once more. Then she let her gaze go slightly unfocused, and put all the elements together in her mind. Double-checked.

A moment later she blinked, and looked at the two men she loved most, along with her king and his son.

She grinned.

"The tunnel goes nearly all the way through the mountain. It stops barely fifteen feet from the outside."

"There's the way to flank them," Dax said.

Tark said nothing; he was staring at the holo projection.

Rina agreed quickly. "Get them into the pass, then come up from behind them. We trap them, and then hold Galatin, we could end this war right now."

Still Tark said nothing.

"I will give what air support I can, from the fighter," Dax said. "I think I can do more good there than on the ground, at least until the *Evening Star* gets here. But if need be, I can set her down almost anywhere."

Rina was watching Tark intently now. She moved to stand beside him, to look at the holo from the same angle. Then she looked at his face.

The truth hit her instantly, tightened her stomach until she felt queasy with it. It was there. That pass, where the battle would take place, was where he had nearly died. Where he and his small band had fought nearly to the death, and then been left to die in fact.

"At least a small force will have to meet them in the pass while the main force goes through the tunnel," Dax was saying, "or they will suspect something. And they will have to be your best, to hold them long enough."

"I will lead them," Tark said, his voice so neutral Rina knew the effort behind it. He was volunteering to march back into the hell that had nearly destroyed him, and against much greater odds.

"You must not," Kateri said sharply.

For an instant Rina wondered if the woman knew. If so, she blessed her silently.

"Who else can?" Tark asked.

Kateri shook her head. "The same reason stands. There will be another battle here, even more fierce now that you have pierced their arrogance. They will be merciless. If the people of Galatin are to stand, you must be here to lead them."

"Are they so wavering then?" Dax asked.

"They have had years of peace to soften them, and no leaders such as you or your king to counter that. But they will fight, if Tark asks it of them." She walked to him, put a hand on his arm. "You must be here," she urged. "I know these people."

"But again, who will lead the force into the pass? Dax is right, he must use that fighter, it will be invaluable in his hands."

"I will," Rina said it without hesitation. She would walk into Hades to save him from going back there.

"No!" Tark's exclamation was quick and forceful. She stared at him. "Do you truly believe I could send you into that and stay here?"

"It could be worse here," she pointed out.

"Stay," Dax said. "You helped him hold Galatin before, help him again. Kateri is right. Do not underestimate the power of the people knowing that the same leaders who saved them before are here again."

Rina felt the moment when Tark let out a breath, giving in to the inevitable. "But again, who then?"

Dax's lips tightened. And with all the knowledge she had gained since the time he had rescued a wild, terrified child whose family had been slaughtered by the Coalition, she realized what he was thinking.

"They have grown much in these few days, Dax," she said softly. "Learned much."

Dax turned to face her. "Enough?"

"There is never enough, not for such as this. But who they are alone will inspire the kind of fighting we need."

"I . . ." For one of the few times in her lifetime, Dax Silverbrake was without a sharp comeback.

"It is time, Dax. For her especially."

He let out a long breath.

"I will still go, if you wish, to be beside her. Or him," Rina said.

Dax looked at her for a moment, then at Tark. Slowly, he shook his head. "No. Your place is here now."

She saw in his eyes that he understood. Everything. "Yes. It is."

She heard Tark's quick intake of breath. Reached to take his hand. Squeezed it in support as he had hers earlier.

"Are you sure, Dax?" he asked quietly. "Your daughter and the king's son, fighting for Arellia?"

Rina knew once Dax decided or was persuaded on a course, he didn't quibble. Yet this was his child, and Dare's, so his voice was a little tight as he spoke. "It is part of what it means to be Triotian," he answered. "We help our friends and honor our pacts. This they know." He looked at Kateri. "Will your people follow the Prince of Trios? And my daughter?"

Kateri's eyes widened. And then, amazingly, she laughed. "Tark holding Galatin, the half-Arellian son of the king of Trios and daughter of the flash-bow warrior on the ground, with Dax himself flying overhead? Oh, yes, they will fight. This is what they needed, all they needed—true leaders. Not those cowards hiding in the next room. Most people are lucky to have one leader they will march into Hades for. Now Arellia has four!"

"How will they get through the end of the cave?" Rayden asked, clearly excited, yet apparently unaware or unconcerned by the swirling emotions and momentous decisions of the adults around him.

Brought back to the practical by the innocent question of a child, Tark grimaced. "Explosives, even small ones, might bring the cave down," he said. "And from what they said in the burst message, the cave is too small and crooked for equipment."

"But not for me," Dax said.

The memory of Dax blasting away a prison wall to save her shot through Rina's mind. It was the first time she had truly seen the full power of the flashbow. But she also knew its cost to the warrior.

"Be careful, Dax. We cannot afford to have you weakened."

Dax snorted. "Fifteen feet? You insult me."

"This will work?" Tark asked. "Without bringing it down around you?"

"The flashbow adjusts to the target," Rina explained. "He can control what the bolt does, how it does it, and with how much power." And the more power he has to give it, the more it drains him, she thought, but did not say it.

"Give me the coordinates for that cave," Dax said. "I must move quickly, for the Coalition will."

Rina keyed them into her communicator and sent them to his.

Tark turned to the table behind him and picked up a laser pistol and handed it to Dax. "From what they said you'll need this, to cut through that screen."

"And be aware," Rina added, "they left Mordred there, trapped."

Dax blinked. "They what?"

She grinned. "I told you they've come a long way."

"There is one other thing," Tark said. "Something I would have you do, if your fighter is capable."

"She can do most things," Dax said proudly.

"Heavy lifting?"

Dax's brow furrowed. "How heavy?"

Tark explained what he wanted. Dax studied him for a moment, then slowly nodded. "You think far ahead," he said approvingly.

"Someone must," Rina said dryly.

"Time," Tark said.

"Yes," Dax agreed, and headed for the door. He paused before opening it and looked back at them. "Good luck."

Tark nodded.

"And," Dax added with a grin at the man Rina knew he'd thought of as more than just a brother in arms, "welcome to the family."

Tark stared at him. Then a small, almost shy smiled lifted one corner of his mouth. Rina could have hugged Dax all over again, were it not for the fact that Tark was right, time was now crucial.

Dax strode through the door and was gone, and moments later the once more visible fighter was rising into the air to the sound of a cheering crowd.

Chapter 48

"HE'S HERE," SHAINA said, feeling the odd sensation that was unique to her father—the awareness she'd always had, but never understood until now. Yet another thing he had kept from her.

"So fast?" Lyon asked. Rina had sent them word, saying that her father had somehow already been in Galatin when their message had come through.

"He must be in the new fighter," she said. "When I left, Larcos was swearing he'd have it finished the next day."

Lyon turned from the gold plate he'd been inspecting for marks of origin. "Are you still angry with him?"

"There is no room or time for that now."

"No. There isn't." Lyon paused, then added gently, "And when there is a chance of dying, I would say there is never any room for it."

Her head came up, but her words this time were calm. "You would have me hold him blameless?"

"No. I would weigh this one thing against all else, all of your life, and decide if it is worth destroying your bond with him for."

As usual, he had found the words. "It is not. Nothing is." What she saw in his eyes then warmed her to her soul. "What did you find?" she asked, gesturing at the treasure.

He shrugged. "Nothing of great note. At least, other than the value of the gold itself." He set down the plate and turned to face her. "What is it you thought of when we first got here this time? That made you frown?"

"I was just trying to figure out why I could see this," she said, gesturing toward the niche. "You, I understand, you're Graymist. And Mordred is not, so it follows he could not see it. But why could I?"

"Because you are beloved by a Graymist?" Lyon suggested.

She felt her cheeks heat; she was still not used to hearing him say it like that, so easily. But then, words had always come more easily to Lyon. She too often spoke rashly, or before she'd thought it through. She would do well to learn his way, and she would, she vowed. She—

"Quite a place."

Her father's voice came from the shadows, and she whirled. She gaped at him, then laughed at herself. Of course he had managed to sneak up on them. He was the vaunted skypirate, was he not?

"The new fighter is not the only thing with stealth, I see," Lyon said mildly.

Her father was grinning as he stepped into the circle of light cast by the torch they had placed on a shelf of rock.

"And you are as unshakeable as ever, I see."

Her father grasped Lyon's shoulder, and nodded. Then he turned to look at her. She held steady under his searching gaze, determined not to hide.

"We will talk, later," he said.

"Yes," she said, and was surprised at the relief that flashed in his eyes.

"Show me the wall," he said, wasting no time.

"Yes, sir," Lyon said and started toward the tunnel entrance.

They traversed the distance quickly, since they had walked it twice now and it was familiar. But it was enough time for her father to explain what was happening. He did not hide the severity of the situation, or play down the coming attack. In this, at least, he seemed to prefer they knew what was coming.

Lyon was right, there was no room for her personal anger now, maybe ever. What her father had done no longer mattered. Right now all that mattered was that they survive to sort it all out. Lyon was right about that, too. The chance of dying changed everything.

They reached the end of the tunnel. Her father took the flarelight and studied the wall.

"This is dense stuff," he said as he ran his hand over it, pausing here, then there. "Really dense." Finally his fingers curled into a fist and he tapped a spot about shoulder high.

"There," he said, and stepped back.

He handed the flarelight to her. "Hold it on that spot," he said.

She knew he could find his target without the light, it was part of the gift, but she also knew it took some energy that would otherwise go to the firing. He swung the flashbow off his back. The silver glinted in the light, from the intricately engraved stock to the metallic string that tensioned the bow itself. It was an elegantly lethal weapon that was fearsome to most who looked upon it, and to all who knew of its power. To her, it was inextricably linked to her father—it was the symbol of his strength, his skill, and his courage.

She glanced at Lyon. He held up six fingers. She countered with five. And the childhood game of guessing how many bolts he would use eased her tension.

"Wagering on me back there?" her father asked casually, without looking, as he took one of the oddly colored, handsbreadth-wide bolts and slid it into the groove on the flashbow. He notched it onto the metallic bowstring, seated it against the charging block, and flipped the lever. It began to hum.

"Yes," she answered. "Don't let me down."

Her father went still. He did not look around, he was into the cycle now and could not, but he answered her.

"I will not. I have already done too much of that."

Shaina's heart seemed to twist in her chest, and for a moment she couldn't breathe. And then he fired; the explosion echoed in the small space, and rock crumbled, sliding to the ground like so much dust. And just like that dust, the last of her anger slid away. He knew what he had done—Lyon was right. As usual.

He went through it again. And again. Each time a couple of feet of the wall fell away. *Fifteen feet*, she thought. Dense, he'd said. It might take more than even Lyon had guessed. And each shot cost him. The bolts seemed to her brighter than ever, and she remembered he had told her the more power he directed to them, the brighter they glowed. The rock must be incredibly dense, for it to take so much.

And each bolt he powered so brightly drained him, exhausting him more quickly. She had seen her father shoot seven, even eight bolts before lagging. But that was in his practice. In reality, he rarely needed more than two or three.

In this reality, with this rock, it was going to take more. Maybe a lot more.

After the fourth shot she saw the slowing, the lag before he reached for the next bolt, the slight delay before it began to glow, and the longer hum before the flashbow was ready. The weapon was inseparable from its master, and useless without him. It drew its energy from him, and each firing left the warrior a little weaker.

He would need recovery time after he got them through this, she thought. It was not something she'd seen herself, but she had heard often enough the tale of his rescue of Denpar, and how he had, in fact, died from firing so many times, and was brought back only by the power of the bow itself.

The very thought made her shiver. Yes, the chance of dying left no room for petty anger.

After the fifth shot the pause was longer, and she saw he was breathing heavily. Finally he reached for the next bolt, fumbling slightly.

It struck her then, with the sharpness of a blow—what he'd wanted to spare her and what she might yet spare him.

"Here," she said, shoving the flarelight at Lyon.

She darted forward, tugged the bolt free of his boot. The instant she touched it it began to glow, more quickly than with her father, since her energy was fresh.

She felt him go still.

"Will it work?"

"I . . . don't know."

So he didn't know if bolts charged by one warrior would fire for another.

"Worth trying," she said. "As long as it doesn't get in a fume and blow us all up."

"I was more afraid of that from you," he said, steadier now.

She met his gaze then. "Not now," she said. And handed him the glowing bolt.

For a split second her father's jade green eyes stayed on her. The eyes that were yet another legacy from him.

And then he lifted the bow. It hummed. And he fired.

Again she charged the next bolt. He seemed to be moving faster again, as if not having to charge the bolt saved more for the firing. But the rock was so dense he was gaining only about two feet per shot. At that rate, it would take two more to get through. And that was if Rina's calculation was exact. But then, she always was.

She could feel the drain herself, just from charging the bolts. She could only imagine what he must be feeling.

He fired again. Wobbled. And then again. This time he staggered, and Shaina jumped to steady him. She hesitated before grabbing the eighth bolt. He needed rest.

"Do it," he rasped out.

Reluctantly, she took the next bolt. When it was glowing, she slid it into the groove of the flashbow herself. Notched the string. Flipped the lever. Left only the firing to him, hoping it would save him enough.

"Wait!"

Lyon's shout rang out, startling them both. And suddenly the flarelight went out, leaving them in pitch blackness.

Almost.

With a gasp, Shaina noticed the tiny prick of light just above the target zone.

Light. From outside.

They were through.

Lyon ran past them, dug at the area around the light. The pinhole grew larger. He crouched and grabbed a heavy, pointed stone and began to hammer at the hole. It began to crumble. And then a full beam of light shot through into the cave, highlighting her father as if aimed.

"It's done," she said to her father. He was still dazed. She could see now the hollow look of his eyes, the sweat on his face, the paleness of his usually golden skin. She realized she had never had any idea of the true cost of who and what he was.

He sank slowly to his knees, his breathing heavy, harsh. The flashbow clattered to the stone floor as he toppled over. With a cry Shaina knelt beside him.

Lyon ran back. "Is he all right?"

"I don't know," she said, her chest so tight she was nearly gasping as her father was. "He needs to rest."

For a moment Lyon looked at them. "Stay with him. I'll scout what's out-side."

"Lyon—"

"You need to be with him. I'll be back."

She nodded then. Lyon kissed her, fleetingly, but it was full of more promise than she'd ever imagined. Then he was gone, through the opening they had made.

Gradually her father's breathing slowed. She put her arms around him as if she could transfer her own strength. Who knew what really was possible between flashbow warriors? She gave him water from her own pack, and he drank without questioning, without even seeming to realize what was happening.

After a few minutes, she saw awareness come back into his eyes. "Shaina?"

"It's all right. Just rest."

He closed his eyes. She looked at him, thought of her mother, watching him fire the bow unto death, and thought that although she had always loved and admired them both, she had never quite respected enough what they had gone through. They had been through worse than this, then fought their way across a galaxy to get home, and then fought for Trios ever since. And now again they were looking at war, and again they had risen to the challenge.

She wondered if her mother could sense his weakness, if she somehow knew. She always seemed to—

A scrape across stone interrupted her thoughts. Lyon, back so soon? She turned toward the new opening.

She smothered a sound of dread. A dark, cloaked shadow stood silhou-etted by the light. She could see nothing of his face. But she knew.

Mordred.

Chapter 49

"AH-AH-AH." THE man who had nearly destroyed her world said it cheerfully, wiggling his disrupter at the downed Dax as Shaina made a move toward her own weapon. She stopped. Her father was still groggy, barely aware.

"And the gods smile at last," Mordred said, booming it out as if he were giving a sermon. He walked toward them, a slow, arrogant strut. Yet she saw a slight limp, saw the blackened spots on his clothing and his skin, saw even more of his lank hair singed. And there was a sort of a burned smell around him that made her nose curl. From throwing himself futilely at the screen, she guessed.

"Both of you," Mordred said with a smile so pleased it made Shaina's stomach churn. "And the famous warrior down already. I shall be the toast of the system. Of all systems!"

Shaina sucked in a breath. Both? Only two? Lyon had gotten clear, then. Out of reach before this rabid flymouse had dropped in on them.

"I wouldn't drink that toast too soon," she said, crouching in front of her father.

"How touching," Mordred drawled. He waved the disrupter again. "Back away."

"Go to Hades."

He laughed. It was an awful, cackling sound.

"Do it, or I'll shoot him right now."

She opened her mouth to repeat her words. He fired. Her father's body jerked, and he made a low sound. The sleeve of his shirt was blackened, his left shoulder bleeding.

"Next one will take out his heart," Mordred promised. "Now back away."

She had no choice. Slowly she moved backward, her eyes darting around, her mind racing, looking for a way out of this.

"You can't escape me. I can't wait to see you as a collared slave. It's always a pleasure to see the spirited ones broken."

"At least I'm safe from you. You prey on little girls, isn't that right, you twisted piece of—"

He shot her father again. This time in the ribs, and the pain jolted him to awareness. She saw his eyes open, then close again.

She also saw Mordred nudge the power lever on the disruptor up to the red zone. If he fired again, it would be lethal. Distracting him with taunts had obviously not been the right course. But she had to do something.

Mordred moved closer, peering at her father with interest, but angling so that he could watch her, too.

"So it is true, what I've heard," he murmured. "Using that thing drains him. How convenient for me."

She had to get him away from her father.

"How did you get here?" she asked, hoping his pride would make him answer. Anything to keep him from firing that last shot. "How did you get past the screen?"

"Past it? It is still here, we are still within it. Quite remarkable. The Coalition must have the technology. I simply went over the mountain," he said.

She didn't miss the smugness in his voice, even as she pondered what he'd said. The screen went all the way up and over, protecting the other side of the mountain as well? Had whoever put it there anticipated one day the tunnel would be completed and the other end would need to be screened as well?

And if Mordred had climbed over that peak and made it down unscathed, in his charred condition, smug or not, she would do well not to underestimate him.

She tensed as Mordred bent over her father. She heard him draw in a sharp breath. He was staring downward, at the tunnel floor.

The flashbow.

It lay on the ground where it had dropped from her father's numbed fingers. Still charged, ready to fire as it had been when Lyon had spotted the light from outside. The glow of the ready bolt must have drawn Mordred's attention.

He reached down to it with his free hand. Shaina held her breath. *Do it,* she urged silently. *Try and take it.*

He touched it.

And screamed.

Recoiling wildly, Mordred staggered backward. He clutched his singed hand to his chest. In the same instant, her father moved. She wasn't surprised; she'd sensed he was more alert than he was letting Mordred see. But what he did shocked her.

He threw her the flashbow.

She caught it instinctively. Expected it to sear her, as it had Mordred. No one could touch an armed flashbow except the warrior.

Instead, it felt alive in her hands. An extension of her, part of her, ready, obedient. And when Mordred moved, clutching the disrupter in his uninjured hand, it snapped into targeting position on her mere thought.

"You think to scare me?" Mordred said. "The entire galaxy knows no one can fire that thing but him."

"And yet I am holding it, as you could not."

Something Lyon had said flashed through her mind.

... he has prepared you for this, every day of your life, even if he kept from you your true destiny ...

She knew her education had been different. All were required to learn at least rudimentary fighting, for self-defense and in case of future attack, but her training, along with Lyon's, had been much more intense. She had always assumed it was simply that she had been raised with the prince, and was taught what he was taught simply because they were inseparable. But now, suddenly, and belatedly, she realized her father had been in fact preparing her all along, without telling her, for the future he had concealed from her. He had made sure she knew what she needed to know; it was merely the final, irrevocable knowledge he'd withheld.

Who would know better what you are facing? The rest of us know only the glory, he knows the danger, the blood, the pain, the weariness. What father would not want to protect his child from that as long as possible?

Lyon's words had only irritated her before. She had still been too angry to hear any defense, any justification.

Now, as she faced the man who had helped nearly destroy her world, she finally understood. He hadn't wanted the choice forced on her before she was ready to choose.

"Put it down," Mordred ordered.

"I think not."

He aimed the disrupter at her father. "Put it down or I will kill him right now."

The energy in the bow seemed to course through her and back into the gleaming silver weapon, as if it were some natural circuit completed at last. Her gaze flicked to her father. He was weak, she could see that, from the firing and the disrupter hits. But he was up on one elbow, looking at her. In the eyes that were the original of her own, something new glowed. Acknowledgment. Encouragement. Pride. Acceptance.

And love.

And she knew, in some newly awakened part of her, what he was telling her. She could fire it.

"The likes of you to take out the greatest flashbow warrior in history? I think not," she said again.

"I said put it—"

"For Trios," she whispered. And fired.

A surge of almost unbearable power shot through her. The clap of thunder and the explosion echoed around the tunnel.

Mordred vanished. Vaporized.

She lowered the weapon, for a moment just staring at the blackened spot where the man who had helped nearly destroy her world had once stood. She wondered vaguely if she was truly stunned, or if it was just by comparison to that incredible surge.

And then she ran to her father.

Chapter 50

"THE FUSION CANNONS are in position. Manned by those who at least remember how to fire them." Tark's voice was brisk as he laid it out for them. "We have a troop ready to head for the pass, a larger one to go through the tunnel and come up behind the main Coalition force."

Dax nodded. Standing beside him, Rina looked him up and down once more. He was bloodied, charred in spots, and looked a bit worse for wear, but he was upright and coherent. She would rather he got some rest, but they'd gotten word the Coalition was moving again, not waiting for nightfall this time.

She wasn't sure of the details of what had happened up on the mountain, but knew when Lyon had flown the fighter back and Shaina had brought her father back in the rover that it had been anything but routine.

"Mordred," was all Lyon said, telling her he didn't know much more, since neither Shaina nor Dax were talking just yet.

"He's dead?" she asked him.

"Very."

And the moment she saw Dax and Shaina together, she knew that whatever anger had been left was gone. She had helped him out of the rover almost tenderly, and he had let her, Rina guessed, not so much because he needed the help but because it was his daughter come back to him and he would not easily let her go again.

And yet, Rina thought now, let her go he must. For the Coalition was returning, in even fuller force this time, on two fronts, and this time the war would end in victory for one side. Galatin, and thus Arellia, would fall back under the yoke of their tyranny, or would hold fast and drive them out once more.

And upon that outcome hinged the fate of Trios.

They had to stop them here. While she knew Trios to be much more prepared, if the Coalition triumphed here, they would not bother to fight Trios, they would simply destroy her. Likely from a safe distance. They would count the loss of her resources as the price for making sure she would never inspire another rebellion.

"The pass isn't covered by the cannons, so they will likely send fighters in there," Tark said.

"I'll handle that," Dax said.

"You are well enough to fly?" Tark asked him.

Rina knew Ardek had treated his wounds, but they had to still pain him. But she also knew better than anyone how strong willed this man was, and ignoring pain was something he had learned long ago.

"I'll fly, my friend," Dax said with a grin as Tark studied him assessingly. "Odd having it reversed, isn't it?"

Rina smiled, guessing he was referring to the time when it had been he himself assessing the young Tark's fitness to fight.

"All right, then," Tark said. "Dax will provide air cover."

If anyone thought it preposterous that one man in a single fighter would hold off who knew how many Coalition aircraft, they said nothing. Such was the reputation of Dax here. And it had only been enhanced by the fact that the new statue stood pristine and untouched while every building around it had taken damage.

"If you're going to use that invisibility function, make sure we have your ID frequency so we don't shoot you down by accident," Tark said.

Dax laughed. "Now that would be an ignominious ending."

"Kateri?" Tark asked. "Are the watchers ready?"

"We will take the pass, to hold them as long as possible. We are one hundred strong now, known fighters all." The woman might not be as young as she'd been, but she was tough, and strong, Rina thought. She would do.

"I scouted the pass on my way back," Lyon said. "There is a point just here"—he pointed to the spot on the holo projection—"that, with a bit of explosive help, could become a choke point."

Tark nodded. "I know this spot. You plan to take the rock face down?"

Lyon looked at Kateri, inclining his head respectfully. "If you will accept my assistance."

The woman looked surprised, and then smiled. "You are a true prince, Your Highness."

"I am but Lyon," he said.

Rina smiled. He had his father's charm and charisma indeed. She stole a glance at Shaina, who was watching him with an expression Rina had never seen on her face before. Dax was watching them both. He'd worked it out. When he felt her gaze and turned, she saw in his face that he, too, was happy with the future of Trios he saw before him.

"Will Dare be pleased?" she whispered to him.

"Yes," he answered. "He knew it just as I did."

"I will go with you," Shaina said to Lyon.

Tark glanced at Dax, who nodded. "I had something else in mind for you."

Shaina looked curiously at her father, but then turned to look at Tark. "Sir?" she said, as respectfully as Lyon had spoken to Kateri. Rina was proud of them both.

"The main force. You know the way to and through the tunnel. And it is no small thing to have you with them. They will rally to you."

She looked back to Lyon. "He is right," he said. "I am an unknown to them, except for my name. You are the daughter of Dax, who fought beside them, who helped lead them to victory. They see your face every day, in that statue on the square."

Dax rolled his eyes at Rina. She smothered a laugh.

Shaina looked at her father again, as if expecting him to protest his girl going into danger. Dax smiled at her, but it was a smile full of the ache of a father's heart when he knows he can no longer protect his child's every moment.

"We seldom have the luxury of choosing our path when the world hangs in the balance, Shaina," he said softly.

"You are right," Shaina said. "I will go with them."

Dax looked a little surprised at her lack of protest. Rina elbowed him. "I told you they'd grown."

"A lot in a hurry," he said under his breath. "I didn't know when my girl left Trios I would next see her like this."

Rina smiled at him. Dax looked from her to Tark and back.

"You are bringing him to Trios when this is over, aren't you?"

She felt herself flush, but her lips curved into a small smile. "I certainly intend to try."

"Then it's as good as done," Dax said.

She hoped he was right. That they would all survive to go home to Trios. She hoped when this was over, there would be a Trios left to harbor them.

RINA WALKED through the outer chamber, assessing the people as she went. Those cowering in the corners, many weeping, she ignored except for a reassuring smile. Those sitting quietly she judged by their expression; the blank stares were of no use, but those appearing angry she made note of. Even those whose faces appeared full of despair, for despair could be turned with the right words, the right motivation.

Those on their feet, or pacing, she took special note of, for those could be driven to motion by the need to do. Something. Anything. And that was what they needed right now.

Many of them were young, barely more than children. But they were chafing at being held here. She heard the mutterings about what they would do, how fiercely they would fight, if only they were allowed.

And it might come to that, if the message the low-flying scout ship had sent was accurate.

"What is happening?" several asked her as she passed.

"Reports are coming in now," she said. "There will be news as soon as we've sorted it all out."

When she returned to the tactical room, Tark was pacing its length himself. She knew he hated this, being here instead of out there. In fact, judging by his glower, she guessed he'd like nothing better than a good hand to hand just now.

He stopped when she came in. And the glower faded as that slow smile she had come to love even more than the flashing grin curved his mouth at the sight of her. For a moment she allowed herself the pleasure of knowing it was for her, but only a moment.

"What did you find?" Kateri asked.

"About half will be of little use," she said. "But the rest, there is some potential. Some, I think, are getting there, by the simple fact that the first attack was repelled. That little foray of yours inspired many."

Rayden grinned, but Tark shrugged it off. "And the rest?" he asked.

"If you want those ready to fight right now, I'm afraid you're looking at the young ones. Many of them are fired and ready."

"They feel they are invulnerable, at that age," Kateri said. "Death is but a concept to them."

"And I would be loath to use that and have them face the reality," Tark said. "But I will, if I must."

Rina hated to think of what that would do to him, that it would add another layer to the scars that were not visible. But Tark was a warrior, and needs must.

"Will you talk to them?" she asked.

He grimaced. "I'm no speechmaker."

"I think you're wrong," she said. "But even if so, you are the hero of Galatin still, and again. They will listen as if you are the greatest orator since the Creonic Age."

She saw his reluctance, but still he stepped out into the chamber. Quiet rippled out from where he stood, as the people noticed he had joined them. He grimaced again as she gestured toward the council podium on the raised platform at the front of the room. But apparently he realized that for them all to hear him, he must be above them, and went up the double steps. Rina followed, but held back. This was his to do, and she knew it.

But if any of them so much as questioned him, or his right to lead, she was afraid she might accidentally blast them.

Tark ignored the grand, elaborate podium. Instead he stood in front of it, putting himself closer to the people crowding in, putting nothing between him and them. Glancing around the room, Rina saw it was a choice not lost on those people.

He began abruptly. "We're holding the gates. And the western lines."

A rousing chant of his name began. He waved them to silence. "It is those leading those fighters you should cheer. Many of you thought them crazy, or too old, and yet they hold."

Somewhat chastened, they quieted to listen as he went on.

"Prince Lyon and our force have slowed them to a crawl at the pass, and the Silverbrakes are carving at them from behind and in the air."

A cheer went up, but he silenced it quickly again.

"There is a cost for us in this success. The Coalition is diverting troops that were headed for the northern plain. But they are now headed directly here."

A buzz went around the room.

"What will we do?" a voice cried out.

"We must assume their goal is to destroy Galatin. We have nothing they need that they cannot get outside the city, and it will matter little to them if there is nothing left of us but debris."

"And it is their way," Rina added, speaking to them for the first time. "Resistance is a personal affront. You are not allowed to stand for yourselves. They want you cowering, on your knees, and begging."

"We drove them out once, we can do it again." It was Rayden, who had gathered a group of his own age around him, and had been doing an effective job of stirring them up.

"We can," Tark said. "But it will cost us. The eastern fusion cannon has been moved, leaving a break in the defenses. They will notice that gap."

"What will you do?" a shaky voice asked, coming from, Rina noticed, one of the men who had been quivering in a corner earlier. She also noticed the difference in the question. He expected Tark to save them. And if he died in the process, would the man even care? She doubted it.

"We will give them what they want. The eastern quarter."

She wasn't surprised by the clamor that went up at that. But she was pleased by the cry that silenced it, from Rayden once more.

"Let him speak!" the boy shouted, echoing Tark's words to him. "This is Tark, have you forgotten?" When he had quieted them, he turned back to Tark. "Finish telling them what will happen when the Coalition has invaded the east," he asked.

For an instant, appearing almost bemused, Tark just looked at the boy. Rina smiled; Rayden was indeed much like Tark had been. An unusually aware soul.

"Then they will be within range of the new position of that cannon in the low hills," Tark said. The hum that went around the room was incredulous. She couldn't blame them, moving a fusion cannon was no small task. But Dax and his fighter had gotten it done, before he'd flown off to the mountain.

"And," Tark added, "the cannon on the south line."

"A trap!" Rayden exclaimed.

"And a crossfire," Tark said. The boy grinned, let out a whoop. The young people around him joined in, and it set the tone for the rest of the crowd. And so turned tides, Rina thought.

Tark raised his gaze to the rest of them. "It will cost us much of that sector," he warned. "I know many of you live there."

"We will rebuild," someone shouted.

"And it must not appear deserted," Tark said, and Rina knew this was going to be the hardest part. "There must be signs of life, or they will guess it is a ruse. They are evil, and cruel, but judge them stupid at your peril."

The only sound that broke the grim silence then was the group of youngsters, whispering among themselves.

"Anyone who is willing, I will take," Tark said. "You will not be asked to stand and fight, just be seen. I cannot say it won't be dangerous, we will likely draw their fire."

"You go yourself?" Rayden asked.

"Yes."

Rina knew his reason, knew that if this failed, there would be little he could do to save what remained of the city. Holding Galatin when he had the *Evening Star* here to control the air was one thing. Holding it when he had a single fighter to keep back a full invading force, even if manned by Dax, was another.

"And you?" the boy asked, shifting his gaze to Rina.

"I go with Tark," she declared. *Anywhere*, she added silently. He glanced at her, his expression as warm as if he'd heard the unspoken word.

"Then take us!" Rayden exclaimed.

A clamor arose anew at the idea of these children doing what so many adults in this room were afraid to do. Tark hushed them much as Rayden had for him.

"Let him speak." He echoed the boy's words. He might not be a speechmaker, Rina thought, but he had instincts about people. He just didn't have much faith in them.

"Why?" he asked the boy simply.

"We are from that sector. We grew up on those streets, we know the buildings. We know every place to hide, and what can be seen from where."

Tark drew back slightly, surprised, Rina guessed, at the boy's cogent description of exactly what would be needed.

"You need them lured in, do you not?" Rayden asked. "We can do that."

"Arellia," Tark said after a moment, "may just have a future after all."

Chapter 51

THE STREETS WERE eerily silent as they dodged from shadow to shadow. *The quiet before the storm*, Rina thought. That it would be a vicious, destructive storm she had no doubts.

They'd gone over the plan in detail before they'd started out, especially with the children. They did not want to be seen moving to the east, it needed to appear as if they had always been there, as if they lived there and were only now fleeing.

They left people—including some adults who had been shamed into it by the courage of their own children—at various places—homes, other buildings along the way—to join in the observable "evacuation" once it began. Once they were all in place and the signal given, they wouldn't hide, but would let themselves be seen, fleeing ahead of the advancing incursion.

The timing would be critical. They had to go fast enough to make it believable, yet slow enough to assure as many of the Coalition enemy as possible were crowded into the sector.

And then they had to escape, get clear before the cannon fire began. Keeping these children safe through it all was going to be the biggest challenge.

"They're as bold as you were at the first Battle of Galatin," Tark said as Rayden darted in front of them into the shadow of the next building. "And not much younger."

"And here I am still," she said serenely. "And ever will be."

His arm slipped around her for a brief clasp. That he would do so now, in the midst of a critical mission, said much of how far they had come.

And then they froze as, in the distance, they heard a howl of sound. Ships. Transport size. They were landing.

The second wave had come to Galatin.

"YOU ARE QUITE insane, you know," Crim observed mildly as they carefully set the armed torpedo in the pilot's seat.

"Thank you," Shaina said with a grin.

In the distance, the fight for Galatin had begun anew, and she had had to put out of her mind her worry about Rina, and Tark, who had quickly become part of the same worry.

This part of the battle had tilted in their favor, thanks in large part to her father's skill and Larcos's brilliant new fighter. On the forward front, Kateri and Lyon and their small force were trying to keep the Coalition from advancing, while her own contingent continued to decimate them from the rear. But the fighters holding the pass were far outnumbered, so she was taking a small group there to assist. She did not know how long they could hold them here. She only knew they had to. They had to hold, until her father's ship arrived. Once the *Evening Star* and her weapons were here, everything would change.

And for the first time she had seen her father in real action, and she was more than a little awestruck. Hearing of his reputation her entire life was nothing compared to actually seeing him fight—fiercely, effectively, and yes, recklessly. He'd flown like that ship was part of him, darting, wheeling, racing forward and dropping back, appearing and then vanishing, until she guessed the Coalition fighters thought they were up against an entire fleet.

He'd kept those fighters off them, enabling them to continue to carve at the ground force from behind. They were divided now, fighting on two fronts, forward and rear; the damaged Coalition fighters had retreated toward the mother ship, and her father had momentarily departed on a mission for Tark over Galatin.

They themselves had had losses, but for every rebel fighter that went down, the Coalition lost twenty or more. So many that the Coalition had had to bring their flagship and her weapons out of the shelter of the moon and expose it.

Which had brought her to where they were now. And caused Crim's admiring words.

Shaina worked quickly, Crim helping. They used various pieces of the transport's own equipment to hold it in place, then Shaina turned to the control panel. It was nearly as familiar to her as a Triotian craft because her father had insisted she learn as much as possible about Coalition weaponry. She also suspected her father had trumped up any excuse to get off the ground. Yet another subtle bit of training, she thought. He had made sure she had the tools, just hadn't told her why she would need them.

Quickly she leaned in and programmed the small transport's self-piloting system, then adjusted the identifier beacon. She rechecked the nitron torpedo they had liberated from the transport's own weapon, then keyed the communicator Kateri had given her.

"Rina? We're set. Coordinates and maneuvers are locked in."

"Stand by."

"How does she do this?" Crim asked.

"She's an exact navigator," Shaina explained. "She can commit any system to memory, call it up, and read all the distances, angles, trajectories, and orbits as if the holo was right in front of her. She'll know exactly when we have to launch to reach the mother ship before it has a chance to disgorge the rest of those troops."

Crim shook his head, whether in amazement or disbelief she didn't know. And it didn't matter.

"Get out now," she told him. "When the moment comes, there will only be three seconds to get clear."

The old man didn't dissent, but hurried to the open hatch and clambered down.

Moments spun out. Shaina was barely breathing. She knew Rina and Tark likely had their hands full, but when they'd come across this intact transport, she'd seen instantly that this was their best shot at spiking the whole operation. It only had to work.

For an instant she closed her eyes and thought of Lyon. She reached out farther, across the distance between them. She'd never tried this from so far before. But at last, she found him.

Slowing them, Shay.

She was still not used to it, this silent communication, and it was fainter at this distance, but it was there. Quickly, she sent him the image of what they were doing. And she heard him, sensed him—whatever this was—laugh.

They don't like our style of fighting. They'd rather we lined up to be mowed down.

She sent a rather terse, suggestive opinion on that. And he laughed again.

"Now, Shaina!"

Rina's command crackled from the communicator's small speaker, cutting through her connection with Lyon. She didn't waste time answering, but turned on the identifier, then slapped the main control and dashed for the closing hatch. She counted down in her head. One, out of the cockpit. Two, to the hatch. Three, headfirst dive to clear the steps that were already retracting.

She tucked in, hit the ground, somersaulted back to her feet. *All those acrobatic classes with Denpar actually paid off,* she thought with a grin as she turned to watch the transport lift off.

The rest of her small band all stood watching as the ship rose, headed for the mother ship. If they were puzzled by the early return of the craft, she hoped the identifier she'd changed, indicating the ship was damaged and needed repair, would distract them enough to take it on board.

They waited. The huge, hovering ship had seemed ominously close until now. Now, she wished it were even closer.

She could hear explosions, and the sound of fierce fighting in the distance. She would have looked toward the city, to see if there was more or less smoke rising than before, but she didn't want to take her eyes off the big ship. She had utter, total faith in Rina, but she was in the midst of that battle and could have been distracted. She had Tark to worry about now. Shaina couldn't help smiling at that. Tough, mischievous, wonderful Rina had finally found her match. If she was only a fraction as happy as she herself was now. . . .

Pay attention, she ordered herself. *The only fraction you should be thinking about is the fraction off that would make this all be for nothing, our best chance wasted.* She stared upward. Waited, barely breathing again. Pictured it in her mind. The transport approaching the mother ship, slowly, entering the launch bay. Clearing the entrance, entering the belly of the ship. Holding steady, her lethal cargo sitting harmlessly in the pilot's seat. Until the program reached the last order she'd given it.

Roll.

The explosion was massive.

Chapter 52

ANY OTHER MAN would show some sign of fear at the thought of what was coming, Rina thought. Tark showed only satisfaction that his calculations had been correct. They had noticed the gap in the defenses where Tark had removed the cannon, and were heading that way.

"Tark!" Rayden's whisper was nearly as loud as if he'd spoken normally, but since it wasn't critical at the moment, they let it pass.

"What, Lieutenant?" He used the informal rank now as if it were official. Rayden smiled so widely at the title coming from his idol that Rina thought she might burst with emotion.

"The tree," he said, pointing to the groundsweeper farther to the east that was tall enough to be visible above the buildings. "If I climbed it, I could see for miles. I could tell you their progress. At least until Dax gets here."

Tark had called for Dax, asking him to flip on that invisibility shield and head out behind the advancing troops, cutting off any possible retreat.

"It looks a bit . . . spindly," Rina said, eyeing the frail upper branches doubtfully.

"It would be if a grown-up tried," Rayden said. "But I climb it all the time. It's a good place to hide because nobody looks up. And the branches hide me anyway."

"You," Tark said then, "are a brilliant tactician in the making."

"Then I can do it?" the boy asked, eagerness making his voice rise again.

"Wait until we reach it. If they aren't here yet, then yes. *If* you understand your orders are to get down and away the moment they reach the perimeter."

"Yes, sir!"

They proceeded, working their way from hiding place to hiding place, leaving others along the way, until they were in the shadow of the building closest to Rayden's tree. The boy looked at Tark, who nodded. With a grin, he darted off.

"His parents would be proud," she said softly. Ardek had told them they had died at Coalition hands some years ago.

"Any parent would be proud of a son like that," he said.

Yours were not, she thought. *And there is no excuse they could give that would make up for that.*

But she said nothing of that to him.

"His grandfather is all he has left," she said instead.

"Yes."

"When he passes, Rayden will be alone." Tark turned his head then. "Or," she said softly, "we could see that he is not."

She heard his sharp intake of breath. He looked at her, and she saw such wonder in his gaze she knew he was daring to for once look ahead. But then Rayden's signal came, a low whistle sounding so like a whisperbird it was uncanny.

They moved forward, leaving one of the older women who had volunteered in the house that had hidden them. Then another, and another as they worked their way toward the edge of the city.

Tark had, of course, saved the most dangerous position, closest to the perimeter, for himself. He tried to leave Rina farther back, where it was marginally safer, but she refused.

"You're not doing this alone," she said.

"But—"

"You got your one. I let you go alone on that cellar run."

There was a pause before he said in dry tones, "You neglected to mention you were going to decide things for me."

"I'm not deciding for you. I'd be a fool to try. I'm deciding for me. And I'm not going to hang back and wait to learn if you've survived or not, ever again."

"Rina—"

A new sound came, a warning, warbling yowl. From above and behind them.

"Unless there's a tree-climbing bark-hound around, they're in Rayden's sight," Rina said.

The directions he'd given had been clear: everyone was to hold in place until the people "fleeing" from the east passed, then join in. The people who began in the safest places would end in the riskiest, within range of the Coalition weapons.

Except for Tark, of course, who would keep himself between them all and those deadly guns and ruthless killers. Rina knew that, because she knew him. And when it came down to it, she wouldn't have him be any other way.

The marching horde of armored Coalition troops cleared the trees and pushed toward the perimeter of the eastern quarter. The sun glinted off the silver metal of polished helmets.

Rina pulled the flare pistol from her belt, but waited, her eyes fastened not on the enemy, but on the man she loved. He watched, and she could almost see him processing, calculating the point at which they would be committed to the action, and the sight of fleeing citizens would lure them onward.

"Now," he said.

She fired the pistol, not into the air where it would be seen by all, but horizontally toward the last building where they had left a volunteer, an old man who had said he had nothing left to lose. She had removed half of the propellant, so the green signal would stay low and drop sooner.

Seconds later the man hurried into the street and hastened away, a bundle of some sort wrapped in a cloth slung over his back, as if he were carrying his most precious possessions as he fled his home.

"Nice touch," Tark said.

"They only needed someone to lead them," she said.

They moved then, working their way back toward Rayden's tree. They were armed with several weapons, Tark weighed down with as much ammunition for his long gun as he could carry, although she knew he knew that if he had to resort to that, the ruse had failed and the battle for Galatin would soon be over.

The process built. A second man joined the first, in the middle of the street. And then a woman from a house across the way. The timing was perfect, as they were clearly visible yet out of the range of Coalition hand weapons as the troops reached the perimeter, crossed it.

Tark and Rina kept moving, but stayed behind the exodus as it moved inward toward the center of the city. The street was filling now, and the troops were picking up speed. Perhaps seeing a nice batch of slaves to pick up, Rina thought. But they had not fired, yet.

"Who is manning the cannons?" she belatedly asked.

"Crim's brother is on the southern position. Ardek is on the one we moved."

The old man had clearly earned Tark's trust on that cellar mission, she thought. She was grateful for that.

They were nearing Rayden's tree when the first blast roared down the street, echoing off the buildings behind them. Rina ducked instinctively, although the troops were still out of range. Barely.

Another blast came; someone up ahead, turning to look, stumbled and fell. Rina held her breath until the man scrambled to his feet and kept going. Another blast, and another. One sent bits of the building they were passing flying.

"Cutting it a bit close there," she said to Tark.

"Have to give them something they think they can hit," he said with a reckless grin that nearly stopped her heart, it was so like the Tark of old. "Lure them on."

She understood; if he could keep them focused on that they were less likely to think of other things. Like traps. But it still made her a bit nervous, dancing on the very edge of being within reach of their weapons. Especially when nothing they had except Tark's long gun could penetrate armor from that distance. She was good enough at hand to hand, but preferred to avoid it with armored troops at these odds, if she could.

In the moment they came even with it, the base of Rayden's tree went up in flames like an oiled torch.

"Rayden!" She broke into a run, Tark at her heels. Somehow she knew the boy would wait for his hero, wouldn't leave without him. Because she knew the feeling.

"I can't see him," she said. Maintaining silence was pointless now, so she yelled the boy's name. The answer came, fear sounding in the young voice for the first time. And then she saw him, about halfway up, through the rising smoke. He must have been climbing down when the blast hit.

The flames were searing. They couldn't get close enough to the trunk of the tree, and the fire was moving steadily upward. She tried to think of something, anything to do—

"Hold on," Tark shouted as he slung his long gun off his shoulder. "Stay where you are, you're going to have to ride it down!"

He raised the big weapon, aimed it at the flaming base of the tree. He fired a rapid burst. The tree creaked. He fired again. It began to lean, and Rina realized he was cutting the tree down from this side, controlling which way it would fall.

Rina glanced down the street. The Coalition force was advancing. A few seconds more, and they would be within range.

The tree shuddered, then gave and began a long arc downward. She could see Rayden clinging to the trunk above the fire. And she suddenly realized he was too close, that the flames would likely flare and engulf him when the tree hit.

Tark realized it in the same instant. Dropping the long gun, he ran forward, into the flames.

"Jump!" he shouted to the boy.

Rayden never hesitated. He flung himself out and down, into Tark's arms. Tark staggered back under the force of it. He managed to control it enough to get clear of the flaming branches. He went to his knees but not down. Rayden quickly scrambled free and stood on his own.

The Coalition opened fire.

Rina lifted the long gun she had grabbed up when Tark dropped it. It was nearly as long as she was tall. And heavy. She barely managed to fire it toward the advancing line. She had the satisfaction of seeing them halt, but the recoil nearly knocked her down.

Tark regained his feet. Grabbed the weapon from her with an oath. Yanked her back out of the line of fire behind the next building.

"What in Hades did you think you were doing?"

"Shooting back?" she suggested, irked at his tone.

"You were right in their line of fire!"

"You were the one who was *unarmed* and in their line of fire!"

"You still shouldn't have—"

"Why in Hades not?"

"Because I love you!"

Rina was ready to fire another retort, but his words took the wind right out of her. In that instant she realized the absurdity of it—here they were, massively outnumbered, under fire, and he chose this moment to say it.

"I swore I'd have those words from you face-to-face, Bright Tarkson, but bedamned you chose a fine moment."

He was looking sheepish now.

"Seems appropriate, actually," she said.

"It does," he agreed.

"I love you, too."

For a moment nothing less than awed wonder flashed in his deep blue gaze. "More fool you, you've made that clear."

It was all the time they had for such things. He took up the long gun once more. Stepped out from the protected corner. Snapped it to his shoulder and fired a long burst. One of the armored men actually went down, two more stumbled. They dodged behind the corner of a building as the enemy returned fire. The ground shook with the explosions, and chunks of the buildings and even the street flew around them.

They dodged from building to building, pausing only to fire back as they worked their way up the street. He was making sure they kept following, she knew. They passed the treatment clinic that had been evacuated in the first wave. This was the building Rina knew was the goal. They had to get them past that. They kept moving, faster now, Tark firing back every few yards, luring them on. She added her own disrupter, more for show than anything, since they were beyond her range.

A hundred yards beyond the clinic Tark stopped. They took cover behind a pile of rubble from the first wave. He rose above the pile, facing back down the street. He fired again, and again. The blasts from the Coalition came nearer and nearer, one peppering them with stinging bits of rock.

The armored men passed the clinic.

"Got you," Tark whispered.

He looked over his shoulder. The others were well out of range now, most of them running, as planned. They would head for cover now, their job done.

The Coalition was squarely in the cannon's field of fire now.

But so were they.

"This way!" Rayden shouted. He dashed between two buildings. Tark grabbed Rina's arm and propelled her into a run. A couple of blocks down, the boy cut to the right. Then left, then right again.

"There's a shortcut," he said as he zigzagged through the narrow back streets, "near the school."

They followed. The boy never hesitated. He led them to a thick grove of trees.

"See?" he said. "This is the back end of the park."

Rina swiftly called up an image of the map she had studied for so long. "Then we're clear," she said.

Tark nodded. She pulled the flare gun out again, this time loading it with a fully powered round. She fired it, upward this time, and the shell burst into a huge blossom of green flame.

The fusion cannons opened up before it had faded away.

The trap had been sprung.

Chapter 53

EVEN FROM THE ground, the explosion on the mother ship was clearly visible as a huge ball of flame and smoke. The massive ship careened sideways, and for a moment Shaina thought it might actually come down. She didn't want that—who knew what or who it might take out. After a tense few moments it steadied, although it was listing now, severely.

The small band of fighters gathered around her, cheering, chanting "Silverbrake!" as the debris from the mother ship rained down around them. They had taken to that after she had led the entire force safely through the tunnel. The screen, oddly, was gone. Perhaps unneeded now that Mordred was dead. Or perhaps it somehow had known they needed access to save the Graymist's beloved Arellia. In light of everything, it didn't seem that odd a thought.

"You are indeed your father's daughter," one of them cried out. She felt a renewed surge of adrenaline. The way the once-uncertain fighters had rallied to her had been proof of their love and respect for her father. And the knowledge did not irk her now, as it might have just days ago. That was past now, vanished with the first firing of the flashbow.

But now they were cheering her, and she couldn't deny it made her blood race even faster. She watched the big ship. Her stunt had crippled it, forced it to leave the rest of the fighters airborne and low on fuel as it retreated.

"That was brilliant!" Crim exclaimed. "Insane, but brilliant."

Shaina gave the grizzled man a grin. "Not my idea. King Darian did it to them, years ago. And then my father, with one of their own fighters full of old liquid fuel. Neither one knew of the other."

"They both did it? Each without knowing?"

She nodded. "I've heard the story so many times, it was my first thought."

The mother ship was in the distance now, the fighters clinging to her skirts like frightened children. They would all be in disarray now, without the mother ship to guide them. If she'd learned nothing else in this battle, it was that the Coalition did not encourage independent thinking. It was why independent thinking, like the trick with the nitron torpedo, worked. Then, and now. It seemed very fitting.

"In the future," Crim said solemnly, "Arellia would do well to be as Trios, to remember rather than pretend this never happened."

"Yes."

"And thanks to Trios, we still have a future."

"You will—"

She broke off suddenly as a tearing pain shot through her. It was so sharp it nearly doubled her over. So sharp she looked down at herself, expecting to see blood from some injury unnoticed until now. She found nothing.

It came again, weaker this time. And this time she knew.

Lyon.

Shaina ran, heedless of the danger, of the fact that she could barely breathe for the tightness in her chest. She took wild chances, leapt over deep gullies where she could have broken a leg or worse, dodged stiff branches and let others whip at her, risked a horrific fall on a narrow trail at the edge of a steep drop-off.

She encountered one of Tark's scouts, who had just taken a position on high ground. Without ceremony she commandeered his airspeeder, telling him he could retrieve it at the pass. The nimble vehicle made short work of the rest of the trip.

It was oddly quiet—no sound of fighting. Dread built in her. Silence did not seem a good sign, not in a battle like this. Was it another lull, the Coalition troops demanding unconditional surrender? Or worse, was it over, was the wrenching pain and grim certainty of disaster not just for Lyon, but for all of them?

She cleared the last grove of trees. She saw the cluster of men, huddled, over a shape on the ground. Her entire body wanted to scream, but with the stubbornness that had gotten her into so much trouble over the years, she held it back. She threw herself off the speeder and ran toward them.

Kateri was there, and tried to stop her. She heard, as a distant buzz, the low voices of the gathered fighters.

"—seen anything like it."

"That entire platoon, by himself."

"And looked like the king himself doing it."

She wrenched free, barreled through the gathered group. Knelt beside him.

He was so bloody she could not at first tell where the worst wound was. When she saw the gaping rip in his side, the steady pulse of blood draining, she knew. Her heart denied the assessment of her mind.

At first she thought him already gone, but she knew she would have sensed it, would have known if he'd passed from this world, from this life. Then he opened his eyes. Those bright blue eyes that were his Graymist legacy, through his mother, from this world. They were dimmer, dark with pain and ebbing life force.

"Shay."

It was so quiet, so weak, that hope curled up and vanished within her.

"Don't try to talk, Lyon," she urged, touching his cheek.

"I must. Must tell you—" He stopped, and she nearly cried out herself at the rasp of his voice and the rattle of his breath. "I wish we had awakened sooner," he finally got out. Another rattling breath. "You. You are the real treasure."

He knew. She heard it in her mind, not in those words, but in the growing faintness of the contact. He knew he was dying.

She grabbed his bloodied hands in a fierce grip. "No. Don't do this."

"Shay . . ."

Desperately, as if they could hold him, she said the words she had never gotten to say before, amid the chaos that had erupted around them.

"I love you."

"Yes. Almost as much as I love you." Urgency came into his voice. "Quickly. You must . . . we must bond."

"What?"

He pulled his hands free, and Shaina realized with a gut-level shock that she could have stopped him, he was so weak. "Bond with me. Now."

He tugged at his ring. The signet that symbolized the royal family of Trios.

"What are you saying?"

"Please, Shay. You must have all rights due my bonded mate."

His gaze compelled her. It was as if he were pouring the last of his strength into convincing her. The royal family had the power to conduct bonding ceremonies, she knew that, but she somehow doubted one had ever conducted his own. Not that that would stop her Lyon.

He smiled at her then, as if he'd heard her very thoughts. As perhaps he had. "We have never played by all the rules, have we?"

He looked over her shoulder, and she instinctively turned. Kateri stood there, tears streaming down her hitherto steadfast face.

"Will you . . . witness?" Lyon asked weakly.

"It would be my deepest honor," the woman said, and knelt beside them. Shay tried to quell the trembling, but it was seizing her now, and she didn't know how long she could hold it back.

Lyon reached for her hands, first one, then the other, as if the effort to take both at once was too much. He began to recite the ancient words, the pledges, the sacred oath that would bind them. The words that would make her forever a part of the royal family of Trios, that would bind that noble lineage and the Silverbrake line into eternity. She could no longer doubt the rightness of it, but the truth of what was happening now, why it was now, was tearing her apart.

She spoke the vows from the depths of a heart that had only so recently awakened, forced the words past the mind that was crushingly, almost cripplingly angry that it had come to this end when it should be only the beginning.

The declarations made, the bonding complete, he slid the bulky ring onto her hand, having to use her index finger because of the ring's size. She leaned down, kissed him gently, then more intensely, as if that could hold him. Already he seemed cold, and the tears she'd been fighting broke through, too much even for she who never cried.

"My fierce Shay, don't cry. Better now than before the meadow."

She choked back a sob. She was unused to crying, and realized now why she had ever fought it. It hurt too much. Too much to bear.

"I love you," she said yet again.

"And I . . . you." His eyes fluttered closed.

He was slipping away. She could feel it, could feel the distance growing between them. She threw herself over him, as if she could somehow protect him that way. In that moment she bitterly thought she knew why her father had never told her who she really was, because he'd known she wasn't up to the task. She had had only to keep Lyon safe, and she had failed completely. He was dying, and she could do nothing. Nothing but hold him as his life ebbed away.

Something was pressing hard against her ribs. She tried to ignore it. No pain could match the pain she was feeling as his breathing grew more labored, slower.

A thought niggled around the edge of her mind, trying to break through the cloud of anguish. She brushed it aside—nothing else mattered anymore. It might never again, for the rest of her life. A life full of endless days without him.

She wondered if a chosen flashbow warrior ever turned it down.

Then again, obviously the choosing wasn't always right. Had anyone else ever failed at the job, or would she be the first in history?

It didn't matter. Nothing did. Not now. But again it tickled, tormented, a fleeting memory of words spoken in an old man's voice. . . .

. . . *the power to heal.*

The orb. That was what was pushing against her ribs. She clawed at his jacket, digging for the inside pocket where he had secreted it. The garment was soaked with his blood, seemed reluctant to surrender the small crystal sphere, but at last she had it free.

Uncertain what to do now, she placed the orb on his chest. Watched it.

Nothing happened.

It would only work for a true child of Graymist, the old man had said. Perhaps he needed to hold it. She tried to rouse him, but he was too far away now. She placed his hands on the orb, hoping somehow he might, even unconsciously, have enough life left to hold it.

His hands fell away.

The labored breathing stopped.

He was gone.

Chapter 54

"RINA, YOU'RE CLEAR? And Tark? Safe?"

Silence. Dax put the fighter into a pivot, to look once more to the east. The Coalition troops were still in chaos.

"We are." At last her voice echoed in his ear through the earpiece, and relief shot through him.

"I'm watching the eastern quarter. I can practically feel the cannon fire from here. They're falling like a swarm of drunken zipbugs. Give Tark my congratulations."

"With pleasure."

It was a common phrase, but something in her voice told him he had been right in his assessment of how things stood between them. It gladdened his heart, to know she had at last found what he had found. She certainly deserved it more than he ever had.

"He's a good man, Rina."

"Yes."

"He'll love life on Trios."

"I hope so. But wherever he is, I will be."

He felt an odd sensation, some combination of satisfaction tinged with loss. They were well launched now, both his girls and Dare's son. They had found their way, their path, and he wasn't sure where he would fit in their lives now. But they would work it out.

"How about my girl?" he said, grinning proudly even though no one but the fighter's computer screen could see him.

Rina laughed. "I knew it had to be her or Lyon the moment I saw the explosion."

Dax laughed. "I felt it first, on my way here." A shock wave had rocked the little fighter from behind. He'd slammed the controls, whipped it around. Scanned the ground, then the sky.

And had stared in shock. The Coalition mother ship had clearly taken a huge hit, by the color of the flames it was from a nitron torpedo. A torpedo their ground forces did not have, and he himself had not fired. In the moment he realized it, a voice had echoed in his ear.

"Dax?" He recognized the voice. Crim, one of Tark's men. *"See anything interesting up there?"*

"I'm looking at it now. What in Hades?"

"*That,*" *Crim said, sounding awed, "was your daughter.*"

He blinked. "Shaina did that?"

"*She said it was one of your old stunts. And the king's. With a torpedo-equipped Coalition transport she just happened to find.*"

He laughed out loud, joyously. He was prouder of his girl in that moment than of anything he himself had ever done.

And more grateful that she had apparently forgiven him than he'd ever been since the day Califa had agreed to bond with him. And his mate would be just as proud.

"I'm heading back to the pass," he said to Rina now. "Congratulations to you all."

While the air fighters hadn't been able to reach Galatin thanks to the fusion cannons, they'd had free space over the pass, and he'd barely had time to breathe trying to keep them off the Arellian forces below. But now his girl, practically single-handedly, had chased off the mother ship, and most of the fighters with it. And then Lyon had managed to block the pass, trapping that force, while Rina and Tark had demolished the forces sent to invade the city. They were winning. Perhaps had already won.

He was thinking how he and Califa might celebrate once she arrived with the *Evening Star,* which should be soon, when a voice on the ground frequency had crackled in his ear.

It was Kateri, who had been directing his fire, and very adeptly, since the start of the fight at the pass. She was a canny thinker, this woman, and had often come through with a direction in the same instant he had seen it from the air. The little fighter had lived up to all of Larc's promises and more, and he was going to buy the genius a lifetime of lingberry when this was over.

"Dax here," he answered.

"Dax . . ."

Something in her voice pulled him out of the pride-induced exhilaration. "What is it?"

"Prince Lyon."

Dax went rigid in his seat. An icy cold swept through him. "What?"

"He was hit. One of the Coalition fighters on a strafing run."

"Where is he?"

"On the ridge, above the slide. He went up to send the rest of it down, to trap the last forces in the pass with no retreat." For a moment he just sat there, unable to move. "It worked perfectly. We have them now."

"How bad?"

"Your daughter is with him. She . . . knew, somehow."

Shaina. His stomach knotted even tighter.

"Dax." The woman's voice held a note he'd heard too often not to recognize.

"No," he said.

"I'm so sorry, Dax. He's gone."

Dax banked sharply, kicking the fighter to full speed. He flew up the pass at low altitude, dodging around corners, barely missing outcroppings of rock, and caring nothing for any of it. He saw the bodies of Coalition thugs strewn thick, and didn't feel a thing. Not even triumph at the obvious victory.

No.

A memory of Lyon as a child, endlessly curious, quietly fearless, shot through his mind. He was the best of Trios, her hope for the future—this could not be.

He careened recklessly around the last corner. He set the fighter down with a thump, heedless of scraping the perfect surface. He popped the hatch and scrambled out.

He saw the cluster of fighters. One of them saw him coming, signaled the others, and they parted to let him through.

His heart gave up its last hope when he saw Lyon's body. He had seen too much death to mistake it here, however much he might wish it otherwise. *Dare*, he thought. *I am so sorry, my brother.*

Shaina was kneeling beside Lyon, staring at some object that lay on his chest. When he reached them, she lifted her head. He never again in his life wanted to see a sight like the look in his daughter's eyes.

He knelt beside her, wishing he had some gift for words, but then realizing no words could ever ease this. He knew from his own nearly unbearable pain that hers must be crippling.

"It was supposed to work," she said brokenly, shifting her gaze down to hands stained with Lyon's blood. "To heal. He said it would."

"What?" he asked, not knowing what else to say.

"That," she spat out. She grabbed up the object from Lyon's chest, the thing he now saw was a small rock that looked made of crystal of some sort. "Bedamned, useless thing. Will you kill me now, for blasphemy? Do you think I care, now?"

Her voice had gone wild, rising as she clutched the polished rock, her knuckles whitening as if she were trying to crush it with her bare hands. The orb, he thought suddenly. This must be the thing they had spoken of, the Graymist Orb.

"You were supposed to heal him," she howled, looking around as if for something to smash it on.

He put a hand on her shoulder. "Shaina—"

She shook him off, raved on. "The old man said you could heal, and here is the truest child of Graymist and you let him die."

He grabbed her then, pulled her close. She sagged against him. He could feel the shudders that wracked her, yet she did not cry. His fierce girl did not cry, although he knew she had to be broken inside, beyond even his imagining. He was filled with the very real fear that he would lose not only the boy he loved as if he were his own this day, but his girl as well.

He reached to take the orb from her, to get this thing that was obviously only adding to her pain away from her.

It was glowing. Faintly. Now stronger. And stronger.

What had been a translucent stone was now a deep, dark red.

"Shaina," he said, but she had already realized.

"It's warm," she said, staring down at her hands. "No, hot. But not blue. Red."

He didn't understand what she was talking about, but sensed silence was his best course, and didn't speak. He had seen some strange things in his wanderings, and whatever this was definitely qualified.

Shaina pulled free, and he let her go. She scrambled back to Lyon's body, the glowing rock still in her hands. She placed it over the grievous wound Dax could barely stand to look at. His girl was made of sterner stuff. His girl was her mother's daughter as much as his.

He felt an odd sort of tingling, much as he had when he'd cut his way through the screen below the tunnel. He knelt once more beside them, his daughter and his prince. He had never doubted they would find each other, in the way they had been meant to. He had seen it himself, had he not, before she had even been born? That they had, at last, had been clear the first time he'd seen them together when he'd gotten here.

But what was the point, if it was to end like this?

"Please," he heard Shaina say, in a voice he'd never heard from her before. "Please."

His proud girl was begging, and he could do nothing. Lyon was gone, and he could do nothing. He'd never felt more helpless.

The orb-like rock she held was bright red now, pulsing. Still she held it in place, although he could tell from her face it was burning her fingers. He wanted to take it from her, but she seemed so intent, as if she knew what was happening.

The orb flashed a starburst of brilliant red. Then faded, returning to its former state almost immediately. Shaina, shaking now, let it drop. Dax held his breath without really knowing why. He wanted to hold her, steady her, but some deep instinct held him back.

He waited.

Shaina waited.

The entire gathering seemed to be holding their breath.

A harsh, shuddering gasp came from that still form on the ground.

And Lyon opened his eyes.

Chapter 55

"BETWEEN YOU all, you left the *Evening Star* little to do but clean up," Califa said. "I had to let the crew chase off a few of those ships just so they'd have some part in it all."

Rina had been smiling from the moment Califa had arrived on the planet, and Dax had raced to greet her. Their joyous embrace had been met with cheers from the crowd; the skypirate and his mate had once more come to Arellia's aid and were celebrated accordingly.

Rina accepted and returned an embrace of her own, savoring the words of the woman she thought of as mother and big sister combined. "Well done, my girl. Very well done."

"I did my part," she said. "But the plans, the tactics, were not mine."

"So I have been told, at length," Califa said, glancing at her mate. Dax grinned at Rina. And winked.

Califa turned then, toward where Tark stood, hanging back. She walked to him, halted before him. Rina sensed his uncertainty, wondered that this man who had been so assured, so decisive in a battle against incredible odds, would hesitate now.

Of course, he was facing the former Major Califa Claxton, the most renowned tactician in Coalition history.

"You took this . . . rather unorganized and reluctant force, a depleted arsenal of outdated weapons, a bunch of untrained civilians, including children, and you not only held off but pushed back the entire Coalition strike force. Commander Tarkson, it is an honor to know you."

Rina grinned at his slightly stunned expression. Califa had not let her down, as she had known she would not. He opened his mouth, but no words came.

"And," Califa added, "you are likely the only man I would deem good enough for our Rina."

Tark's mouth snapped shut, and he nearly winced. Rina barely managed not to run to him as he turned his head slightly, in the way she had come to know. He was hiding the scar, the patch. But she held—her position and her breath.

Califa reached out, and with one slender hand, touched his scarred forehead, then his cheek. Gently, she turned his head back.

"I know something of this," she said softly. "Of scars carried for life, of hating the pity of others, of thinking yourself less because you are no longer whole."

Rina saw Tark suck in a breath. Califa's limp was most times barely noticeable, but it was there, and she knew a man as observant as Tark would not have missed it.

He also would not have missed the sheer joy of Dax's reunion with his mate, making it clear the scars she bore had nothing to do with them.

"It means less than nothing to her," Califa said. "I know this, for I know her."

He held her gaze then, and Rina sensed it took as much, if not more, courage than facing down row upon row of armored Coalition men.

"I cannot say it would restore your vision, but if you wish the scar repaired, we have a physician who could do it."

Rina didn't care for the idea. If it would indeed restore his vision, perhaps, but she found nothing repellant in his appearance, or in the scars he carried. Tark glanced at her, saw her reaction in her expression. He turned back to Califa.

"Have you done so?" he asked quietly.

Califa smiled, a slow, warm smile. With a glance at Dax, she said, "No."

Tark gave a nod that included both she and her mate. "Then I must accept that Triotians are indeed different."

Califa laughed then. "Indeed they are." And then, abruptly, "You love her?"

Rina almost wished she had not asked, not in so public a place. Almost.

"I do," the man who had first sent those words through a boy in battle said, in front of all and without hesitation. "I would die for her."

"I think," Califa said with a laugh, "she would much prefer you live for her."

Rina crossed to him then, heedless of the onlookers, or the cheerful clamor that arose when she put her arms around him.

"Indeed I would," she said. "I, and all of us, have spent more than enough time thinking you dead."

Califa smiled, stepped back, and Dax slipped his arm around her. She looked up at him.

"I told you," he whispered.

"You were right, my love. He is perfect for her." She gave Rina another smile. "Now, where is my daughter?"

Rina, Tark beside her, led the way quietly to the room where Lyon slept, weary but miraculously alive, his grievous injury already healing. Shaina, who had never left his side, was now lying asleep beside him on his uninjured side, her arm and one leg crossed over him protectively. The orb that, if the incredible story were to be believed, had saved him sat on the small table at the head of the bed where the two were sleeping.

They had been through so much, these two she loved as if they were her blood.

Outside in the square, they were being celebrated as heroes, he for trapping the main Coalition force with that second landslide, risking and nearly losing his life to do it, she for helping carve them up from the rear, and that family stunt with the mother ship.

The acclaim was rightfully theirs, but Rina knew what was most important to them was right here, in each other's arms. Just as what was most important to she herself was beside her now.

"He's resting well," Tark said quietly as Dax and Califa slipped through the door behind them.

"And she would likely slaughter anyone who tries to disturb him," Rina said.

"That's my girl," Dax said, grinning.

"And yours," Rina said to Califa. "I think she's proven that."

"As he has proven he is the king's son," Tark said with a nod toward Lyon.

"When you get to know Shaylah, I think you'll find he's got a bit of her in him as well," Dax said.

And Rina nearly laughed again at Tark's nonplussed expression as they casually assumed he would, of course, get to know the queen personally.

"They will want to take him home as soon as possible," Califa said.

"Of course," Rina agreed. "Nothing will do him more good than being home." She felt Tark go still. "And I cannot wait for you to see Trios," she said to him.

"I—"

"You are as much a hero on Trios as this rascal," Califa said, teasing her mate.

Rina could have kissed her. She had told Tark this, but sensed hearing it like this made it more real to him.

"Hero," Tark muttered with a shake of his head.

"Indeed," Rina said, "so get used to it."

There was a stir outside, so loud she feared it would wake Shaina, if not Lyon. She consulted her internal clock. *Yes, about right*, she thought.

"They're here," she said softly.

The four of them moved to flank the door just as it opened. And the King and Queen of Trios walked into the room.

SHAINA WOKE TO the stir. Her parents were beside them as the royal couple paused to give Rina a hug. Rina's Tark looked uneasy, and rather stiffly made the traditional bow of the head to them.

"No, Bright Tarkson," Dare said firmly. "I will have no bow from you.

Besides, I'm told you will soon be family."

Tark's gaze shot to Rina.

"Well?" she said, an impish grin on her face.

Tark's expression softened in a way Shaina wouldn't have thought possible. "Yes. If you are fool enough to want me, yes."

Lyon shifted restlessly, and Shaina sensed he was close to waking up. The royal couple turned to cross the room, the queen pausing to kiss Tark on the cheek—his scarred cheek, Shaina noticed, no shrinking away for this queen—making the hardened warrior flush.

She didn't move from Lyon's side as his mother sat down on the edge of the bed beside him. The woman who was as a second mother to her gave her a smile as she smoothed the hair back from his forehead tenderly. King Dare stood beside her, looking down at his son, his jaw tight with emotion.

"You told them?" Shaina asked her father, who along with her mother, had come to stand on the other side of the bed.

"As best I could," he said.

"It was . . . a bit of an odd recounting," the king said.

"It was odder in reality," she said.

Lyon moved again, as if he'd sensed his parents' presence. After a moment his eyes fluttered open. When he saw them there, he smiled. But when Shaina moved as if to rise, his arm came around her to hold her close.

"Quite an adventure you've had," Dare said to him.

"More than you know," Lyon said. His voice was much stronger, almost normal, Shaina thought in relief. "I don't know if I'll ever fully understand."

"No matter, it was well done," Dare said. "By both of you."

Lyon started to sit up. Everyone leaned forward to help him. He waved them off. But he allowed Shaina to pull cushions behind him.

"It was Tark. He and Rina," he said with a smile at them, "they master-minded the plan."

Tark ducked his head, but Rina grinned.

"Only you, sir," Lyon said, looking at the scarred warrior, "could conceive and fight a four-front battle with such a small army, and win."

Tark's head came up. "I had help."

"You and your help left nothing for my force to do but chase the stragglers," Dare said. "Who, by the way, are still at a dead run for the far reaches."

Lyon smiled as his mother agreed.

"We are so very, very proud of you all. And," she added with a glance at the ring Shaina now wore, "glad you two have found your way to each other."

"It was difficult for her," Lyon said. "You know how she hates being told what to do."

She nearly elbowed him, would have had she been more recovered from his near death.

"I had not noticed that," her father said dryly.

Even Shaina laughed at that, although part of her reaction was sheer joy from hearing Lyon laugh. He was sounding stronger by the minute.

"I'm afraid she got that from both of us," her mother said.

"You must admit," Shaina said, "all that old talk about destiny was rather the epitome of being told what you will do."

"No," her father said quietly. "Learning—far too late—you are the next flashbow warrior is that."

Her gaze shot to her father's face. In his eyes she saw the love that had always been there, more than a little pain, and a fierce regret. Lyon urged her, with a nudge at the small of her back, and slowly she got to her feet. She faced the man she had come here hating, but now loved even more because she understood so much more.

"I understand, now. I still wish I had known, but I understand. And I realize that you have been teaching me, giving me the tools I will need, all my life. That it was only the final knowledge you withheld. And that you did it out of love."

Her father stared at her. She saw moisture glistening in his eyes. "Ah, Shaina," he whispered, and she had never heard such a broken sound from this man who had guided her life, who had been ever strong, tough, and sardonic. And then she was hugging him, and he her, so tightly she doubted either of them could breathe.

Her mother hugged them both, and Shaina felt the dampness of tears that had spilled over on her cheeks, mingling with her mothers. After a long, jubilant moment, her father drew back. Only then did Shaina see that Lyon's mother was crying too, and Dare's eyes were damp as well. Rina was simply beaming at them.

Tark looked a bit stunned, as if he'd never seen such family love and forgiveness before. For a moment she locked gazes with him.

Welcome, she thought, and put as much of the word as she could into her smile. After a moment he smiled back at her, a smile so full of awe she knew he'd realized this was his now.

Her father had crossed the room and taken up something Rina had had behind her. Now he brought it back and stood before her.

"There will be a formal ceremony when we return to Trios," he said, "but I've already waited too long. This is yours now."

Shaina stared. In his hand was not the traditional apprentice weapon, but his own flashbow, gleaming silver as he held it out to her.

"But this is yours," she said.

"And now it is yours."

"But you—"

"I think I can make do with my secondary bow."

She had no doubt of that, he was, after all, the greatest flashbow warrior Trios had ever known. But this?

"But—"

"You saved my life with this, Shaina. And put an end to the man who helped guide the near destruction of Trios. You've more than earned it."

"For what it may be worth, your king agrees," Dare said when she still hesitated. It was part of the form—the warrior chose, the king approved, but it still took a moment before she could move. And then Lyon got to his feet. With amazing steadiness, considering, he stood beside her.

"As do I," he said softly. "And I am the one who shall have to deal, am I not?"

At last she put a hand on the elegant, lethal weapon. Unarmed now it lay quiet, yet she thought she could feel a slight tingle along her fingers.

"Were it not your right," her father said, his voice low and husky, "it would not respond to you."

She took it then, felt an electric sort of snap as a current seemed to run through her. Then it settled, and it was merely a tool in her hand. A very special, very powerful tool. Waiting to come to life at her command.

"A queen and a flashbow warrior," Dare said with a wondering shake of his head.

Shaina's breath caught. She hadn't thought of that. Bonding with Lyon meant she would one day be queen. Her gaze shot to his face.

"I think Trios can withstand it," he said with a grin.

Her mouth quirked. "I'm not queen material," she said ruefully.

"I think you and I need to have a talk, my dear," Shaylah said dryly.

"You are precisely queen material, my love," Lyon whispered into her ear, making her color as his breath tickling her ear made her wish he was well enough to think of other pursuits.

The door to the room swung open. Eight heads snapped around, eight hands streaked to weapons. Instinctively, Shaina glanced at the orb, as did Lyon. It sat quietly. No enemy warning here.

An old man stepped out of the shadows.

"How in Hades did he get in here?" Tark growled, his weapon aimed at the old man's head.

"You!" Shaina exclaimed.

"You know this man?" Dare asked, his disrupter aimed squarely at the newcomer's chest. The king of Trios had lost none of his reflexes.

"Yes," Lyon said. He looked at his mother. "And so, I believe, do you."

Shaylah frowned. "I do?"

The old man smiled at her. "I'm not surprised you do not recognize me, little sunbird. It has been a very long time."

The queen's brow furrowed. Then cleared as her eyes widened. "Theon? Theon, is it truly you?"

At the delight in her voice all weapons came down. She ran forward and threw her arms around the old man. After a moment, he drew back and looked at her.

"It has been too long, little Shaylah. But your blood is strong, and you have passed the essence on to your son. I am glad he is recovering."

"He almost didn't," Shaina said starkly. "When I first laid that orb upon him it did nothing."

The old man turned. "They say to heal it must be held by a still-living Graymist."

Shaina opened her mouth, but could not say the words, as if speaking them would make it all too real, all over again. Lyon spoke them for her.

"And I was not."

Shaina felt the spike of pain in the very air of the room as those who loved him reacted.

"So I had heard," the old man agreed easily.

"I still do not understand why it worked, then," Shaina said, fighting off the painful images of Lyon lying bloody and broken on a field of battle. "I am only thankful that it did."

Theon walked over to the orb, glanced back at Shaylah. "If I may?"

"Why ask?" she said with a smile. "You seem to know more of it than anyone."

"What I know was told to me by your grandmother, who had a great fondness for the tales."

"I remember," Shaylah said softly.

"You have not held it?"

"No. I've been . . . distracted."

"Of course." He smiled at her. "Your grandmother told me the orb spoke to all Graymists, but to the head of the family most of all. And you are, now, the oldest of the Graymist clan."

"Well, I'm feeling much older than I did a few days ago," Shaylah agreed wryly with a glance at Lyon.

"Then take it," Theon said, holding it out.

The queen took the orb. The crystal leapt to life with a fierce, steady glow. And held, longer than either Shaina or Lyon had seen before. Shaylah looked startled, and for a long moment stared down at the orb in her hands. Then her head came up, and the smile on her face lit the room. She gave her mate a swift hug, and then went to Shaina and Lyon. She took her son's hand.

"Oh, my dear Lyon, it did not work for you." She turned to Shaina. "It worked for you."

"But I am not Graymist."

"No." Her queen, the woman she loved second only to her own mother, put a hand to Shaina's cheek. Her smile was radiant. "But your son is."

"My—"

Her breath caught. Her eyes widened. Shock numbed her. Lyon's arm steadied her. And then she felt a flood of heat rising from deep within her, coloring her chest, her neck, her face as the others reacted, the men with a blankness she thought was probably typical, the women with gasps followed by slowly growing smiles.

Rina was the first to recover. "Well. That's a fine way to find out."

"But . . . already?" Lyon said, sounding a little shaky. "And after only—"

He broke off before he would have truly earned that elbow, Shaina thought, still feeling a little numb. It was enough that it had been announced to all and sundry, without the details of how it had come about. She stole a glance at her father, who looked shell-shocked. The king looked nearly so.

And then her mother was there, hugging her, then Lyon, then Shaylah. Rina joined them, her teasing laugh a joyous thing.

A child. She was carrying a child. Lyon's son.

She had to believe it. The orb had done everything promised, had been right about everything. Dear God. The very thought made her shiver. Lyon's arm tightened. She leaned into him, feeling suddenly weak.

Ridiculously, the first thing that occurred to her was that this explained why she had not been able to see through the screen, but had been able to see the treasure. She was already pregnant, even then.

"I think," old Theon said, "that soon I may have to take up my brush again."

"I would count it an unmatched favor if you would, my dear old friend," Shaylah said, still smiling so widely Shaina couldn't help but feel the warmth of it. "We need a portrait of our king at last. We have sadly missed having an artist of your talent."

"And in time," Theon said, "a portrait of this entire family, for the thought of this combination of Graymist and Trios royalty, of Claxton and Silverbrake, will give an entire galaxy hope for a final and lasting peace. And perhaps one day this child will assure it."

"That's a lot to lay on a baby who's not even here yet," Rina said, bringing them all back to practicality.

"I think," the queen said briskly, "there are two people here who need some time alone."

"I think," Rina said with a grin, "there are four sets of two people here who need some time alone."

The laughter eased the emotions. And at last Shaina was alone with the man who was her destiny, who had always been her destiny. Her bonded mate.

And the father of their child. A child who had his own magnificent destiny, if the old man was to be believed.

She believed him.

Epilogue

KING DARIAN OF Trios arose early. He walked quietly to the window of the royal bedchamber and looked out at the pink and orange streaks that heralded the coming sunrise. He smiled as in the distance he saw a familiar silhouette against the sunrise. A kingbird, soaring. They were returning, as Trios healed.

The grounds were still deserted at this early hour. For a moment he simply savored the peace of it. A peace hard won. The cost had been high, many had died to do it. He doubted anyone would take it for granted, here or on Arellia, ever again.

A movement caught his eye. Two people stepped out of the lower palace doors, into the courtyard. Close together, arm in arm, dark head bent to golden, they walked in silence, as if they were savoring the peace as was he. Rina and her Tark, Dare thought. The hero of Galatin, twice over. He could not have picked a better man for her.

When Rina had told him, privately, of the isolation he had endured, of the way his own people had rejected him as a symbol of a time they wished to forget, he was incensed. He had moved quickly to offer him that rarest of things, a royal offer of immediate citizenship.

"You mean . . . become Triotian?" Tark had asked, seeming startled.

"I do."

"But I know what is required. I can bring nothing of value you do not already have."

"You would be welcome even if you were not already a hero, a legend among us." Dare liked him even more for the way he shook his head in bemused doubt at that. "You would be welcome because you have brought joy to someone very important to many Triotians. Rina was a symbol of what we nearly lost, a child regained, hope renewed."

"I do not deserve her," he said. "But I do love her. Beyond measure."

"I believe that. That and my respect,for you as a man makes you someone I greatly wish to stay."

"I thought . . . more was required to become Triotian."

"I should think the word of the king would do," he had said dryly then. "And if not mine, then the hundreds of others who would line up to put their name down for you. We have peace once more, and there is no one on Trios who does not know we have you to thank for it."

He had meant it. He meant it still, as he watched the couple walk toward the lightening sky. Thanks to Tark the enemy had been pushed back again, perhaps forever. They had never expected the resistance that had met them on Arellia. They were in a shambles, and word had come last night that they appeared to be retreating from the sector altogether.

They had never even set foot on Trios this time.

And they never would. He would see to that. And when his time was past, Lyon would see to it. And then his son after him.

His chest tightened. For the first time, he saw his years as a slave as insignificant. If that was the price for the joy he had now, he would pay it again, gladly.

It had been a long, hard journey since the Coalition had first invaded and conquered this gem among worlds. His people had been slaughtered. He had endured his father's brutal end, then the guilt and horror over the death of his childhood love, Brielle, Dax's own sister, followed by his own enslavement. For a very long time, when he had believed there was no one else left alive, he had wished for death, for an end to the torment.

He turned to look over his shoulder to where Shaylah lay sleeping. She had, with her courage, her conviction, and her unfailing sense of what was right, changed everything. Not merely his fate, but he himself. In one of his few fanciful moments, he once had thought that when he had first seen her was the instant when everything started to change, when the momentum shifted, leading them to this time.

Through Shaylah had come Califa, once his fiercest enemy, now a trusted friend. He would have forgiven her much for what she had done for Dax, the man who had ever been his brother in spirit if not in blood. But now he accepted her for herself, for a woman who had changed herself at the very core, for the love of a once-tortured lost soul. Dax, who had been lost to Trios as so much had, but had finally come home and was now all Dare had known he could be. The greatest flashbow warrior Trios had ever seen. At least, Dare thought with a smile, until his daughter took over one future day. He thought Shaina, her father forgiven and her path now straight and true, would match him.

And most of all Lyon, so strongly certain of himself and his destiny. Dare acknowledged the ache inside at the tragedy they had so barely escaped, but it was eclipsed by the pride that filled him at the man his son had become.

They had fulfilled that destiny, these two, and were without doubt the pair to fulfill the new one, they and their child.

His grandson.

He felt a shiver as memories swept him, of the days when his mind, his body, his very soul had not been his own. Of the days when the treatment he had endured had made him doubtful he could ever sire children.

Shaylah slipped up behind him, slid her arms around his waist, and held him tightly. All the memories vanished at her precious touch, replaced by the warmth and joyfulness only she brought to him.

"It is well done, my love."

He put a hand over hers. "None of it would be as it is now, if not for you."

"Us," she said. "None of it began until there was us."

"And our son, and then our grandchild will see Trios into the future."

"He will."

"I love you, my queen."

"Would you care to prove that, your majesty?"

With a joyous laugh he turned, took into his arms the woman who had saved him from so much more than slavery.

"Indeed I would," he said, and swept her up in his arms and carried her back to their bed.

And he found joy almost unbearable as the sun rose over Trios.

The End

About the Author

"Some people call me a writer, some an author, some a novelist. I just say I'm a storyteller."
—Justine Dare Davis

Author of more than sixty books (she sold her first ten in less than two years), Justine Dare Davis is a four-time winner of the coveted RWA RITA Award, and has been inducted into the RWA Hall of Fame. Her books have appeared on national best-seller lists, including *USA Today*. She has been featured on CNN, taught at several national and international conferences, and at the UCLA writer's program.

After years of working in law enforcement, and more years doing both, Justine now writes full time. She lives near beautiful Puget Sound in Washington state, peacefully coexisting with deer, bears, raccoons, a newly arrived covey of quail, a pair of bald eagles, and her beloved '67 Corvette roadster. When she's not writing, taking photographs, looking for music to blast in said roadster, or driving said roadster (and yes, it goes very fast), she tends to her knitting. Literally.

Find out more at her website and blog (where she posts some of those photos) at justinedavis.com, Facebook at JustineDareDavis (which also gets photos), or Twitter @Justine_D_Davis (which mostly gets odd observations, favorite quotes, interesting links, and the occasional question flung into the ether).

CPSIA information can be obtained at www.ICGtesting.com
Printed in the USA
LVOW07s0437130215

426868LV00003B/28/P

9 781611 945560